The Poydras Ring

Ed Lee

The Poydras Ring

**HISTRIA
FICTION**

Histria Fiction

Las Vegas ◊ Chicago ◊ Palm Beach

Published in the United States of America by
Histria Books
7181 N. Hualapai Way, Ste. 130-86
Las Vegas, NV 89166 USA
HistriaBooks.com

Histria Fiction is an imprint of Histria Books. Titles published under the imprints of Histria Books are distributed worldwide.

Certain characters in this work are historical figures, and certain events portrayed did take place. However, this is a work of fiction. Names, characters, places, and incidents are either the product of the author's imagination or are used fictitiously. Any resemblance to actual persons, living or dead, is entirely coincidental.

Library of Congress Control Number: 2024944039

ISBN 978-1-59211-501-3 (softbound)
ISBN 978-1-59211-517-4 (eBook)

Preface

This is a work of fiction set primarily in colonial Louisiana. Certain historical figures appear in the story under their real names. While many of the events involving the characters are historical, the scenes and dialogue are invented. Any other usage of a real person's name is coincidental. Any resemblance of the imaginary characters to actual persons, living or dead, is unintended and fortuitous. A central character in this novel, Julien de Lallande Poydras, was a remarkable and accomplished developer, poet, entrepreneur, philanthropist, and political leader of early Louisiana. The references in this story to his involvement with the cult of Voodoo are all fictional, and not intended to besmirch his reputation and accomplishments in any way.

There are many historical references in this novel to the institution of slavery and the complex systems of racial segregation and racial stratification that existed in the early history of Louisiana and the South. These racism references are used to give a complete historical context and setting for the characters and events that occurred, not to in any way dignify them. As historian David McCullough noted, "History is who we are and why we are the way we are." And to paraphrase the philosopher George Santayana, if we ignore or forget our past, we do so at the peril of repeating its faults. So, if there are passages herein that make you feel uncomfortable or incensed, that's as it should be.

For Debi and the Vieux Carre

Part I
Beginnings

A bad beginning makes a bad ending.

– Euripides

Prologue

Viet Cong anti-aircraft fire riddled the low-flying, olive-green helicopter, first striking a fuel tank and causing a cabin fire. The starboard door gunner was doused with burning jet fuel and began to scream. The next few hits got the engine and sliced off one blade of the main rotor.

The pilot pulled helplessly at the controls as smoke filled the chopper's cockpit. As the jungle floor rushed toward him, Jim Noyan knew he was going to die.

The last thought that went through his mind, as his Huey impacted near Pleiku, was, *"God! Why didn't I bring the ring with me?"*

Chapter One

One of them was going to die this morning. There was no way to avoid it. Despite all his obvious advantages, Emile Poydras was nervous, limping on his bad leg as he paced the ground under "The Oaks." The pink and yellow rays of dawn went unnoticed by Emile as he hobbled back and forth. These giant live oaks, cloaked in Spanish moss, were on the plantation of Louis Allard, located just outside New Orleans.

Emile wondered how many duels had been fought on the grounds of the Allard Plantation. *Would Monsieur Allard care that more blood is about to be spilled on his land?* While these thoughts raced through his head, Emile realized he was compulsively pulling at the corners of his slightly graying mustache, first one side and then the other.

Trying to shake off his jitters, Emile gazed at the double gold band on his left ring finger. *With Uncle Julien's ring*, I cannot lose, he thought. Besides, as the challenged man, he had named the place, the weapons, and the firing distance. All the circumstances were of his choosing. No one doubted his skill as a marksman. *So,* he concluded, *why should I be doubting myself?*

A spurt of bile rising from his stomach escalated Emile's misgivings. He tried to distract himself by thinking unrelated, positive thoughts. Emile rubbed the gold ring on his finger and pondered, *Uncle Julien, what an incredibly generous man he was. Thank God he is not alive to see how I've shamed the name of Poydras.* It struck Emile that he was so anxious that he was having trouble remembering when his uncle had died. *It was only three months ago, wasn't it?*

Emile ran his fingers through his sweaty, dark hair and paced back to his younger half-brother, Benjamin, who was acting as his second once again. Benjamin was leaning his stocky frame against one of the giant oaks, his arms folded across his half-opened shirt. His wide chin rested on his chest, and his eyes were closed.

Softly, Emile asked, "Benjamin, are you asleep?"

Benjamin opened his eyes and rolled his head to work the stiffness out of his neck. "Asleep, hah! Who could sleep in this heat? I shall never get accustomed to this damn humid climate."

"Benjamin, when did Uncle Julien die?"

"That's an odd question to ask just before a duel, dear brother."

"Benjamin, please! I must — "

"June 23rd. My God, Emile! How can you forget? He died in our very arms."

"Yes. Yes. I remember that. It's just that I couldn't recall…"

"Emile, you must get ahold of yourself."

Benjamin left the tree he was leaning against, walked over, and put his big hand gently on his brother's neck. "It is not too late to call this off. Noyan really has no stomach for this fight. An adjustment may yet be reached."

Pulling away from his brother's grasp, Emile shook his head. "Oh, Benjamin, how can any adjustment be reached? His wife carries my child!"

"Are you certain it is your child, Emile?"

Emile's blue eyes flashed with anger. "Benjamin, speak no more of Nicole, or I shall be compelled to call you out for such comments."

"Hah! And who would be your second then?"

Sighing, Emile quickly apologized. "Forgive me, Benjamin. You know I didn't mean that. It's just… I just can't seem to get command of myself."

"And why is that?"

"I don't know! If I knew, I would be able to control my feelings."

"I think you know, Emile. I think that is why you are so troubled."

"What are you talking about, Benjamin?"

"Guilt! Guilt, Emile. Before all your other duels, your heart was always filled with righteous indignation, or at least with the thrill of showing off your skill. It is not so today. Today, you feel guilty for shaming Nicole, for shaming yourself, and for goading poor Henri Noyan into a duel with pistols — a duel to the death."

Emile dropped his head, unable to look Benjamin in the eyes. "You are right, Brother. I do feel guilty. I forced Noyan into issuing a challenge so… so I could kill him and have Nicole to myself. But, you see, pricking him with a sword would solve nothing. Nicole would still be his wife, and still be carrying my child. And

Henri refuses to give her a divorce, so the only way to solve the problem is for one of us to die."

"One of you could leave New Orleans! You could come back with me to Pointe Coupee. You could even leave Louisiana for a while."

"I will not give her up, Benjamin. She loves *me*, not Henri. Henri is a cruel and boorish husband. Nicole cannot endure his mistreatment any longer."

"As you wish. Just make certain Henri's first duel with pistols is his last. I should not like to lose the only family I have left in this country."

Emile smiled. "I shall not leave you yet, Brother."

The sound of approaching carriages gained the attention of the two brothers. Two coaches pulled into the grove of oaks. Henri Noyan's second, Frederick Maury, and his surgeon for the occasion, Dr. Valsin de Rivière, exited the first coach. One man remained in the coach. Emile couldn't see the man clearly, but assumed it was Henri Noyan. The second coach contained Henri's father, Paul, and three other men of the Noyan family whose names Emile could not recall.

The dapper Frederick Maury and Dr. de Rivière walked towards Emile and Benjamin. The bald-headed doctor was not carrying his black medical bag, but an armload of wooden stakes. Benjamin moved to meet the men at mid-field. It was a sullen Maury who spoke first, pulling on his coat lapels as he said, "It is my duty, Monsieur Poydras, to inquire one final time if an adjustment can be reached?"

"Are the terms unchanged, Maury?"

"Yes, your brother must leave New Orleans forever, and never attempt to contact Madam Noyan again."

"Then no adjustment is possible," Benjamin said firmly.

"Very well." Maury motioned for Dr. de Rivière to step forward. "Then we shall stake out the firing distances. I believe we have agreed on a range of twenty paces?"

"Yes. That is correct."

Frederick Maury took one of the wooden stakes and shoved it into the damp soil. Then the men began walking toward Emile, taking giant, stiff-legged steps. When they had stepped off ten paces, a second stake was set. Ten more paces were walked, and a third stake was set. Then all three men returned to the first stake and repeated the process in the other direction.

Despite the oppressive heat and humidity, Paul Noyan and the other men standing outside Henri's coach all wore coats or long capes. Surveying the men, Benjamin said, "Pardon me, Monsieur Maury, but I must request that you ask your party to open their cloaks."

Maury seemed taken aback. "Whatever for?"

"So I may confirm that they are unarmed. You know the Code. Only the participants and their seconds may carry weapons on the field of honor."

His face flushing, Maury replied, "How dare you! How dare you even insinuate that I would allow such a thing?"

Taken somewhat aback by Maury's volatile response to his perfunctory request, Benjamin tried to pacify the man. "I mean no disrespect, Frederick. I know you would not condone a violation of the Code. But I have my duty to perform."

Without releasing Benjamin's eyes from his cold stare, Frederick spoke in a loud voice to the other men. "Gentlemen! Monsieur Poydras has requested that you remove your cloaks!"

None of the other men replied. They hesitated a moment, and then one by one removed their capes and coats and threw them inside the open coach. With that, a tall, thin man with ash-colored hair exited the coach. Henri Noyan's face was pallid, and his eyes were red, as if from crying. He raised a shaking hand and finger, pointing at Benjamin.

"As you can see, Monsieur Poydras, my family is unarmed. I… I demand satisfaction for your insulting accusation."

Benjamin bowed ever so slightly. "I did not mean to offend, monsieur. But I shall be happy to make myself available, should my brother's aim be off today."

The elder white-headed Noyan grabbed his son's trembling arm and stepped between him and Benjamin, saying, "Enough! Bring your damn pistols."

Benjamin turned on his heel and marched back to Emile, who was waiting for him with the leather-covered case containing his matched set of French dueling pistols.

Emile had overheard part of the vocal discussion at the other end of the field, and inquired, "Are the Noyans to be trusted today?"

"I could see no weapons."

"They might be in the coaches."

"Yes, but Henri's father is a man of honor. I don't believe he would allow such a violation of the Code."

"Honor has its limits, Brother. And Henri is his only child."

"Have you forgotten Paul's brother?"

"Ah yes, the great hero, Jean Baptiste Noyan, who chose honorable death with his comrades before the Spanish firing squad."

"Emile, Henri is barely able to control himself. His whole body trembles. Yet his father commands me to load the pistols. It's like Jacob delivering Isaac to the altar."

"Yes, I suppose you are right. If any man would sacrifice his only son to save family honor, it would be Paul Noyan. At any rate, I feel better now that I see Henri is far more nervous than I am. No doubt he's been drinking as well. Well, let's get on with it."

Benjamin checked his two pistols stuck in his belt to verify they were both primed for firing. Then he took the small case containing the dueling pistols and returned to the center of the field. Frederick Maury was waiting for him by a small folding table, on which he had placed a jar of gunpowder, lead shot, wadding, and loading instruments.

Everyone watched as the seconds measured out equal amounts of powder and as Benjamin loaded the first pistol, and Maury the second. The long-barreled pistols were then placed back in the case, and the seconds motioned for the duelists to come forward.

When Emile saw Henri Noyan up close, his first feeling was one of sympathy. The man was visibly shaken. Then Henri lashed out. "Tell me, Monsieur Poydras, where did you learn the art of seducing other men's wives?"

"Monsieur, if you had not been such a brutal husband and incompetent lover, your wife would not have felt the need to leave your bed for mine."

"Monsieur, you pride yourself upon an animal faculty, in respect of which the Negro is your equal, and the jackass infinitely your superior."

Emile was thankful when Benjamin interrupted the verbal exchange, because he was having a hard time thinking of a good retort to Noyan's derogatory salvo. It seemed Henri might yet find his courage. Benjamin raised a hand between the two antagonists. "Gentlemen, let us proceed. I shall toss the coin, and Monsieur Maury shall call it in the air."

Benjamin threw a silver dollar in the air, and Frederick Maury called out, "Heads!"

"Heads it is," declared Benjamin. "Monsieur Maury, you shall have the honor of calling the fire. Emile, you may designate which side of the field you wish to take."

Emile said, "As we stand now shall be fine."

Maury held out the case containing the pistols. "Henri, you have the first selection, as the choice of weapons was by Monsieur Poydras."

Emile watched as Henri took the bottom pistol from the case. Emile then removed the top one.

Benjamin then gave the men their final instructions. "Gentlemen, you shall now move to your firing positions, as marked by the far pegs on each side of the field. Remember, once you have reached your positions, you may not move, except upon the command of Monsieur Maury. If you move from your position, your opponent's second is free to fire upon you. Do you each understand these instructions?"

Both duelists nodded in the affirmative, and each turned and marched off to his respective position. When the firing positions were reached, each man turned his body in profile toward his opponent, pointing his pistol barrel down at arm's length.

Frederick Maury's first command echoed across the field. "Gentlemen... men, cock your pistols... ols!"

Each duelist pulled back the hammer on his pistol, neither taking his eyes off his adversary.

"Gentlemen, aim your pistols! After I give the command to fire, I will count to three. You are free to fire as soon as I begin the count." After a brief pause, Maury yelled, "Fire! One, two..."

Maury never got to the count of three. He was interrupted by the loud retort of Henri's pistol. Benjamin immediately turned to his brother. Emile was just standing there, arm extended, his pistol aimed at Henri. *Why didn't he fire?* thought

Benjamin. Then Benjamin noticed the hammer on Emile's pistol. It was down. Benjamin ran to his brother's side.

"Emile, what happened? Are you hurt?"

"No, no. Henri was so off target, his shot must be in the next parish by now — my damn pistol misfired!"

Benjamin grabbed the gun from his brother's hand and pulled back the hammer.

"Emile! There's no cap. The percussion cap is missing."

"What?"

"Emile, this is the pistol Maury loaded. Henri took the one I loaded."

Emile glared across the field at Maury. "Of course, Maury and Noyan knew he had first choice of weapons."

"Emile, forgive me. I should have noticed. I — "

"No, dear brother. It's not your fault. It all comes to light now. The argument that Noyan started with me at the loading table, it was all meant to distract us, so Maury could tamper with my pistol."

"Thank the Lord they did not succeed."

"Yes," agreed Emile. "But Noyan is such a terrible shot, he couldn't hit me even knowing I would not be able to return his fire."

"You chose your firing distance well, Brother."

Emile meditated a moment before speaking again. "Benjamin, when you return to Maury, do not mention anything about the tampering with my pistol."

"What?"

"Simply tell Maury I demand a second fire and tell them I wish to shorten the firing distance to ten paces. And Benjamin, this time, when the pistols are loaded — "

Benjamin held up his hand in mock protest. "Say no more. If Maury so much as looks crossly at your pistol, I shall shoot him where he stands."

When Benjamin returned to the loading table, Maury would not meet his eyes when he was addressed. "My brother demands a second fire, Monsieur Maury, and a firing distance of ten paces."

"Sir, I must protest — "

"There is nothing to protest, Maury. It is his choice, not yours. Both men must declare themselves satisfied, and my brother is *far* from satisfied. And Frederick, I shall load my brother's weapon this time."

Emile turned his attention from the loading table to his opponent. Henri had returned to his coach and was waving his hands as he spoke with his father and other family members. Emile could see the elder Noyan shaking his head at his son.

When the pistols were reloaded, Benjamin carried Emile's to him. "Here you are, Brother. I promise you it will fire this time."

The duelists resumed their positions at the far stakes. Then Maury made the announcement. "Gentlemen, a second fire has been demanded, and the challenger has requested that the firing distance be shortened to ten paces. Therefore, at my command, advance to your new firing positions. Ready? Advance!"

Benjamin put his right hand on one of the pistols in his belt and silently cocked the weapon, as Emile and Henri Noyan marched toward each other and halted at the first set of wooden stakes.

Maury continued with the commands. "Gentlemen, cock your weapons. Gentlemen, the firing count remains unchanged. Now, aim your weapons!"

As the men raised their pistols, Benjamin turned his attention to Paul Noyan and the other Noyan men, while Maury gave the commands. He saw no suspicious activity. He turned to look at Henri as Maury began the command to fire. Henri's face was still ashen, but his aim appeared much steadier than during the first fire.

"Fire! One…"

Before Maury could count "two," Henri fired his pistol. Benjamin saw Emile quickly cup his left ear in his hand. When Emile dropped his hand, Benjamin noticed blood trickling down his brother's neck. Emile kept his pistol trained on the now trembling Henri. Then, he suddenly turned his pistol skyward and fired it. Henri looked shocked and relieved at the same time. But his relief was short-lived.

Emile yelled, "I demand another fire!"

Henri yelled back, "Monsieur, you shall have it with pleasure!"

Maury turned to Benjamin and said, "This is barbaric. It needs to end now."

"Emile could have killed Henri where he stood," replied Benjamin. "Tell Henri to give it up, before it is too late."

"No! You tell your brother to withdraw his demand for another fire."

"He will only do that if Henri agrees to leave New Orleans — without his wife."

"He will never do that."

"Then we reload the pistols."

When Benjamin went to retrieve Emile's pistol, he saw that his brother's wound was very minor. The bullet had grazed his brother's head, just above his left ear. Emile dabbed at the slight bleeding with his handkerchief.

"Emile, why didn't you shoot him?"

"I don't know. Henri looked so wretched and vulnerable. I just couldn't… Besides, I can afford to wait for the proper time to — "

"Damn it, man!" said Benjamin, interrupting his brother. "If Henri's shot had been an inch closer you would be dead right now. I will not allow this duel to continue if you are just going to stand here for Noyan's target practice."

"I will fire this time, Benjamin. I know he will fire on the first count again, and so shall I."

Benjamin studied his brother's face for a moment, as if to ascertain whether Emile was ardent. He then took the pistol off for reloading without speaking another word.

When the two men faced each other the third time, Benjamin forgot about watching the Noyan family. Instead, he concentrated on his brother's face, looking for the slightest sign of indecision.

For the third time, Maury gave his command. "Gentlemen, aim your pistols! Ready? Fire! One…"

This time, two shots rang out simultaneously. After Benjamin was certain his brother had escaped injury, he turned toward Henri, who had dropped his pistol and was clutching the center of his chest with both hands. As Henri sank to his knees, his father and Dr. de Rivière came running up to him. Benjamin could tell from the amount of blood spurting between Henri's fingers that the wound was a mortal one.

Paul Noyan grasped his son's hand and held it until Henri became motionless. Then Paul arose and started walking toward Emile. This aroused Benjamin's suspicions. He followed Paul Noyan and eased his cocked pistol from his belt.

Paul Noyan spoke first. "Monsieur Poydras, my son is dead."

Emile said, "I am truly sorry this had to happen, Monsieur Noyan."

"You need not apologize, monsieur. Your conduct on the field today has convinced me you are a man of honor. You were more than fair with my son. So, as one man of honor to another, I have a request. Will you hear it?"

"But of course."

"As you know, Henri was my only child. I have no other descendants, except for the child Nicole carries. If Nicole gives birth to a son, I beg you to give him the Noyan name, and I promise you that the child will inherit all that I have."

Benjamin gasped, overcome with surprise. Amazingly, Emile did not seem shocked at all. However, Emile did take some time before responding to Paul Noyan's stunning proposal.

"Monsieur Noyan, surely you know that the child Nicole carries is mine?"

"So you say, monsieur. But that is not important. What *is* important is that my family's name lives on. On the blood of my dead son, I implore you to grant me this request."

Emile handed his pistol to Benjamin and then held out his open right hand to Paul Noyan. "Very well, I promise you, monsieur, that the name of Noyan will not die."

As Henri's body was being loaded into his coach and Emile and Benjamin were preparing to leave the dueling field, a figure came out of the shadows of the oak trees. No one paid any attention to the tall, slender Negro woman in a worn purple dress as the duelists' entourages and other spectators were focused on the loading of Henri's body. But then, one of the Noyan Negro servants walked by the woman as he carried the folding table and other implements of the duel. As the servant walked past the young woman in the purple dress, he stopped, did a double take, dropped his burdens, and fell to his knees in front of her, head bowed.

Immediately, the woman spoke to the servant in sharp, hushed tones. "Get up, you fool! I don't want them to know I'm here."

Chapter Two

Celeste Noyan pressed her feet down hard on the floorboard and braced herself with both hands on the dash of her fiancé's old Toyota Corolla. The car lurched to a stop, just inches from the bus in front of them.

"Jesus, Mark! I'd like to live long enough to get our marriage license."

Mark Richards grinned as he started the car moving again and made the turn onto Eighth Street. "Sorry, babe, I didn't mean to scare ya."

"It's okay. I just wish you wouldn't follow so close. Have you ever had rear-enders driving like that?"

Mark shrugged his shoulders. "One or two."

"Well, are you suffering from a learning disability, or what? Do I need to drive?"

Mark reached across the car with his right hand and squeezed Celeste's arm. "Ah, come on, Celeste. Let's not have an argument right now. I think this spring heat wave is getting to us. Is that the courthouse coming up on the right?"

Celeste turned her attention from her fiancé's blue eyes and blond hair to the brick building appearing outside her side window.

"Yeah, that's it, the West Baton Rouge Parish Courthouse. There's public parking on the other side," said Celeste, pointing with her right hand.

"*Parish* courthouse?"

"Yeah, in Louisiana we have parishes instead of counties."

"How come?" Mark inquired as he pulled into the public parking lot.

"I don't know for sure. I think it goes back to the days when the French ruled the state."

Mark parked his faded blue Toyota and hurried around to open Celeste's door. Celeste was tugging and pushing on her seat belt buckle as Mark opened the door.

"Damn, Mark. Doesn't anything work in this car?"

Mark reached in and released the buckle with two fingers. "I promise you, babe, as soon as I find a job, this car is history. No more student lifestyle for us."

Celeste smiled as Mark helped her out of the car. "Aww, I guess it isn't such a bad machine, Mark. We did have some good times in this car."

"Yeah, especially in the back seat."

"Come on, handsome. It's time to make me an honest woman."

Mark paused a moment as Celeste walked ahead. He loved to watch Celeste's behind as she walked. Her pert ass twitched ever so slightly in her tight blue jeans, and her shoulder-length brown hair bounced rhythmically against her neck. Celeste stopped in her tracks and looked over her shoulder at Mark, catching him gawking.

"Come on, you letch. You've seen it all before."

"Sorry, thought I had spotted Natalie Wood walking to the courthouse."

"Natalie Wood's dead. Now come on."

Mark trotted up to Celeste and took her hand. "What office are we looking for?"

"Mom said we fill out the application at the Parish Clerk's Office."

When Celeste and Mark entered the Clerk's Office, they walked up to a counter where a gray-headed black woman was writing in a large ledger. Celeste spoke first.

"Excuse me? Can someone please help us apply for a marriage license?"

The clerk looked up from the ledger. "I can help you." As the clerk spoke, she reached below the counter and pulled out a printed form. "Are you gettin' married in this parish?"

"No, ma'am, in Baton Rouge," replied Celeste.

Looking at Mark, the clerk asked, "May I have your full name, sir?"

"Mark Clark Richards."

Celeste looked at Mark with surprise. "Clark?"

Mark's face flushed pink. "Yeah, my mom had this thing for Clark Gable."

Both women smiled at Mark, and the clerk said, "Do tell. And your name, miss?"

"Celeste Nicole Noyan."

"Noyan? Were you born in Louisiana?"

"Yes, ma'am, right here in Port Allen."

The clerk laid her ballpoint pen on the counter. "I have not heard that name in a very long time. Do you know — are you a descendant of Jean Baptiste Noyan?"

"Who?"

"Jean Baptiste Noyan, the hero of the French colonial revolution against the Spanish."

"I'm afraid I don't know. I've never heard that name before, or of that revolution."

Mark, feeling left out of the conversation, decided to ask a question of the clerk. "Say, I took American history in college, and I don't recall studying about a French revolution in Louisiana. When was it?"

The clerk didn't hesitate with her answer. "1768. France had ceded the Louisiana Territory to Spain a few years earlier, and the colonists finally rebelled after the Spanish took over the colonial government in New Orleans."

Mark was impressed by the clerk's power of historical recall. "You sure know your history, ma'am."

The clerk picked up her pen again. "Excuse me, I'm takin' up your time. It's just that Louisiana history is my hobby."

Celeste said, "No, please. You're not keeping us from anything, and I've always wondered about my family history. My father died when I was very young. So, I've never learned much about his side of the family. Who was Jean Baptiste Noyan?"

"I'm afraid I can't tell you all that much, dear. I just remember that he was one of the leaders of the rebellion and that the Spanish executed him and the other leaders by firing squad. Legend has it Noyan had a chance to save himself but chose to die with the other rebels."

Before Celeste could inquire further, a phone rang on the desk behind the clerk. The woman turned the form towards Celeste.

"Would you all mind to finish fillin' out this application? I'll be right back. Please print."

Celeste filled in the blanks on the application. As she wrote, "May 20, 1987" in the space for the date of the application, Mark removed his checkbook from the hip pocket of his jeans and wrote a check for the license fee. Then they both signed the bottom of the application, just as the clerk hung up her phone.

The clerk quickly read the completed application. "This looks just fine. I see, Ms. Noyan, that you are still a resident of this parish. Would you also like to apply for your dowry?"

With a puzzled look, Mark asked, "Dowry?"

"Yes, the Julien Poydras Dowry Endowment." Looking to Celeste, the clerk inquired, "Have you not heard of it?"

"Well, I've been away to college the past four years, but I do recall reading about it in the paper some years back. I didn't know it still existed."

"Oh, yes. The principal is never touched." The clerk reached under the counter again and handed Celeste another form. "Here, take an affidavit with you. Just make sure you return it before the end of the year, or you lose your eligibility."

Mark leaned over and looked at the form in Celeste's hand. "Dowry. Now that's a tradition from by-gone days. How much does she get?"

The clerk said, "Actually, the payment notice will be mailed to you, sir."

"Really? Of course, dowries were paid to the husband, weren't they?"

"Yes. Now the amount paid varies from year to year. The Police Jury divides the interest earned each year by the number of eligible brides. Last year, each girl received a little under a hundred dollars. The year before that, I believe it was around a hundred and twenty dollars."

Celeste caught a slight look of disappointment as it crossed Mark's face. "Sorry, my dear. You're still gonna have to work to support me." They all chuckled at Celeste's little joke.

Celeste asked, "When was the dowry fund set up?"

"Oh," said the clerk, "around 1825 or 1826. Julien Poydras's will left the parish thirty thousand dollars to establish the fund. His will instructed that the unfortunate girls of the parish, who had no dowries, be given preference. But now, the

Police Jury awards the dowries to all brides who apply and who are residents of the parish."

Celeste's curiosity spurred her continued inquiries. "Why did Mr. Poydras's will give a preference to poor girls?"

The clerk removed her glasses and studied Celeste's face a moment before answering. "Honey, that's a long story, and you have to remember that, in those days, women had to provide dowries if they wanted to marry into the upper class. Anyway, the legend is that before Julien Poydras left France, he was in love with a poor girl who couldn't provide a dowry. So, his family prevented the marriage. Supposedly, Poydras never got over it because he never married."

"How sad," said Celeste.

Mark, becoming bored with all the talk about Louisiana history, began drumming his fingers on the counter. Celeste picked up his sign of impatience and gently laid her hand on top of his fingers. Then she began her farewell to the clerk, "You've been most kind and helpful, ma'am. May I ask your name?"

"Sure, honey," said the clerk, extending her right hand. "It's Reba, Reba Moore."

"Well, thank you again, Reba. We've really enjoyed talking with you." Celeste gently kicked Mark's ankle.

Mark took the hint. "Yes, Reba. Thank you and thank you for my dowry."

"Don't thank me, honey. Thank Julien Poydras."

Chapter Three

Julien Poydras groaned as his dream and sleep were interrupted by someone shaking the rope at the foot of his canvas hammock. It was one of the crewmen Julien had not yet met. The drowsy Julien started to pull himself up out of his hammock but let himself fall back, covering his eyes with his wrist. At age twenty-eight, Julien had an unusually long face with deep set eyes and pencil thin lips. No one would ever call him handsome.

"Please, remove your lantern from my eyes."

The other crewman, a plump young Frenchman about Julien's age, obliged the request and lowered the oil lantern to his waist.

"Come on, Poydras. You and I have the watch."

Julien sat up, pressing back his matted brown hair. "What time is it?"

"Almost twelve-bells. Now come on. That first officer will have us punished if we are even a moment late."

When the still groggy Julien dropped from his hammock, his clothes drooped on his bony frame. He looked at the sailor's pudgy face. "Do I know you?" he asked.

"No. Come on. Grab your boots and let's get on deck before we wake the other men."

Julien nodded his assent, and the two men walked softly out of the crew's quarters and up the wooden ladder to the forecastle of the Dutch brig *Aries*. The men reached the bridge just as the ship's bell began to ring midnight. The ship's first officer, an Englishman named Hawkins, met the two sailors at the top of the ladder.

"You men were almost late reporting. Don't let it happen again."

"But, sir — ," Julien began.

"No buts, sailor! Next time you shall find yourself on report. Am I understood?"

Both seamen answered in unison, "Aye, aye, sir."

"Very good. Now, assume your duties."

When the first officer was out of earshot, Julien spoke. "I was about to say that no one informed me that I had this watch."

Julien's shipmate snorted and shook his head. "Humph! Hawkins wouldn't care if your mother had just died. I hate all Englishmen."

"So do I," was Julien's quick reply. "By the way, you seem to know my surname, but my Christian name is Julien, Julien Poydras."

"Georges Mazureau," said the sailor, as he shook Julien's outstretched hand. "We Frenchmen must stick together among this crew of mongrels."

As he pulled on a halyard to make certain the line was taut, Julien inquired, "What part of France are you from?"

"Marseille, and you?"

"From the other coast of our country, near Nantes — in the Parish of Rezé."

"Ah, yes, Brittany. I have sailed by those bleak shores many times, and every crew I served with had a different tale about Norman pirates and the spirits of the murdered priests."

"Well," said Julien, "I lived there for the first seventeen years of my life and never saw a single ghost."

"Hah, no ghosts, eh? Well, now we find ourselves headed for Nouvelle France — to Nouvelle Orléans. Have you been there before?"

"No, but I have read a great deal about the colony," answered Julien.

"Read?" queried Georges. "I knew you must be an educated man when I heard you speaking all those languages, and interpreting orders for the crew. When I first saw you, I thought you were German or Dutch. Where did you learn to speak German — and English? You speak English nearly as well as one of those devils."

Julien frowned. "In prison — in a damn English prison. My ship was captured during the war, in the fall of 1760, and I spent the next three years in a dirty English prison. There was nothing to do there except talk to the other prisoners, and many of them were German and Dutch."

"So how did you end up in Santo Domingo, on a Dutch ship, bound for Nouvelle Orléans?"

"One day, I was on a work detail outside the prison, and I hid in the open hold of a merchant sloop. As fate would have it, the sloop was bound for Santo Domingo."

"So, you had no idea where the ship was headed when you hid on board?" asked Georges, shaking his head.

"No, none at all. I just knew it was headed away from England. That was good enough for me."

Georges motioned for Julien to follow him toward the ship's bow. "Come on, we'd better go check the forward rigging... Now, Julien, how did you come to be a member of our crew? I was surprised the captain signed you on just before we sailed. We already had a full company."

"I convinced the captain he needed an interpreter. I speak every language on board but Spanish. Don't tell the captain. I told him I speak it as well."

"Hah. No doubt you will learn Spanish before we reach port."

"No doubt I must learn Spanish since our king has ceded the colony to Spain... Now," continued Julien, "let me ask you a few questions."

"But of course, mon ami. What do you wish to know?"

"Have you ever been to Nouvelle Orléans before?"

"Yes. I was there just this past winter, and a terrible winter it was. It was so cold the great river froze from bank to bank, and I'll wager all the orange trees were killed as well."

"Well," said Julien, "if the trees survived, they should have borne fruit by now. What about the great river? I understand it flows all the way to the Canada colony, and that the Indians call it the father of all waters?"

"Yes, they call it 'Mes-cha-ce-be.' That is how the river got its name, Mississippi."

"What about the fever? Before I left Santo Domingo, I heard that a plague had stricken the city."

"Yellow fever," answered Georges. "It had not occurred when I was there last. They say it only comes in the spring and summer. So, we should be safe since it is nearly the end of October. But yes, I have heard those stories too. One sailor told me hundreds have died. Another man told me half of the citizens had become diseased."

"That's over fifteen hundred people!" said a startled Julien.

"Correct. I see you *have* studied about the colony. Yet, knowing about the plagues, you still chose to come on this voyage?"

"Yes. I've heard there is much fertile land along the great river, and that the price is cheap."

"Land? You plan on staying in the colony and becoming a farmer?"

"That is my dream. I don't intend to stay in Nouvelle Orléans any longer than I have to."

Georges grinned and laid his hand on Julien's shoulder. "Speaking of dreams, when I woke you for our watch, you must have been having a fine dream. You had such a smile on your face."

Julien pulled away from Georges, grabbing the railing of the ship's bow, and stared out at the ocean. "Yes… It was a good dream."

Georges knew intuitively what Julien's dream was about. "Ah, mon ami. And who is this woman of your dreams?"

A few seconds passed before Julien answered. "A girl from Nantes. We were engaged to be married, but my father called it off."

"But, why?"

"Her family could not provide a suitable dowry."

"Dowry?" exclaimed Georges. "What, am I in the presence of nobility?"

Julien laughed. "Hah! Very poor nobility, I assure you. My full name is Julien de Lallande Poydras, but when I joined the French Navy, I left all that behind me."

"And what of your fiancé? How could you just leave her behind?"

"I had to, Georges. I couldn't be near her and not have her. If fortune is with me in Nouvelle France, I will send for her."

Georges could see the pain in his new friend's face, so he was kind enough not to spoil Julien's dream any further. But Georges did think, *Poor devil, he will never send for her. No woman will wait that long. It's already been at least five years.*

"Come, Julien. We'd best return to the bridge before that damn Englishman misses us."

Chapter Four

After applying for their marriage license and dowry, Celeste and Mark returned to Celeste's mother's house. This was Mark's first overnight stay in Celeste's home, and he found himself impressed with its character. The Noyan home was a huge, white Victorian frame house, located just west of Baton Rouge in one of Port Allen's older, established neighborhoods. After spending the night alone in one of the spare bedrooms on the top floor, Mark kidded Celeste and her mother about all the strange creaks and wind noises he heard during the night. He told the women the house reminded him of the one in Alfred Hitchcock's *Psycho*.

As they drove up, Mark saw Celeste's mother's car was in the driveway, so he parked in the street to keep from blocking her in. When the couple entered the house, Mrs. Noyan was not to be found in the living room, kitchen, or any place downstairs.

Mark asked, "Where's your mom? At a neighbor's house?"

"I doubt it. I can smell the roast cooking in the oven. Mom never leaves the house when she's cooking. Let's look upstairs."

Mark followed Celeste up the wide staircase as she called out, "Mom! We're back!"

When they reached the top of the stairs, Celeste called again, "Mom! Where are you?"

A faint reply came from above. "Up here, darlin'. In the attic."

Celeste started toward the stairs leading to the third floor of the house, but Mark grabbed her arm and gave her a very serious look.

"Wait. Don't we need garlic or a cross or something before we go up *there*?"

Celeste pulled her arm free and shook her head. "Come on, will ya? And no more haunted house jokes in front of Mom, okay?"

Realizing he had milked his house humor for all it was worth, Mark meekly answered, "Okay."

Two flights of stairs later, Celeste and Mark found Mrs. Amy Noyan on her knees in the dusty attic, rummaging through a trunk of old clothes. Amy Noyan was a youthful looking woman in her mid-fifties. She had her short, graying brown hair covered with a large red bandana, and she wore an old blue work shirt and jeans. This was the first time Mark had seen his future mother-in-law in pants, and he was impressed with her petite figure. *That's a good sign*, thought Mark. *No middle-age-spread. Maybe Celeste will take after her mom.*

"What are you doing, Mom?" asked Celeste.

Amy looked up from the trunk and seemed a tad embarrassed that Mark was with Celeste. "Oh, dear. I thought I'd be finished before you two got back. I don't want to frighten your future husband off."

Celeste smiled. "You look fine, Mom. Now, what are you looking for?"

"My weddin' dress. I thought you might like to use my veil, or some of the lace."

"I get it," said Mark. "Something borrowed?"

"That's right," replied Amy. "I know it's old fashioned — you don't have to use any of — "

"I'd love to use your veil, Mom. Let me help you look."

"Can I help?" Mark asked.

Amy looked up and thought a second. "Well, perhaps you can, Mark. I don't recall which trunk I stored my dress in." Amy pointed toward the opposite end of the attic. "Would you be a dear and pull that other trunk out from under all those boxes?"

"Sure," said Mark as he walked over to the stack of cardboard boxes filled with miscellaneous dishes, old shoes, and pots and pans. Mark was very careful in picking up the boxes and restacking them, but as he lifted the last box of pots and pans, the bottom fell out, and the contents hit the floor. The sound it made was a combination of crashes, bangs, and rattles.

Amy and Celeste looked up from their trunk with startled expressions, but neither woman spoke.

"Sorry," said Mark. "I guess the box was rotten." He noticed Celeste was now giving him her standard dirty look.

Amy Noyan was quick to put Mark at ease. "Oh, don't you worry about that junk, hon. You can't hurt it. Just pull that trunk out from the wall so we can open it."

Mark did as Amy requested and opened the lid on the ancient looking tinplated trunk. Inside was a stack of yellowed newspapers, several old books, and bundles of old letters tied with ribbon and string. The letters looked so brittle that Mark thought they would crumble if touched. Mark could also see the handle of a sword sticking out among the newspapers, and a glass jar containing some tarnished brass buttons. But what attracted Mark's immediate attention was a military flight helmet, painted olive drab. Stenciled in black on the front of the helmet were captain's bars and the name "J. NOYAN." The helmet looked out of place among the other artifacts in the trunk — like it was from another century.

Mark hadn't realized he had been staring at the contents of the trunk until Celeste finally asked, "Well, Mark, what have ya found?"

"Oh, just a bunch of old books and papers… No clothes unless you count this." Mark held up the flight helmet.

From the look that flashed onto Amy Noyan's face, Mark knew he had uncovered something that caused her distress. Mark realized his puzzlement must have shown because Celeste answered his unspoken question. "It's my dad's. It's his old flight helmet. He was in Vietnam."

Mark felt dense and helpless. He couldn't think of anything appropriate to say, but the silence that fell in the attic compelled him to speak. "Oh, I'm sorry. Was your dad killed in the war?"

"MIA," said Amy. "His helicopter was shot down in 1968… three years after Celeste was born."

As Mark gently laid the helmet back in the trunk, Celeste got up and walked over to look at the trunk's contents.

"Say, Mom, what is all this other stuff? It looks really ancient."

Amy forced a smile. "That trunk belonged to Jim's great-grandfather Noyan. Jim said it contained the family history. He was always going to compile it and translate it all, but he never got the chance to finish."

Celeste asked, "Translate?"

"Yes. Most of those old letters and papers are in French. There's even an old diary in there and a French Bible."

Celeste and Mark could sense how uneasy Amy Noyan had become since Mark had discovered the trunk's contents, so Celeste gave her mother an opening to escape the melancholy that had pervaded the attic.

"Say, Mom, why don't you go down and check your roast? Mark and I can clean up this mess."

"But... but we haven't found the weddin' dress."

Celeste glanced around the attic and spotted a third trunk partially covered by an old rug. Pointing to it, she said, "Look, there's another trunk. We'll find your dress and veil and bring them down to you. Okay?"

Amy sighed softly. "Thanks, darlin'. I guess I had better go check the roast. I'd hate for it to dry out." As Amy started down the steps, she turned back to Mark. "Thank you for your help, Mark. And don't you fret about openin' that trunk. I told you to do it."

"Thanks, Mrs. Noyan."

"Please, call me Amy — we're practically family now."

Mark dutifully replied, "Thanks, Amy."

When Amy Noyan's steps could no longer be heard, Mark asked, "How come you never mentioned your dad being in Vietnam?"

Celeste didn't answer for a second or two. "I guess it's just a defense mechanism. For years, when I was growing up, Mom kept the faith that Dad would be found alive in some prison camp. When I was little, I didn't understand. I hardly remembered my dad. It... I just found it was easier to tell people he died when I was very young. That way I didn't have to endure a bunch of painful questions I couldn't answer."

Mark gently put his arm around Celeste's neck. "Look, babe. If you don't want to talk about it now, that's okay with me. I just want you to know that I'm ready to listen, if you ever feel the need."

Celeste smiled and stroked Mark's cheek. "Thanks." Then Celeste knelt down and started sorting through the old books in the open trunk. "Hey, look at this. It's an old family Bible."

The old Bible's binding had come apart in several places, and the back of its black leather cover was missing. As Celeste started thumbing through the first pages, Mark noticed it was indeed a French Bible, printed in a large Gothic style. Celeste stopped turning the pages when she came to an ornate illustration of a tree, on the limbs of which were handwritten names in faded gray ink.

"Look, Mark. It's the Noyan family tree."

Mark pointed his finger at one of the tree's upper limbs, saying, "Jean Baptiste Noyan. Say, that's that revolutionary guy the lady in the Clerk's Office was talking about."

"You're right. I guess I am related." As Celeste's eyes read down the trunk of the tree, she noticed an entry beside the name Nicole Laure Noyan. One name had been crossed out and another written above it. "Isn't this odd? Someone has drawn lines through this man's name. Can you make it out?"

Mark studied the entry for a moment. "Looks like it was Henri-something-Noyan. I can't make out the middle name."

"What about the name written above it, Emile something? The last name looks like it starts with a P… Pay-dress?"

Mark replied, "Maybe that's an O. Poy-something."

"Poydras!" exclaimed Celeste. "It's Poydras."

"You mean like the man who set up the dowry fund?" joined Mark.

"Maybe a relative of his. I'll bet back then there weren't too many Poydras families in colonial Louisiana."

"No," agreed Mark. "There couldn't have been. It's a pretty unusual name."

"I wonder what this means? Do you suppose this Nicole Noyan married a Poydras later in life?"

"That's plausible," agreed Mark. "But look underneath at the name of their child. Someone has also changed the child's last name from Noyan to Poydras. Why do that?"

"I don't know. I suppose that Emile Poydras could have adopted the boy. That is a boy's name, isn't it? Jean?"

"I guess it could be either," said Mark. "But look. If you follow the lineage, the descendants of the Jean Noyan-Poydras are named Noyan. So, he had to be male, and his real name must have been Noyan."

"Yes. You're right. If Jean had been adopted, his descendants would have been named Poydras. How strange. It's like someone tried to rewrite part of my family's history."

Mark glanced at his watch. "Say, babe, hadn't we better find the wedding dress and go down and join your mom? I don't think she needs to be alone right now."

"You're right. And thanks for being so considerate. I have one more favor to ask, after we find the wedding dress."

Mark stood up and bowed before Celeste. "At your service, Mademoiselle Noyan. What is your desire?"

Celeste grinned and took Mark's hand as she rose from the attic floor. "Later, would you help carry this trunk downstairs with me? My family curiosity has got me now. I want to see if any of those old letters or papers will explain why someone would alter my family tree."

Mark shrugged his shoulders. "Sure, glad to. But I didn't know you can read French."

Celeste blushed. "Good point. Guess I'm gonna have to learn."

"Speaking of language and family history, I've noticed you don't have the Louisiana accent that your mom and people around here have. It only slips out once and awhile. How come?"

Celeste shrugged her shoulders. "I made a conscious decision to lose it when I went away to college. I even went to a speech coach my freshman year at Mizzou. I wasn't ashamed of being from the South, but I just didn't like being labeled as 'Southern.' I didn't like people thinking they knew what kind of a person I was based on my southern accent. Paranoid, huh?"

Mark smiled at her and nodded. "No, I get it. Some college students can be pretty high-and-mighty and judgmental. They think every white person from the South is a racist. I'm impressed you were able to complete your... transition before we met our sophomore year. But, just between you and me, I think it's sexy when you talk southern."

Blowing Mark a kiss, Celeste replied, "Thanks, babe. Now, I better go check on Mom. I'll be back to get the wedding dress."

As Mark moved to uncover the trunk containing the wedding dress, he suddenly felt overcome with a feeling of apprehension about the trunk containing Celeste's family history. At first, he thought it was caused from stirring up Celeste's painful memories of her dad. But, in the back of his mind, there was a nagging angst that the old trunk contained more than one painful memory, maybe a lot more.

Chapter Five

The *Aries* docked in New Orleans on October 25, 1769. From the wharf, Julien Poydras and Georges Mazureau could see that a large crowd had gathered opposite the levee in the city square, called the Place d'Armes. Since the men had no duties to perform while the ship was being unloaded, they decided to investigate all the commotion there.

Spanish soldiers had surrounded the square and were holding the crowd back from its center. Occasionally, a citizen would press too close to a soldier. He would be met with a threatening bayonet point or a clubbing from the butt of a musket.

As Julien and Georges walked up to the top of the levee, they could see five men mounted on mules being led into the Place d'Armes. Each of the five had his arms tied behind his back and his mule led by a Spanish soldier.

"My God!" said Georges. "It looks like some sort of public execution."

A grisly looking old man standing next to Julien answered Georges. "Yes, that's exactly what it is. The Bloody Irishman is standing them before a firing squad."

"Them? Who are they?" asked Julien.

The old man didn't answer at first. He rubbed the stubble on his chin and gave Julien and Georges a good looking over. "You men sailors?"

Georges answered, "Yes, we just came in on the — "

"That explains it," interrupted the old man. "But you men are French. Surely the news of the revolt has reached France?"

Julien said, "We didn't come from France. We came on a Dutch ship from Santo Domingo."

The old man looked a little stunned. "You mean you have not heard about the revolt of last October, when Noyan and the Acadians drove Governor Ulloa and the Spanish from the city?"

"No," explained Julien. "I knew that the colony had been ceded to Spain, but I heard the local French government had been left in place."

"That was true until about three years ago, when Spain sent Governor Ulloa and Spanish troops to set up a new government. We tolerated the tyrant for two years. Then, last October, Jean Baptiste Noyan, Attorney General Chauvin, and others led a revolution. On the night of October 28th, Noyan and his men took the Tchoupitoulas Gate and spiked the Spanish guns there. Ulloa and his troops retreated to his frigate anchored in the river."

"What happened then?" asked Julien.

"Nothing, for a while anyway. The rebels cut the anchor cables to Ulloa's ship, and he fled to Havana. Then, this August, Governor O'Reilly arrived with twenty-four warships, three thousand crack troops, and fifty pieces of artillery."

"O'Reilly?" inquired Georges. "Spain sent an Irish governor?"

"Yes, Don Alexander O'Reilly. A bloody mercenary — the devious bastard! At first, he recognized our Superior Council and acted like all was forgiven. Then, he held a great reception and invited Noyan and all the other leaders of the revolution. During the dinner, O'Reilly arrested them all. After a farce of a trial, Noyan and five other leaders were sentenced to hang."

"Hang? I thought you said the Spanish were forming a firing squad?" queried Julien.

The old man shook his head. "You see, when the death sentences were handed down, Louisiana was without a public executioner. No colonist would take the job, and the law forbids the conscription of anyone to serve as hangman."

"So, the *good* governor changed the sentences to death by military firing squad?" replied Julien.

"Exactly," replied the old man.

Georges pointed toward the Place d'Armes. "Look, the Spanish are building a fire in the square."

All three men fell silent, as did the crowd encircling the Place d'Armes. They watched as the firing squad charged their muskets. To the left of the prisoners, a fire was kindled, into which a Negro threw several bundles of papers. As the fire blazed up, the governor's official crier walked over to the fire. He was a little old man in a large, dusty black robe.

The crier began walking in circles around the fire, shouting, "This, the memorial for the planters of Louisiana, is, by order of His Excellency Don Alexander

O'Reilly, thus publicly burnt for containing the following rebellious and atrocious doctrines: 'Liberty is the mother of commerce and population. Without liberty there are but a few virtues!'"

After the crier finished his announcement, he went over to a large, uniformed man with graying red hair. Julien surmised he must be Governor O'Reilly. O'Reilly nodded to the officer in command of the firing squad. The officer stepped forward and ordered the condemned men to line up before a row of cotton bales. The officer then went to the first prisoner and offered him a blindfold. The rebel refused, as did all the others. One prisoner even spat on the Spanish officer when the offer was made.

When the officer had returned to the firing squad, the old crier stepped forward again and faced one of the doomed prisoners, a young man with a clean-shaven face.

Speaking again in a loud voice, the crier proclaimed, "Jean Baptiste Noyan! Because of your prior service to this colony, and because you are the nephew of Jean Baptist Le Moyne Sieur de Bienville, the great founder of Nouvelle Orléans, His Excellency, Governor O'Reilly, has authorized a pardon of your life!"

Many in the crowd cheered and gasped with relief upon hearing the announcement. But, before the crowd could even begin to rejoice in the pardon of their hero, Jean Noyan pulled away from the two soldiers who had come forward to release him from his bonds.

Noyan turned and faced Governor O'Reilly, shouting, "With my comrades I fought! With them I die!"

The crowd fell silent again, except that a few women could be heard wailing. Julien could not see that Noyan's defiant words had any effect on Governor O'Reilly. The governor didn't speak or alter the blank, cold expression on his face, but with a wave of his hand, revoked his pardon.

The Spanish soldiers put Jean Noyan back in line with the other four prisoners and returned to the firing squad. The firing squad then lined up in front of the condemned men, with their backs to them. The officer in charge gave the command to order arms. Then there was a pause in the action. To Julien, it seemed like long minutes, but in actuality, it was only seconds. As the flames from the paper fire died down, the soldiers suddenly wheeled and fired on cue. Julien flinched as all five men recoiled from the simultaneous musket fire and fell back against the wall of cotton bales.

Even from where Julien stood on the levee, he could see the blood soaking the front of Jean Noyan's white shirt.

The old man standing next to Julien put his face in his hands and began to weep unashamedly. Julien put his hand on the old man's shoulder. "Monsieur, come with us. Perhaps a drink will calm you?"

Georges pointed up the levee. "Come on. I know a barrelhouse not far from here."

As the men walked up the levee, Julien noticed that most of the houses were nothing more than crude cabins constructed of rough-hewn cypress planks and logs. He also saw that large areas of swamp remained within the city. Julien thought there was nothing about the city even remotely like its namesake in France.

A block north of the river, the men came to another log building with shuttered windows. As Julien opened the door, the foul odors that hit him made him stop in the entry. The room smelled of sweat, urine, and rotten meat. It was dark, except for the light of a few candles. The barrelhouse had a dirt floor and consisted of a single room. Three walls of the bar were lined with large barrels and casks of wine and rum. The patrons consisted of sailors, longshoremen, and just about any kind of derelict one could imagine.

"What is this place, Georges? It smells as if something has died here."

Georges smiled. "Oh, I forgot that I was in the presence of royalty." The old man squeezed past the two other men and left them standing in the doorway. "Come on, Julien. You'll get used to the smell. The barrelhouse is the poor man's tavern, but they give you a large measure for your money."

Georges led Julien to the table at which their old companion had seated himself. Georges pulled up a bench so he and Julien could face the old man.

A filthy young man in leather breeches and a torn shirt came up to their table, asking in English, "What'll it be, gents?"

Julien answered in English, "Rum. Three rums."

When the young man left to get their order, Georges told Julien, "There's your answer, Julien."

"What?"

"The smell. It's that bloody Englishman."

They all chuckled at Georges's joke, even the old man. When the men were served their wooden cups filled with dark rum, Julien asked the old man, "What is your name, monsieur?"

The old man took a gulp of rum before answering. Wiping his mouth with the back of his hand, he spoke. "Paul, Paul Tremé, at your service."

"Monsieur Tremé," continued Julien, "I do not wish to upset you. But I must understand what has happened here. I have come to make New France my home."

The old man shook his head. "You mean, *New Spain*, monsieur…?"

"Poydras, Julien Poydras, and this is my shipmate, Georges Mazureau. Now tell us. What has happened? I read such great things about the colony."

"Hah! Well, Monsieur Poydras, I don't know what you have read, but I have lived in New Orleans since the city was founded, and I can tell you that some of our French governors make Bloody O'Reilly seem like a feeble woman."

"What?" exclaimed Georges.

"Yes, I was here in 1754 when the troops stationed at Cat Island mutinied. I was in the colonial militia. Our governor then, Governor Kerlerec, also held a public execution in the Place d'Armes. But a simple firing squad would not do for Kerlerec. He had two of the mutineers broken on the wheel. A sledgehammer was used to break their bones, one at a time. The third man was nailed alive in a coffin. Then they sawed him in half!"

"My God!" declared Georges.

Julien nodded his head. "A terrible punishment, I agree. But surely there was just cause for such retribution?"

"Cause!" scoffed the old man, slamming his cup down on the table. "Cause? The cause was that the commander of Cat Island — Duraux was his name — he sold his troops' provisions for his own gain. He starved us, beat us, mutilated us, tied us naked to trees for the flies and mosquitoes… When some of us escaped and came to Kerlerec for justice, the governor sent us back to Duraux."

"I'm sorry," said Julien. "I had no idea such things happened. Please forgive me and let me buy you another drink." Julien held up the old man's empty cup to alert the waiter of their need.

Georges pressed the old man for more information. "I take it you served on Cat Island? How did you survive?"

"I got the plague — yellow fever."

"What?"

"Duraux had me tied to a tree in the swamp, and I came down with the fever. A few days later, my comrades led the rebellion, and Duraux was killed. But I was too ill to participate."

"And what of your comrades?" asked Julien.

"They fled to the Georgia territory, but Kerlerec sent the Choctaws after them. When the captives were brought back to the city, the governor held his grand execution. The public never knew the truth. So, the crowd was cheering and shouting for the blood of my comrades."

The men fell silent as the waiter came to refill their cups.

"I see what you mean now," said Julien. "Bloody O'Reilly is a *humanitarian* when compared to your Governor Kerlerec."

The old man only nodded and continued to drink.

"But tell me. What do you make of young Noyan refusing his pardon?"

The old man grunted. "Huh! Noyan was a fool. He should have taken the pardon — no matter what the terms. Then he might have lived to raise a new army to fight the Spanish pigs."

Julien replied, "Perhaps he felt his honor would not allow that?"

"Honor? Take my advice, Monsieur Poydras. If you are going to live here, forget about honor. The only thing honor will lead you to is an early grave. If you want to survive in this Godforsaken land, you'd best learn Voodoo. That will serve you here far better than honor."

Chapter Six

As Mark's old Toyota chugged to a stop in front of the Noyan house, Celeste saw all the parked cars and cursed. "Damn it, Mark! Everybody's here already. I needed to be here to help Mom."

Mark nodded as he set the parking brake. "I know, I'm sorr — "

Celeste cut him off. "Why didn't you tell me we had to take the organist home? I would have ridden with Mom."

Mark grasped Celeste's hand and looked her in the eyes. "Look, babe. I didn't know the organist was expecting a ride until the rehearsal was over, and I sure as hell didn't know she lived twenty miles out in the sticks."

Celeste jerked her hand free and exited the car without responding. She slammed her car door and waited for Mark to get out and come around to her side of the car. "Well, all I can say is it's pretty bad when you're late to your own rehearsal dinner. Mom must be going nuts, especially with your folks not getting here."

Mark took Celeste by the arm and led her toward the front door of the house. "Come on, will ya? We're only fifteen minutes late. Besides, we're the guests of honor. We're supposed to make an entrance."

Celeste continued to pout as they walked up the front brick walk. She didn't answer Mark, but as soon as Mark opened the front door for her, it was like someone threw a switch. A smile came on her face, and she immediately gave the first person she saw a warm greeting. However, Mark could tell Celeste was still pissed at him, for she left him helpless at her side for a few moments before introducing him to the dapper white-haired and mustached gentleman she was conversing with.

"Mark, I'd like you to meet my grandfather, Justin Noyan."

Mark extended his hand. "A pleasure, sir. Until yesterday, I had no idea I was marrying into such a distinguished family."

Justin Noyan returned Mark's firm handshake. "The pleasure is mine, young man. Celeste's mother has spoken so highly of you that I was lookin' forward to meetin' you."

Mark chuckled. "Hah. Well, you can't believe everything your mother-in-law says. Do you live in Baton Rouge, Mr. Noyan?"

"No. I live in N'aw Arlens. I do hope you and Celeste will come for a visit. With my son and my wife both departed, I have plenty of room for company, and I do enjoy showin' guests the city."

"You've got a deal," said Mark. "Celeste has been bragging that New Orleans has the best food in the country."

Justin smiled and nodded his agreement. "That's no boast, Mark. Just give me two days, and I'll have you convinced our Cajun and Creole cookin' is unbeatable."

Celeste tugged at the coat sleeve of her grandfather's blue pinstriped suit. "Speaking of cookin', guys, it looks like everyone is heading for the dining room. Shall we?"

Mark followed Celeste and Justin into the dining room. Amy Noyan had reserved seats for Mark and Celeste at the center of the long table. Mark ended up at the seat across from Celeste and next to Justin Noyan. Before the guests were seated, Amy introduced herself as Celeste's mother, and then asked everyone around the table to introduce themselves. Mark concentrated on absorbing as many names and relationships as he could. When the introductions were complete, Mark's best man, Tony Hamilton, stood and raised his wine glass.

"Ladies and gentlemen!… A toast to the bride and groom."

"Here, here," said Justin, standing and raising his glass.

The dinner was southern comfort food, buffet style, and Mark ate until he was stuffed. Pushing his plate aside, he patted his stomach and spoke to his mother-in-law to be.

"Amy, that was a wonderful meal. You outdid yourself."

"Why, thank you, Mark, but your folks and I had it catered. I'm so sorry your parents didn't get to join us."

Mark blushed and thought about the hard time Celeste had given him for not getting her back in time to help with the dinner.

"Me too, Amy. Those darn airlines don't care what happens to people when they cancel a flight, but they will be here in plenty of time for the wedding tomorrow."

Amy stood up, taking Mark's empty plate. "I did make the dessert though — cheesecake. Would you like a piece with your coffee?"

Mark hated cheesecake, but answered, "Why thank you, Amy, I'd love a piece, but not too big, please. I'm so full."

Amy nodded and left the table. Mark glared at the grinning Celeste. "Thanks for not telling me the food was catered."

Celeste waved her wrist at Mark. "Did I not tell you, darlin'? It must have just slipped my little ole mind. You know, in all the confusion over takin' the organist home."

Mark wanted to tell Celeste to cut the damn Scarlet O'Hara routine, but he couldn't in front of Celeste's grandfather.

The tension between Mark and Celeste did not escape Justin Noyan. He took his spoon and tapped his water glass so it rang like a small bell. "Now, now, children. We can't have you fightin' now. All these good people are expectin' a weddin' tomorrow."

"Oh, we're not really mad at each other, Granddad. We just like to tease each other."

Mark decided it would be a good idea to change the subject of the conversation. "Say, Mr. Noyan. I was really intrigued to learn about your revolutionary ancestor, Jean Baptiste Noyan."

Justin took a sip of coffee before answering Mark. "Jean Baptiste Noyan. Now, I haven't heard that name in a very long time. Who told you about him?"

"The Parish Clerk, when we applied for our marriage license and Celeste's dowry," answered Mark.

"Ah yes, the Poydras dowry. It's hard to believe it still exists after a hundred and fifty years."

"Granddad?" asked Celeste. "Are the Noyan and Poydras families related?"

Although Justin's expression remained unchanged, Mark sensed that the question bothered him. "Whatever makes you ask that question, dear?" he replied.

"Well, yesterday we were in the attic, and we found an old trunk — Mom said it was your father's. Anyway, in it was an old family Bible and a handwritten journal that appears to be the diary of someone named Emile Poydras."

Mark interjected, "Yeah, and in the old Bible we found the Noyan family tree, and someone had written the name of Emile Poydras over the name of one of your ancestors — Henri Noyan, wasn't it?" asked Mark, as he looked to Celeste.

"Right, Mark, Henri Noyan and his wife Nicole. Did your father ever tell you about that part of our family history, Granddad?"

It now became obvious to both Mark and Celeste that Justin did not want to talk about the family history. Justin began to fidget in his chair, and he stared into his coffee, avoiding Mark and Celeste's eyes. There was a long pause before Justin answered Celeste.

"I told your father to leave that trunk be, Celeste, but he didn't listen to me." As Justin looked up from his coffee, Mark and Celeste saw tears starting to form in his eyes. "Now, I ask you to do the same. Please stay out of it. No good will come of it."

Celeste was stunned by the effect her question had on Justin. "I'm sorry, Granddad, I didn't mean to upset you. It's just that I know so little about our family history."

Justin stood up. "Please keep it that way, Celeste. For everyone's sake, please just keep it that way. Now, if you'll excuse me." With that, Justin left the dining room.

Celeste and Mark gave each other bewildered looks. Mark spoke first. "I'm sorry, babe. It seems that every time I bring up that trunk, I step on somebody's feelings."

"It's no more your fault than mine, Mark. I'm totally baffled as to why he got so upset."

"Yeah," agreed Mark. "How could something that happened over a hundred and fifty years ago upset anyone like that?"

Celeste shook her head. "I don't know, Mark. But I want to find out."

Chapter Seven

The sun had been up for less than an hour as Julien led his two packhorses into the open-air French Market. Already, the women of New Orleans were there with huge baskets on their arms, scrutinizing the butchers' meats, smelling and feeling the fruits and vegetables, and haggling over prices.

The merchants offered everything one could imagine: brightly colored parrots, alligators (live and skinned), monkeys, canaries, patent medicines, rat-traps, crockery, cheap glass jewelry, and all kinds of hardware and trinkets. The vendors who did not have a stall lined the lanes and edges of the market and hawked their wares.

Julien tied his packhorses next to a stall that contained tools, hardware, and cutlery. The proprietor, an olive-skinned Spaniard with thinning black hair, came out from behind the counter to greet Julien.

"Julien! Back already? You had another successful trip, I trust?"

Julien shook the hand of the middle-aged merchant and returned the greeting in Spanish, "Si, gracias, Garcia. I had a most successful journey — I finally purchased the land at Pointe Coupee I told you about."

"There on the banks of the False River?"

"Yes," answered Julien. "It will be perfect for my trading post, and the alluvial soil there is the richest in the territory."

"So, Monsieur Poydras is to become a gentleman farmer?"

Julien smiled. "Yes, hopefully. I have grown weary of these constant sales trips to the plantations and Indian tribes. Besides, by building a trading post at Pointe Coupee, I can sell to all the local planters and shorten my trading trips to all my customers on the west bank of the Mississippi."

Garcia sighed. "Then you will have no more need of a humble merchant such as myself?"

Julien shook his head. "No, no. I will still need hardware for my trading post — even more than I have been able to sell by horseback. I've come to order my new stocks from you."

Señor Garcia rubbed his palms together with glee. "Fantastic, my friend. I will make you a good price — the more you buy, the less the charge."

"Good. Then I can lower the prices to my customers."

"Lower!" Garcia raised his eyebrows and threw up his hands. "You could get twice the price you charge those planters. Now you're going to lower your prices?"

The men's conversation was interrupted by the shrill scream of a young Negro woman in the china stall across from Garcia's booth.

"Ah-ee! Gris-gris! Curse of Sanité Diable! Ah-ee!"

Despite the protests of the red-bearded crockery vendor, the black woman ran from the booth and out of the French Market. Julien and Garcia watched as the merchant threw a small leather bag and cord on the dirt street and swore.

"Damn you! Damn Voodoo!"

Garcia knew the crockery vendor and walked over to him. Julien followed.

"Juan," asked Garcia, "what is the matter?"

Juan Roxas, the rotund china merchant, stomped the little leather bag with one foot. "Damn Voodoo! Now that girl won't be worth anything. I'll have to whip her to make her work here. And I'll have to close up shop to go find her."

Garcia repeated his question. "Juan, what has happened?"

When the runaway slave girl had disappeared from sight, Juan finally took his eyes off the street and acknowledged Garcia's presence and question. "When we came to open up the shop this morning, Lydia found that Voodoo bag nailed to the booth." Juan pointed to the leather bag in the dust at his feet. "I tried to tell her it wasn't meant for her — that it's all just superstition, but she became hysterical and ran off."

Julien stooped over and picked up the trampled leather bag and emptied it into his hand. It appeared to contain some yellow ochre, some red hair, cayenne pepper, and a piece of snakeskin. Looking up from his hand, Julien spoke to the two Spaniards. "This is the dreaded gris-gris? It seems harmless enough." Juan Roxas eyed Julien cautiously. "Excuse me, you look familiar, señor. Have we met?"

Garcia jumped in with an introduction. "This is Señor Julien Poydras, Juan, a good customer of mine. Julien, allow me to present Señor Juan Roxas."

Juan relaxed his stare. "Ah yes, the French trader. I have heard Garcia speak of you. Do you know of Voodoo, Señor Poydras?"

"Not really. Only what I have heard at the various plantations I trade with. I understand the cult was brought here by the African slaves imported from Martinique and Santo Domingo."

"Yes, and Guadeloupe," added Juan. "All of them *French* colonies, Monsieur Poydras."

Julien ignored Juan Roxas's not so subtle insult to his nationality and changed the subject back to Voodooism. "Who would want to place a curse on you?"

"Sanité Diable herself," replied Juan. "I drove her from my shop last week. I told her she may be a free woman of color, but that I would not sell to her kind — free or not!"

"And for that she cursed you?" asked Garcia.

"When she refused to leave until I waited on her, I took out the switch I use to discipline Lydia and whipped her legs until she left my shop. But she stopped in the street and screamed at me. She said she would take my soul for what I had done. Then, as I turned my back on her, she took a knife out of her skirt, rushed forward, and cut off a lock of my hair before I knew what happened."

"Then, this is your hair?" asked Julien, extending his open palm.

Juan glanced at the contents of Julien's hand. "Yes, I suppose it is."

"And this little bag of hair and powders is supposed to cause your soul to leave your body — and go where?" continued Julien as he dumped the contents of the gris-gris bag into the street.

Juan Roxas shrugged his shoulders. "Believers in the cult say the soul must be trapped in some object the moment it leaves the body — if the Voodoo priest is to be able to control the body of the cursed person."

Garcia inquired, "Who is this Sanité Diable?"

Juan looked at Julien. "Tell him, Frenchman."

"The name means saint of the devil, Garcia. I have heard that she is the queen of all the Voodoo cults in the colony, but that's all I know about her."

"It's true," said Juan. "Sanité Diable has become Voodoo queen — by killing or cursing all those who opposed her."

"Why hasn't she been arrested?" asked Garcia.

Juan shook his head. "Nothing could be proven. Sanité Diable always made sure she was in some public place, with lots of witnesses, when her enemies were disposed of. Remember, under the Black Code, manumitted slaves have the same rights and immunities as freeborn persons — they can even own property."

"So, originally she came here as a slave?" Julien asked Juan.

"Yes, from Martinique. The rumor I heard is that Sanité Diable enticed her master to bed and made him *her* slave. Once she got him under her spell, she made him give her her freedom."

Juan looked back up the street his slave girl had run up. "Damn you, Lydia! When I find you, I'll give you such a whipping you'll forget all about Voodoo." Turning to Garcia, Juan asked, "Will you be so kind to watch my stall for a little while? I must go and report my runaway before she leaves the city."

"Certainly, Juan, take as long as you need."

Juan Roxas grunted a thank you to Garcia as he started up the street. After taking only a few steps, Juan turned around and ran back to his shop and brought out a thick willow switch. Then he trotted on out of sight. When Juan was out of earshot, Garcia spoke first. "Well, none of Juan's spirit seems to have left his body yet."

Julien chuckled. "Yes, so much for gris-gris. Now, shall we finish making my new order?"

Chapter Eight

By 10:30 p.m. all the rehearsal dinner guests had left, except for Mark and Tony Hamilton, who were both spending the night at Amy Noyan's house. Celeste helped her mother clear the tables and load the dishwasher. Despite Celeste's repeated reassurances, the whole time, Amy kept telling her not to help — to go and be with Mark and Tony, who were in the living room watching MTV and drinking beer.

Celeste finally got her fill of her mother's protests and decided to trick Amy into changing the subject. "Mother! I've got to spend the rest of my life with Mark. It's okay if I want to spend a little of my last single evening talking to my mother."

Celeste figured her satirical declaration would distract her mother in one of two ways: A. It would flatter Amy and make her nostalgic for the days when Celeste was her little girl, or B. Amy would do her old trick of reading too much into a statement and jump to the conclusion that Celeste was having second thoughts about marrying Mark. It was B.

"Celeste, what do you mean you've *got* to spend your life with Mark?" Amy laid her dishtowel down and turned to face her daughter.

Celeste smiled to herself before she raised her eyes to her mother. "Nothing, Mother dear. Mark and Tony are watching some stupid music videos on TV and going through the last rites of bachelorhood. It's just not the place for me right now."

Amy had to probe a little deeper to be convinced a major crisis was not at hand. "Celeste, are you sure that's all it is? You know, a little dose of cold feet is normal, but if it's — "

Celeste interrupted by tickling Amy's ribs. "No but-ifs, Mom." Now Celeste gently took ahold of her mother's shoulders and looked her square in the eyes. Amy was grinning at her daughter now. "Everything is fine. The rehearsal went perfectly. Your dinner was perfect, and the wedding will be perfect too."

Amy leaned into Celeste and hugged her neck. "I just want you to be happy, baby. That's all."

"I know, Mom. I love you too."

Just as this touching scene was concluding, Mark came sauntering into the kitchen with two empty beer bottles in each hand. Mark stopped in his tracks when he saw Celeste and Amy in their embrace.

"Oops, sorry, I didn't mean to intrude."

Celeste and Amy gave each other one more squeeze and then separated. Amy spoke first. "You weren't intrudin', dear. Mothers just get a little sentimental when their daughters get married."

Celeste walked over and took the empty beer bottles from Mark. "I can't believe you and Tony are in there watching TV. This is your last night as a free man. Don't you guys want to go out and paint the town red or something?"

"You mean you don't mind if we go hit a few clubs?"

Celeste checked the whites of Mark's eyes to see if he was already drunk. "No, I don't mind. Just promise me you'll take a cab. So Mom and I don't have to worry about you driving."

Mark nodded his head. "It's a deal, but you're sure you don't want to come along?"

"I'm sure, but thanks for asking. Now, don't drink up your cab fare, 'cause Mom and I ain't gettin' out of bed to come and pick you guys up when the bars close."

"Deal!" Mark started to exit the kitchen but stopped, turned around, and took Celeste in his arms and kissed her. "I love you, babe. It just dawned on me that the next time I see you will be our wedding day."

"You just make sure you get to the church on time, handsome. If you're late, I'll just have to marry the first available man."

Mark pinched Celeste on the butt before he let go of her and headed out of the kitchen. "I'll be there, babe. I'll be there with bells on."

When Celeste turned her attention to her mother, Amy had her back to the room, rinsing dishes in the sink.

"Mom, you mean you don't like to watch your daughter and future son-in-law make out?"

"I could see everythin' in the reflection in the window," answered Amy. Then both women laughed.

"Say, Mom?"

"Yes, honey."

"Did you speak to Granddad after dinner?"

"Why… no, now that you mention it. He didn't even say goodnight to me. Isn't that odd?"

"Yes," agreed Celeste. "It is odd. In fact, Granddad was acting very strange tonight."

"Oh? I wonder why?"

"Well," continued Celeste, "he seemed fine until Mark and I started asking him about Dad's old trunk and the Noyan family history."

Amy stopped washing the dishes but didn't turn to face Celeste. "I've been meanin' to talk to you about the trunk, dear."

"What about it, Mom?"

"I really wish you wouldn't sleep with it in your bedroom."

"Why not? What's wrong with the old trunk?"

Amy turned from the sink to face Celeste. Her expression was one of trepidation. "Honey, I've never told you this before, but… the last night your father spent in this house — before he went to Vietnam — we slept with that trunk in our bedroom. Jim had been translatin' parts of that old diary. Anyway, that night, Jim had a terrible nightmare. I woke up to see him sit straight up in bed, screamin' bloody murder. 'No! No!' he kept yellin'. When I finally calmed him down, all he would tell me was it was just a bad dream. I assumed it was just a bad case of jitters — the subconscious fear of goin' to the war."

"So? What did Dad's nightmare have to do with the trunk?"

"I don't know for sure. The connection didn't hit me until after Jim had left. But, that last night, after he had his nightmare, Jim put everything back into the trunk and hauled it back to the attic before comin' back to bed. When I asked him what he was doin', he said he had meant to do it earlier. That he wasn't goin' to leave all the clutter in our bedroom while he was gone. But now… now I've realized there was somethin' in that trunk that scared Jim — that caused his nightmare. And he didn't want to leave it in the room with me."

Celeste reached out and took her mother's hand. "Oh, Mom, I'm so sorry. If I'd known that trunk had such bad associations for you, I would have left it in the attic. Please don't worry. I slept with the trunk in my room last night, and I slept like a baby. But if it will make you feel better, I'll have Mark and Tony put it back in the attic when they get back. Okay?"

Amy squeezed her daughter's hand and forced a smile. "Thanks. That would make me feel better. Now, enough of this cleanin'. We both need to get our beauty sleep."

Celeste smiled. "You're right, Mom. We can't have circles under our eyes on my wedding day."

Celeste felt too keyed up to sleep. She decided a nice hot bath would relax her. But the whole time she soaked in the tub, her mind kept spinning about her dad's old trunk. *What had Granddad meant? Why is he afraid of it? Why is Mom still so upset about it?*

Celeste finally realized she was never going to get to sleep until she at least partially satisfied her curiosity, so she decided to inventory the contents of the trunk. Celeste didn't even wait to dry her hair or put her nightgown on. She just threw on her bathrobe, wrapped her wet hair in a towel, and headed for her bedroom.

Chapter Nine

Two days after witnessing the gris-gris curse of Juan Roxas in the French Market, Julien was crossing the Place d'Armes. As he walked toward the province's government building, known as the Cabildo, Julien sighted another merchant friend exiting the stately structure. It was the plump American trader from Philadelphia, Oliver Pollock. Oliver did not see Julien approaching, so he called out before Oliver turned the corner and got out of sight.

"Mister Pollock! Wait up!"

Oliver Pollock stopped in his tracks and turned to face Julien. His smooth cherub's face did not show recognition until Julien extended his hand in greeting.

"Julien? Julien Poydras! I almost didn't recognize you in those fine clothes. Business has been good I take it?"

"Yes, yes, thank you, Oliver. How goes your colonies' war for independence? Is there any news?"

Oliver Pollock shrugged his shoulders. "Alas, no good news, I'm afraid. The war is nearly two years old, and the British still control nearly all the major ports. But I have great hopes. It seems likely France will come to our aid."

"And what of our Spanish government?" asked Julien. "Any new aid from Spain?"

"Governor Gálvez is sympathetic to our struggle. In fact, he has granted the right to trade with all of the American colonies, and any port in Spain or France."

"Then the Mississippi has been opened to free trade with the Americans?"

"Well... it's not *free* trade," replied Oliver. "There are many restrictions, and the tariffs have been set at extremely high rates."

Julien's expression became one of concern. "The governor has not revoked your special license, has he?"

"Oh, no, the king of Spain himself gave me the right of free entry for all my goods, but I cannot begin to supply the needs of our war effort."

Julien nodded. "Yes, of course. If you think it would help, I will speak to the governor about lowering the tariffs?"

"Yes, thank you, Julien. It might just help. The governor is fond of you, I think."

Julien chuckled. "Yes, it's amazing how a few lines of poetry will turn a politician's head."

Oliver grinned and shared Julien's laugh. "Yes, the governor does enjoy flattery, I've noticed. But you, Julien, you carried it to new heights. What was the poem you wrote for him? Wasn't it about his victory over the English at Baton Rouge Hill last year?"

"Yes, it is called 'La Prise du Morne du Baton Rouge par Monseigneur de Galvez.'"

Oliver Pollock smiled and shook his head. "Even the title is enough to make one lightheaded. You must translate it for me sometime. My French still leaves much to be desired. What is the English translation of the title, please?"

"'The Taking of Gloomy Baton Rouge by Monseigneur de Galvez.' It describes the governor's valor in great detail." Julien grinned.

"Is it true you did not sign the poem when you sent it to him?"

"Yes, that's true. Flattery is much more poignant if the giver at least appears to be modest."

"There is much I can learn about New Orleans' politics from you," said Oliver. "But, enough of my troubles. Two hardworking and patriotic merchants such as we deserve a little entertainment, do we not?"

"What do you have in mind, my friend?"

Looking around to make sure no one else was in earshot, Oliver asked, "Do you know what today is?"

Julien answered without deliberation, "June 23, 1778?"

"That is the date, Julien. But what *day* is it?"

Julien thought for a moment. Then it dawned on him as he noticed worshipers leaving the St. Louis Cathedral. "Of course, it is St. John's Eve. Are church services your idea of entertainment?"

"Not church services, Julien. Voodoo services."

"What?"

"St. John's Eve is the most important date on the Voodoo calendar," replied Oliver. "Tonight, all the Voodooiennes will gather for their great conclave. I've heard that by the end of the ceremonies it turns into a total orgy."

Julien was beginning to think he did not know his friend Oliver Pollock as well as he thought. Oliver responded to the perplexed look that came across Julien's face. "I'm not suggesting we participate in the ceremonies, Julien. Merely that we go and observe. We won't be the only spectators."

Julien relaxed a little. "We can really gain entry? I thought that outsiders are not welcome at Voodoo ceremonies."

"That is not a problem. My valet, Nathan, is a member of the cult. He assures me that, for the right price, any white man may observe the rituals."

"You know where the ceremony is to be held?" asked Julien.

"Yes, tonight, in the old, abandoned brick yard on Dumaine Street. You can come to my house for dinner tonight, and afterwards Nathan will escort us there." Seeing the reluctance on Julien's face, Oliver added, "At least come to dinner and meet Nathan. Then you may decide for yourself."

Julien felt he could not turn down his friend's invitation, despite the unsettling feeling that had come over him. He couldn't help but wonder why he was having so many encounters with Voodooism recently. "Very well, Oliver. How can I refuse you? Anyway, I must admit, I too am curious as to what transpires at those Voodoo gatherings. What time shall I call on you?"

"Eight o'clock is dinner, but please come by earlier if you can, so you can meet Nathan before the other guests arrive."

"Other guests? I don't wish to — "

"No, no," interrupted Oliver. "You will not be intruding. I'm just entertaining the Spanish trade ministers in hopes of enlisting their support. After all, we can't all be poets."

Julien chuckled at Oliver's quip. "Very well, I shall be there by half past seven."

Chapter Ten

Finding some paper to write on was the first thing Celeste did upon reaching her room. She settled for the blank pages of her checkbook register. Then she lay on her stomach across the bed, looking down into the open trunk.

First, she took out her father's flight helmet without further examination. Celeste didn't even bother to write it on her list. Next, Celeste removed the old sword. It had a cane handle with no hilt, and its blade was dull and tarnished. Celeste looked for a name or initials engraved on it but could find none. She listed it as: "One old sword." Then Celeste took out and listed an ancient-looking, hardback journal ("Emile Poydras diary") and the family Bible she and Mark had examined in the attic.

When Celeste picked up the small glass jar containing brass buttons, she noticed that among the tarnished uniform buttons was an antique gold wedding band. Celeste strained to open the old jar, the lid of which was brown from age and rust. Finally, the lid snapped free, and she poured the contents into her hand. The wedding band was in fact two interlocking bands of gold. When Celeste tried to twist them apart, they would not budge. Suddenly, Celeste felt a pain shoot up her arms — like when you hit your funny bone — and she dropped the ring on the bed. The pain immediately ceased. Celeste decided her concerted twisting on the rings must have pinched a nerve or something. She picked up the wedding band and examined the inside. There were some faint initials and an engraved date. Celeste studied the markings and made a note: "Double gold wedding band, engraved with date September 21, 1824 and initials E. P. ? on one band and N. N. on other."

Returning the ring and buttons to the glass jar, Celeste continued with her inventory. She pulled out a bundle of old letters and found they were all written in French. Carefully leafing through each letter, so as to not break or tear the dry, brittle paper, Celeste noticed that many of the letters were written to some woman named Nicole and were signed Emile. *Of course!* thought Celeste. *Emile Poydras and his wife, Nicole. That's their wedding rings in the jar. Damn, wish I'd taken French in college instead of German.* Not all the letters were dated, but the ones that were ranged in age from 1824 to 1829. Celeste made a note of the number and age of the letters. Then she made an additional notation by the wedding band: "? Emile Poydras and Nicole Noyan."

Next, Celeste removed three modern books from the trunk. All had her father's name written on the inside cover. Without further examination, Celeste added the books to her list: "One book on the history of the French Quarter and two books about Voodoo in New Orleans."

All that remained in the trunk was another bundle of old letters, a big stack of old newspapers, and some old baby clothes and blankets that smelled like mothballs. Then Celeste noticed that the other letters were in English.

At last! she thought, *something I can read.*

These letters were written by her great-great-grandfather, Randolph Noyan, and all were addressed to her great-great-grandmother, Wilma. All the letters were written while Randolph was stationed in France during the First World War. One interesting letter recounted Randolph's chance meeting with a distant French cousin of the Noyan family. Celeste quickly scanned the letters. Instinctively, she felt the answers she sought were not in her great-great-grandfather's war experiences, but she kept reading anyway. Then in the next to the last letter, dated September 14, 1918, she ran across a paragraph that made her pause. She re-read it carefully three times:

I don't want to worry you, dear, but I had the dream again last night. In fact, I've had it several times since I landed in France. It seems so ironic. With all this death and misery caused by the war, I have nightmares about a man who died eighty-eight years ago. It's almost like his ghost followed me to France. Please don't think I've turned into a lunatic, but I have concluded that the dream is connected with the ring Grandfather gave me for good luck. He swears it protected him during the War Between the States. At any rate, I feel the charm may be having the opposite effect on me. Thus, I return the ring to you with this letter. Please put it in the trunk with the Poydras diary. When I return from this war, we will decide whether to proceed or to destroy the ring and the diary.

Now, please don't worry about me. I'm not trying to be a hero. I'm coming home to you in one piece. That's a promise.

Your loving husband,

Randolph

Celeste read the last of her great-great-grandfather's letters, but it was dated earlier and contained no reference to the ring, the Poydras diary, or his nightmares.

When Celeste turned the last page of the last letter, she found that a folded and yellowed newspaper article had adhered to the back of the letter's last page. She carefully removed and unfolded the article. It was obviously from a local Baton Rouge paper because it was about the local men who had served in France during World War I. Celeste noticed her great-great-grandfather's name was underlined in the article, and she skipped to that paragraph:

Killed in action during the Meuse-Argonne Offensive was Corporal Randolph Lewis Noyan of Baton Rouge. It is reported that Corporal Noyan was shot by a sniper while guarding his company's headquarters on the night of September 30th, 1918. The local men wounded during this final offensive include…

A cold shiver ran through Celeste's body. She laid the newspaper article down and picked up the jar containing the wedding band and brass buttons. This time, she examined the ring through the glass.

Celeste glanced at her alarm clock. Its red digital numbers read 1:03 a.m. Seeing how late it was caused Celeste to realize she was now very fatigued and sleepy. The information she had discovered during her inventory had raised more questions than it had answered, but Celeste felt she was too tired to think clearly about things. She decided to sleep on it. She quickly loaded all the items back into the trunk and closed the lid. Then Celeste threw off her bathrobe and pulled on her long Garfield the Cat nightshirt. She quickly brushed her hair a few strokes and jumped into bed. Celeste reached up to switch off her lamp but stopped. She got up, walked around to the trunk, pulled it away from the edge of her bed, and then pushed it against the wall farthest from her bed. Celeste fell back into bed, turning off the lamp as her head settled into the pillow. She was so exhausted she fell sound asleep within minutes. In her sleep, Celeste heard her name called out. "Celeste. Celeste. Are you alright?"

Celeste opened her eyes. There was a man standing over her bed. The only light came from the hall, behind the man, so his features were completely in the dark. The man sat down on the edge of the bed, took ahold of Celeste's hand, and spoke again. "Are you okay, babe?"

Celeste was starting to scream, but then she recognized the man's voice. "Mark? Is that you?"

"Yes, it's me. Who were you expecting? Freddy Krueger?"

"No. No, I'm fine. I guess I was just having a weird dream."

"I'll say," replied Mark. "I could hear you moaning at the bottom of the stairs. It sounded like you had some dude in here with ya too."

"What?"

"Yeah, I could hear you calling out some name, or should I say *moaning* out a name. And I could hear the bed squeaking like you were really gettin' it on."

Celeste reached up and brushed her hair and forehead. Her bangs and face were damp with sweat. "Yeah, it was quite a dream, all right. Tomorrow night, I'll definitely be ready for the real thing."

"So, you were dreaming about doing it?"

"Yes…Yes, I was." Celeste pulled herself up in bed and snapped on her bed lamp. "Will you please shut the door, Mark? I don't want to wake Mom — and Tony?"

"Out like a light."

Mark did as Celeste requested, closed her door, and returned to the edge of the bed. "So?" he asked.

Celeste smiled at him. "Okay, Dr. Freud, if you must know. As I recall, I fell asleep dreaming about you — do you feel better now?"

"Go on," Mark replied and gave her an intoxicated grin.

"Well, I was dreaming about the week we spent together last Spring Break — you know? How we never hardly left the hotel room… Now comes the strange part. There I was, in bed with you at the Fort Lauderdale Holiday Inn. Then, all of a sudden, I'm in a different room, in a bed — and with a different man."

"What?"

Celeste continued, "Yeah, it was really strange. The room was full of French antiques, and I was on this huge, four-poster bed with a canopy and mosquito netting."

"What about the man?" queried Mark.

"Well… I never saw his face… He was on top of me. All I could see was the back of his head."

"Then how do you know it wasn't me?"

Celeste blushed. "Because I could feel his mustache against my neck and ear."

"Oh," said Mark in a dejected tone of voice.

Celeste leaned forward and hugged Mark. "Now, come on, handsome. You're the one I'm marrying. You can't be jealous of some silly dream."

Mark returned Celeste's hug and then began to kiss her neck and run his hand across her breasts. Celeste kissed him once on the lips and pulled away from Mark's advances.

"Sorry, honey. But it's too late to get something started. Besides, we agreed to keep up appearances for Mom." Celeste glanced at her alarm clock. "And we have to get up in less than five hours and look our best."

"Okay," said Mark. "But I promise you — you won't have time for your *dream man* tomorrow night."

Celeste giggled. "You've got a deal, Casanova."

As Mark started to rise from the bed, a sudden thought entered Celeste's mind. "Wait a minute," she said.

Celeste jumped out of bed, went to the trunk, and removed the jar containing the buttons and wedding band. She poured the contents of the jar onto the bed and handed the ring to Mark.

"What's this?" asked Mark.

"You know the Bible and family tree we looked at the other day?"

"Yeah?"

"Well, that's the wedding ring of Emile Poydras and Nicole Noyan."

"How do you know that?" asked Mark.

"It's a long story — I read some of the old letters in the trunk. It's Emile's ring. Anyway, I have a favor to ask."

"Sure, anything for you, babe."

"Can we use this ring in our wedding ceremony tomorrow?"

Mark's face fell. "You don't like the bands we picked out?"

"No. No. I love them — and that's the ring I'll wear forever. But this ring has been in my family for something like eight generations. It would really mean something to me if we could use it just for the wedding ceremony. You know, something borrowed and old?"

Mark gave her a puzzled look. "I thought your mom's wedding veil was for that?"

"Well, yeah, it covers borrowed. The ring is for old."

"Have you tried it on — how do you know it'll fit?"

Celeste realized she had not tried the ring on, but then she answered, holding out her left hand. "It'll fit."

Mark slid the double band onto Celeste's second finger. It was a perfect fit.

"See!" said Celeste triumphantly.

"Huh? Emile Poydras must have had real small hands. Okay," Mark agreed reluctantly. "If it means that much to you, it's fine with me." Mark pulled the ring off and slipped it into his shirt pocket. "I'll give it to Tony in the morning."

Now, suddenly, Celeste felt anxious about what she had convinced Mark to do, but she couldn't bring herself to admit her instantaneous flash of doubt to Mark. All she could do now was follow through on her impulse. "Thank you, Mark. Now, if you don't mind, I think I need to try and get some beauty sleep."

Mark stood up and then bent over and kissed Celeste's forehead. "Sure, babe. Sleep tight." As Mark walked out the bedroom door, he turned and said, "And hold that moaning for tomorrow night."

Celeste had no more dreams that night, but she did recall the lover's name she had been calling out in her sleep, and she was thankful Mark had failed to press her for it.

Chapter Eleven

Julien did not have an opportunity to discuss the Voodoo ceremony with Oliver Pollock and his servant prior to dinner, for the other guests had arrived before Julien.

The dinner conversation was dominated by discussions of the war in the American Colonies, and by Oliver's arguments for less restrictions and lower tariffs on trade with the American rebels. Although these subjects were of great interest to Julien, he had a difficult time keeping his thoughts on the conversations. True, the petty Spanish officials were pompous and boring, as always, but Julien was used to that. It was something else that kept distracting Julien, a combination of anxiety and, at the same time, intense curiosity about attending the St. John's Eve Voodoo ceremony. Thus, by the time the other dinner guests had departed, Julien needed no more convincing to accompany Oliver and Nathan to the Voodoo rituals.

Nathan, a mature mulatto with white hair and stooped shoulders, led Julien and Oliver to the gate of the abandoned brickyard off Dumaine Street. As they approached the gate, Oliver motioned for Julien to pull the hood of his long black cape over his head, and Oliver did likewise. The hooded men waited at the gate while Nathan spoke in hushed tones to the two burly gatekeepers. Julien's eye caught the glint of silver as money changed hands. Then he and Oliver were ushered into the walled brickyard.

Since it was after eleven o'clock by the time they arrived, the ceremony was already under way. As the men approached a large, barn-like structure, Julien looked through the open double doors of the building. There was a raised bonfire burning in the middle of the stone floor, and African drumming and chanting could be heard.

Eh! Eh! Bomba hen hen!

Canga bafio te,

Canga moune de te,

Canga do ki la!

Canga li!

The men hurriedly entered the building and found a place among the other spectators at the back wall, just to the left of the doors.

The first thing that attracted the men's attention was a built-up square of bricks on which the compact, but intense, fire was burning. The only other light in the building came from lighted dips in a few sconces on the walls. These flickering flames added little to the yellow light of the brick pyre. The dancing shadows cast by the pyre's flames gave the room an eerie atmosphere. The temperature in the room was stifling, with the heat from the bonfire on top of the humid summer air.

Julien estimated there were about seventy-five worshipers in the building. The majority were Negroes and Negresses. There were also handsome mulatresses and quadroons. The sex of the company seemed to be about evenly divided between male and female. Julien was shocked when he observed about a dozen white men and three white women among the chanting pagans. He turned to Oliver to point out his discovery, but he could tell from the look on Oliver's face that he too had spotted the white members of the cult.

Each male cultist had a white kerchief tied around his forehead, and all the women's heads were covered by the traditional madras handkerchief, or tignon. Most of the men were bare-chested, and some wore nothing more than knotted tignons tied over their loins.

Behind the fire was an even higher platform of bricks where two wicker chairs sat with a low table in between. The table was covered with a black cloth, and on it sat two burning candles plus an ornate wooden chest.

The crowd of worshipers had formed a semicircle in front of this pagan altar, and they were still repeatedly chanting the same words that Julien had heard as he approached the building, but the pace and volume of their chant had intensified.

Eh! Eh! Bomba hen hen!

Eh! Eh! Bomba hen hen!

Suddenly, the chanting ended in a chorus of shouts:

Sanité Diable!

Sanité Diable!

The attention of the crowd had focused on a striking black woman and muscular black man ascending the altar, hand in hand. The woman appeared to be in her early twenties and was tall with long black hair and a well-endowed figure. She wore a costume made of red tignons sewn together with a blue cord tied about her waist. Around the woman's neck was a thick gold necklace. Her male companion was naked from the waist up. He too wore a blue cord tied around the waist of his brown leather breeches. From the looks of his strong physique, Julien guessed the black man to be a field hand or laborer. Only the woman wore anything on her head. It appeared to be a red silk scarf with dark fringe.

Oliver motioned for Nathan to come between him and Julien so both men could hear his answer to Oliver's whispered question. "Who are these people, Nathan?"

"The queen and king, Sanité Diable and King Soto."

"So that's Sanité Diable," replied Julien. "I expected a much older, more wicked looking person."

Oliver grinned and snorted at Julien's remark, but Nathan's blank face made it clear he did not find the comment amusing. "I assure you, gentlemen. Sanité Diable is wicked enough — and powerful enough — to rule the sect."

It was apparent from the way that Soto deferred to Sanité Diable that it was she, the queen, who ruled the ceremonies. Soto led Sanité Diable to one of the platform chairs and knelt before her. The queen made a cabalistic sign over the king's head, and then she pointed at the chest on the table. Soto jumped up, raised his arms about his head, and addressed the crowd in French. "L'Appé vini, le Grand Zombi! L'Appé vini, pou fe gris-gris!"

Oliver shook his head and turned to Julien as the worshipers took up this new chant. The men could no longer whisper and be heard, as the chanting was now accompanied by loud drumbeats.

"What are they saying, Julien? I can't make out any of this French."

Julien turned and spoke directly into Oliver's ear. "He is coming, the Great Zombi. He is coming, to make gris-gris magic."

Because of the noise of the chanting and drumming, the men did not attempt to converse further. They stood and watched as Soto removed the chest from the table. Soto then knelt again before the standing queen, holding the chest above his head. Sanité Diable opened the chest and withdrew a large, spotted snake, holding it over her head with both of her fully extended arms. Julien had seen such snakes before in African ports. It was a python. Sanité Diable held the snake behind its head and placed her other hand about three feet from the head. Even though she held the reptile as high as possible, its tail draped over Sanité Diable's left shoulder, nearly touching the floor. Julien guessed the python was around eight feet long.

The appearance of the python brought about a variation in the chanting by the cult members and an increase in the volume of the chants and accompanying drums.

Le Grand Zombi!

Le Grand Zombi!

Aie! Aie!

Voodoo Magnian!

Next, Queen Sanité Diable slowly brought the head of the great serpent toward her face. Julien watched spellbound as the slender, forked tongue of the snake darted in and out of its mouth. When the python began to lick the cheek of the queen, a great cheer was raised by the cult, and the chanting ceased. With a background of now low drumbeats, Sanité Diable let the python drape itself around her neck. Then she grasped the outstretched hands of King Soto and brought him to his feet. Another cheer came from the worshipers, and as if on cue, they formed two lines before the altar. In single file, each member of the cult ascended the altar and received a two-handed handclasp from either King Soto or Queen Sanité Diable.

Julien took advantage of the lull in the proceedings to question Nathan about the ceremony now taking place. "It is the passing of the power," replied Nathan. "We believe the first man and woman came into the world blind, and it was the serpent — the Great Zombi — who bestowed sight upon the human race. From the kiss of the serpent, the queen has again received the vision and the power to lead us and be our oracle."

Before Julien could inquire further, Nathan excused himself and marched off to join the lines of worshipers at the altar. Oliver and Julien gave each other simultaneous looks of bewilderment. When Nathan returned to join his master and Julien, after receiving the blessing from Sanité Diable, Julien thought the slave's eyes had a glint in them that had not been there before.

Oliver asked, "What is next on the agenda?"

Nathan pointed to four persons who had come forward and formed a crescent before the altar with their backs to the crowd. King Soto was in the process of scratching a circle around the four in the brick dust on the floor of the building.

"Those four are going to be initiated into the cult. But first, they must be tested. They must not leave the circle during the ceremony of the testing, no matter what."

Julien observed that the four initiates consisted of two young black men, a slender Negress, and one stout white man. The three men were stripped to the waist. The black woman was dressed only in a long camisole. Julien watched as Sanité Diable descended the steps of the dais and faced the neophytes. The python had been returned to its chest. The queen made cabalistic signs over each of the new disciples. Then she sprinkled them vigorously with some liquid from a calabash made from a long-handled gourd. The anointing completed, the queen raised her hand, and the drums recommenced their faster beat, but not nearly as loud as before.

King Soto came forward with a large wooden paddle and began striking each of the initiates on the head and shoulders. As he did so, Soto chanted in a low, muffled voice. Julien could not make out any of the words of the chant, but he recognized that it was in an African dialect. As Soto alternated the blows between the candidates, Julien noticed that Soto was gradually increasing the force of the blows each time he began a new round of paddling. Soon, the intensity of the strikes caused Julien to cringe in sympathy for the initiates. The slap of the wooden paddle could easily be heard over the drumbeat.

The black girl was the first to collapse from the beating. As she fell to the floor, she began to jerk and tremble. Soon, the two black men fell from the intensified blows, and all three of the felled candidates writhed on the floor.

Amazingly, the white male initiate seemed immune to Soto's strikes. Even from where Julien stood, in the back of the room, he could see blood begin to fly from wounds opening on the man's neck and back. Soto's blows did stagger the man, but each time he rose to willingly receive the next hit, and never once did he cry out or give any indication of the pain he was surely feeling.

Oliver turned to Julien. "My God! They're going to kill him if he doesn't stop soon."

Before Julien could reply to Oliver, Sanité Diable raised her hand and shouted, "Assez!"

With nothing more than a wave of her hand, Sanité Diable summoned forth two black handmaidens who proceeded to slaughter a live chicken on the altar's table. One woman held a shallow pewter bowl while the other held the decapitated chicken above it. Apparently, the heart of the chicken was still beating, for its blood gushed into the bowl in rhythmic spurts.

When the bowl was filled with blood, it was handed to Sanité Diable. As the Voodoo queen approached the four initiates, King Soto pulled the three fallen candidates to their feet. Sanité Diable held the bowl of blood above her head, then drank some of it. With that, the crowd again began to chant in a combination of French and African.

Eh, yé, yé Sanité Diable!

Ya, yé, yé, li konin tou, gris-gris;

Li té kouri lekal, aver vieux kokodril;

Oh, ouai, yé Sanité Diable...

Next, Sanité Diable held the bowl of blood to the lips of each initiate as they drank from it. As soon as all had received the pagan communion, Soto turned each new disciple to face the chanting crowd. Julien was surprised to see expressions of joy and tranquility on the bloody faces of the new cult members. But when King Soto turned the white male neophyte toward the crowd, there was no expression at all in the man's red-bearded face. It was completely blank — completely dead.

Suddenly, Julien recognized that dead face. This recognition made him gasp and grab Oliver's shoulder for support. For a moment Julien thought he had merely succumbed to the heat in the building, and that his eyes were playing tricks on him. *That can happen when one feels faint,* thought Julien. However, this was not the case. For when Julien recovered enough to look again at the white man's face, he was forced to admit his eyes were not deceiving him. For there, standing rigid, was Juan Roxas, the china merchant, while a smiling Sanité Diable smeared his face with more of the chicken blood.

Part II
Submission

Yield not to evils, but attack all the more boldly...

It is easy to go down into Hell; night and day,

the gates of dark Death stand wide;

but to climb back again, to retrace one's

steps to the upper air — there's the rub...

— Virgil, *Aeneid*

Part II
Submission

Yield not to evils, but against all the more boldly

...

...

...

...

Chapter Twelve

Celeste and Mark's wedding was a traditional Catholic service, but without the full nuptial mass. The ceremony took place in Baton Rouge's old St. Joseph Cathedral, with about a hundred and twenty-five guests in attendance. As Celeste processed down the aisle with her grandfather, Justin Noyan, Mark blushed with pride. Despite her lack of sleep, Celeste was every bit a beautiful bride. Her green eyes sparkled, and her face just seemed to radiate happiness. To please her mother, Celeste wore Amy's white lace wedding veil, although Celeste really preferred the big white hat she had picked out.

The only member of the wedding party who looked a little worse for wear was the best man, Tony Hamilton. Celeste noticed his eyes were still bloodshot from last night's carousing with Mark. Tony was so out of it, it seemed to take him forever to fish the old wedding band out of his vest pocket and hand it to Mark.

Yet the ceremony came off without a hitch. Before Celeste could fully realize she was actually getting married, she found herself kissing Mark at the altar and running down the aisle with him, hand in hand.

Celeste thought, *All these months of planning, and it happened so fast I didn't get to really enjoy it — wish weddings could be in slow motion.*

The reception followed the afternoon ceremony. It was held at the old Knights of Columbus Hall near Amy Noyan's house. The reception was totally a Cajun affair. The music was provided by a Cajun zydeco band, complete with an accordion player. The hors d'oeuvres consisted of Cajun shrimp and crawfish, fried oysters and bouchettes — spicy meatballs made with chopped onion and sweet peppers. The caterers made certain that the cold beer and wine flowed freely, and it did not take long for the wedding guests to get into a festive mood.

The dancing commenced with another Cajun tradition, the bride's dance. Mark and Celeste waltzed solo for one number. Then all the guests were welcome to take the floor. Any male guest who wished to dance with the bride was free to cut in, for a price. The tradition was to pin some folded money to the bride's veil or dress to pay for the privilege of the dance. Celeste's dress was soon covered with ten- and twenty-dollar bills. Mark kidded her, telling Celeste she looked like a dancing Christmas tree.

Justin Noyan displayed none of the moodiness he had shown at the rehearsal dinner, and Celeste noticed he was laughing and joking with the wedding guests — the charming grandfather she had always known. Justin waited until the end of the bride's dance to take his turn with Celeste. Justin pinned a hundred-dollar bill to the bottom of Celeste's veil as he began his dance.

"You're a beautiful bride, my dear. I suppose everyone has told you that. But I waited, so I could be the last one to say it."

Celeste hugged her grandfather's neck. "Thank you, Granddad. Thanks for everything. I felt so proud when you were walking me down the aisle."

Justin beamed at Celeste. "So did I. So did I. I just wish your dad was here to see how beautiful you are." Quickly changing the subject before Celeste could reply, "Do you think everyone is enjoyin' themselves?"

"Oh my, yes, Granddad, the reception is wonderful. Mom told me you were a great help in arranging and helping to pay for things. Thank you so much!"

Justin shook his head. "You are most welcome, my dear. I wasn't sure how Mark's family would relate to our Cajun ways, but from the way they've been eatin' and drinkin', I think they'll fit in this family just fine."

Celeste giggled and nodded her head.

"Where are you two goin' on your honeymoon?" asked Justin.

"Nassau — Paradise Island."

"Wonderful. Your grandmother and I went there the year before she died. And what about after your honeymoon? Will you come to visit me in N'aw Arlens for a few days?"

"We'd love to, Granddad, but I'm not sure how long we can stay. Mark and I really need to get back to our job hunting, and find an apartment — "

Justin interrupted, "I thought your mother told me you both had jobs in St. Louis?"

"No, I had a job offer, but the paper folded. Mark had interviews with a couple of local TV stations. But, so far, they haven't made any offers."

"Have you made up your minds that St. Louis is where you want to live?" asked Justin. "Surely there are other markets for two outstanding journalism graduates?"

"I'm sure you're right. St. Louis just seemed like the place where we both had the best chance of landing a job. The MU Journalism School had the listings and helped us with our job searches there."

"Well," said Justin, "I don't want to interfere, but the city editor of *The Times-Picayune* is a friend of mine, and he's always sayin' the paper needs good reporters. Why don't I ask him if he could set you up an interview when you come to visit me?"

Celeste thought for a moment, and said, "That's very generous of you, Granddad. I… I just don't know if…"

"If, what, sugar?"

"Oh, Granddad, you know I love you and New Orleans. But I'm just not sure I'm ready to come *home* yet."

Justin pulled his head back to study his granddaughter's face before he responded. "I understand. Let's just take it a step at a time. You and Mark come for a visit, and we'll see how things go? No pressure, I promise."

Celeste forced a smile. "Okay, Granddad, deal. I don't know what Mark would think about living in New Orleans. Before he met me, he'd never been farther south than Branson, Missouri."

"Don't you worry about that, sugar. When we get done winin' and dinin' that young man of yours, he'll be so in love with the Big Easy he won't want to live anywhere else. Oops, I said no pressure, didn't I?"

Celeste grinned and hugged her grandfather's neck once more as they turned on the dance floor. "Thank you again for everything, Granddad. I'll really think about your offer to help us. I don't know what I'd do without ya."

Justin smiled and returned Celeste's hug. "No thanks is required, sugar. I have my own selfish reasons for wantin' to help. I'm tired of my only — and favorite — granddaughter bein' so far away from me." *You're all I've got left,* thought Justin. "Mark majored in broadcast journalism, right?"

"Yeah, he wants to be a TV sportscaster."

"Well, from what I've seen on local television, there is surely a need for a good sportscaster."

Celeste grinned again, shook her head gently, and placed her index on her grandfather's lips. "No pressure, right?"

As Justin finished speaking, the dance ended, and Mark walked up to retrieve his bride. Justin spoke first, "Mark, I was just tellin' Celeste that I really do want you two to visit me in N'aw Arlens after your honeymoon. In fact, I won't take no for an answer."

Mark was receptive to the invitation. "Sounds great to me, Mr. Noyan, I — "

"Justin, please call me Justin. After all, we're all one family now."

"Okay, Justin. I've always wanted to visit New Orleans."

"Granddad lives in the French Quarter, Mark," interjected Celeste. "Wait till you see his house. It's like a museum."

Justin uttered a gracious little laugh. "Well, my house is over a hundred and fifty years old, but I believe it'll last till your visit."

Celeste gave Justin a feigned look of disgust. "Oh, Granddad, you know what I mean. I was referring to all the beautiful antiques and paintings you have."

Justin smiled and replied, putting his hand on Mark's shoulder. "Don't worry, Mark. I promise I won't let your bride lock you in the slave quarters."

Mark looked intrigued by Justin's comment, "Slave quarters?"

Celeste answered his question, "It's okay, Mark. The slave quarters are now a guest house."

"What? The chains and whips are gone?" retorted Mark.

"Well," said Justin. "It's settled. I'll expect you in N'aw Arlens on the…?"

"We'll be in Nassau five days," said Mark. "And we had to fly out of New Orleans anyway. So, that will put us back in New Orleans Friday afternoon."

"Wonderful," said Justin. "Just call me when your flight arrives, and I'll pick you up at the airport. Now, I'll leave you two alone. After all that dancin', the bride looks like she could do with a little sit-down."

Justin took Celeste's left hand to give it a parting kiss. As he brought it to his lips, he stopped abruptly. Both Mark and Celeste looked taken aback. They watched Justin freeze in motion as the color rapidly left his face. Finally, after an awkward pause, Justin summoned the breath to speak.

"The ring! Where did you find that ring?"

Celeste slowly withdrew her hand from her grandfather's trembling fingers. "It was in the old trunk, Granddad. Why? What's wrong with this ring?"

Justin ignored Celeste's questions. "You… you used that ring in your weddin' ceremony?"

Mark responded with concern in his voice. "Yes, Mr. Noyan. What's going on here?"

Justin ignored Mark's question as well, and looked Celeste directly in the eyes. "You know whose ring this is?"

Celeste took a second, but answered with a hesitant, "Yes."

Justin followed with another question. "And you accepted the ring willingly?"

"Well, yeah," replied Celeste. "We just used it for the ceremony. We have my personal ring for… But what is…?"

Justin dropped his head and shook it at the same time.

Mark finally forced his way back into the conversation. "Will someone please tell me what the hell is going on here?"

Justin raised his head. Mark could see a look of panic in his gray eyes. Justin took both Mark and Celeste's hands into his before answering Mark. He looked hard into Celeste's eyes. "We can't discuss it here, children. I'll explain when you get to N'aw Arlens. For now — for God's sake — just promise me you won't take the ring off. Not even to wash your hands."

"What!" exclaimed Mark. "Celeste, what's going on? You said you were only gonna wear that old ring for the wedding ceremony."

Celeste ignored Mark and nodded her head at her grandfather. She felt a sudden, overpowering chill run down the length of her spine. "I understand, Granddad. I promise. The ring will not leave my finger."

Chapter Thirteen

Julien's first encounter with Voodoo had caused him no ill fortune, far from it. In the seventeen years that had elapsed since attending Sanité Diable's ceremony, Julien Poydras had become one of the wealthiest men in the Louisiana Colony. He now owned six large plantations, several properties in New Orleans, a cattle company, the first bank in Pointe Coupee, his trading company, and some 3,700 slaves.

Within the same seventeen years, Julien had reveled in the success of the American Revolution and had become bitter over the gory revolution in his homeland. The French Revolution, which was inspired by that of the American Colonies, failed miserably as far as Julien Poydras was concerned. For not only had the French Revolution murdered the monarchs to whom Julien gave allegiance, it had brought economic and social chaos.

Julien's plans for a triumphant return to France were dashed to pieces by the revolution. So too was his improbable dream of perhaps finding and winning the woman he had wanted to marry before he left France all those years ago. Now, the Reign of Terror and the "sans-culottes" (men without fancy knee breeches) made it all impossible, even in Julien's dreams.

Julien's great success in his business ventures in Louisiana was substantial consolation for his self-imposed exile. He had become a respected and wealthy leader in the colony. Even without the revolution, in France Julien would have never been more than a presumptuous nouveau riche. Thus, Julien resolved to make Louisiana his permanent home and to invite his family to join him in the prosperity to be found in the New World.

The first relative to accept Julien's invitation was his nephew, Emile Poydras. Emile was the illegitimate son of Julien's brother, Godfroi. When Julien first heard of his nephew's adversities, his heart went out to him. From his days in the English prison, Julien remembered what it was like to be treated with disdain — like a bastard. When Emile Poydras rose above his bad fortunes and pursued education and the banking trade, Julien was convinced that paying for the young man's passage to Louisiana would be a good investment.

Consequently, on March 19, 1795, twenty-two-year-old Emile Poydras stood on deck of the Spanish merchant ship, the *Aztec Conquistador,* as it approached the New Orleans wharf. Emile was apprehensive about making a good impression on his uncle Julien, and at the same time grateful his sea voyage was complete. His early spring crossing had been an unpleasant one, and the small quarters on the ship made him claustrophobic.

Emile had put on the clean, dark blue suit he had saved for the occasion of meeting his uncle. He hoped the eight-day delay in his crossing had not caused him to miss connecting with Julien in New Orleans.

The new immigrant appeared more youthful than his years. His frame was tall and slender, and he had a smooth face and dark complexion that made it hard to guess his age. Emile kept his long dark hair pulled back and knotted with a purple ribbon behind his neck. His mustache was trimmed pencil thin.

As the ship came within sight of the wharf, Emile removed a folded letter from inside his coat pocket. All he knew of his uncle Julien came from their correspondence. This particular letter meant a great deal to Emile. Julien had written it two years earlier, shortly after the execution of King Louis XVI. The failure of the revolution to bring about a constitutional monarchy had shattered Emile's dreams, as well as his uncle's, and Emile had found wisdom and solace in Julien's words. Emile re-read two passages from the letter:

Tis not the whole of life to live; nor all of death to die…

Men gifted with reason, who with sangfroid shed torrents of blood, are not worthy of the name of men…

Emile refolded the letter and put it back into his pocket. He gazed ahead at the outline of New Orleans, and felt his apprehensions being replaced by feelings of great expectations.

Julien Poydras was also experiencing a slight case of nerves as he awaited the arrival of Emile. Word had come from down river that Emile's ship was nearing New Orleans. Julien paced the dock scheduled to receive the *Aztec Conquistador.* In the years since his arrival in Louisiana, Julien had kept his tall, sinewy figure. His long, clean-shaven face had acquired a few lines, but Julien's strong, plain features remained unchanged.

The biggest change in Julien's appearance was in his dress. During the reign of Louis XV, Julien had adopted the dress of a subject of the prior king of France, right down to his satin knee breeches; silver buckles; and queue, or pigtail wig. Julien had chosen a peacock blue frock for today's occasion.

As the passengers from the Aztec Conquistador disembarked, Julien and his Negro body servant, Andrew, studied the faces coming ashore. Emile had no trouble recognizing his uncle Julien. After all, Julien's elaborate attire certainly made him stand out in a crowd.

As Emile approached Julien, he saw an expression of recognition come upon his uncle's face.

"Uncle Julien?"

Julien smiled and extended his arms to hug his young nephew. "My dear boy. It is so good to finally lay eyes on you. Welcome to Nouvelle Orléans."

"Thank you, Uncle. I hope the delay in my passage has not inconvenienced you?"

"No, not at all my — Emile. But I am afraid we will have to wait for another occasion for me to show you the city. We must leave immediately for Pointe Coupee, for I am obliged to leave for Philadelphia next week and have much to do before I depart."

"Philadelphia?"

Julien nodded and pointed Emile toward the far end of the wharf. "Yes, I am scheduled to meet my friend Monsieur Pollock there — the American trader. I believe I wrote of him to you?"

"Yes, yes, you did, Uncle. He was the first American allowed to trade in New France, wasn't he?"

"Yes, that's the man. Oliver Pollock. He and I are seeking to expand our trade with the new United States government, and we are scheduled to meet with their trade officials in Philadelphia. But, come along. My galley is standing by at the end of this pier. My man, Andrew, will claim your baggage."

Emile laughed. "Hah! That won't be necessary, Uncle. All I have is in these two bags I carried off the ship."

Julien patted Emile on the back. "Don't feel inadequate, my boy. When I came to New France I had only *one* old sea bag." Julien turned and spoke to his servant. "Andrew, carry Monsieur Emile's bags for him please."

Andrew acknowledged Julien's command with a nod of his head. Picking up Emile's valises, he walked on ahead of the men.

Emile was dazzled when they reached his uncle's riverboat. It was not your ordinary keelboat. This boat was painted lavender and gold, and six black oarsmen stood at attention as Julien and Emile came aboard. All the oarsmen were in matching ornate, purple uniforms. Emile thought that these black slaves had finer uniforms than line officers in the Royal French Navy. The river galley was lavishly furnished inside and out. Even the deck chairs were upholstered in fine brocades.

After Emile was shown to his private cabin, with its own toilet, he joined his uncle on deck. They sat at a small table under a white canvas canopy, and Andrew served them wine as the boat got under way. Julien received reports on the welfare of Emile's father and other members of the Poydras family. Then he asked Emile for the latest news of the revolution in France.

"Pray, tell me, Emile. How goes the revolution? In your last letter to me, you wrote that Robespierre and his followers had all been guillotined."

Emile took a long drink of wine before answering his uncle. "Yes, that is true, Uncle Julien. The sans-culottes gave them a farce of a trial, convicted them all of treason, and that same day executed them all. The heads of twenty-three men were decapitated by the guillotine in less than two hours. What I did not write was that I actually witnessed the execution of Robespierre. It was beyond the pale — beyond any brutality I could even imagine."

"What do you mean?" pressed Julien.

"You see, when the mob came for Robespierre, he tried to shoot himself in the brain, but all he succeeded in doing was shattering his jaw. For six hours, he was left bleeding while the Revolutionary Tribunal debated his fate. No physician was allowed to treat him. Then, when Robespierre was led upon the scaffold, the executioner ripped the rough bandage from his jaw, and the crowd laughed and cheered as Robespierre shrieked with pain."

"My God!" said Julien. "It is true what they say — that the whole country has gone mad. The dogs have turned upon themselves."

"Actually, Uncle, when I left Paris, the situation had improved somewhat."

"How so?"

"The Girondists are calling for a new constitution, and — "

"Hah! How many constitutions has the revolution produced?" interrupted Julien.

Emile continued, "There is hope that the Reign of Terror is over. The so-called Watch Committees have been disbanded. The National Guard now controls the capital, and the sans-culottes have lost their control of the government."

"But for how long?" questioned Julien. "France must have a king again, a single strong leader, or the bloodletting will never be brought to an end."

"I agree, Uncle. I agree, and so does your entire family."

"What do you mean?"

"Your brothers, Godfroi and Claude, and my half-brother, Benjamin, have been in contact with the Duke of Orleans."

"I thought the duke was executed two years ago?"

"He was. I am speaking of his son, Louis Philippe." Emile lowered his voice and leaned closer to his uncle before continuing. "I could not dare write you about this, but I am carrying a letter from the new duke."

"Go on," prodded Julien.

"The duke has heard of your great success, and he requests your assistance in his quest for the throne."

"But what can I do from here in Louisiana?"

"You can grant the duke asylum and help him raise money for an army."

Julien was taken aback. "The duke wishes to come here? To New France?"

"Possibly. Here or in the new United States. He feels it would be safer for him to leave France for a while. As the heir to the throne, there are many rebels who wish to kill him before he can organize the royalists. Also, the Duke knows there are many loyal subjects here who would contribute to his campaign, and he requests your assistance in enlisting these men."

"I am flattered," responded Julien, "that the duke would call on my services. I am ready to do all that I can, and the duke is welcome in my home any time he likes."

Emile smiled at his uncle. "Somehow, I knew that would be your answer. I have only to write to Benjamin a coded letter, and the duke will be notified of your offer of assistance."

"How long do you suppose it may take for him to come here?"

"That's hard to say, Uncle. The duke is closely watched, and his travel is restricted. The journey cannot be accomplished without subterfuge. And, as I said, he may not be able to come directly to New France."

"I shall pray for the duke's deliverance," said Julien. "Now, you may wish to rest and clean up before we reach the plantation of Monsieur Barren. We will dine there and spend the night."

"I am much too excited to rest, Uncle. Please, tell me more about Pointe Coupee and your new bank."

"The bank is nothing like those in Paris, Emile. I hope you will not be disappointed in its unrefined operations. At any rate, I have another challenge in store for you."

"And what might that be?"

"I have recently acquired a new plantation near Pointe Coupee, Alma Plantation. It consists of over two thousand acres, and I am determined that it shall become the richest sugar plantation in the territory."

"But what does that have to do with me?"

"I intend for you to manage Alma."

"What!" exclaimed Emile. "I'm a mere bank teller. I know nothing of farming and managing such an operation."

Julien chuckled. "Neither did I when I came here, Emile. But don't worry. I shall teach you, and I'll see to it that you have all the slaves that you need."

"Slaves? I don't know the first thing about overseeing slaves. Why, I'd never even seen more than a handful of Negros prior to my voyage here."

"Slaves, unfortunately, are a necessary evil of the New World economy, Emile. There are three rules in dealing with them. Demand their respect! Respect their human needs, and never let them practice Voodooism."

"Voodooism? What's that, Uncle?"

"A pagan religion; I will explain it to you later. Right now, I want you to go with Andrew and have him fit you with proper clothes for dinner this evening. I had to guess on the sizes, but hopefully one of the ensembles will fit. First impressions are important in the quest for success, and Monsieur Barren is a very influential man. And…"

Emile smiled and stood up. "Say no more, Uncle. I readily admit my attire is rather shopworn. Thank you, again, for all you have done — and are yet to do."

Chapter Fourteen

Justin Noyan picked up Mark and Celeste thirty minutes after they called him from the New Orleans International Airport. Justin pulled up to the curb in a brand new, black BMW four-door sedan and jumped out to help the honeymooners load their luggage.

"Welcome to N'aw Arlens," greeted Justin as he kissed Celeste on the cheek. "How are you, Mark?"

"Fine, sir," Mark said as the men shook hands. "Thank you for picking us up, but we could have taken a cab."

"Nonsense, I've looked forward to this. Besides, it was no trouble. We should even beat the rush-hour traffic on the way home."

As Mark and Celeste got into the back seat of the BMW, Celeste inhaled the new car smell and complimented her grandfather. "Love your new car, Granddad, but isn't this rather *yuppie* for you?"

"Hah! Yuppie I'll never be, sugar. I just decided I could navigate better in the Quarter with a smaller car. I'd still rather have my old Lincoln, but this car is a lot easier to turn and park."

"So is a Honda, Granddad, and it's a heck-of-a-lot cheaper," teased Celeste.

"Never could bring myself to buy one of those Jap cars… I suppose, if I'd fought the Germans durin' the war, it'dah been the other way around."

"How long have you lived in New Orleans?" asked Mark.

"All my life, Mark. In fact, I was born in my house. My mother didn't have time to get to the hospital."

When they reached the New Orleans business district, Justin exited I-55 and drove down Canal Street, toward the river. He pointed to the left when they stopped at a red light at St. Charles Avenue. "To the left, this street becomes Royal Street. The French Quarter is all to your left."

"Where's Bourbon Street?" asked Mark.

"Bourbon is the street we just passed, one block behind us. Don't worry, Mark. I only live a couple of blocks from Bourbon Street. All the honky-tonks are within walkin' distance."

"Sounds great," replied Mark. "Where do you live?"

"Right behind the St. Louis Cathedral, on Orleans. I'm gonna turn left down here at Decatur and drive you past the cathedral and Jackson Square. Then we'll circle around to my house."

After Justin's quick tour of the French Quarter, he pulled his BMW up in front of a rather run-down-looking, red-brick, two-story residence at 821 Orleans. "We're lucky to find a parkin' place on the street," said Justin. "Come on in. I'll put the car away later."

Justin got out of the car and unlocked a black wrought iron gate in front of the premises. Celeste and Mark followed Justin past the front of the house and through a dim, narrow passage that led to a square garden with a hexagon-shaped fountain in the center. The garden was surrounded by the house on three sides, and a brick wall on the fourth side. It was jammed full of flowering plants, hanging ferns, and huge banana trees.

"This is beautiful," said Mark. "I love how the balconies are built facing your garden and courtyard. You have quite a green thumb, Justin."

"Thank you, Mark. Things grow well down here. It rarely gets cold enough to harm even the tropical plants."

"You ain't seen nothing yet, Mark. Show him the dining room and parlor, Granddad," requested Celeste.

"Certainly," said Justin as he turned and opened the double French doors leading into the dining room. The dining room was dominated by a long, polished walnut table that was set with china and silver for eight people. Two crystal chandeliers were suspended over the dining table, and the walls were lined with oil paintings of local landscapes and bygone portraits.

"Are you expecting a lot of people for dinner?" asked Mark.

Justin smiled. "No, just you two. My wife always left the table set to display her china, and I have maintained the tradition. Come on in and sit down in the parlor, and I'll fix us somethin' cool to drink. I hope I have the air conditioner on cold enough for you?"

"Feels great, Granddad. I'm always surprised by the humidity when I visit you in the summer."

Justin ushered Celeste and Mark into the adjoining parlor. It had a single, but larger, chandelier hanging from its sculptured plaster ceiling. The floor was covered with a thick Persian rug, and the room was full of antique French provincial furniture. If it weren't for the console television in front of the sofa, Mark could imagine that they had stepped back in time a hundred years.

Justin pointed at the sofa and matching armchairs. "Please, sit down, and I'll bring the drinks. What would you like, Mark?"

"A cold beer would be hard to beat."

"Certainly. And you, sugar?"

"Have you got the makin's for a mint julep, Granddad?"

"Of course, honey. Comin' right up — I have everythin' prepared."

Celeste laughed. "You know me like a book."

When Justin returned with the drinks, the men settled in the armchairs. Celeste kicked off her shoes and pulled her legs up underneath her on the sofa. During a lull in the conversation, Mark set his beer down on the coffee table and turned to face Justin. "Justin, since we're all one family now, there's a question I need to ask you."

"Certainly, Mark."

"Celeste has not taken off that old wedding band since we got married, not even when we went to the beach. But, when I tried to talk to her about it, she only says she's just wearing the ring to humor you — that you're superstitious about the ring causing bad luck if she takes it off… Only, I saw how upset you got at our wedding reception. I think there's more to it than you being superstitious. Am I wrong?"

Justin shook his head and paused a moment before answering Mark. "No, unfortunately, you're not wrong, Mark. It's not just a superstition. It's a family curse."

"Curse?" responded Mark incredulously. "I'm sorry, Justin, but I just don't believe in curses and witchcraft and — "

"Not witchcraft, Mark. It's a Voodoo curse," interrupted Justin. "I can appreciate your skepticism." Turning to face Celeste, Justin asked, "What about you,

Celeste? Have you encountered anythin' disturbin' or supernatural about the ring?"

Celeste avoided her grandfather's eyes. "I don't know what you mean, Granddad."

"Then answer me this. Have you had any strange dreams — dreams about colonial Louisiana — since you put on the ring?"

"Not since… Not since…Well, yes, I've had a couple of odd dreams, I guess. But I figured they were caused by my research into the Noyan family history."

"And was there a young man in your dreams — a handsome man with long dark hair and a mustache?" pressed Justin.

"Yes! Yes!" exclaimed Mark. "She told me about that dream the night before our wedding. It was the night she found the old ring in her dad's trunk. Do you know what these dreams are all about?"

Justin sat his drink down before answering. "The ring belonged to Emile Poydras."

"Poydras, right," affirmed Mark. "The Emile Poydras we found written in the Noyan family tree."

"Yes, that's the man. Emile Poydras fell in love with the wife of Henri Noyan and got her pregnant. Henri Noyan challenged Emile Poydras to a duel, and Emile killed him and married Henri's wife, Nicole. Out of guilt, or for some reason, Emile promised Henri's father, Paul Noyan, that his unborn child would carry the Noyan family name."

"How come?" Mark asked. "That's a pretty bizarre request."

"Because Paul Noyan had no other children or lineal heirs, and he wanted to ensure the Noyan name would live on. Anyway, after the child was born — it was a son they named Jean…"

"After Jean Baptiste Noyan, the revolutionary?" queried Celeste.

Before Justin could answer, Celeste quickly continued, "Wait a minute! You mean we're all descendants of Emile Poydras? We're not really Noyans?"

"Yes, that is so," replied Justin. "Anyway, Paul Noyan became very possessive about young Jean and demanded that the boy live with him. As I recall, he even wanted to adopt him. Emile wrote later that was Paul's plan from the beginning.

Anyway, when Emile and Nicole refused to give the child up, Paul Noyan is said to have employed a Voodoo queen to put a curse on Emile and Nicole."

"What kind of curse, Granddad?"

"Actually, there was more than one curse. First, Nicole fell ill suddenly and died of a fever in a matter of days."

"That's not so supernatural," interjected Mark. "People dropped dead of yellow fever and all kinds of diseases back in those days. Didn't they?"

"That's true, Mark. It's what happened after Nicole died that convinced Emile Poydras Voodoo was involved... You see — and this is documented by police records — the night after Nicole was buried, someone stole her body from her crypt, and it was reported to Emile that Nicole was seen thereafter takin' part in Voodoo ceremonies."

"What!" Mark cried. "Are you telling us Nicole Noyan-Poydras was turned into a zombie?"

"Exactly," replied Justin. "Emile went to a gatherin' of the cult and saw Nicole with his own eyes. But, alas, Nicole did not recognize him when Emile saw her."

"What did Emile do?" asked Celeste.

"He went straight to the Voodoo queen and demanded to know who had Nicole cursed. The queen told him Paul Noyan hired her. Then she offered to release Nicole's soul for a price."

"Boy, sounds like that bitch liked to work both sides of the street."

"Yes, she did. Most of the Voodoo practitioners were known to do that. Extortion was the most lucrative part of their trade. Anyway, Emile paid to have Paul Noyan done in by a curse, and to have himself and Nicole released from the curses Paul had put on them."

"What happened to Nicole, Granddad?"

"She was beyond rescue, but Emile did get her body released from the zombie curse, and had it buried in a secret location. Only then was her spirit free to seek its eternal peace."

"This is all very interesting..." Mark smirked. "But what does this have to do with the old wedding ring?"

"Apparently, the Voodoo queen double-crossed Emile in addition to Paul Noyan. First, the queen demanded that Emile give her the possession he valued most in the world, if he was to save Nicole from the zombie curse."

"His wedding ring?" proposed Celeste, holding up her left hand.

"Yes, sugar, his weddin' ring — or alliance ring, as they called them back then. The very ring you now wear. Emile loved Nicole dearly, but their weddin' ring was precious to him for more than that reason. It has protective powers. Anyway, besides wantin' the ring for its protective powers, it seems the queen planned to use the ring to gain control of Emile. Emile wrote in his diary the queen was trying to blackmail him for a fortune and have him killed if he refused. As I said, the queen used extortion to get the ring. Emile only gave up the ring to free Nicole from the zombie curse."

"Who was this Voodoo queen, Granddad?"

"Marie Laveau. The most famous — or should I say, infamous — of the Voodoo queens."

"Yeah, I've heard stories about her. Wasn't she supposed to have lived more than one lifetime? I thought she was just a fictional character?"

"Oh, I assure you she was a real person, sugar. And most of the stories about her are probably true."

"So, did Marie Laveau kill Emile?" Mark asked.

"Well, not exactly… Emile figured out what she was doin' and nearly killed her while reclaimin' his ring. And then he died in a duel shortly after gettin' his ring back. So, I suppose, it was the Voodoo queen's curse that in fact killed Emile Poydras."

"Oh, how sad," remarked Celeste.

"Unfortunately," continued Justin, "Emile's soul did not find rest. His spirit is trapped in the ring."

"Come on, now!" scoffed Mark. "You expect us to believe the ghost of Emile Poydras lives in that ring? All that happened over a hundred and fifty years ago. Besides, if it is a *haunted* ring, why didn't someone throw it in the Mississippi a century ago?"

"Because of the power that goes with the ring, Mark. As long as one wears the ring, they will never die. But, once the ring is gifted, and accepted, you can't give it up without sufferin' certain death."

"I'm not trying to be disrespectful, Justin," continued Mark, "but this is all too far-out for me. It's like some lost episode of the *Twilight Zone*."

Justin turned to Celeste. "What about you, sugar? Do you find it all unbelievable?"

Celeste shook her head. "I don't know what to believe, Granddad. I read your grandfather's letters…"

"Randolph's?"

"Yes, the letters he wrote from France during World War I. Randolph wore the ring because he thought it would protect him in battle. Didn't he?"

Justin nodded. "Yes, that's correct. Randolph was the last Noyan to wear the ring — until now."

"What happened to Randolph?" asked Mark.

"He was killed on guard duty, a few days after mailin' the ring home," replied Justin.

Mark rolled his eyes and looked incredulously at Celeste. She ignored his scornful gestures and kept her attention focused on her grandfather.

"Granddad? How do you know so much about this family curse? I've never heard any rumor of this ring before."

"From my father. He first warned me about the ring. But many of the details came from *your* father's work. Jim had nearly completed the translation of the diary of Emile Poydras when he came to me for help. Reluctantly, I agreed to help him finish it. But I never finished it before he died."

"Translation? There was no translation in the trunk."

"Your father left it with me before he left for Vietnam. He was afraid Amy would find it and worry even more about him."

"Then Celeste's dad wore the ring to Vietnam?" supposed Mark.

"No, Mark. I persuaded him not to… I convinced Jim it would drive him insane… like it has nearly everyone who has ever tried to wear the ring. That's why Randolph sent it home. He was startin' to lose his mind."

"Oh, this is great!" said Mark. "Let me get this straight. If Celeste takes the ring off, she's gonna drop dead, but if she continues to wear the ring, she'll go crazy?"

"Lighten up, Mark," retorted Celeste. "At least I'll live forever."

"I wish I could share your amusement," Justin said solemnly. "But this isn't a jokin' matter. If you two don't take this seriously — *now* — there is nothin' I can do to help you."

Celeste released her smile and looked at her grandfather earnestly. "Suppose we believe you, Granddad. What can you do about a Voodoo curse that's lasted over a hundred and fifty years?"

"Not me, personally. But, while you two were on your honeymoon, I did some research, and I've located someone that I believe can help."

"Don't tell me. There's a Department of Voodoo Studies at Tulane?" taunted Mark.

Justin refused to take Mark's baiting. "No, Mark. The help we need can't be found at any university or medical center. It can only be obtained from those who still practice Voodoo."

Chapter Fifteen

The fertile acres of Alma Plantation lay in the floodplain of False River Lake. The lake had once been the main channel of the Mississippi, but the river's constant meanderings had turned it into a dead-end lake.

After a brief tutorial in plantation operations, Julien left for Philadelphia, leaving Emile in charge of the plantation's management. At that time, the thousand and some odd slaves at Alma were busy with the tasks of clearing land, planting sugar cane, digging irrigation ditches, and building a sugar mill. It just so happened that a number of the slaves working at Alma had come from the French colony at Santo Domingo, on the Island of Hispaniola. Julien had acquired them at a bargain price after the slave revolt there three years earlier.

Julien had also acquired Alma's current slave overseer from Santo Domingo, a fat, devious man by the name of Nathan Cabot. Cabot claimed his lineage came directly from one of the French colony's founding families. Julien suspected that Cabot was a bastard of mixed blood, but it didn't matter to him, as Cabot had experience managing these slaves and the operations of sugar plantations. Until Emile came to Alma, Nathan Cabot had been the de facto manager of the entire plantation, and he resented having to relinquish that authority to the young and inexperienced Emile.

Of course, Nathan Cabot was not foolish enough to express his resentment openly to Julien or Emile. His practice was to take out his frustrations on some of the slaves he oversaw. Unfortunately for Emile and Julien, Cabot would not limit his expressions of discontent to mistreating the slaves. He had resolved, and he plotted, to take control and loot the area plantations by fostering a slave uprising as he had witnessed in Santo Domingo. In fact, Cabot had been actively pursuing and planning the rebellion long before the arrival of Emile Poydras. He had already helped organize confederates among the slaves on most plantations in the vicinity of Pointe Coupee, and he had enlisted some other disgruntled white men in the area — those that resented the wealth of the gentry of Pointe Coupee.

One of the main obstacles to inciting a slave rebellion at Pointe Coupee was the slaves themselves. While the blacks in the area outnumbered the whites by over two to one, for the most part, they were treated much better than the slaves had been in Santo Domingo, especially the slaves at Alma and Julien Poydras' other plantations. This made the majority of the slaves there reluctant to risk the consequences of rebellion. To help induce the slaves to support the rebellion, Cabot gave favors to those that supported his cause, cruelly punished those that dared speak against it, and appealed to the superstitious natures possessed by most of the slaves in the area. The superstitions of the slaves had been a factor in causing the slave revolt in Santo Domingo as well, for the colony at Santo Domingo had been a hotbed of Voodooism.

After making his evening report to Emile at the main house, Nathan Cabot walked directly to the slave quarters. Near the end of one of the rows of crude shacks, which made up Alma's slave lodgings, Cabot entered one of the one-room shacks without knocking. The room was dark, except for the light of a single candle burning on a small, low table, but Nathan could hear the sound of creaking wood coming from the far corner of the room.

Cabot mopped the sweat off his bald head and neck with a dirty handkerchief and called out to the darkness. "Sally? You in here?… Speak to me, girl."

From a dark corner of the room, a high-pitched voice answered, "I'm here, Nathan."

"Well, come over here by the light so I can see you. How can you sit alone in the dark all the time? It's down-right eerie, if you ask me."

"Nobody asked you, Nathan," answered Sally as she struck a match and lit another candle next to the rocking chair she was seated in. The light of the second candle disclosed a young black woman slowly rocking in a creaking, oak rocking chair. Sally was tall and slender with jet-black hair, and her skin was the color of India ink. There was no mixed blood in her veins. She was pure African. She was also stark naked.

"Jesus, Sally!" exclaimed Nathan. "Cover yourself up. I can't talk to you like that."

Sally cackled and walked over to her bed and jerked the sheet off of it. She wrapped herself loosely in it and sat back down in her rocking chair. Then she motioned for the gawking Nathan to sit down in the cane-bottomed chair next to her. Nathan tested the bottom of the chair with his hand before he sat his wide ass in it.

"Do we still make our move tomorrow night?" asked Sally.

"Yes. There was some disagreement at the last meeting, but April 15th is still the agreed date. But it depends on you. Can you dispose of young Poydras by…"

"Emile Poydras no longer has a will of his own," interrupted Sally. "I can *dispose* of him whenever I please."

"You know what I mean," continued Nathan. "You must kill him. We can't have him raising the alarm before we march on Pointe Coupee."

"I will enjoy killing Monsieur Poydras. He thinks of me as his little black whore. The fool! It was my gris-gris that seduced *him*. And I made him think it was all his idea to take me as his lover. The idiot actually believes he's in love with me. The plan has not been changed, has it? All the white pigs are to be killed?"

Nathan pulled out his handkerchief again and wiped his brow before answering. "Just remember who organized this revolt, Sally. Don't you get no ideas about killing *all* the whites."

Sally snorted and gave Nathan a sly little smile. "Of course, I didn't mean you and the other comrades, Nathan."

"The plan is unchanged, Sally. All the slave owners and their children will be massacred tomorrow night in their beds. All except the adult females."

"Yes!" exclaimed Sally. "Let those fine ladies learn what it is like to be treated like a whore — the whore to some black stud! What's the final count of slaves who will join us?"

"From Alma?"

"Yes."

Nathan thought a moment before answering. "Twenty, counting yourself."

"Only twenty? Twenty out of a thousand?"

"Only twenty I can count on," answered Nathan. "But more will join us once they see that slaves from all the other plantations are involved. When we take the armory tomorrow night, they will all come running to join us. Now, you are certain that Poydras suspects nothing?"

"Of course I'm certain!" snapped Sally. "I serve the man his dinner every evening and sleep with him every night. Neither Poydras nor any of his house guests have given any indication that they suspect our uprising."

"Good," responded Nathan. "Hey. It's getting late. Won't Poydras wonder where you are?"

"Hah! Not tonight he won't. I drugged his food. By now, he should be passed out in his chair."

Nathan nodded his head as he again wiped at his sweat. "That explains it. When I made my report this evening, I thought he was acting oddly. I thought he was drunk."

"It wasn't the wine, Nathan. It was my gris-gris powders."

"Is that how you're going to kill him — poison his dinner tomorrow?"

"Oh, no," rejoined Sally. "I want to see the expression on his face as he dies. I want him to know that I have killed him. I will wait until he takes me to bed tomorrow night. Then I will slit his throat and cut his heart out!"

Nathan could not keep from shuddering as Sally expressed the delight she anticipated in murdering Emile Poydras in his bed. "You have a colder heart than mine, Sally."

Sally's eyes flashed at Nathan's remark. "You forget that I was forced to watch as the French pigs hacked my parents to death! That will turn any heart to stone."

"I too saw many people die during the rebellion in Santo Domingo, Sally. Both black *and* white." Nathan stood up and headed for the door. "And we must be on our guard, or we will all meet the same fate as your parents."

"I will not fail you, Nathan. Make certain you do not fail *me*, or not even death can save you from my vengeance."

***

A knocking sound awakened Emile on the morning of April 15, 1795. It was only the houseboy checking to see why Emile had slept through breakfast, but the pounding in Emile's head was amplified by the gentle rapping on his bedroom door.

"Monsieur Poydras? Are you awake?"

Emile sat up in bed and rubbed his forehead with one hand. Opening his eyes, he noticed he still had on most of the clothes he wore at dinner the night before. "Come in, Gérard. I'm awake."

The small Negro houseboy opened the bedroom door just enough to stick his head in. "Are you alone, Monsieur Poydras?" Seeing Emile alone in his bed, Gérard continued, "I thought Mademoiselle Sally might be with you."

Emile motioned for the boy to enter the room. "It's all right, Gérard. I'm alone. What o'clock is it?"

"It's nearly noon, monsieur. I was afraid you were going to miss your lunch, as well as your breakfast. Your guests are inquiring as to your wellbeing."

"Noon! How can that be? Thank you for checking on me, Gérard. Tell them I'm fine and that I'll be down in just a few minutes."

"Can I do anything else for you, monsieur?"

"No, no, thank you, Gérard. I'll be fine."

Upon Emile's dismissal, Gérard bowed slightly and left the bedroom, softly closing the door behind him.

Emile struggled to his washbasin and splashed some cold water on his face. As he stared into his shaving mirror, he tried to recall the events of the prior evening. He didn't recall getting drunk. And yet, his head pounded with the worst hangover he had ever experienced. *I don't remember having over two glasses of wine with dinner,* thought Emile. *Surely that could not have done this to me?*

Emile shook his head and wiped his face with the towel hanging by the mirror. As he changed into a fresh white shirt, he continued to ponder his current predicament. It dawned on him that he had been acting rather strange the past few weeks. Things had happened so fast, so many different things. There was meeting his uncle Julien, being thrown into management of his uncle's bank and huge sugar plantation, and then there was his whirlwind romance with a young slave girl, Sally Francis.

Checking his appearance in the mirror, Emile stared at himself. He shuddered to think what his relatives in France would think of his open liaison with a black slave. Emile had to admit that he found it impossible to resist the charms of Sally. To him, she was the most beautiful and the most sensuous woman he had ever met. It seemed that every time he made love to her, it only made him want her more. In fact, last night was the first night that they had not slept together in the past two weeks. Emile thought, *I must get ahold of myself... I can't carry on like this when Uncle Julien returns.*

After brushing back his long dark hair and tying it in a ponytail with a fresh red ribbon, Emile left his bedroom and descended the stairs. As he entered the dining room, he was greeted by a smiling Sally holding out a steaming cup of coffee.

"Good morning, Monsieur Poydras. Are you feeling better now?"

Chapter Sixteen

"Ah!" said Justin. "We're in luck. There's hardly any line at all."

It was the second day after their arrival in New Orleans, and Justin had insisted on taking Celeste and Mark out to dinner. Upon Justin and Celeste's strong recommendations, Mark had selected Galatoires Restaurant, which was a short six-block walk from Justin's house.

As they stood in line, Mark read the address on the plain exterior of the restaurant out loud. "209 Bourbon Street — say, we've walked almost to the end of Bourbon Street, haven't we?"

"Yes, Mark," confirmed Justin, pointing behind them. "That big street you see up ahead is Canal. Bourbon Street and the French Quarter end there. Of course, there is the section of Bourbon known as the *wild side*. It's the opposite direction from my house."

"Wild side?" asked Mark. "Sounds interesting."

Celeste giggled and said, "Believe me, Mark. You wouldn't be interested."

"Huh! Just because I married you, don't — "

Celeste interrupted Mark before he swallowed his foot even further. "The wild side is the gay district, Mark."

"Oh!"

Justin confirmed Celeste's revelation. "She's right. When we walk that stretch after dinner, I'd not advise droppin' in one of those clubs for a drink."

"I'm with you guys," agreed Mark as he tugged at the neck of his white dress shirt.

Justin recognized Mark's discomfort. Even after sundown, the heat and humidity were intense. "Sorry about the coat and tie, Mark. Most of the fine restaurants have a dress code in the evenin'. I promise you, it'll be worth your discomfort — and it's nice and cool inside."

Celeste was just about to suggest that Mark remove his jacket while they waited when they were ushered inside the restaurant. Galatoires consisted of one long dining room, the side walls of which were covered with mirrors and brass fixtures. The tables were placed close together, and all of them occupied. Numerous waiters in black tuxedos maneuvered efficiently between the packed patrons. Celeste, Mark, and Justin were seated next to one of the mirrored walls, directly under one of the ceiling fans.

"Ah. That fan feels great," said Mark. "It makes air conditioning even better." Glancing at his menu, Mark asked, "What do you recommend, Justin?"

"The crab dishes are very good, and so is the Trout Marguery."

Celeste read the blank expression on Mark's face. "I'm afraid we're going to have to ease Mark into Creole cuisine, Granddad. He's one of those midwestern meat-and-potatoes boys."

Justin nodded. "Never fear, Mark. They serve the best steak in the Quarter here. They can turn a hunk of beef into a work of art."

After they had ordered dinner and were enjoying their wine, Celeste brought up the main reason for their outing. "Granddad, can't you tell us anymore about who you're taking us to see tonight? I didn't think people still practiced Voodoo in New Orleans."

Justin shook his head. "I want you two to approach this with an open mind. That's all I ask. If you don't like what you hear, we can leave. And I'll figure somthin' else out. But please, please believe me. You are in real danger."

"I believe your warnings are sincere, Granddad, but there are still too many unanswered questions for me. For instance, you said that everyone who wore the ring went insane. But, in Randolph Noyan's last letter from France, he mentioned that his grandfather had given him the ring and that it had protected him during the Civil War."

"That's correct," agreed Justin. "Randolph's grandfather was Jean Noyan — Emile's and Nicole's son — and he did wear the ring durin' the War Between the States. He was in the thick of fightin' at both Antietam and Gettysburg, and he never got a scratch, while the rest of his regiment suffered seventy percent casualties."

"Did Jean Noyan die when he gave Randolph the ring?" asked Mark.

"Yes, but not immediately," answered Justin. "I believe it was cancer."

"Cancer!" scoffed Mark. "That hardly seems like the work of Voodoo. After all, Jean Noyan had to have been pretty old when he died?"

"I suppose he was in his early nineties," admitted Justin.

"But, what about his mind, Granddad? Did the ring drive Jean Noyan insane?"

Justin lowered his eyes and stared at his wine glass. "No, evidently Jean Noyan did not go insane — at least, there is no record of him havin' mental problems. He restored the family plantations and became quite successful after the war."

"Then," continued Celeste, "how can you be so sure the ring will drive me crazy?"

Justin looked up from his wine and looked directly into Celeste's eyes. "Not all of our family history is to be found in your father's old trunk, sugar. There were stories about Jean also bein' involved with Voodoo. There was even a scandalous newspaper article accusing him of bein' involved in a break-in of the tomb of Marie Laveau. In my opinion, Jean Noyan didn't go insane because he didn't try to fight the curse. He accepted it for what it was. He submitted to its will and became its servant. Is that what you want? To lose your free will and serve some Voodoo curse?"

"You make it sound like he sold his soul to the Devil," chimed in Mark.

"In a way he did, Mark. And if we can't find help soon, Celeste will be faced with the same decision. The power of the ring can be quite seductive."

Celeste asked her grandfather, "Why didn't you complete the translation of Emile Poydras's diary?"

"I tried to work on it several times. But, after Jim was killed, I couldn't bring myself to finish it. So, I just put it back in the trunk after Jim's funeral. I was..."

Celeste laid her hand on top of Justin's. "What, Granddad? Why couldn't you finish Dad's translation?"

"I was afraid I would find somethin' in the diary — some secret that would have allowed Jim to wear that ring without sufferin' from the curse... I couldn't bear to know that I might have had it in my power to save his life but was too stubborn to use it."

"Then, it sounds like we need to finish translating the diary," suggested Mark.

"You're right," said Justin. "I've been workin' on it while you two were in Nassau. I showed it to Celeste while you were out shoppin' this morning."

"But I thought the diary was in the old trunk at Amy's house?" asked Mark.

"It was. I picked it up after the weddin' reception, without tellin' Amy… Of course, I've had photocopies of portions of it for years — Jim gave them to me before he left for Vietnam."

Celeste held up her wine glass when Mark offered the wine bottle. "Just about half will do, babe. Thanks. You know, I can't remember exactly how my dad put it. But, when I was reading part of what he had translated, I concluded that Emile Poydras owned the ring before he was married. There was some comment about it having protected Emile in duels he fought prior to his marriage."

Justin confirmed Celeste's observation. "Yes, that's correct. Last night, I was re-readin' the part of the diary leadin' up to the death of Julien Poydras. It was Julien Poydras who originally owned the ring. And he gave it to Emile, just before Emile fought a duel with a very skilled fencer by the name of Cuvillier."

"What happened to Julien Poydras?" asked Mark.

"He took ill and died about seven months after givin' the ring to Emile. The diary didn't mention the exact nature of Julien's last illness, just that he lingered for quite some time."

"And what happened in the duel with Cuvillier?" continued Mark.

"Emile was victorious. He didn't kill the man, but he cut him up pretty good. Emile claimed he was never touched by Cuvillier's blade. That with the ring on, he was able to parry every thrust his opponent made."

"I wonder where Julien Poydras got the ring?" interjected Celeste.

"That's a story in itself. Emile reported that his uncle saved the life of one of the early Voodoo queens — I believe they called her Sanité Diable."

"Saint of the Devil?" asked Celeste.

"Right, that's the name she went by. Anyway, Sanité Diable gave the ring to Julien Poydras as a reward for saving her life. She also made Julien a member of her Voodoo cult."

"So where did the Voodoo queen get the ring?" asked Mark.

"As I recall, she created the ring especially for Julien Poydras. Sanité Diable had some kind of magic gold necklace that protected her. And it gave her the power — or it contained the magical incantations — that allowed her to make other charms like it."

"What kind of necklace was it?" Celeste asked.

"Julien described it to Emile as being solid gold, very massive, and very old. I don't recall for certain, but I don't think Julien ever knew the origin of the necklace."

"I don't get it," added Mark. "If Sanité Diable had the necklace, how could Julien Poydras save her life?"

"Seems like she dropped it, or the necklace got torn off in the attack on her. Somethin' like that. It's been a while since I've read that part of the diary."

The waiter suddenly appeared with the entrées, and the topic of the conversation shifted back to the delectable cuisine they were about to experience.

After dinner, Celeste, Mark, and Justin walked back down Bourbon, past all the jazz clubs, striptease bars, and massage parlors. When they passed St. Peter Street, Mark pointed at the green neon sign proclaiming, "Pat O'Brien's."

"When we come back, can we stop in there for a drink? A buddy of mine used to say those hurricane drinks they make there are something else."

Justin laughed. "Indeed they are, Mark. Pat's is a real fun place, but I'll pass on the hurricane tonight. Besides, you two newlyweds need to have some time by yourselves."

For the next six or seven blocks, as the trio walked to the east end of Bourbon Street, Celeste noticed that Mark became uneasy, and he seemed to really stare if they passed a group of men walking together.

"Don't worry, Mark," kidded Celeste. "I won't let any of 'em git you."

Mark made a comic face back at Celeste, and said, "How do ya know some dyke won't step out of the shadows and grab you?"

Justin chuckled at their antics. "More likely some purse snatcher will make a grab for Celeste's handbag. Just keep on walkin' — the next street is Esplanade. We're almost there."

As they turned right onto Esplanade, Mark and Celeste walked behind Justin, past the alternating well-kept and run-down houses, all of which appeared very old. Abruptly, Justin halted in front of a freshly painted old mansion with a postage-stamp front yard. The house was painted a dull gray, but it had red shutters and handsome wrought iron balconies on its three visible sides. The large porch was dimly lit, and as they came up the walk, Mark saw that the cast iron gate had the figure of a dancing cupid in its center.

When they came up onto the porch, Mark noticed that the drapes on all the windows were completely closed, and they could hear Jerry Lee Lewis's "Whole Lot-A Shakin" being played loudly on a stereo. Mark was going to ask Justin if he was sure he had found the right house, but just as he started to open his mouth, the front door opened, and a very large black man stepped out onto the porch He unbuttoned his navy-blue suit coat as he came out the door. "Can I help you folks?"

Justin gave their reply. "I'm Justin Noyan. I have an appointment with Madame Dauphine."

The black man nodded. "Wait here for moment, please." Then he went back inside, closing the solid walnut door behind him.

Mark took the opportunity to address Justin. "*Madame* Dauphine? Justin, what is this place? If I didn't know better, I'd guess we were about to enter a brothel."

"You're right, Mark. This is a bordello, but don't let that concern you. Madame Dauphine is no common streetwalker. She is one of the Quarter's most respected madams and practitioners of Voodoo."

"You speak as if you've known the woman for some time?" commented Celeste. She grinned as she watched her grandfather begin to blush. Before Justin was forced to respond to Celeste, the door reopened, and they were ushered into the foyer. To their left was a large, softly lit parlor. There was a bar at one end and two couples leaning against it, drinking. At first, Celeste thought the two women had on long cocktail dresses, cut low in the front. Then she realized they weren't dresses, but very sheer negligées.

Before she could gawk at the other people in the parlor, Celeste felt Mark tug at her elbow. When she looked, she saw her grandfather entering the open door of another smaller parlor. The black man was holding the door open and giving Mark and Celeste a rather impatient stare.

Mark and Celeste quickly followed into the room, just as Justin was shaking hands with a very attractive and buxom black woman. This parlor was furnished with reproductions of French provincial antiques and was well lit. Mark could see the woman's face clearly. Her skin was the color of milk chocolate, and her short dark hair was coiffured in an updo. She appeared to be in her mid-forties and was wearing a stylish but conservative navy-blue dress. Mark was surprised when he heard the woman return Justin's greeting, for she didn't have the syrupy accent that the natives of New Orleans spoke with. In fact, she had no accent at all. She spoke so precisely, it almost sounded British.

Justin turned and pointed at Mark and Celeste as they entered the room. "… and this is my granddaughter, Celeste, and her husband, Mark Richards."

The madam extended her hand to Mark. "Ah yes, the newlyweds. Welcome to you both. I'm Ethel Stern." Responding to Mark and Celeste's simultaneous looks of puzzlement, the woman continued, "That's my real name. To my customers, it's Madame Dauphine."

Mark gently pressed Madame Dauphine's extended hand. "A pleasure to meet you… ah… ma'am. Thank you for taking the time to see us."

"You're welcome, Mark. You feel free to call me Ethel or Madame Dauphine. Whatever you're comfortable with."

Pointing to a red velvet loveseat and matching stuffed chairs, Madame Dauphine nodded to Celeste and bid everyone to be seated. She sat down behind an antique writing desk and pressed a black button tacked to the back edge of it. Almost instantly, the black doorman reappeared. As he entered the room, Madame Dauphine instructed him, "Tyrone, please hold my calls." Then, looking at Justin, she asked, "Can I offer you all something to drink?"

Justin spoke for them all, "No, thank you, Ethel. We just finished dinner."

Madame Dauphine then dismissed the doorman with a wave of her hand.

Justin immediately got the conversation onto the purpose of their visit. "Do you recall the ring I told you about last week, Ethel?"

Madame Dauphine nodded and leaned over her desk toward Celeste. "Yes. Yes, of course. May I see it please?"

Celeste extended her left hand. Madame Dauphine held it under her green desk lamp and examined the ring with her fingertips, rubbing and rolling the ring between her index finger and thumb. Everyone waited for Madame Dauphine to speak next.

Finally, she said, "It is very old, and *very* powerful. Where did this ring come from?"

Justin answered, "As I told you, it has been in my family for generations —
since colonial times."

Madame Dauphine looked slightly annoyed as she let go of Celeste's hand and
ring. "Yes, yes. I understand that. But last week you told me the ring had been
cursed over a hundred and fifty years ago by one of the old Voodoo queens. Which
queen was it?"

Justin looked uncomfortable with the question. His answer was hesitant. "I
haven't been able to absolutely confirm it, Ethel. But our old family diary indicates
it was Marie Laveau."

Madame Dauphine was visibly startled by Justin's answer. "Marie Laveau! My
God! Was it *the* Marie Laveau, or her daughter?"

Justin shook his head and exhaled hard before answering. "That's what I'm not
certain of, but the dates — the early 1820's — would lead one to conclude that it
had to be the original Marie Laveau, and not someone merely tradin' on her name
and reputation."

Celeste finally felt compelled to enter the conversation. "Will someone please
tell me why you all are freaking out about Marie Laveau? You two speak of her as
if she was the Devil incarnate or something. There were plenty of bad voodoo
queens — right?"

When Justin hesitated in answering Celeste's question, Madame Dauphine
spoke, "'Bad' doesn't begin to describe Marie Laveau. She was one of the most
powerful and the most malevolent of *all* the Voodoo queens. She may have reigned
the longest, and she was known to be very ruthless, and very cruel. She was so
famous and powerful that others used her name after she retired and for many
years after her death. But no other queen has been able to replicate her unique
charms and curses."

"So, she was a superstar among Voodoo queens," added Mark. "You two are
talking like she could come back from the dead and butcher us."

Madame Dauphine looked Mark in the eyes when she answered. "It's not Marie Laveau's ghost you need to be concerned about, but what she did while she was
alive. Some of her curses were known to last for many years, even past her death."

Mark was beginning to feel frustrated. "Well, you knew we were dealing with an *old* curse before we came here. Why is an old curse by Marie Laveau so much worse than any other old curse?"

Madame Dauphine didn't answer for a moment. She first got a pen and paper out of her desk and wrote briefly. Then she looked up at Mark. "Mark, I'm not sure I could ever make you understand that. For now, you'll just have to believe me when I tell you that it is not in my power to help you and Celeste."

Before Mark could reply, Madame Dauphine folded the paper she had written on and handed it to Justin. "Justin, I'm sorry. If I could help you, you know I would. But you and I know time is critical, and I don't want to waste any of the time Celeste may have left. I have written down the name and the address of Mama Vance. She's the only person I know of who may have the power to help you."

"*May* have the power to help?" entreated Celeste.

Madame Dauphine turned to Celeste. "Yes, my dear. You must understand. There are many practices and skills of the old religion that are unknown today. The Voodoo of a century ago was a much stronger force than what exists today. The name I have given you is of one of the old-ones. The last one I know of."

"Old-ones?" asked Celeste.

"Yes. We call them old-ones because they lived when Voodoo was still a powerful force in the city, many years ago. And because they are the only ones who know the old secrets of Voodooism."

"Wait a minute," interjected Mark. "Just how old a person are we talking about?"

Madame Dauphine kept looking at Celeste when she answered Mark. "Very old, Mark. No one knows for sure. Just don't ask her. It annoys her when people ask questions about her past."

"Okay," agreed Celeste. "Can we call her now and set up an appointment?"

"Mama Vance doesn't have a telephone, my dear. Besides, you don't need to call her. I have an idea she's already expecting you to call on her."

Chapter Seventeen

After serving lunch and assisting with the departure of Emile's visiting sugar mill suppliers, Sally returned to the kitchen, which was located in a small building behind the main house. As she was finishing up the lunch dishes, Nathan Cabot came to the kitchen door.

"Sally, are you alone?"

"Yes. The other girls are in the main house."

Nathan stepped into the kitchen and closed the door. "We've got a problem."

"What do you mean, Nathan?"

"Some of our slaves are trying to back out. They've turned yellow."

"How many?" asked Sally as she wiped her hands on her apron.

"Right now, only two. But if we let them get away, others are sure to follow."

Sally took off her wet gray apron and threw it on the table. "Who are they, and where are they?"

"Anthony and William," answered Nathan. "I've got them cleaning out the stables right now."

Sally threw open the kitchen door so violently that it bounced off the wall and closed again. Nathan grabbed her hand as she started to reopen the door.

"Hold on, girl. Where's Poydras?"

Sally threw off Nathan's hand. "I told you before, don't ever touch me!"

Nathan let go of her and took a step back. "Alright, Sally, alright. We've just got to be careful. We're too close to tip our hand now."

"Don't worry about Poydras. He just rode off to check on the sugar mill construction. Now, let's go see about our two reluctant rebels."

Sally marched out of the kitchen and down the hill towards the stables with Nathan walking about two steps behind her. They found the two offending slaves, Anthony and William, pitching fresh straw into the horse stalls. Nathan stood watch at the stable doors as Sally proceeded inside. The two slaves did not see Sally as she came up behind them. "I hear you two have deserted our cause!" declared Sally.

The two slaves were startled by Sally. As they spun around to face her, the younger of the two, Anthony, dropped his pitchfork and began to slowly back up into the stall he had been cleaning. The older slave, William, stood his ground, pointing his pitchfork at Sally.

"We don't want no trouble with you, Sally," said William. "Just leave us be!"

Sally's eyes flashed at William's defiant stance, but her speech became calm and measured. "I'm afraid I can't do that, William. You made a blood promise — an absolute commitment to the revolution. I can't let you back out now. Today is *the* day."

William remained defiant. "I won't say nothin' about the revolt, Sally. But I'm not gonna risk the gallows for it."

"You knew the risks when you gave your promise, William. Do you recall the commitment ceremony we had?"

"You can't scare me with that Voodoo talk, Sally. I don't really believe in it."

Sally shook her head. "Well then, William, I'll just have to make you into a believer."

Sally turned her back on William as if she was leaving. Suddenly, she spun around and threw some white powder in his face. William let out a scream, dropped the pitchfork, and clawed at his eyes. Nathan heard the scream and turned to see blood trickling out of William's eyes and down his cheeks.

After his scream, William yelled, "I'm blind! Oh, God! She blinded me!"

William staggered backwards as he scratched at his eyes and fell over a bale of straw that was behind him. While William struggled to get to his feet, Sally picked up his pitchfork, walked over to him, and calmly plunged it into his throat.

Sally turned to the cowed Anthony and ordered him to bury William under the floor of one of the empty stalls. There was an implicit understanding that Anthony had rejoined the cause. At first, Anthony trembled so violently he could hardly break the soft ground with his shovel. But Sally's impatient stare soon quickened his pace.

By the time William was buried and Sally and Nathan had spread fresh straw over William's blood, it was late in the afternoon. Sally knew she had to get back to start supper, or the other girls would miss her. When Sally returned to the kitchen, her helpers had the cooking underway, but no one dared ask why she was late.

***

The fresh air and horseback ride had seemed to clear Emile's head. As he rode back from the mill site, Emile realized he would be seeing Sally very soon, and he wondered if his resolve to distance himself from her would dissipate once more. *There's no resisting Sally,* he sighed, as he spurred his mount into a fast trot.

When Emile came down for dinner, he noticed Sally had the table set for two, as she had given herself the privilege of eating with Emile at the master's table when there were no guests at the house. Emile's visitors had departed early that afternoon. It made Emile realize he must make Sally understand that she could not behave in such a fraternizing manner when Uncle Julien returned, which could be any day now.

Sally entered the dining room carrying a silver tray with a whiskey decanter and two glasses on it. Emile noticed she had on his favorite dress — a white cotton shift, which Sally wore tightly belted to her slender waist. The dress really wasn't so special. It's just that it was very sheer cotton, and Sally wore nothing underneath it.

Sally held up an empty glass. "Drink, Emile?"

Emile shook his head. "No, thank you, Sally. Sally, you do understand that you cannot address me by my Christian name when others are present?"

Sally bowed her head slightly before replying. "Yes, I know, Emile — Monsieur Poydras. I'm sorry, I didn't — "

"You don't have to apologize, Sally. If it were up to me, you could eat with me every night, but… I'm a newcomer in this territory, and I must respect the customs."

Sally looked up. "And so shall I, Emile. Tonight, I shall only serve you supper. Then, later — if you have enjoyed the service? Perhaps you can reward Sally?"

Emile could not restrain himself from smiling at Sally's seductive question. "Oh, Sally, whatever am I going to do with you?"

Sally returned Emile's smile, and without speaking another word, she adjourned to the pantry to order the other servants to start serving dinner.

For the main course, Sally stood at the sideboard and cooked fresh crepes, which she stuffed with shrimp in a wine and cheese sauce. It was Emile's favorite dish. It was Sally's secret pleasure that Emile was so enjoying his food, without any inkling that it was his "last supper." After stuffing himself on Sally's delicious crepes, Emile insisted that Sally sit down and eat, but she politely refused. She did, however, agree to join him for coffee and cognac. When Sally leaned over the table to caress his hand, Emile fixated on her taut nipples showing beneath her tight dress.

As they walked up the stairs, arm in arm, Emile said, "My love, it is I who must visit your lodgings, when Uncle Julien returns."

Sally only smiled her reply. When Sally got undressed, she made certain she dropped her belt close to the edge of the bed.

While Emile was fully engaged in his passion, with his face buried in the pillows, Sally dropped her arm to the floor and pulled at the buckle of her belt. By grasping the buckle and shaking it, she withdrew a concealed straight razor. As Emile reached his climax, Sally brought the razor up toward his neck.

At that very instant, the sound of four rapid gunshots rang in through the open window. Emile jumped to his feet before the stunned Sally could react. Running to the window as the sound of galloping horses came out of the darkness, Emile made out five or six riders coming toward the house. All the horsemen were in uniforms, and two of them were carrying torches.

One of the riders spotted Emile's head sticking out of the second story window and pointed, calling out, "Señor Poydras!"

Then another rider, in an officer's uniform, addressed Emile in French. "Monsieur Poydras, are you alright?"

"Yes! Yes, I'm fine. What is going on here?"

"The Parish Commandant sent us," replied the officer. "He sent us to warn you of a slave rebellion."

"What!"

"Yes. The leaders are right here on your plantation. You were to be murdered tonight!"

Emile wheeled to look at Sally and froze in front of the open window. For the first time, he saw the glint of the straight razor in her hand. It took a few seconds for Emile to process what was happening. *Was I being used and manipulated all these months? What an idiot I have been!*

"Sally! Why, Sally? Why?"

Sally got out of bed and came toward Emile, threatening the naked man with her outstretched razor. "You are a fool, Emile!" she screamed. "You actually thought I loved you!"

Emile stood still at the window and replied in a steady, firm voice. "Sally, put the razor down. The soldiers are coming into the house now. It's all…"

Before Emile could finish his sentence, Sally rushed towards him with her razor raised above her head, ready to strike. Emile, naked and defenseless, stumbled backwards in front of his washstand. Grabbing the china water pitcher, the only item available with which to defend himself, Emile hurled it at Sally's head. The pitcher hit Sally in the forehead and caused her to stagger backwards and drop her razor. At that moment, they heard the sounds of the soldiers entering the house and pounding up the stairs. Ignoring the bleeding gash on her forehead, Sally grabbed up her razor, took a step back, and cursed, "Damn you to Hell, Poydras! I curse you and all your lineage. I'll see you in Hell!" With that, Sally slashed deep into her own throat and fell backwards across the bed. Emile ran to her but saw there was nothing he could do. The blood spurting from Sally's severed jugular vein splashed against his bare chest.

Chapter Eighteen

After leaving Madame Dauphine's "house," Mark, Celeste and Justin retraced their steps back down Bourbon Street. When they came to St. Peter, Justin insisted that Celeste and Mark take a break and go to Pat O'Brien's. He told Mark he might also be interested in checking out the Dixieland jazz in Preservation Hall, which was right next door to Pat's.

Celeste led Mark into Pat's Piano Lounge, the club's most popular bar. There were two grand pianos on the mirrored stage in the lounge, where two singing women pianists lead the crowd in group singing. As Mark and Celeste waited for a table, the crowd was singing "The Yellow Rose of Texas." A group of what had to be Texans whooped and waved their cowboy hats in the air as they sang. As the song ended, a green-jacketed waiter came and led Mark and Celeste to a table occupied by two other couples. Before they had a chance to exchange hellos, the roar of the singing began again. That was fine by Celeste. She wasn't in the mood to make conversation, not even with Mark.

Celeste really wasn't in the mood to party either. It was sinking in that her grandfather's concerns were not just Voodoo superstitions, and that her dreams about Emile Poydras were more — much more — than some fixation on her family history. Celeste realized she was really becoming frightened about what the ring was doing to her, and what it could do to her relationship with Mark. *I've got to stop thinking this way, or I'll go crazy,* she thought as she pulled her tall, red cocktail toward her. After quickly consuming one of Pat O'Brien's famous hurricane drinks — all twenty-nine ounces of it — Celeste felt her troubling thoughts drift away.

She noticed that Mark was really enjoying the club. He joined the singing in a loud voice and ordered two more hurricanes when the waiter came to check on them. About halfway through his second hurricane, Mark leaned over and spoke directly into Celeste's ear, "Wow! What's in these things? All of a sudden, I feel like the floor has dropped out from under me!"

Celeste grinned and put her mouth to Mark's ear, so he could hear her reply, "A whole lot of rum, sugar! After we finish this one, we'd better head home, while we can still walk!" Mark nodded in agreement and went back to sucking the straw in his tall, red drink.

When Celeste and Mark staggered out of Pat O'Brien's, Mark glanced at his watch as they turned the corner. Bourbon Street was still bustling with other drunks, tourists, and street performers.

"Man! Past one-thirty, and this place hasn't begun to slow down. Don't they ever close the bars in this town?"

Celeste lifted her head off Mark's shoulder to make her reply. "Yeah, they close up around four — just long enough to sweep the drunks out, hose down the street, and get ready for the morning crowd."

Mark shook his head. "I thought I was hearing things last night when I got up to go to the bathroom. But it was just the music drifting in from Bourbon Street."

"Well," said Celeste, "after two hurricanes, I'd say we could sleep soundly in the middle of the dance floor at Papa Joe's."

"Yeah, you don't need to worry about having your dream tonight. After all that wine and rum, we should sleep like rocks."

Mark's prediction could not have been further from the truth. Not only did Celeste repeat her dream about making love to Emile Poydras, the dream progressed into a totally new and really frightening chapter. Celeste was sitting upright in bed, experiencing a cold sweat, when she realized she had been so terrified that she screamed out loud in her sleep.

Mark was gently shaking her shoulders, telling her everything was okay, when Justin ran into their bedroom, pulling on his bathrobe as he came through the door.

"What's the matter?" asked Justin.

Mark shrugged his shoulders and looked back to Celeste.

Both men waited patiently for Celeste to gather her wits and respond to Justin's question. After a long pause, Celeste relaxed her rigid body and leaned back against the headboard of the bed. Finally, she answered, "I had the dream again, but this time it changed, all of a sudden I — "

Justin interrupted her, "No, wait. Don't tell us now. Let's all go down to the study so we can record your recollections. The details you recall now may become important later."

Mark thought that Justin was being overly dramatic about Celeste's nightmare, but they dutifully put on their robes and followed Justin downstairs.

Justin sat Celeste behind his desk and put a new tape in his cassette recorder. He plugged in the microphone and sat in the side chair in front of the desk. When the red record light came on and the tape was turning, Justin turned and faced Celeste.

"Now, sugar, describe every detail of your dream to us."

Avoiding eye contact with her grandfather and Mark, Celeste took a deep breath and spoke into the microphone. "Well, at first my dream was the same as before — I'm in the four-poster bed making love to Emile Poydras — "

"You never told me you *knew* it was Emile Poydras," interjected Mark.

Justin held up his hand. "Please, Mark. Don't distract her. We must get this on tape while it's fresh in her mind."

"Sorry," mumbled Mark.

"Anyway," continued Celeste, looking uncomfortable and visibly blushing. "The dream was exactly the same, the lovemaking was the same, my climax came at the same time — which is where my dream has always ended before — when we both climax." Celeste glanced at Mark from the corner of her eye. "But, this time, after the climax, Emile got up and held out his hand and motioned for me to follow, but I was afraid to take his hand. Then, suddenly, I found myself in an old cemetery — alone — and at night. The odd thing is, I wasn't scared, at first. When I said I was alone, I meant Emile wasn't with me. The cemetery was actually crowded with people — and children. There were children running around and playing. The children were dressed in costumes. The people all held candles and lanterns, and they were decorating the graves like it was Christmas time. I mean... the *tombs* — it was an old New Orleans cemetery because all the graves were above ground... Where was I?... Oh, yes. All the tombs had beautiful wreaths and flowers on them. Some of them were draped in black crepe and velvet. At the far end of the cemetery, I saw a procession of people following a Catholic priest. The priest appeared to be blessing the tombs. I guess? It looked like he was sprinkling holy water or something as he walked and chanted in Latin. I was enjoying the dream. Then, I was *really* alone in the cemetery. All the people and children — except for one child in a ghost costume — had vanished. As I turned to observe the tomb I was standing in front of, the child in the white costume ran behind it. It was one of those stacked tombs — oven vaults! That's what they call 'em. You know, the kind that have three or four vaults stacked on top of each other?"

Justin nodded his head to Celeste and answered, "Yes, oven vaults. Go on."

Celeste closed her eyes as she continued to describe her dream. "The tomb I was facing had been freshly painted — white. And it had a bright green flower holder attached to each side of it. There were numerous candles, different colored candles, burning in front of and on the tomb itself. Suddenly, all the candles began to flare up, and I heard the sound of drums beating — and chanting. But no one was to be seen."

"What kind of chanting?" asked Justin.

"I don't know. I didn't recognize the language. It was like something from a jungle movie. Then I noticed the slab, or name plate, that covers the opening to the top vault. It had little crosses crudely drawn all over it. Some were in pencil, some in chalk, and some looked like they were drawn with a piece of red brick. As I moved closer to examine the slab, it began to glow. Not a constant glow, but a pulsating yellow-green glow — like a big firefly. Then, I started to really feel frightened, and yet, at the same time, I was drawn to the glowing vault. I wanted to read the name on the plate, but I couldn't make it out. I could only see that it's a long inscription, and that it's in French. So, I bent over and picked up one of the candles and moved closer to read the name…" At this point in her narration, Celeste became visibly distressed. She began wringing her hands and furrows appeared in her forehead. She squeezed her eyes shut even tighter. In an almost trance like state, she relived the climax of her dream.

"… I have the candle right next to the inscription — I'm touching the stone with my fingers! But my mind won't work! I can't read the name." Celeste's eyes flew open. "Then it happened!… As I'm desperately trying to read the name on the tomb, a hand bursts through the glowing slab and grabs my hand. But it's not really a hand that grabs me. It's a skeleton. That's when I started to scream."

Justin leaned over and switched off the tape recorder. Then he walked behind Celeste's chair and patted her gently on both shoulders. "I'm sorry," he said. "But what you've given us may help solve this curse. Now, let's all go back to bed."

Celeste reached up over her shoulder and grabbed one of her grandfather's hands. "I'm scared to go back to bed, Granddad."

Justin squeezed her hand. "Not to worry, sugar. The dream never comes but once a night. But I have some sleepin' pills upstairs if you want one?"

Celeste accepted the offer of the sleeping pill and fell asleep, exhausted, in Mark's arms. Mark didn't sleep a wink the rest of the night. He just lay there, staring into the darkness, listening to the pattern of Celeste's breathing — waiting for the telltale sign of another nightmare coming on.

Chapter Nineteen

Upon his arrival in New Orleans, Julien was greeted with news of the slave rebellion at Pointe Coupee. The city was seized with fear that the uprising would spread throughout the colony. Governor Carondelet had been compelled to send so many of his troops to put down the rebellion that the New Orleans garrison was nearly depleted. All the citizens could talk about was how under-protected they would be if the local slaves joined the rebellion. Already, petitions were being circulated, asking the governor and the Cabildo (city council) to ban the importation of new slaves.

The fact that the rebellion had emanated at his Alma Plantation made Julien's presence unwelcome in the city. Therefore, at dawn on the day after his arrival, Julien set out on his barge for Pointe Coupee. The voyage upriver proved to be a gruesome one, for at the prominent points and bends in the Mississippi, Julien observed the decaying and bloated corpses of Negro slaves hanging from trees or makeshift gallows. He counted twenty-three bodies between New Orleans and Point Coupee, a number of whom Julien recognized as his own slaves.

After landing at Pointe Coupee and briefly checking to see that everything was under control at his home plantation, Julien rode out to Alma to check on Emile and conditions there.

Emile, having heard that Julien had arrived in Pointe Coupee, nervously awaited his uncle's coming. As he paced the floor of his study, Emile reflected on his arrival in New Orleans. He had been nervous that day, but it was nothing compared to the anxiety and shame he felt now.

Gérard, the houseboy, rapped on the study door and entered without waiting for permission. "Monsieur Poydras, your uncle is coming up the road. He's almost here."

"Thank you, Gérard. Fetch one of the grooms to take Uncle Julien's horse."

"Yes, monsieur," replied the boy as he turned and ran out of the study.

Emile stood at attention on the portico as Julien rode up. As the waiting groomsman took the reins of his horse, Julien dismounted, came up the steps, and threw his arms around Emile's rigid shoulders.

Julien spoke first. "My dear boy, I'm so relieved to see you. The commandant told me you were nearly murdered the night the rebellion began."

Emile felt his knees go weak upon receiving his uncle's warm embrace, and tears welled up in his eyes. He returned Julien's hug before replying. "Oh, Uncle, I am so ashamed. I have failed you completely. Can you ever forgive me?"

Julien led Emile over to the wrought iron table and chairs located to the left of the front door. He sat Emile down at the table and motioned for the nearby Gérard. "Gérard, bring cognac and water, and two glasses please."

Gérard nodded and disappeared into the house. Before Julien could remove his riding gloves and three-cornered hat, the houseboy returned with the cognac, a pitcher of water, and two crystal glasses.

Julien nodded his approval of Gérard's speedy service. "Thank you, Gérard. After you pour us each a drink, you may leave."

Even after taking a long pull on his cognac, Emile could not look his uncle in the eyes. He spoke into his glass. "I… I suppose the commandant told you how it came to pass that I was nearly murdered?"

"Yes. Yes, he told me, Emile. And that Sally cut her own throat rather than be captured."

"So, you know," continued Emile, "that I was having an affair with her while she was plotting the slave rebellion."

"Yes, I know that, Emile, and it is I who should ask your forgiveness."

For the first time, Emile looked his uncle in the eyes. "What!… Surely, you jest? You must know what my mismanagement has cost you."

Julien shook his head. "I should have warned you about Sally. I knew she was a Voodooienne, but I had no idea she was so dangerous."

"Please, Uncle! Don't make excuses for me. I knew it was wrong to get involved with her, but — "

"But you couldn't stop yourself," interrupted Julien. "You see, you didn't have a choice. I suspected Sally probably had designs on Cabot, but I never dreamed she could have been behind a full-fledged slave revolt. So, don't blame yourself. This revolt took all the planters by surprise."

"How do you know I couldn't resist Sally? Is there some flaw in my character that is apparent to others but blind to me?"

"No, Emile. There is no flaw in your character. The error was mine. I was in such a rush to leave for Philadelphia that I didn't take the time to warn you of the tricks and practices of Voodoo women. I left you here like a babe in the woods."

Emile rolled his eyes. "This is preposterous, Uncle Julien. My recklessness has cost you twenty slaves and sullied your good name. And *you* apologize to me?"

"Emile, the plot for the uprising was widespread, and the planning was undoubtedly well underway before your arrival in the colony."

Emile took another drink of his cognac. "I don't deserve your understanding, Uncle. But I promise you, I will not fail you again."

"Nor I you, Emile. I promise you that I will teach you enough about the dark side of this New World for you to protect yourself. Now, give me your accounting. You say twenty of the slaves were executed for involvement in the rebellion?"

"No, only sixteen were executed, but four others are missing. We found one of them buried in the stable."

"A victim of Sally and the other rebels, no doubt," mused Julien. "Was there any other loss or damage here?"

"Not really. There was some limited damage from the fighting in the slave quarters on the first night of the rebellion, but no damage to the main house or new mill. Most of the fighting took place later in Pointe Coupee."

"When the rebels tried to free their other leaders from the garrison's prison," confirmed Julien.

"Yes. Had it not been for the reinforcements sent by Governor Carondelet, the rebellion might have succeeded."

"Well," said Julien. "Your first year at managing Alma will certainly not be a profitable one. All the slaves we lost cost at least 30,000 piasters. But I would gladly have lost the entire plantation to see you unharmed."

"I don't deserve your magnanimity, Uncle. I will strive to make 1796 a fruitful year and to be worthy of your benevolence someday."

"I know you shall, Emile. Now tell me, how did the commandant come to learn of the revolt in time to arrest its leaders and save you from Sally's razor?"

"It was the wife of one of the white overseers involved. I don't recall which plantation she was from. Anyway, she feared the rebellion would fail and went to the commandant. She informed in return for her husband's life."

"And what of Cabot and the other conspirators?"

"Twenty-five rebels died trying to break Cabot and the other ringleaders out of jail. When the revolt was finally put down, Cabot and the rest of the insurgents were tried and hanged the same day. The rebel slaves that did not take up arms were only flogged and returned to their owners. Uncle?... Do you really believe that Sally had me under some spell? That she was able to completely take away my free will?"

"You already know the answer to that question, Emile. So, put away your blame and your guilt. And, while you're at it, all your preconceptions about religion — Heaven and Hell — life and death. For all kinds of spirits, good and evil, roam the roads of New France, and the Voodooiennes who worship them and their queens can be found not only in the slave quarters, but also in some of the finest families in the colony. I know you can't begin to understand what I'm talking about. Nor could I, until I saw the living dead with my own eyes. I shall show you what you dare not let yourself believe."

"I don't understand, Uncle," replied Emile with a perplexed look.

"Of course not. Where are those dueling pistols you brought with you from France?"

"In the study, but what do they — "

"Never mind now, I'll explain later. Just fetch your pistols, load them, and meet me in the old hay barn. It's still empty, isn't it?"

"Yes, but — "

"Just bring your pistols, Emile. I'll go ahead and make certain there are no slaves around to observe us."

Emile did as he was instructed and brought his dueling pistols to the vacant hay barn west of the main house. As he entered the barn, Julien closed and latched the wooden doors and walked to the middle of the barn, about five paces from Emile. Turning to face Emile, he asked, "Are your pistols loaded?"

"Yes, Uncle. I keep them loaded."

"Are you a good enough shot to hit me where I stand?"

"What!" exclaimed Emile. "I would never consider such a thing!"

"Don't worry, Emile. No harm can possibly come to me. Please, fire away."

"Uncle, please do not jest with me in this manner. If you have some point to make, make it plainer to me."

"Very well," said Julien as he walked over to Emile, who was cradling the case of pistols in his arms. He withdrew one of the pistols from its padded leather box then walked back to the center of the barn and cocked the pistol. "Are you certain this pistol is fully loaded?" asked Julien.

For a second, Emile did not answer. He was suddenly seized with a new fear, that his uncle had gone mad and was about to do himself harm.

"Emile, are you certain this pistol will fire?" reiterated Julien.

Finally, Emile made himself answer after deciding the truth was the safest answer to give. "It will fire, Uncle. I loaded it myself. Please be careful."

"I shall be careful; just promise me you will not rush me and try to stop my firing. That could cause an accident."

Emile felt an awful sinking feeling hit his stomach, but he answered Julien. "As you wish, just — please don't do anything — "

Before Emile could finish his sentence, Julien raised the pistol barrel to his temple and pulled the trigger. Emile could take but one-half step toward Julien before the hammer struck home. But the pistol didn't fire. The only sound was the metallic click of the hammer striking home. Emile was so shocked that the weapon did not fire that he froze in his tracks. Before he could react further, Julien had re-cocked the pistol and fired it into the dirt floor beside his right foot. The sound of the pistol discharge was deafening in the closed barn, and the acrid smoke stung Emile's eyes. Finally, Emile laid the pistol case down, walked to his uncle, and took the pistol from Julien's extended hand.

"Uncle, you are undoubtedly the luckiest man alive. You would have died had the pistol not misfired."

Julien gave Emile a knowing smile before answering. "No, I would not have died. If you don't believe me, just hand me the other pistol and I'll prove it again."

Emile was flabbergasted. "Prove what? My God! Have you gone mad? No one could survive two such attempts to affront death."

"I can, Emile…. I can because death has no power over me. Only I have the power to choose the time of my death. Until I so choose, no real harm can come to my person. No contagion can infect my body — no curse can be imposed on my spirit."

Emile became convinced his uncle was insane but tried not to let it show. "Uncle, that is not possible. Only God can choose the time of our deaths."

"I told you that you must put aside all your conventional beliefs about religion, if you are ever to understand the power of Voodoo." Julien extended his left hand, holding it up to Emile's face. "Have you ever noticed the alliance ring I wear?"

Emile took Julien's hand and went through the motion of examining the ring. "Yes, I've noticed your ring. It looks like a wedding ring."

"And it didn't strike you as odd that I should be wearing a wedding ring when I have never been married?"

"Yes," agreed Emile. "I must admit I wondered why you wore the ring, but I did not feel I had the right to pry into your private affairs."

"This is no ordinary wedding band, Emile — not anymore. It is the most powerful Voodoo charm of its kind. I believe there is only one other charm like it in existence. Whoever wears this ring is immortal until the ring is removed. If the ring is lost, or given to another, the protection is lost, and death will have its way."

"Where did the ring come from?" Emile tried not to sound incredulous.

"The ring itself? I brought it with me from France. I had purchased it for the girl I wanted to marry in Nantes. But the power of the ring came from Sanité Diable, the greatest Voodoo queen to ever walk the earth. Only she knows how to make such charms."

"This… this Voodoo queen, is she the only other person to have such a charm?"

Julien shrugged his shoulders and gave an elusive smile but did not directly answer Emile's question.

Emile looked dubious and released Julien's hand. "Uncle, why tell me all of this? Even if it's true, what does it have to do with me?"

Julien responded to Emile's apparent skepticism. "I don't expect you to understand all this yet — nor to even believe me. You are the only other living soul who knows what this ring really is. By telling you about it, I have placed my life in your hands.... I have shown it to you because I have decided to obtain such a charm for you — so I don't have to worry about you ever again falling prey to evil Voodooiennes. But I warn you. The power and protection the ring offers has its price. It cannot be worn by any man who is not willing to pay that price... If you're interested in learning more, tell me. If not, I shall respect your decision, and we shall never discuss the subject again."

"I don't know what I believe, Uncle. But I do know that I trust you with my life. Pray, tell me more about your ring."

That evening, in his bedroom, Emile filled several pages in his diary before he went to bed. It was nearly dawn before Emile could stop thinking about the dramatic events of the day and drift off to sleep.

Part III
Wishes and Consequences

We would often be sorry

if our wishes were granted.

– Aesop, *The Old Man and Death*

Chapter Twenty

The morning after her nightmare, Celeste awoke to an empty house. It was 10:30 when she got up and went into the bathroom. Mark had taped a handwritten note to the vanity mirror:

Baby,

Sorry I had to leave you, but I had an interview scheduled for 9:00. I should be back by noon.

Love,

Mark

P.S. Your granddad was gone when I got up.

Celeste shook her head and brooded, *I sure had him figured wrong. I thought with all this Voodoo ring business, Mark would want to get as far away from New Orleans as possible. Granddad, you are a force to be reckoned with.*

By 11:45, Celeste had showered, styled her hair, and put on makeup. As she descended the stairs, Justin came through the front door. He smiled at Celeste as she stepped down into his view.

"You look much improved," said Justin.

"Thanks, Granddad. That was a compliment, wasn't it?"

Justin blushed slightly. "Just like your grandmother — always remindin' me that I'm too stingy with my approbations."

"I was just goin' to make some coffee," said Celeste. "Can I bring you a cup?"

"No thank you, dear. I've had my limit but help yourself. I made a fresh pot just before I left the house. It warms up great in the microwave."

When Celeste exited the kitchen, she noticed her grandfather had seated himself in the garden on a wrought iron bench opposite his fountain. Justin was just staring at the fountain, seemingly lost in thought. He had left the dining room doors open, so Celeste took it as an invitation to join him.

"Where were you off to so early?" asked Celeste.

Justin turned to face her and patted the empty seat next to him on the bench. "Come and sit down, and I'll tell you all about it."

Justin put his arm behind Celeste's back as she sat down, then cleared his throat before answering the question. "I went to find Mama Vance."

"And did you?" inquired Celeste.

"Yes. I found her livin' in an old house on the edge of Bayou Fatma — it's on the other side of the river, past Gretna. I took her the tape of your dream."

"What did she say about it?"

"Nothin' really. She told me she was willin' to meet you, but that she would not interpret the dream until… she meets you."

"So, she said she could interpret my dream?"

Justin nodded. "Yes. She even said she recognized the tomb you saw in your dream."

"What's she like, Granddad? Does she strike you as a charlatan?"

"Well… she's very old and very eccentric, but I believe she is no fraud."

"I trust your judgment, but it would help me if you could explain why you believe her."

"Certainly," agreed Justin. "You see, when I knocked on her door, she called me by name. She said, 'Come in, Monsieur Noyan.' I opened the screen door and found her sittin' in a rockin' chair, facin' away from the door. She never turned toward me when I entered. When I asked how she knew who I was, she would only say that she'd been expectin' me for quite some time."

"Okay, that's all a little weird," said Celeste. "But maybe she saw you drive up — maybe Madame Dauphine told her you were coming."

"Yes, one would think that's possible," agreed Justin. "Except, Mama Vance is stone blind."

Celeste had no comeback for that disclosure, so Justin continued after pausing for a moment. "There's something else I must tell you. Before Mama Vance will help us, we all must go through an initiation ceremony."

"What!"

"It's really quite harmless — we don't have to renounce God and worship the devil — nothin' like that. But we all must become members of her cult before she will help us."

Celeste couldn't sit still any longer. She jumped up, walked to the fountain, and turned to face Justin. "Granddad, this is getting out of hand — Mark'll never go along with that."

"If Mark doesn't want to join us when we go to Mama Vance's, I understand. And if you don't, I'll understand that as well. But, before you make your decision, ask yourself how many more nights like last night you care to experience."

Celeste slumped down and sat on the edge of the stone fountain. "Okay, you win. When do we go?"

"Late tonight. We are to be there at eleven o'clock."

Celeste shook her head and blew out a heavy sigh. "Just let me tell Mark. He'll do it for me." With a miffed tone, she added, "By the way, *thanks* for helping him land the job interview."

***

It was 10:45 when Justin, Celeste, and Mark turned off onto the dirt road leading to Mama Vance's. The road was pitch black. There were no streetlights or other houses to give any illumination to the dense vegetation growing along the bayou. The only glint of light came from the reflection of the moon off the waters of Bayou Fatma, which paralleled the left side of the road. Celeste noticed it was a full moon.

Just when Celeste was thinking they might be lost, Justin pulled over and parked the car. Then, as she started to ask where they were, she caught sight of an old, rundown bungalow. It was partly obscured by a group of tall banana trees and tall weeds. Celeste wouldn't have noticed the house at all, except for the light of a single candle burning behind the front window.

Mark was alone in the backseat and couldn't see the house. "This is it?" he asked.

"Yes," replied Justin.

Celeste turned and leaned over the front seat to speak to Mark. "I really appreciate you coming with us, Mark."

Mark muttered, "You're welcome," and quickly exited the car, almost slamming the car door. Celeste looked at Justin, shrugged her shoulders, and got out and joined Mark.

Still pouting, Mark said nothing as they walked up the grassy path to the house.

As they walked along, Celeste asked her grandfather, "Has there been a power outage?"

"No, Mama Vance doesn't have electricity in her house."

Breaking his self-imposed silence, Mark commented, "From the looks of this shack, it was built before electricity was invented."

As they stepped up onto the sagging front porch, they could see other flickering candles through the screen door. This time, when Justin rapped on the door, he was greeted by a big black man wearing overalls and no shirt. The man's shaved face and head made it hard to judge his age, but Celeste estimated he was in his mid-fifties.

The black man filled up the open door frame but didn't move out of the entrance, never saying a word.

Finally, Justin said, "I'm Justin Noyan. Mrs. Vance is expectin' us."

A shrill voice came from inside the house. "Cupid can't answer you, Monsieur Noyan, he got no tongue."

When Cupid moved aside, Justin stepped inside first and addressed Mama Vance. "Mrs. Vance, I've brought my granddaughter, Celeste, and her husband, Mark Richards."

"Wonderful. Come ta me, ma chérie. I've been so anxious ta meet you."

Celeste stepped through the door and saw a frail, little black woman sitting in a high-backed walnut rocker. Mama Vance had stooped shoulders and short, kinky gray hair. She appeared to be about eighty to ninety, but it was hard for Celeste to make an accurate estimate of Mama Vance's age in the faint candlelight. The old woman wore a bright yellow housedress that buttoned up the front. It looked to be about two sizes too large. She held out her hands as Celeste approached her chair.

Mama Vance smiled as she took ahold of Celeste's hands. Suddenly, Celeste felt as if she was going to faint. But when Mama Vance released her hands, her dizziness quickly dissipated.

"Cupid, git dis girl a chair," ordered Mama Vance. "And for de gentlemen too."

Cupid dutifully brought out three old straight chairs from the kitchen and seated Celeste next to Mama Vance. Justin and Mark ended up opposite the two women.

There was a pause after everyone was seated. Celeste broke the silence. "Mrs. Vance — "

"Call me Mama Vance, ma chérie, everyone calls me Mama Vance."

"Sure," continued Celeste. "Mama Vance, my grandfather said you can tell us whose grave I dreamed about?"

"Dhat I can, ma chérie. I can tell you dhat and much more. But first, we must bring you into de fold."

Mark couldn't restrain himself any longer and let out a disgruntled snort before asking, "And how much is that gonna cost?"

Mama Vance cackled with laughter and rocked back hard in her chair before answering Mark. "I'll let you decide dhat, Monsieur Richards. You tell me how much your wife's soul be worth. But, no worry, I don't want your money."

"Let's get on with it," was Mark's terse reply.

"As you wish, Monsieur Richards… Cupid! We be ready."

Cupid came back into the room carrying a large wicker basket covered by a folded white tablecloth. He spread the tablecloth on the floor in the center of the room. Then Cupid stepped off to the side and started removing his shoes and socks.

As if on cue, Mama Vance said, "You-all must do everytin' Cupid do, otherwise dis ceremony not work."

Mark muttered, "Oh, brother." However, he started removing his shoes when Justin and Celeste complied.

"Make sure nothin' be crossed," continued Mama Vance. "If your legs or arms be crossed, de spirits won't come near us."

As everyone removed their shoes and socks, Cupid removed a framed picture of Saint Peter from the basket and stood it in the middle of the tablecloth. Then he began spreading out the other articles from his basket. He performed his tasks quickly and with an air of precision, as if it were a well-known routine.

He stood green and white candles on each end of the tablecloth. Candles of various other colors were placed around the sides until he had constructed a ring of candles around the picture of Saint Peter. Cupid stood a quart bottle of apple cider on one side of the circle. On the other side, he stood a bottle that appeared to contain grape soda or Kool-Aid. Next, a number of saucers were laid out, seemingly at random. One appeared to be filled with steel dust, another dried basil. Other plates contained biscuits, gingersnaps, and birdseed. Celeste could not discern the contents of some of the dishes. They appeared to contain dried animal or other vegetable matter. A bowl of dingy looking liquid was placed on each side of the cloth, and a small bottle of olive oil was set at the far edge on the left side. Behind the olive oil, Cupid sat a five-pound sack of sugar. On the right edge of the tablecloth, a bunch of bananas were placed next to a bowl of red apples. A branch from a camphor tree was carefully laid in front of St. Peter's picture. Finally, Cupid pulled the last two items from his "bottomless" basket — a pint of gin and a dusty bottle of Jax beer.

Mark had bitten his tongue several times during the display to keep from making snide comments. He'd promised Celeste he'd go along with the ceremony, so they could hear what the old witch had to say.

Cupid pulled a Bic lighter from the bib of his denim overalls and proceeded to light all the candles. His face seemed to light up with the candles. Until now, Mark had thought Cupid was old, dull-witted, and sullen as he observed how Cupid went about the mechanical motions of setting up the display. But now, Cupid's eyes glittered in the bright candlelight, and he didn't look nearly as old as he first appeared. Then he gave a broad smile, and his lips pulled back in a grin that exposed pointed canine teeth, like a dog's.

Cupid knelt on his knees before the candlelit Voodoo altar, and everyone did the same, except Mama Vance. She just scooted her rocking chair to the head of the tablecloth. Next, Cupid rapped on the floor three times. He looked at Mark when he failed to follow suit. Mark took the hint and slowly rapped his knuckles on the plank floor three times, following Justin and Celeste's compliance.

Now, Mama Vance took charge of the ceremony. She recited the Lord's Prayer in Creole French. Cupid looked at Justin, and he reiterated the prayer, also in Creole, but not nearly as rapidly as Mama Vance.

There was a pause. Then Celeste spoke up for her and Mark. "Mama Vance, we can't speak Creole."

Mama Vance nodded. "Dhat's alright, ma chérie. You two can say de prayer in English."

Mark hated to admit his ignorance, but was forced to ask, "What prayer are we reciting?"

"It's just the Lord's Prayer, Mark," responded Celeste. Then she led Mark through the litany. "Our Father, who art in Heaven, hallowed be thy name…"

When the praying ended, without any visible cue from Mama Vance, Cupid sprang up and began to dance around the tablecloth and the kneeling novices. As Cupid danced, Mama Vance began to chant in Creole, and another language Celeste didn't recognize.

Eh, yé, yé, Sanité Diable,

Ya, yé, yé, li konin tou, gris gris;

Li té kouri lekal, aver vieux kokodril;

Oh, ouai, yé Sanité Diable…

After repeating the chant three times, Mama Vance began a new chant of:

L'Appé vini, le Grand Zombi,

L'Appé vini, pou fe gris gris!

When Cupid heard this new chant, he returned to his place and began turning in slow circles. As he started his turning, Cupid motioned for them to join him. All the participants, except Mama Vance, stood and imitated Cupid's slow turns until Mama Vance quickened the pace of her chant. Cupid, likewise, sped up the revolutions.

Mark got so dizzy from turning circles he had to stop or he knew he would fall down. When the room stopped spinning for Mark, he noticed Celeste had sat back down in her chair, and that Justin was holding on to the back of his chair for support.

Cupid just kept spinning away, faster and faster. He flung his arms out over his head. Then he tilted his head back and glared at the ceiling. Suddenly, he too stopped and stood with his eyes shut, his whole body shaking and quivering, seemingly in a trance. Abruptly, Cupid's body ceased its shaking, and his eyes closed. At the same instant, he let out a loud grunt, which was followed by a rapid sequence of other guttural sounds that startled the dizzy neophytes.

"De spirit is on him," said Mama Vance, in a shrill whisper. "He's speakin' de unknown tongue. Aie, Aie! Voodoo Magnian! Aie! Aie! Voodoo Magnian!"

Upon hearing Mama Vance's repeated Creole command of "Voodoo Magic," Cupid ceased speaking in tongues, bent over, and picked up the pint of gin. Throwing down the cap, Cupid took a hard pull on the bottle, consuming about a fourth of the liquor in a single swallow.

Now, Cupid began a new dance, sort of a back-and-forth shuffle, that brought him directly in front of Mama Vance's rocking chair. Stopping before her, Cupid took another gulp of gin and spewed it directly into her face.

"We have it now!" Mama Vance screamed. "We have it now!"

Before Mark had time to react, he too was treated to a spray of gin from Cupid's mouth, likewise a startled Celeste and Justin.

Now, for the first time, Mama Vance got out of her rocking chair and knelt before the tablecloth altar. When Cupid followed suit, everyone else did the same. When all were kneeling, Mama Vance began a new chant:

C'est l'amour, oui maman, c'est l'amour!

C'est l'amour, oui maman…

Everyone else picked up the chant, *even Cupid*, and it was repeated ad nauseam. When Mama Vance ended the chant, she instructed everyone to return to their chairs.

Cupid went to the kitchen and dragged in an old-fashioned washtub. Into it he poured the contents of the cider bottle, the beer, and the grape Kool-Aid. Next, he added in a little of the contents of each of the saucers on the altar, plus the olive oil and two handfuls of sugar. After mixing this solution with his hand, Cupid pulled the tub to Mama Vance's feet and washed them in the murky liquid. This ritual was in turn performed on each of the participants. The rite was conducted in complete silence. The only sound was the soft sucking noise the out-of-breath Cupid made drawing air in and out between his pointed teeth.

When the foot baths were complete, Cupid began to pass out the candles that had been used on the altar to Mark, Celeste, and Justin. As he handed out the candles, Cupid passed the flame of each through his mouth to extinguish it. When he had finished, everyone had possession of a white, green, and red candle. With that, the initiation ceremony came to an end. Cupid picked up the washtub and withdrew to the kitchen.

"Now, my children," said Mama Vance, "what it be you wish ta know?"

Chapter Twenty-One

After supervising the spring planting at his Pointe Coupee plantations, Julien decided it was time Emile got acquainted with New Orleans. He'd been too rushed for time to show the boy the city upon his arrival. Besides, he felt the urge to enjoy New Orleans's cosmopolitan environment, and Julien thought he needed to check on his properties there as well.

Thus, on the 30th of June, 1795, Emile saw all of New Orleans. He also smelled New Orleans. In fact, the smell was the first thing he noticed during the carriage ride from the wharf to Julien's house.

"Uncle? What is that horrid odor?"

Julien pointed at the edge of the narrow dirt street. "The garbage ditches. I'm afraid plumbing is as yet unknown to this city, and because we are below sea level, the ditches never drain properly."

"Are they never cleaned?" asked the still offended Emile.

"Yes, occasionally, by Negro convicts. Don't worry, my boy. You'll be accustomed to the smell by tomorrow."

"Wonderful," muttered Emile, who was sarcastically thinking that Pointe Coupee with its slave uprisings might be preferable to a stay in the unbearable stench that penetrated his nostrils.

As they rode along, Emile noticed that none of the streets were paved. The narrow dirt thoroughfares seemed to be choking beds of dust, with occasional quagmires at low, wet points. The banquettes, or raised walkways, beside the streets were nothing more than mud covered planks or logs pegged into the ground. Emile found the architecture not unappealing, though. He liked the houses with open porticos, balconies, and red tile roofs; here and there, the Spanish style seemed to be refined by French ironwork and other accents.

When their carriage passed through a street that seemed to be lined with nothing but coffee houses and cafés, it made a left turn at the end of the block and stopped in front of a rather plain-looking, but large, two-story brick residence. Emile and Julien were immediately attended to by two Negro servants in blue uniforms who unloaded their luggage. They were also greeted by the house manager, an effeminate, middle-aged Frenchman by the name of Maree.

After a brief consultation with Monsieur Maree, Julien, followed by a gray-haired maid carrying a tray of wine, joined Emile in the parlor. When the maid had served the wine and withdrawn, Julien checked to make certain no servants remained in the hall and closed the parlor door. Julien's secretive acts allowed Emile to guess what the topic of their conversation would be. Subsequent to a short discussion about where they would dine that evening, Julien got down to what was on his mind.

"After dinner, I hope you will excuse me, Emile. I have some business to attend to."

"And what business might that be, Uncle?" inquired Emile with a knowing tone in his voice.

Julien smiled. "You are a perceptive young man, aren't you? Yes, I intend to seek out Sanité Diable."

"The Voodoo queen who made your ring?"

"The very same," answered Julien.

"Is it wise to seek her out alone, Uncle?"

"Not to worry, Emile. Two of my trusted servants will accompany me. Believe me, it is better that I go without you this time. As they say, 'to test the waters.'"

Emile decided to pursue the subject of the ring. "Uncle, you have yet to tell me how it came to pass that Sanité Diable showed you such favor."

Julien took a mouthful of the red wine and leaned back in his chair. "It was seventeen years ago next week. The week before, on St. John's Eve, I had been taken to view my first Voodoo ceremony by my American friend, Oliver Pollock. At first, I could not believe what I saw. That a man I knew — a man of strong will and an enemy of Sanité Diable — could be cursed into becoming the queen's slave — like a walking dead man he was... Anyway, when I heard of another meeting of Sanité Diable's sect, I decided to go — to see if what I witnessed had been some elaborate hoax, or if the man had been merely drugged..."

When Julien paused too long in his narration, Emile encouraged him. "And was it a hoax?"

Shaking his head, Julien replied, "It was no hoax. I met the man again, face to face — a Spanish china merchant by the name of Roxas. And he was dead to the world — a mere shell of his former self."

"What did Roxas have to do with you obtaining the ring?"

"Nothing, really. It's just, if I hadn't gone back to see him, I would never have met Sanité Diable. The second gathering of the cult I attended was not open to outsiders. Thus, I was compelled to bribe my way in and to hide from view in the back of the hall. I had secreted myself behind some barrels just inside the door. When Sanité Diable and her entourage entered, the queen was arguing with her king — King Soto was his name. Anyway, I never knew what the argument was about, but as they came past my position, King Soto became enraged, and he tore from Sanité Diable's neck the thick gold necklace she always wore. When the necklace broke and hit the ground, Sanité Diable immediately fell to her knees to recover it. At that very instant, Soto drew a dagger from the back of his pants and lunged at the queen's exposed back... To this day, I don't know why I decided to intervene. I suppose it was a reflex reaction. I shoved the stack of barrels I was behind onto Soto — knocking him down and the dagger from his hand. When Soto recovered himself, Sanité Diable had retrieved her necklace and was on her feet with loyal followers coming to her aid. Seeing that, Soto fled the premises."

"I see. The gold necklace is Sanité Diable's charm of protection?"

"Exactly, and the source of her great powers."

"So, you saved the Voodoo queen's life," commented Emile.

"Yes. Yes, I did. I'm not certain I should have, but I did save her."

"And your reward was the ring?"

"Exactly," answered Julien. "Sanité Diable embraced me and insisted that I join her cult."

"What!"

"Yes. It happened before I could object. Sanité Diable made a few cabalistic signs over my head, sprinkled me with some liquid from a calabash, and voilà, I was initiated... She abbreviated the induction ceremony for me."

"Another favor for saving her life?"

"No doubt. It was after the meeting had adjourned that Sanité Diable took me aside. She asked me for some item I held dear — preferably a piece of jewelry."

"And you just handed her your alliance ring? Without asking what she wanted with it?"

"Yes. Yes, to both of your questions. I know that must seem odd. At the same time, I felt I could not refuse her, even had she asked for the house we sit in."

"When did she return the ring?" asked Emile.

"It was several days later. She came to my lodging one night... She told me that she was giving me my life in return for saving hers. Then she went on to warn me to never remove the ring, if I decided to wear it. I didn't — I couldn't believe what she had given me at first. But as soon as I put the ring on, I felt its power rush through my body. And in these past seventeen years, I have truly lived a charmed life."

"I'm curious, Uncle. Sanité Diable's gold necklace, do you know where it came from or how she came to possess it?"

"No, she never told me. The necklace itself was like nothing I'd ever seen. It was very old and massive. It had a large gold moon disk on one side and a lotus flower of some sort engraved on the other. Some sort of ancient writing was etched into the links. I assumed it was an artifact from some ancient civilization... ancient Egypt perhaps? But, as I said, it is Sanité Diable's protective charm — as the ring is mine."

"Of course," said Emile. "That was why she immediately fell to retrieve the necklace, rather than trying to fend off Soto's attack." After a sip of wine, Emile asked, "How long has it been since you have seen Sanité Diable?"

"Seventeen years," answered Julien. "I had no desire to see her again and possibly be trapped into becoming one of her acolytes."

Julien's fear of Sanité Diable suddenly hit home with Emile. "Uncle Julien, now that I understand what kind of a — what kind of evil you are dealing with, I must protest your efforts to seek such a charm for me."

"Nonsense, my boy, she will not harm me. She still holds me in good regard, or so I've been told."

"But, Uncle — "

"No more of her, now. Let me suggest some entertainment for you while I am occupied this evening. Monsieur Maree tells me there is a Bal du Cordon Bleu this evening at the Condé Street Ballroom."

Emile looked puzzled. "What kind of ball is that?"

"They are better known as the quadroon balls. It will be an opportunity for you to see the most beautiful women in the colony, if not the whole of the new world."

"But aren't the quadroons mixed blood, Negro slaves?" asked Emile.

"They are of mixed blood, but they are not actually slaves or Negros. They are of the gens de couleur libres. Only pure-blooded Africans are referred to as Negros."

"Free colored people? How did that come to pass?"

"There has always been a shortage of white women in the colony, particularly in the early days. So, men took Negro women as their mistresses. The mistresses, and the mulatto children that were born to these relationships, were often set free by the slave owners. Of course, all the offspring of a freed slave are born free. Thus, was born the gens de couleur libres."

"Then the free colored have all the rights of free whites?"

"No, not at all," answered Julien. "But they are protected under the Black Code. For example, they may own property and slaves of their own, but the gens de couleur are not allowed to marry a slave."

"I'm confused," admitted Emile as he poured himself another glass of wine. "Where does one draw the line between the white and the colored? Does any fraction of Negro blood make one a member of the gens de couleur?"

"That is a matter of much debate," replied Julien. "The octoroons are the top class of the gens de couleur, and they are one-eighth Negro blood. I contend that less than one-eighth Negro blood is not enough to classify a person as colored."

"I had no idea the colored society was so stratified. Who is at the bottom of their class order?"

"They are called the griffe — the offspring of a mulatto and a Negro. They are even looked down on by the pure Negros."

"So, these women at the quadroon balls, they are three-quarters white?"

"Yes, beautiful breeds of French and Spanish Blood — but it's not what you might think. The admission is twice the price of white society balls, and the girls are all chaperoned, usually by their mothers."

Julien's last disclosure perked Emile's interest in attending the ball. He pressed the subject with another question. "I assume only white gentlemen are invited to attend?"

"You are correct, Nephew." Julien grinned. "As long as you have the price of admission."

"Just how much is admission?"

"The admission is nothing. I've sent one of the servants for tickets. The real price is paid if you decide to take one of the girls as your mistress. Until you pay the mother *her* price, you will never be left alone with the quadroon maiden. And that's just the beginning of your expense. You are expected to provide at least a modest home for your lover. Many of them are installed in houses near the ramparts."

"I see what you mean, Uncle. One chooses his dancing partners carefully at these balls."

"Oh, you may dance with them all if you like. Just obey all the protocols you would at any formal ball. And be mindful of jealous suitors. Many a duel has been fought over a beautiful quadroon."

"What time is the ball tonight?"

"Eight o'clock, I believe. They've been known to last well past midnight. I shall drop you off, while I attend my business with Sanité Diable. Hopefully, I will be finished early enough to join you at the ball later."

Emile splashed down the last of his wine. "I'm beginning to think I've misjudged New Orleans, Uncle. In fact, the city is already starting to smell sweeter."

Chapter Twenty-Two

After the Voodoo initiation ceremony was complete, everyone put their shoes and socks back on. Mark used his socks to wipe the smelly bath water off his feet and put his brown boat loafers back on, sans socks.

Mama Vance picked up a corncob pipe, and Cupid lit it for her with his Bic. Then he sat on the floor by Mama Vance's feet like a dutiful pet. When Mark got a whiff of the smoke from Mama Vance's pipe, he immediately looked at Celeste. She returned his knowing glance. They both recognized the sweet, pungent odor of marijuana.

Justin began questioning Mama Vance. "Mama Vance, how is it that Cupid was able to join in the chantin'? I thought you said he had no tongue?"

"Cupid," Mama Vance ordered, "open your mouth." Cupid obeyed the command, and Justin was able to observe that he, in fact, had no tongue.

"But how did he do those chants?" continued Justin.

"De voice you heard come from Cupid's mouth was not his own," answered Mama Vance. "It be de voice of le Grand Zombi."

Celeste decided to focus on getting the information they had come for. She already had her fill of Mama Vance's house, especially the stares she kept receiving from Cupid. "Mama Vance, whose tomb did I dream about? You said you knew."

"Dhat's easy, ma chérie. Without no doubt, it be Marie Laveau's tomb."

Turning to her grandfather, Celeste asked, "Isn't that the Voodoo queen who cursed Emile Poydras and his wife?"

"Yes," replied Justin. "She's the — "

Before Justin could elaborate, Mama Vance let out another of her piercing cackles and said, "Yes, sir. Dhat Marie Laveau was one mean bitch, alright. She never minded de taste of blood neither."

Mark's curiosity finally got the better of his sour disposition, and he joined the questioning. "Was it Marie Laveau who really made the ring?"

"Hah! Never! Marie Laveau could never do dhat. She wanted de ring for herself, 'cause she could never make such a charm... Only Sanité Diable could make such charms."

"Then other such rings — charms — exist?" Justin inquired.

"No, Monsieur Noyan. Sanité Diable make no others, besides de ring she give ta Julien Poydras. She not wish ta share her power, and dhey say she take de secret of makin' such charms ta her grave."

Justin's facial expression showed Mama Vance's answer had somewhat surprised him. "How did you know the ring was originally owned by Julien Poydras?"

Mama Vance took a small puff on her pipe and smiled before answering. "Monsieur Noyan, de history of de Poydras ring is well known ta me. De ring was given ta Julien Poydras in gratitude for savin' Sanité Diable's life."

"But our family diary," interjected Celeste, "Emile Poydras's diary. It says Marie Laveau cursed Emile Poydras."

"Dhat be true," confirmed Mama Vance. "Marie Laveau make certain dhat Emile Poydras's soul never rested when he stole de ring back from her. Hah! Dhat Emile Poydras was one crafty man. Few mortals ever got de best of Marie Laveau. But, in de end, it was Marie dhat got de best of him."

"I've often wondered," mused Justin, "why there is no record of Marie Laveau tryin' to get the ring back after Emile Poydras died in the duel. It doesn't make sense that she would just give up after bringin' about Emile's death?"

It was clear from her annoyed expression that Mama Vance did not like Justin's query. She ignored it and then finally responded when no one else broke the silence. "Dhere is good reason for dhat, Monsieur Noyan. But dhat is all I can tell you now."

Celeste decided to get the conversation back onto the interpretation of her dream. "Mama Vance? Does the tomb of Marie Laveau still exist?"

"Sure does, ma chérie, though her real name ain't on it. De slab belong ta one of her daughters. But Marie's bones still be dhere in de Basin Street graveyard. You know where dhat be?"

Justin nodded and answered the question. "I know exactly where that is, Mama Vance. It's only a few blocks from my house. But I recall readin' an article that said the true location of the tomb was lost."

"Hah!" snorted Mama Vance. "What fool write dhat story? I've heard 'em all. Some say Marie's buried in St. Louis Cemetery No. 2, instead of No. 1 on Basin Street. Others claim her tomb be in No. 3, in St. Roch's, Holt, or Girod Street cemeteries. Hell, every cemetery in N'aw Arlens has tried ta claim de tomb of Marie Laveau. Most dem damn stories you read — ha! Dose fools who write dem — dhey's too stupid ta know more dhan one Voodoo queen claimed ta be Marie Laveau — her own daughter stole her name first."

"Whose name is on the tomb?" Justin asked.

"Like I say, her daughter, Marie Glapion."

"Glapion?" asked Justin.

Mama Vance nodded as she pulled the pipe from her lips. "De slab on de crypt — its de top crypt — say 'Marie Philomen Glapion.' But, at de top, it say famille Paris. Marie Laveau was married ta a Paris. Fact is, most people called her 'Widow Paris.'"

Celeste felt compelled to make certain Mama Vance knew what she was talking about. "Mama Vance, I mean no disrespect, but how can you be sure the tomb in my dream is Marie Laveau's?"

"You described it perfectly, ma chérie, a whitewashed over vault with green flower holders. And all dem markings and candles. Hell, I may be blind, but I ain't deaf. I heard your tape machine."

"Then, it was Marie Laveau's... hand... that grabbed me?"

"Dhat ghost grabbed your ring hand, didn't she?"

Celeste nodded her reply, then remembered to answer verbally, "Yes."

"Ma chérie, Marie wants de ring back, and you must give it ta her. Dhat's all dhere is ta understandin' your dream."

"Wait a minute," interjected Mark. "We're supposed to go bust open this tomb and give the ring to a woman that's been dead over a hundred years?"

Mama Vance's vacant eyes suddenly flashed at Mark's rhetorical comment. "You shall become a believer yet, Monsieur Richards! Hah! Dhat be for sure... If you have de courage ta see your wife through."

"See me through *what?*" pleaded Celeste. "Please tell me, Mama Vance. Just tell me what I must do — to rid myself of this ring." Celeste extended her ring hand to the blind woman's face. "And to end my nightmares. I don't — I'm not sure how many more times I can face that dream."

Instinctively, Mama Vance reached out and took Celeste's hand. "You must be strong, ma chérie. Remember, de ring will protect you from everyone — but yourself. I can feel dhat you believe. Listen ta your dreams. Listen for Emile Poydras. I can feel his love for you. All he asks of you is dhat you help him free his soul from de ring… He wants only ta join de spirits of his wife and family." With that pronouncement, Mama Vance let go of Celeste's hand. Celeste let her arm fall into her lap. She felt suddenly drained and faint again.

Observing Celeste's pallid face, Justin intervened. "Is there nothin' more specific you can tell us, Mama Vance?"

"De dream tell you, Monsieur Noyan. De way de tombs are decorated, de vigil lights. De priest blessing de dead."

"Of course!" exclaimed Justin. "All Saint's Day. I used to go to the cemetery every year with my parents and help clean and decorate the tombs of our relatives."

"Oui, Monsieur Noyan. But I believe your granddaughter's dream take place on All Saint's Eve. I recalls her describin' de children in der costumes."

"Yes," agreed Justin. "So, you're sayin' the ring must be returned on All Saint's Eve?" Seeing the puzzled look on Mark's face, Justin quickly added, "Halloween night."

"No, Monsieur Noyan," answered Mama Vance. "I'm not sayin'. Emile Poydras is sayin'. He tellin' you it must be when de sprits are movin.'"

Celeste had recovered enough to rejoin the conversation, "But, Mama Vance? If I take the ring off and give it back, what will happen to me?"

Instead of answering Celeste's question, Mama Vance handed her pipe to Cupid, grabbed the arms of her chair, leaned her head back, and began rocking. After a long pause, Celeste asked again. "Please Mama Vance? Tell me."

"I'm sorry, ma chérie. If you just give away de ring now, you surely die."

Celeste dropped her head upon hearing Mama Vance's pronouncement. Justin took up her cause once more and asked, "Mama Vance? There must be a way to give back the ring and save Celeste. Otherwise, there's no purpose to these dreams."

"Oui, I feel you be correct, Monsieur Noyan. And I truly wish I could help. But I must know more."

Feeling hopeful again, Celeste asked, "What more do you need to know, Mama Vance? We'll find it out."

"I must have de curse Marie Laveau placed on Emile Poydras and de ring — de exact incantation. Since de ring was never freely give up by Marie Laveau — perhaps I can come up with a spell dhat will safely release you from de ring. I feel dhat Emile Poydras will help you ta your freedom, if we can also free him from Marie's curse."

"Is there anythin' else you require?" offered Justin.

"No, Monsieur Noyan, not now. Bring me de composition of de curse — we'll see where dhat leads." Sensing that Justin and Celeste were worried they could not find the curse, Mama Vance added, "Pray ta Marie Laveau. She'll help you. She wants de ring back. Make a wish on her tomb."

"What? How do we do that?" Celeste asked.

"You just knock three times on her crypt and ask your favor, ma chérie. It helps if you bring her some offerin' — flowers or money, and burn a candle. But, before you leave, you must make de sign of de cross on de tomb — three times."

"Yes," added Celeste. "That was in my dream. The tomb was covered with crosses in chalk and pencil, and brick dust — and candles were burning everywhere."

"You see, ma chérie. De answers you seek be in your dreams. Listen for dem."

After Mama Vance had put Mark in his place for uttering his skeptical comment, he had remained out of the conversation. Now he decided to test her once more. "Mama Vance, the way you talk about Marie Laveau — did you ever meet her?"

It was apparent that Mark's new question was also irksome to Mama Vance. She continued to rock for a moment. Then, a sly grin came across her face, and she answered, "Oui, I meet her once. Although, I didn't know who she be at first... I was in de old drugstore dhat used ta be across from de Basin Street graveyard. While Mr. Williams was gittin' my order, a wrinkled old woman in a long white dress, with a blue tignon, came in behind me. I didn't pay her no mind. But all of de sudden, I see Mr. Williams had quit workin' on my order. He wasn't even listenin' ta me. He just stared at de old woman behind me. Dhen he took off runnin' ta de backroom. I didn't know what had happened, so I turns around and look at de old woman. She just looked back. Dhen, she starts laughin' like some crazy person. Pretty soon, she say, 'Don't you know me?' I say, 'No, ma'am, I don't.' Well, dhat make her mad. Her eyes — dhey shoots sparks at me. And before I knows it, she hauls off and slaps me in de face… Dhen things went crazy. De old woman jump up and hang suspended in de air. De door ta de store flies open by itself, and she went flyin' out de door backwards and disappear over de top of de graveyard wall… When Mr. Williams hears de door bang shut, he peeks out and sees dhat de old woman done gone. So, I asks him who de old woman be?"

"Marie Laveau," answered Mark.

Mama Vance nodded. "Mr. Williams, he say, 'Girl, you just been slapped by Marie Laveau. Why ain't you dead?'"

Realizing that Mark was irritating Mama Vance, Justin decided to bring the session to a close. "Thank you for all your help, Mama Vance. Are you sure we can't pay you somethin'?"

"No, Monsieur Noyan. As I say, I have no need of your money."

"Well," continued Justin, "may we call on you again?"

"But of course. I will see you all again — very soon."

Mama Vance started to stand when she heard her guests rise to leave. As she did, she tripped over Cupid's feet. Cupid sprang forward and caught the old woman at the waist before she could hit the floor. Still, the jolt Mama Vance received caused the front of her loose-fitting housedress to gape open, exposing a portion of a massive gold necklace around her neck.

After asking if Mama Vance was all right, Justin and Celeste thanked her again and bid her goodnight. Mark said nothing as they went out the door.

During the drive back to New Orleans, there was little conversation in the car. Justin made a couple attempts to discuss Mark and Celeste's job prospects, but both Mark and Celeste declined to pursue the topic.

It was nearly 3:00 a.m. when they got back to Justin's house, but Celeste went directly to the living room and switched on the TV. Mark and Justin gave each other a knowing look. Justin excused himself and went up to bed. Mark went to the kitchen, got a couple beers, and joined Celeste on the couch. Mark and Celeste fell asleep in each other's arms, and during a rerun of "Gilligan's Island," Celeste had the nightmare again on Justin's couch.

Chapter Twenty-Three

After an exquisite dinner at a French bistro around the corner from Julien's house, Emile and Julien returned home to dress for the quadroon ball. When Emile entered his bedroom, he saw that the servants had laid out his clothes on the bed. The clothes were brand new and freshly pressed. There was a long, plum colored frock coat, white knee breeches, white silk shirt and stockings, a pair of black patent leather dress shoes with silver buckles, and a pair of fancy stitched black boots. At the foot of the bed were a leather raincoat and a walking cane with a silver grip.

Emile smiled when he picked up the ebony cane. Giving the handle a quick jerk, Emile produced a razor-sharp sword, wide near the hilt, but tapering to a rapier-like blade at the tip. As Emile was admiring the sword-cane, Julien entered the room.

"Ah, I see you have discovered your colichemarde," said Julien. "I trust you find the remainder of your attire to your liking?"

Emile slid the sword back into its cane scabbard. "Yes, of course, Uncle. Your generosity has shown itself again. I was concerned that I did not have the proper attire for the ball."

Julien beamed at his nephew. "You're quite welcome, my boy. I do hope everything fits properly. The tailor was working on rather short notice."

"I'm sure everything will be fine, Uncle. I'm curious though. Why have the servants laid out both shoes and boots for me?"

"You won't need the boots or the raincoat tonight," replied Julien. "I'll drop you off in the carriage. But, to answer your question, because of the poor streets and banquettes, we wear our boots when walking to a social function. The raincoat is to protect your clothes from being splattered with mud. Normally, the servants precede us carrying a lantern and our shoes and clean stockings."

Emile nodded his approval and changed the subject. "Uncle Julien, are you certain that I should not accompany you on your meeting with..." Emile stopped himself before uttering Sanité Diable's name.

Julien held up his hand. "I'm certain, my boy. I'm not even sure I will find her tonight. The servants tell me her exact whereabouts are uncertain."

"Very well, Uncle. I will not press the matter further. But I do hope you can join me later at the ball."

"Oh, indeed. I plan on it," responded Julien gleefully. "It's been much too long since I attended a Bal du Cordon Bleu."

***

The Conde Street Ballroom was not at all like the image Emile had conjured up in his mind. The ballroom was a plain wooden frame building, approximately eighty feet wide. The furnishings and fixtures were as unadorned as the building's exterior. Emile observed that the orchestra consisted of five ragged looking gypsies, whose musical skills left much to be desired. Standing just inside the entrance to the ballroom, Emile surveyed the dancers in motion. The attire of the dancing couples contributed the only color to the drab hall. Emile mused about the last ball he had attended in Paris, and he realized Julien — and New Orleans — had decidedly lower standards for the production of a grand ball.

As Emile surveyed the young women in the hall, he surmised that many of them were adolescents still in their teens. While many of the girls were in silk or satins of gay colors, just as many of the girls wore modest white muslin dresses, some adorned with a colored sash. Emile was forced to agree with his uncle Julien's description on one point. When Emile appraised the faces and figures of the quadroon girls, he had to admit that he had never seen so many beautiful young women in one room before. Most had full, sylphlike figures, and their complexions were as fair as the haughty Creole females Emile had encountered.

Directing his gaze above the turning dancers, Emile viewed the tiers of boxes on the walls overlooking the dance floor. Here roosted the girls' mothers and chaperones, watching their young like protective mother hawks. Below the boxes were rows of chairs for the girls, and directly behind their seats was a narrow runway that went the length of the hall. Here the Creole gentlemen conversed and waited their turns on the dance floor.

Before approaching any of the quadroon mademoiselles, Emile heeded Julien's advice about studying the suitors vying for the attentions of the young women he might be interested in dancing with. Spying the punch bowl, located in a corner of the hall, Emile decided to continue his observations there, as it was surrounded by Creole gentlemen fetching drinks for their ladies and themselves. The hot humid air in the ballroom made the punch vendor much in demand.

Emile patiently waited his turn for a cup of wine punch, and just as it came, another Creole "gentleman" cut in ahead of him and snatched the cup from the server's hand. The young man even had the gall to stand there and drink it with his back to Emile. His face flushing red, Emile used the tip of his cane to tap the man on the back of his blond head. "Pardon me, monsieur!" said Emile. "That was my cup you took."

The blond-headed man turned to face Emile. He studied Emile a moment before responding. Then he sat the empty cup down and said, "Excuse me, monsieur — I did not realize. Please allow me to buy you a cup." The blond Creole turned again to face the table and obtained two more pewter cups of warm punch. Handing one to Emile, he introduced himself. "Allow me to introduce myself. Anton Francois Cuvillier, at your service." Anton finished his self-introduction with a slight bow.

Emile nodded, his temper having abated. "Thank you, Monsieur Cuvillier. Emile de Lallande Poydras, at your service."

Recognition flashed across Anton Cuvillier's face. "Poydras? Are you by any chance related to Monsieur Julien Poydras?"

"Yes. He is my uncle. You know him?"

"I'm afraid I've not had the pleasure. But everyone has heard of your uncle. He is one of the wealthiest men in the colony — I don't believe I have seen you at any of the other balls."

"No, you haven't," agreed Emile. "I have only recently arrived from France."

"What part of France?"

"Paris."

"Paris!" blurted Anton. "How goes the revolution?"

"That, Monsieur Cuvillier, depends on which end of the guillotine you are on."

Anton snorted at Emile's black humor. "I think I'm going to like you, Monsieur Poydras. Come, let us adjourn from this crowded table, and I'll tell you about these beautiful quadroon women you are about to meet."

Smiling, Emile replied, "Thank you. I would like that."

As Emile and Anton were weaving out of the crowd around the punch vendor, a commotion broke out at the orchestra stand. Both men turned to face the orchestra of gypsies as they heard someone repeatedly yell, "Contredanses anglaises! Contredanses anglaises!" These demands, even though in French, were being made by a young, and obviously intoxicated, Spaniard, in a full-dress military uniform.

"Who the devil is that?" inquired Emile.

"Governor Carondelet's nephew, Manuel de Salcedo. He knows we French despise the English contradances. So, when he's drunk and when the governor's not around, he delights in flaunting his authority by commanding the orchestra to play English tunes."

"And everyone lets him get away with such rude behavior?"

"I'm afraid so," answered Anton. "You see, the governor's nephew is also Captain of the City Guard."

Emile and Anton stood in silence a few moments, watching the dancers stumble as they went through the unfamiliar steps of an English contradance. Emile felt his temper rise again as the Spaniard smirked and joked with his companions. Emile could not hear what the Spaniards were saying, but he was certain they were making fun of the troubles the dancers were encountering while attempting to perform the unfamiliar English dance.

After the dance ended, the orchestra returned to playing French contradances, Manuel de Salcedo and his companions having made their way to the punch table.

Sensing that the hot-blooded Emile might have taken personal offense at the actions of Manuel de Salcedo, Anton diverted Emile's attention to the edge of the dance floor. Discreetly pointing, Anton said, "See the girl in the red satin dress?"

Emile turned his head to follow Anton's finger, and he saw why Anton had pointed her out. She appeared to be a little older than most of the girls in the hall. She was tall, with a beautifully sculptured figure and long black hair, which she had plumed with red feathers. Her eyes were dark and lively, and her gait and movements on the dance floor were elegant. *She is probably the most beautiful woman I have ever laid eyes on,* thought Emile. "Who is she?" he asked.

"Aurora Béluche. Isn't she exquisite?"

"Yes," agreed Emile. "She seems somehow older or more sophisticated than the other girls."

"She's really no older — only nineteen. But I agree. She does stand out from the pack, so to speak."

"Does she belong to anyone yet?" asked Emile.

"Not yet. Though many have approached her, she has yet to take any man up to negotiate with her mother. And if she ever did, I doubt that many men could meet her mother's price."

"I must meet her," said Emile. "Will you introduce me?"

Anton smiled to himself. "But of course, my friend. Follow me. This dance is just ending."

Following the beautiful quadroon to her seat, Anton bowed before her and introduced Emile. "Mademoiselle Béluche, please allow me to introduce Monsieur Emile de Lallande Poydras. Monsieur Poydras has only recently arrived from Paris."

Without rising, Aurora Béluche looked up at Emile and smiled, extending her hand. "Poydras?" she asked. "Are you Monsieur Julien Poydras's son?"

Once again, Emile was grateful for his uncle's standing in the community. "No, he is my uncle, Mademoiselle Béluche. I realize you have only had a moment to rest, but would you do me the honor of the next dance?"

"I would be delighted, Monsieur Poydras," said Aurora as she rose from her chair.

As they began their dance, Emile tried to make small talk, "Your gown is quite stunning, Mademoiselle Béluche. Did you have it shipped from Paris?"

With a demure smile, Aurora gave her reply. "Why thank you, Monsieur Poydras. But, no, my mother made this gown for me. She does study the latest fashion publications from France though."

"Well, your mother is a magnificent seamstress, then. I would be honored if you would introduce me to her?"

"Oh, monsieur, we have only just been introduced," Aurora said politely. "I don't believe it would be appropriate to have an introduction to my mother just yet."

Before Emile could plead his cause any further, Manuel de Salcedo began anew his demands on the orchestra. "Contredanses anglaises!" he yelled for all to hear.

Emile's heart fell and temper rose at the same instant, for he didn't know how to dance any English contradances. Challenging the young Spaniard's demand, Emile shouted out, "Contredanses francaises! Contredanses francaises!" Soon, all the other Creole men in the ballroom joined in Emile's counter-demand, and a loud chant arose that drowned out the Spaniard's demand for English dances, "Contredanses francaises! Contredanses francaises!"

Manuel de Salcedo locked eyes with Emile for a moment then stomped out of the ballroom with his entourage. As the Spaniards left the hall, the orchestra struck up a French contredanse, and the crowd let out a triumphant cheer. Emile's victory was short-lived, however. Before his next dance with Aurora had ended, Manuel de Salcedo re-entered the hall. This time he was accompanied by twelve Spanish grenadiers, who entered the ballroom with muskets and fixed bayonets. With an order from another Spanish officer, the orchestra was silenced, abruptly ending the French dance it was playing. Again, Manuel de Salcedo loudly commanded, "Contredanses anglaises!"

This affront was more than the collective honor of the Creole men could endure. Numerous cries and insults rang out at the Spaniards, and many of the Creoles scrambled for their swords. Others picked up chairs or whatever could be utilized as a makeshift weapon. The tumult grew louder and was increased by the influx of many other Creole men who flocked in from nearby cafés and gaming halls.

A dangerous standoff developed with Manuel de Salcedo and his grenadiers on one side of the dance floor and the infuriated Creole men on the other. Whereupon Manuel de Salcedo ordered his troops to fire on the crowd unless it immediately dispersed.

While all this was taking place, Emile escorted Aurora from the dance floor toward her mother's waiting arms. On the way, Emile made his apologies. "Mademoiselle Béluche, please forgive me for exposing you to this madness. May I call on you and your mother later this week?"

Aurora smiled at Emile but said, "Monsieur Poydras, as I said, since we have only been introduced, I'm not sure it would be proper for you to call on me as yet. But I will speak to my mother about it." Stopping and turning back before reaching her impatient mother, Aurora added, "Good luck, Monsieur Poydras! God be with you!"

As the quadroon girls and their chaperones retreated from the hall, Emile made his way to the place where he had left his colichemarde. Drawing the sword from his cane, he marched towards the dance floor to help confront the Spanish soldiers.

After the governor's nephew had ordered his troops to fire on the crowd, it seemed certain that what had started as a rude farce was about to become a bloody confrontation. It was at this critical moment that three young Creoles appeared in one of the boxes that lined the dance floor. One of these men was Anton Cuvillier. Anton and the other two Creoles pleaded with and exhorted the crowd with elegant words and firm tones, urging peace and civility in the interest of the females and other innocent persons who might fall victim to an outbreak of violence. The speeches of Anton and the other men succeeded in causing all the antagonists to lower their weapons and gradually withdraw and vacate the dance floor.

As the conflict subsided, Emile's attention was drawn to the entrance of the ballroom. There, standing just inside the door, was his uncle Julien, visibly distraught and ashen faced.

Chapter Twenty-Four

When Justin came downstairs at 7:45 the next morning, the TV was off, and Celeste and Mark were still asleep on the couch. Celeste's head was lying against Mark's chest, while Mark's head was bent backwards against the back of the couch. Justin thought the couple looked very uncomfortable in their sleeping positions, but he tried not to wake them as he tiptoed into the kitchen.

Trying to minimize the noise of the splashing water, Justin filled the coffee maker with a slow stream from the faucet. Turning from the sink, he bumped into someone behind him and almost dropped the coffee carafe, sloshing some of the water out.

"Oh, Mark," whispered Justin. "You startled me. Sorry, if I got you wet?"

"No problem," replied Mark, brushing at the water soaking into his wrinkled blue jeans.

"I hope I didn't wake you up? You look like you've had a pretty rough night."

Mark shook his lowered head and rubbed the back of his neck. "No, really, I was awake. I was dying to get up — my neck is stiff as a board."

"Is Celeste still asleep?"

"Yeah, she didn't fall asleep till about two hours ago."

Justin finished refilling the carafe and turned on the Mr. Coffee before he asked, "Then Celeste had the dream again?"

"Oh, yeah."

"How did she do?"

"A lot better than the night before," answered Mark. "We had a couple beers before trying to sleep. We talked about it being an opportunity to maybe find out more information about Marie Laveau. Then, I promised her I would stay awake and hold her during the dream. That seemed to calm her some."

"Were you able to stay awake the whole time?"

"Pretty much. I dozed off and on at first, 'cause Celeste seemed to be in a deep sleep. But, when I heard her breathing rate pick up fast, I knew it had started."

"I didn't hear a thing," commented Justin. "Did she cry out at all?"

"No, not this time. Although, she did let out a low moan or two during the first part of the dream."

Justin blushed, saying nothing at first, as he realized Mark was referring to the part of the dream in which Celeste makes love to Emile Poydras. "What about the cemetery dream? Did she recall anythin' new or different?"

As Justin finished asking his last question, Celeste lumbered into the kitchen, rubbing her eyes. She answered for Mark, "Not really, Granddad. Although it all seemed much clearer now — it made more sense after talking to Mama Vance."

"Celeste, sugar," responded Justin. "You must be exhausted. Why don't you go upstairs and try to get some more sleep?"

Celeste brushed at her matted hair with her fingers. "No, thanks, Granddad, I would like a nice long, hot bath though. Then I want to go to the Basin Street Cemetery."

***

St. Louis Cemetery No. 1, or the Basin Street graveyard as the locals call it, was located on Basin Street at St. Louis, one block north of Rampart. The old walled cemetery enclosed one city block and adjoined a subsidized housing development. The gang graffiti on the cemetery walls and the broken liquor bottles on the sidewalks put visitors on notice that this was not a neighborhood to linger in.

After treating Celeste and Mark to a leisurely brunch at Brennan's, Justin led the couple on a brisk walk to St. Louis Cemetery No. 1. As the gate of the cemetery came into sight, Justin remarked, "Ah, we're in luck. The sexton is here today. They keep this place locked a good deal of the time."

Entering the gate on Basin Street, Justin spied a small table holding a donation box and a stack of cemetery maps. Justin shoved a five-dollar bill into the box and picked up a map. At the same moment, an elderly man in starched, blue coveralls came out of the sexton's tool shed.

"Afternoon, folks," he said. "Thanks for your donation."

"You're welcome," replied Justin. Glancing down at the map's very small print, Justin asked, "Excuse me, Mr....?"

"Lefebvre, Felix Lefebvre's the name."

"Pleased to meet you, Mr. Lefebvre," responded Justin. "Could you please direct us to the tomb of Marie Glapion?"

The sexton smiled and nodded. "You lookin' for the tomb of Marie Laveau?"

"Why, yes," answered Celeste. "Is it really her tomb?"

Shrugging his shoulders, Mr. Lefebvre replied, "Some say it is. Some say it ain't. All I know is that tomb sure gets the most visitors — especially at night. Folks climb the walls to get to her tomb."

Feeling reassured, Celeste asked, "Is it hard to find?"

"Nope, you're practically there." Pointing to the walk behind him, the sexton continued, "Just stay on the path — don't make but the one turn. It's in the Catholic section. So, if you find yourself on the other side of the dividin' wall, you've gone too far."

"Thank you," replied Justin, starting up the path. As he turned to follow Justin, Mark thought he caught the sexton giving them a creepy look. Walking single file up the narrow pavement, the party had to squint in the bright afternoon sun reflecting off the closely packed tombs, nearly all of which were painted white. The tombs and vaults were made of either stone or whitewashed bricks. In some places, the tombs were built so close together a person would have to walk sideways to get to the row behind the tombs adjoining the path. There was practically no grass or vegetation to break the stark atmosphere of the cemetery.

The intense June sun, pouring down on the white surfaces of the tombs, made the heat in the cemetery stifling. Mark felt the sweat running down his back turn from a trickle into a steady stream, and he began to feel like he was trapped in some sort of carnival maze as the path they were on seemed to wind through the tombs without plan or design.

Celeste noticed that most of the tombs were topped with a cross, usually constructed of iron or stone. Several of the graves they passed had dates from the early 1800s. Occasionally, they would pass a tomb that was empty, or one that had crumbled into nothing more than a mound of bricks. Wild ferns grew in some of the empty vaults. Giant spider webs choked other openings.

Upon reaching a low interior wall, Justin turned around and pointed back the way they had come. "We must have missed it. Let's retrace our steps."

Just when Celeste felt like she was going to faint from the heat, Justin halted their parade in front of a three-tiered, whitewashed oven vault with queer green flowerpots extending on both sides of the top tier.

"This is it!" declared Celeste. "This is the tomb in my dream."

"Are you sure?" asked Mark as he wiped his forehead with the back of his wrist.

"Yes. This is it. Look at all those cross marks on it. And see at the bottom — there's a little brass plaque stating this is Marie Laveau's tomb?"

Celeste then pointed to the top slab that read:

FAMILLE VVE. PARIS

née Laveau

Ci-Git

MARIE PHILOMEN GLAPION

decédée le 11 Juin 1897

agée de soixante-deux ans

Elle fut bonne mère, bonne amie et

regrettée par tous ceux qui l'out connue

Passants priez pour elle

"Can you read all that, Granddad?"

Justin replied, "Yes, it says, 'Family Paris and Laveau. These lying down, Marie Philomen Glapion. Died June 11, 1897, age 62 years. She was a good mother — good friend. Missed by all the ones who knew her. Passer-by, pray for her.'"

"Huh!" scoffed Mark. "That's quite an epitaph for a Voodoo queen."

"Remember, Mark," corrected Celeste. "Mama Vance said the epitaph belongs to Marie Laveau's daughter."

"Then where is the real Marie Laveau's body?" asked Mark.

"Most likely in the bottom of the tomb," answered Justin. "They call it the receiving vault. It's where they deposit the old remains to make room for new burials. The tomb is certainly well maintained," added Justin. "It looks freshly painted, except for…"

Justin didn't finish the sentence, but Celeste and Mark noticed what Justin was staring at — a splattered pattern of rust-colored spots at the base of the tomb. No one had to speak the word. They all recognized the spots as dried blood.

"Are you ready?" continued Justin.

Celeste nodded her answer. She opened her purse and withdrew a short pink candle. She set it on the ledge, at the base of the tomb, and lit it with a match. Next, she took four quarters from her coin purse and dropped two of them in each of the green flower holders on the sides of the oven vault.

"Why pink?" asked Mark.

"The lady at the candle shop said pink candles are for love," answered Celeste.

Mark rolled his eyes.

Next, her hand shaking slightly, Celeste rapped her knuckles three times on the top stone, and read from an index card, "Marie Laveau, queen of all the Voodoos, hear my prayer. Show me how to free my spirit and return the ring to you. Please, great queen, only you can show us the way. Lead us to the key of deliverance. Reveal your curse to us, so all spirits may be at peace."

Celeste paused for a moment, trying to decide if she should add anything else to her prayer. Then she pulled a lipstick out of her purse and used it to make the sign of the cross three times on the tomb's face.

"Well," said Mark. "No skeletons this time. The old girl must like pink candles after all."

Neither Celeste nor Justin responded to Mark's weak attempt at humor. Justin finally said, "Let's get out of here before we melt like that candle."

"Yes," Celeste agreed. "I'm dying for something cold to drink."

"A cold, dark bar sounds good to me," added Mark.

As Celeste bent over to pick up her purse, a chameleon lizard darted out of a crack at the base of the tomb and ran across her wrist. Instinctively, Celeste jerked her hand back, dropping her purse. Observing Celeste's adverse reaction, Mark made an attempt to stomp on the lizard, but the chameleon was too fast for him. The quick green critter disappeared around the corner of the tomb before Mark's foot could make contact with the pavement.

"I'm sure glad you missed him," said Justin.

"Huh?" replied a puzzled Mark.

"Chameleons are good luck — at least that's what my mother always said. We used to sit and rest our hands against tombs and wait for the chameleons to crawl onto our fingers."

"Oh, ick," commented Celeste. "I can't stand to touch snakes or lizards."

"Just the same," continued Justin. "It's a good omen. I'm sure of it."

Chapter Twenty-five

Julien did not talk during their carriage ride home from the ballroom. Emile took Julien's silence as a sign of his disapproval of Emile's actions at the quadroon ball. When he attempted to inquire as to the cause of his uncle's anxious state, Julien shook his head and said only, "When we get back to the house." So, Emile made no further attempt at conversation during their trip.

Upon their arrival at Julien's house, Julien dismissed the servants and asked Emile to join him in his study for a cognac. Emile nodded his assent, assuming he was now to be chastised about his behavior at the ball. Emile kept quiet as Julien poured their drinks. When Julien finally spoke, Emile was caught off guard again by his uncle.

"I'm sorry, my boy. It will not be possible to obtain a charm for your protection."

Emile blinked with surprise. "Uncle, you never cease to amaze me. I dishonor you by provoking a near riot at the ball, and here you stand apologizing to me again. Perhaps you are 'heaping coals of fire upon my head?'"

Julien took a long pull on his drink before answering. "I suppose your near disaster this evening should be my immediate concern. But it is not. I only ask that, in the future, you do not confront Manuel de Salcedo. We do not want to have the governor and his nephew as enemies."

"I will do my best to honor your request, Uncle. But you are obviously upset. What do you mean, it is not your 'immediate concern?'"

Julien fell back into his desk chair and took another drink of his brandy. "My demeanor has nothing to do with your activities tonight, Emile. I am distressed by my own experiences."

"You found Sanité Diable?"

"Yes. I found her. Although she calls herself Sanité Dédé now."

Emile waited for Julien to explain, then said, "Well, don't keep me in suspense, Uncle. What happened?" From his uncle's pained expression, it was obvious Julien was quite apprehensive about their discussion.

"At first, I was told that Sanité Diable was dead, or that she had gone back to Santo Domingo. But, after a few well-placed bribes, I was taken to the home of the current Voodoo queen."

"Sanité Dédé?"

"Yes. When I entered the house, a Voodoo ceremony was in progress. The likes of which I have never seen before. Most of the celebrants were white women, with a few quadroon men. Each participant carried a burning brand. The women were all elaborately dressed. Some were in bridal costumes… At one end of the room a white male corpse lay exposed."

"It was a funeral then?" asked Emile.

"No, it was no funeral. The chest of the corpse had been cut open, and his heart removed."

Emile's eyes widened. "My God! You mean you witnessed a human sacrifice?"

"I cannot be certain. The corpse may have been dead before the ceremony began. But I certainly began to worry if I would be allowed to leave the ceremony alive. Then, I saw her."

"Who?"

"Sanité Diable. She wears a turban now and dresses differently. But as soon as she ascended the dais, and I saw her face, I knew it was her."

"You are certain it was the same woman?" asked Emile. "It's been seventeen years since you last saw her?"

Julien nodded. "It was her. She still wore her great gold necklace, and…"

"And what, Uncle?"

"And she had hardly aged a day since I saw her last. As God as my witness, she still had the same face of the young woman I met seventeen years ago."

"Well, some of these Negro women age quite well, I hear."

"I suppose. At any rate, when I talked to her after the ceremony, she admitted to me that she was Sanité Diable."

"She remembered you then."

"Yes, yes. She stroked my face and said she could never forget the man that saved her life."

"Did you ever find out what the ceremony with the corpse was about?"

"Yes… Sanité Diable explained a young Creole girl had been jilted by her fiancé. She had come to Sanité Dédé to curse his heart so he could never love another woman."

"Ahh, um… and did she succeed?"

"I don't know," answered Julien. "During the ceremony, the girl appeared en chemise and barefoot. All the celebrants were required to dance around a basket that contained hissing snakes. In turn, each dancer touched the head of one of the serpents. When they did so, they seemed to become intoxicated and mad with excitement. The jilted Creole girl took her turn last. When she touched the snake, she fell down in a convulsive fit, foaming at the mouth like one possessed by the devil."

"She must have been bitten by a serpent?"

"No! I saw it clearly. The serpents struck at no one."

"What happened to the girl?" asked Emile.

"When she fell, the mad carnival came to a halt, and the girl was carried, half-dead, from the scene by the quadroon men. I never saw her again."

"It was after that when you spoke to Sanité Diable — Dédé?"

"Yes. She had me wait until everyone else had left her house. Then we talked."

"Did you ask her about the corpse?"

"No," admitted Julien. "I did not want to know, but…"

"But what?"

"I believe I found out anyway — indirectly, when I asked her about making a charm for you."

"I'm afraid I don't follow you, Uncle?"

Julien became visibly agitated. He sprang from his chair and went to the sideboard to pour another cognac. Downing half the drink in one gulp, he turned to face Emile once more. "Have you ever heard the expression 'a goat without horns'?"

"No," answered Emile. "What does it mean?"

"It means a human sacrifice. Specifically, the sacrifice of a young white child."

"What! You're not serious? The Voodooiennes sacrifice children in their ceremonies?"

Julien held up his ring hand and grimaced. "Only in very *special* ceremonies... such as the ritual of creating a charm of eternal protection."

Emile was horror-struck. "My Lord, Uncle. You mean some child was murdered to create your ring?"

Julien nodded slowly and dropped his hand. "And now I am doomed to live with that knowledge for the rest of my days."

"Can nothing be done?"

"I'm afraid not. I begged Sanité Dédé to take the ring back when she told me about the child. She reminded me that I may never remove the ring, or I will surely die. Now, I'm not sure I can stand to live with myself."

***

When Emile arose the next morning, Julien was already out of the house. If the servants or Monsieur Maree knew where Julien had gone, they weren't telling. Shortly after noon, Emile had a caller. It was his new friend, Anton Cuvillier, whom he had met the night before at the quadroon ball. When Anton was shown into the parlor, Emile rose to greet him. "My dear Monsieur Cuvillier, I'm so happy you have come calling. In all the commotion last night, I didn't have the chance to say good night and to thank you for helping avert violence at the ball."

Shaking Emile's hand, Anton replied, "Please, call me Anton."

"Yes," agreed Emile. "After what we experienced last night, we should be on a first name basis. Please, sit down. May I offer you something to eat or drink?"

"Thank you, no. I was on my way to meet some friends at a nearby café, and I thought you might like to join us — we're going to the cockfights later."

"Wonderful. I was feeling rather bored. I'll fetch my hat and colichemarde, and we'll be off."

As they walked, Anton said, "Actually, my friends are dying to meet you, Emile. The whole city is buzzing about your confrontation with Manuel de Salcedo."

Emile rolled his eyes. "Please, don't remind me. My temper nearly caused a riot. If it were not for you and the other cooler heads, bloodshed surely would have resulted. I feel that I have shamed myself and my dear Uncle Julien."

"Nonsense!" replied Anton. "No doubt de Salcedo and the other Spaniards have ill regard for you today. But to the citizens of French blood, you are the hero of the day. That is why so many readily rallied to your cause last night. We all were fed up with the insolence of that Spanish pig."

Having never attended a cockfight before, Emile and his money soon parted company. Even so, Emile was fascinated by the bloody sport, and he found it amusing how some of the contestants cried unashamedly when their favorite rooster fell, mortally wounded by its opponent's razor-sharp spurs. Emile wondered if the arena's losers ended up on their owner's dinner table that night.

After an afternoon of gambling, drinking, and carousing at the cockfights, Emile, Anton, and his Creole friends adjourned to a nearby cabaret on Royal Street. The cabarets of New Orleans were nothing like the fashionable music halls Emile had frequented in Paris. The particular cabaret Emile found himself in was called the Maison Coquet. It combined an amateurish songstress performance with a grocery store, dram-shop, gambling den, and house of prostitution all under one roof. A poster by the door of the establishment stated:

Maison Coquet is operated by the express permission

of the Honorable Civil Governor of the City.

Soon the conversation of the men turned from cockfighting pits to proposals for that evening's entertainment. The attributes of other local bordellos were discussed, but Emile declined all invitations to join the men on their lustful quests. In all honesty, he felt a little queasy from all the cheap wine he had consumed that day.

Taking Anton aside, Emile asked, "Do you know where Mademoiselle Béluche lives?"

"Yes, she and her mother live in a small house on Rampart Street."

"It is far from here?"

"No, only four or five blocks. It's rather late to go calling, though, don't you think?"

"Yes, I know it is," said Emile. "And after all I've had to drink, I'm in no condition to meet Aurora's mother. But... I thought if I walked by her house, I might catch a glimpse of her. That would be enough to sustain me until tomorrow."

Anton grinned and shook his head. "My dear Emile, are you love-struck already? You didn't even get to finish your last dance with the girl."

"I cannot logically explain how I feel about her, Anton. I only know she is the most enchanting and beautiful woman I have ever laid my eyes upon, and I must see her again — now... to confirm that what I saw and felt last night was not a dream."

"Come on then. I'll show you the way."

"No," protested Emile. "I will not deprive you of your friends' company. Just give me directions to her — "

"Nonsense," interrupted Anton. "I have no money left for the bordellos. Besides, it is not wise for a gentleman to walk alone after dark."

As Emile and Anton began their walk, the sun had just finished setting. Strolling north, they passed a lamplighter on a ladder, firing up one of the dim oil lanterns that served as the city's streetlights. Reaching Rampart, the men turned west and walked a block and a half. Anton stopped in front and pointed at a small, white frame house with green shutters.

"That is the Béluche house. Unfortunately, the shutters are closed. Alas, there will be no glimpse of your — "

Anton didn't get to finish his sentence. For at that very instant, the front door of the Béluche house opened and out stepped two men in Spanish military uniforms. It was too dark to clearly see the men's faces, but that wasn't necessary. Both Anton and Emile recognized one uniform as belonging to the captain of the Spanish garrison, Manuel de Salcedo.

Chapter Twenty-Six

Celeste, Mark, and Justin felt immediate relief upon exiting the Basin Street grave-yard. Even though the humidity was high and the temperature was in the 90s, just getting out from between the white ovens of the cemetery made things feel cooler.

"I can see why people prefer to visit this place at night," commented Mark as he pulled at his shirt, which was soaked with sweat and clinging to his chest.

Walking four blocks south on St. Louis, the party was back on Bourbon Street. Mark suggested they go into Papa Joe's for drinks, but Justin excused himself, saying he had business to attend to and that he would meet them at home later.

Mark and Celeste sat under a ceiling fan in Papa Joe's for two rounds of gin and tonics, talking about Mark's recent job interview at the local NBC television station. Mark seemed so excited about his prospect of landing the assistant sports-caster position, Celeste didn't say anything discouraging, even though she knew she didn't want to stay in New Orleans when — if — their ordeal was over. Feeling refreshed, the couple walked the last few blocks to Justin's house.

They found Justin at the desk in his study, pouring over the diary of Emile Poydras.

Celeste spoke first. "Oh, Granddad, give yourself a break. You'll drive yourself crazy over this if you're not careful."

Justin looked up and smiled, saying, "I'm fine, sugar. I took a cool shower and changed clothes. It's just, seein' those blood stains at the tomb just now made me recall an entry Emile Poydras made at the time his uncle Julien gave him the ring."

"What entry are you referring to?" Celeste asked.

Justin pointed at the yellowed page before him and translated the entry out loud for Celeste and Mark. "Emile said, 'Knowin' that the ring is based on the sacrifice of the goat without horns, how can I live with the guilt?'"

"What kind of goat has no horns?" asked Mark.

"A baby goat?" offered Celeste.

"I'm afraid you're bein' too literal in your interpretation of the term," responded Justin. "It's a metaphor for… a sacrifice."

"What kind of sacrifice, Granddad?"

Justin picked up a reference book lying on his desk and handed it to Celeste. Glancing at the cover, she read out loud, "*Voodoo in New Orleans* by Robert Tallant. There's a copy of this in my dad's trunk."

"Yes, I know," replied Justin. "Look at the third chapter."

Turning to the table of contents of the book, Celeste read, "The Goat Without Horns." Flipping the pages to the beginning of the chapter, Celeste read silently for a moment. Looking up with alarm, she said, "Oh no, Granddad! You mean the ring came from the sacrifice of a *child*?"

Mark grabbed the book from Celeste's hands and began reading.

"All we can say for certain," answered Justin, "is that Emile Poydras believed that to be the case."

"Wait a minute," interjected Mark. "It says in here that 'there is little proof of human sacrifice ever having been used in Louisiana.'"

"Yes. That's true," agreed Justin. "But if you read on, you'll find that there were a few reported cases of what can be termed child sacrifice."

Celeste slumped down into one of the chairs facing her grandfather's desk and put her face in her hands. "Oh, this is becoming more than I can bear. To think that the blood of some innocent child is on this ring…."

"I know. It's a terrible revelation," confirmed Justin. "But we have to look at it as findin' one more piece to this puzzle we're workin' on. This information may help Mama Vance break the curse."

Dropping the book onto Justin's desk, Mark said, "I'm getting confused. This goat without horns business has to do with the creation of the ring. I thought Mama Vance wanted to know about the curse Marie Laveau put on Emile Poydras?"

"You're right," answered Justin. "But remember, Marie Laveau's curse was on the ring as well as on Emile Poydras. So, I have a hunch that the spell used to create the ring is related to the curse of Marie Laveau."

"Okay," said Mark. "Suppose they are related. Where do we find Marie Laveau's curse?"

"We start," said Justin, "with the diary of Emile Poydras. In my gut, I feel the key is in here somewhere." Justin tapped on the open diary with his index finger for emphasis. "You two can help by goin' to the libraries and researchin' every available reference on Marie Laveau and Voodoo. Look for references to human sacrifices and charms of protection."

Mark looked down at Celeste, still slouched in the chair. "Do you feel up to hitting a library this afternoon, babe?"

Celeste's reply was nonresponsive. "It's true, you know."

"What's true, babe?"

Celeste looked up. Ignoring Mark, she spoke to her grandfather. "The child sacrifice, it really happened."

"How do you know?" asked Justin.

"It was in my dream. Although I didn't recognize it until now. Remember, I said all the people in the cemetery suddenly disappeared, except for one child in a ghost costume?"

Justin nodded. "The child that ran behind the tomb of Marie Laveau."

"Right," said Celeste. "It didn't click with me until now. But now I realize that the child wasn't wearing a costume. Her skin was too pale, and the bloodstains on her clothes were too real. It was like blood was still oozing through her dress."

"You never mentioned the child's sex before," said Justin. "Are you certain it was a girl?"

"Yes. She was a beautiful little white girl, with curly blonde hair. She was the goat without horns."

***

Unable to come up with any better idea, Celeste and Mark followed Justin's suggestion that they research Marie Laveau. Since it was getting late in the afternoon, they decided to start with the closest library, the New Orleans Public Library located at the corner of Tulane and Loyola Avenues.

While Mark and Celeste found several reference books dealing with the history of Voodoo, few reported the components of specific Voodoo charms or curses. They found nothing that described the type of curse Marie Laveau had placed on

Emile Poydras. Nor could they find any reference to the Poydras ring or similar charms created via human sacrifice.

After nearly three hours of fruitless research, Mark and Celeste took a cab back to Justin's house. When they arrived, they found Justin as they had left him, sitting at his desk, studying the diary. Looking up as Celeste and Mark entered the study, Justin asked, "How'd you two do?"

"We struck out," answered Mark. "How 'bout yourself?"

"Not much better, I'm afraid." Justin dropped his pen and arched his back in his chair to relieve his tired back muscles. "After all, Emile Poydras couldn't have written about the curse that killed him and trapped his soul. He really couldn't have realized what Marie Laveau did to him until he was already dying."

"What I don't understand," said Celeste, "is how Marie Laveau succeeded in killing Emile Poydras. According to his diary — and Mama Vance — Emile stole the ring back from Marie Laveau. Why didn't it protect him in the duel and from Marie's curse?"

"That same question crossed my mind," answered Justin. "We know the ring has not lost its power. So, why didn't it save Emile Poydras?" Justin picked up the diary and gently turned back through the brittle yellow pages. "I believe I may have found the answer.... Yes, here it is, in the entry dated April 25, 1795. This was the day Julien Poydras first told Emile about the ring. He proved the power of the ring by tryin' to shoot himself in the head with Emile's duelin' pistol. The pistol misfired. Anyway, Julien told Emile that... 'Once the ring is accepted, it may not be removed, except on pain of death. If the ring is lost or given to another, its protection is forfeited.'"

"We already knew that," interjected Mark. "How does that — wait a minute. You mean, once the ring is intentionally given to someone else, it will no longer protect the giver — even if he gets it back?"

"That has to be it," agreed Justin. "Since Emile was only the second person to wear the ring, there was no way for him to know that. And don't forget, Emile stole the ring back from Marie Laveau. She didn't gift it back to him."

Celeste, staring down at her ring finger, said, "This is all very interesting, guys. But it doesn't get us any closer to finding the curse of Marie Laveau."

"Maybe it doesn't, sugar," said Justin. "But learning more about the ring can't hurt. I do have a suggestion though."

Celeste waved her ring hand. "Let's hear it."

"Mama Vance said it. She said the answers we seek are in your dreams. That you should listen for guidance from Emile Poydras — because she felt Emile's love for you."

"I don't understand what you're suggesting, Granddad?"

"You must take control of your dream tonight. Become an active participant. When Emile comes to you in the first part of your dream, ask him to show you where we can find the curse."

Celeste shook her head. "You don't understand, Granddad. I don't control my dreams — they control me. Besides, I don't want to have that dream again."

Justin rose from his chair, walked over to Celeste, and gently took her face in his hands. "I know you don't want to have the dream again, sugar. I'd give my right arm if I could have it for you. But there's no other way... You have to try and ask Emile for help. Remember, he wants to help. He loves you."

Chapter Twenty-Seven

As Manuel de Salcedo turned from the front door, he caught sight of Emile and Anton standing in front of Aurora Béluche's house. Anton tugged at Emile's elbow to leave, but Emile stood his ground, never taking his eyes off the approaching Spaniards.

When the governor's nephew got within a couple of steps of Emile and Anton, recognition flashed across his face.

"What are you two doing — loitering out here?" Manuel demanded in fluent French.

Anton quickly answered, before Emile could. "Nothing, Captain de Salcedo, we are just on our way home from the cockfights."

Manuel laughed. "Hah! I did not realize you lived in the colored part of the city, Monsieur Cuvillier." Then, looking to Emile, he said, "Or is it your companion that is of mixed blood?"

Up until now, Emile had been struggling with his temper and contempt for de Salcedo and his promise to Julien. But Manuel's direct insult made Emile's decision easy. "Monsieur," replied Emile, "your insolent and crude behavior compliments well the cowardice you displayed at the ball last night. If I challenge you for your uncouthness, must I wait for you to call your troops to do your battle again?"

Even in the dim streetlight, Anton could see Manuel's face flush red in reaction to Emile's sarcastic retort. Anton felt his heart sink, for he knew a duel could not be avoided now. Manuel went for his saber, but the other officer with him grabbed his hand before Manuel could pull his sword from its scabbard.

"Not here, my captain," the officer said in Spanish.

His eyes flashing at Emile, Manuel screamed, "You need not challenge me! I challenge you! Name the time and your weapons."

"I choose *now*!" rejoined Emile. "Our swords will suffice."

Holding up his hand and stepping between the men, Anton spoke. "Gentlemen, as the lieutenant has pointed out, you cannot cross blades on the public street. Come, it is but a short walk to St. Anthony's Square. The lieutenant and I will serve as seconds."

With a grunt of agreement, Manuel de Salcedo and his lieutenant marched off toward St. Anthony's Square. As Emile and Anton followed the officers, Anton pulled on Emile's shoulder to slow his pace, so he could speak without being overheard.

"Emile, have you gone mad? I can understand why you had to challenge the pig, but your colichemarde is no match for his heavy cavalry saber. He'll slice you to ribbons."

"I'll manage, Anton."

"You'll manage! You don't understand. Not only does Salcedo have the advantage in weapons, he's an expert with the saber. I've seen him in action."

Emile halted and threw his hands out to his sides, turning to Anton. "What are you suggesting, Anton? That I withdraw, like a coward?"

"No, no, not at all, my friend. Just let me approach the lieutenant and inform him that I demand more equal terms for you."

Shaking his head, Emile walked on. "No! Even that would give the appearance of cowardice. I must stand behind my words."

"Or die by them," Anton muttered to himself as he followed behind the hurried Emile.

***

St. Anthony's Square was a modest garden located directly behind the St. Louis Cathedral. It consisted of a small clearing concealed from Royal Street by a heavy growth of shrubbery. Even though dueling was illegal within the city, the square was the scene of almost daily duels. During or after the balls, gentlemen sometimes had to wait and watch one or more duels before their turn could be taken. It seemed that vying for the affections of certain Creole or quadroon ladies could lead to a duel quicker than any other cause. Many high-spirited Creoles would even invent a reason to challenge one of their friends, if no one else was available for them to fight. St. Anthony's garden had even been the scene of duels fought over such a slight disagreement as the beauty of the moon on a particular evening. The Creoles dueled strictly according to the French Code; honor was deemed to be satisfied when the first blood was drawn, however slight the wound inflicted, unless the wounded man demanded further combat. Thus, few sword duels resulted in death. The victor usually returned to the ball or café boasting of his conquest, while the vanquished opponent went home to bandage his laceration and seek the solace of drink.

Upon entering the empty garden, Manuel shook off his uniform jacket and threw it to the ground. He had his saber drawn and ready as Emile and Anton entered.

As Anton helped Emile remove his coat and loosen his shirt, the Spanish lieutenant came up to them. Addressing Anton, he spoke to him in Spanish. "Señor Cuvillier, I wish to confirm that this contest shall be held strictly according to the Code. When first blood is drawn, the combat shall end."

"But of course," answered Anton. "My friend and I are both well aware of the requirements of the Code."

Turning to Emile, the lieutenant asked, "My captain wishes to know the name of the man he is to engage?"

Emile gave Anton a blank look. "What did he ask me? My Spanish is very lacking."

"The captain wants to know your name."

Emile replied, "Monsieur Emile de Lallande Poydras, at your service," and he nodded once to the lieutenant. The lieutenant returned his nod and marched off to report to Manuel.

When the two men squared off, Anton's worst fears were quickly confirmed. Emile was immediately forced to take the defensive. It was all he could do to parry Manuel's powerful saber strikes. At one point, Anton thought the blade of Emile's colichemarde would snap under Manuel's relentless assault.

Anton did notice that Emile was quick on his feet and with his sword. A couple of his thrusts came close to striking home. One even snagged the sleeve of Manuel's shirt. However, the skillful Spaniard and his heavier sword soon had Emile retreating and back-stepping around the garden. Suddenly, Emile tripped and fell backwards over a low stone bench. Emile's head and shoulders hit the ground with a loud thud, while his feet and legs remained elevated on the bench. The impact with the ground dazed him and caused his sword to fly from his hand.

Emile's predicament did not deter Manuel's continued attack. Stepping on Emile's right hand, so he could not retrieve his sword, the Spaniard leaned over his face. Then, before Emile could even raise his other hand for protection, Manuel slashed his cheek open with the tip of his saber.

"There," declared Manuel, "you insolent French peasant. Now you have something to remember me by."

"Poltroon!" declared Emile, holding his hand on his bleeding face. "You strike the defenseless?"

Enraged by Emile's charge of cowardness, the Spaniard drew back his sword to attack the defenseless Emile again, but Anton ran up to confront de Salcedo.

"Foul! Coward!" shouted Anton, drawing his own sword cane. "That, señor, is the most cowardly act I have ever seen, and a blatant violation of the Code. You will have to answer to me now!"

"Gladly!" screamed Manuel, as he turned and swung his saber at Anton's head. Anton adroitly dodged the assault and countered with his own attack. By now Emile, still holding his bloody cheek, had pulled himself to a kneeling position behind the stone bench. He was dazed from his fall and Manuel's ruthless attack. But he was soon mesmerized by Anton's masterful assault on Manuel.

Anton was like an unleashed demon with his sword. He whipped and slashed so rapidly his blade sang as it ripped through the air. It was now Manuel's turn to go on the defensive as he parried Anton's repeated strikes at his face. Then, just as it appeared that the Spaniard might beat back Anton's attacks, Anton parried each strike and doubled the speed of his ripostes.

Anton's colichemarde suddenly struck home, slashing a wound to the left side of Manuel's face. Anton started to drop his guard, as he assumed the duel to be at an end. However, Manuel flew into a fury at the sight of his own blood, and he lunged hard at Anton. Like a matador evading a charging bull, Anton sidestepped Manuel's onslaught, and as Manuel passed by, Anton jabbed his sword into his opponent's right shoulder, causing Manuel to cry out in pain and drop his saber.

The lieutenant ran forward, placing himself between Anton and the bleeding Manuel. "Enough! Enough!" the officer cried. "The matter is at an end!"

Anton saluted the lieutenant with his sword, and said, "For now, Lieutenant. For now, it is at an end. The rest is up to your captain."

***

Anton helped Emile back to Julien's house. The houseboy, who opened the door for the men, cried out when he saw Emile covered in blood. "Monsieur Poydras! Come quick! Come quick!"

When Julien came into the foyer and caught sight of Emile, he dropped his newspaper and his mouth fell open. Recovering, he ordered, "Odeo, go fetch the bandages — and hot water. Hurry!" Motioning toward the dining room, he said, "Bring him in here — to the table."

After Anton helped Emile into a chair at the head of the dining room table, Julien gently lifted Emile's bloody handkerchief from his cheek. Examining the wound, he exploded with questions. "What happened? Who has cut you? And why are you limping?"

Emile mumbled, "I'll be all right, Uncle." From the groan in his voice, it was evident it pained Emile to speak. So, Anton spoke for him.

Extending his hand to Julien, he introduced himself. "Anton Cuvillier, Monsieur Poydras. Perhaps I can answer your questions."

"Please do, Monsieur Cuvillier," said Julien as he sat down in the chair next to Emile.

"It was a duel, monsieur. In fact, we both were in a duel tonight — with the same man."

"Duel? What duel?" asked Julien.

"With Manuel de Salcedo."

"What! You both dueled with the governor's nephew?"

Anton nodded. "Yes, I'm afraid so. We had no choice. He accosted us both as we passed him in the street. Well… actually, he challenged Emile first. Then he committed the most cowardly act I have ever seen on a field of honor. Your nephew had tripped and fallen, and de Salcedo held Emile down and cut him. He was preparing to strike again when I intervened."

At this moment, Odeo came in with a bowl of steaming water, a towel, and a roll of gauze bandages. Julien dipped the towel in the hot water and began cleaning Emile's face and wound. "And your limp?" he asked.

Anton answered again. "I believe it's merely a sprain. He must have turned his ankle when he fell during the duel."

Turning to face Anton, Julien asked, "You say you also fought a duel?"

"Yes, I did. When I saw the cowardly acts de Salcedo committed, I rushed forward and challenged the pig. I was acting as your nephew's second."

Eying Anton again, Julien nodded and said, "Well, Monsieur Cuvillier. You look as if you fared much better in your duel than my nephew did in his?"

Forcing himself to speak, Emile said, "He saved my life, Uncle. And what a swordsman he is. His sword is quicker than a cat. He cut de Salcedo worse than I am."

Julien nodded. "I thank you, monsieur, for all you have done for my nephew. May I offer you a drink? Or something to eat?"

"Thank you, monsieur. But I really should be on my way. That is, unless I can be of further assistance to you?"

Julien waved his hand. "No, you've done more than one could ask, Monsieur Cuvillier. Just be on your guard. The governor is very fond of his nephew. He may have you and Emile arrested for dueling."

"The governor wouldn't dare send troops into your house, Uncle," muttered Emile.

"I wouldn't be so sure," replied Julien. "At any rate, Monsieur Cuvillier, you are welcome to spend the night. In the morning, I suggest we all leave the city for a while. You both should be safe from arrest at my Pointe Coupee plantation. I imagine it will take some time for the Spaniards' blood to cool down."

"I cannot leave," protested Emile, "and be called a coward. Besides, I must see Aurora."

"Aurora?" queried Julien. "Who the devil is Aurora?"

Ignoring Julien's question, Anton spoke to Emile. "You are no coward, Emile. You took on de Salcedo and his saber with your colichemarde. As for Aurora? No woman is worth a prison term. Besides, if you are arrested, her mother will never let you near her."

Anton's logic and the pain in his cheek silenced Emile.

When Odeo came back to check on the men, Julien instructed him, "Odeo, take Monsieur Cuvillier to the guest room and see to his needs."

"Thank you, Monsieur Poydras," said Anton as he shook his head. "But if I am to accept your invitation to leave the city, I must go home and advise my parents of these developments and pack for the trip. I live but a short distance from here."

"Then I bid you good night, Monsieur Cuvillier. Please be back here no later than noon for our departure."

Alone in the dining room with Emile, Julien wrapped a bandage around Emile's wound. "I'm afraid you'll have a nasty scar."

Emile sighed. "Maybe it will serve as a reminder of my foolish temper, Uncle. I've failed you again, and nearly gotten myself killed to boot."

Squeezing his nephew's shoulder, Julien said, "Oh, my dear boy, if I could only give you this damn ring. You, I fear, truly need its protection. But, alas, it seems I am condemned to wear it or die."

Chapter Twenty-Eight

Celeste woke up early after having her dream. She lay perfectly still on her back and stared at the ceiling in thought. After a moment, she turned her head and looked up at Mark. He had tried to stay awake for her again but was too exhausted from sitting up with her the night before. He'd fallen asleep in an upright position, his head resting on the wooden headboard of their bed. Mark had kept the bed lamp on but had fallen asleep in spite of the light in his eyes.

Seeing Mark asleep, it dawned on Celeste that she must have had the dream without crying out. Knowing what to expect had helped Celeste face the dream. But it was more than that. Each time, the dream was becoming less frightening. She enjoyed the lovemaking sequence. She was even a little ashamed that she looked forward to it. As Celeste fell back to sleep, she heard a little voice in the back of her mind. It was warning her she was beginning to like her dreams too much.

Later that morning, sitting down to biscuits and coffee in the kitchen, Justin asked Celeste for a report on her last dream. "Did you notice anythin' new in your dream last night, sugar?"

"You mean, was I able to ask Emile Poydras for help?"

"Yes, that too," admitted Justin.

"The answer's yes," confirmed Celeste. "You had a good idea. I believe Emile is directing us to the curse."

"What?" interjected Mark. "I didn't even know you had the dream last night."

"I know, babe," replied Celeste. "You were so exhausted you slept right through it. Besides, it didn't scare me as bad last night."

Justin picked up on Celeste's last remark. "You were less frightened last night? Good. Perhaps that will be a trend."

"I think it already is," conceded Celeste. "Anyway, I got a good hint on the curse."

"Tell us," encouraged Justin.

"Well," began Celeste, "when Emile started to leave our bed, he held out his hand again and gave me that same imploring look. But, this time, I made myself grab his hand, and I asked him for help. I said, if he wanted my help, he must show me how to find the curse Marie Laveau placed on him."

"Did he answer you?" asked Mark.

"Not directly." Celeste stared down at the milk clouds in her coffee. "But he understood my question. He nodded his head."

"That's it?" pressed Mark.

"No. Then I found myself in the cemetery again. The dream was the same, at first. But, when the little girl — the ghost — appeared, she motioned for me to follow her around to the side of Marie Laveau's oven vault. I guess she was doing that all this time. Anyway, when I came around the corner, she was writing on the side of the tomb."

"Writin' what?" Justin asked.

"In her own blood," answered Celeste. "She kept dipping her finger into her chest wound and rubbing it on the wall of her tomb. But I can't tell you what it said."

"You can remember nothin' else about the writin'?" nudged Justin.

"Not really, Granddad. I... I remember there were several lines to the message, and the lettering was big. It nearly covered the entire wall."

"Can you recall what language?" asked Justin.

"I'm pretty sure it was French or Creole. But it's like the other part of my dream. I can't recall any specific words at all."

Justin rubbed at his beard stubble with one hand, then said, "Well... looks like we take another trip to the cemetery."

Mark shook his head slightly. "Great, I'll wear my swimsuit this time and work on my tan. Can we go at high noon? The sun's better then."

Mark's sarcastic comments triggered something else in Celeste's memory. "One more thing, when the little girl appears, I always hear the cathedral clock strike the hour. Have I mentioned that before?"

"I don't think so," said Justin. "What hour is the clock strikin'?"

Celeste grinned. "Midnight, of course."

Justin stood up and gulped down the remainder of his coffee. Setting his cup down, he said, "You two relax, or explore more of the Quarter, if you like. I've got a little errand to run this mornin'."

When Justin got back, he found Celeste and Mark on the couch. Celeste was half asleep, and Mark was watching a Cardinal's baseball game.

"We're all set," announced Justin.

"Set for what?" asked Mark.

"Here," said Justin, handing Mark the paper sack he carried in. "Do you know how to work one of these?"

Mark peered down into the sack and asked, "A flashlight?"

Justin chuckled. "No, not the flashlight, the Polaroid camera."

Mark pulled the box out of the sack and examined it. "Yeah, sure, my dad had this same model. What am I taking pictures of?"

Celeste yawned, stretched her arms above her head, and sat up, joining the conversation. "Yeah, Granddad. What's the camera for?"

"To take with us to the cemetery tonight."

"To photograph ghosts?" Mark quipped. "I hope you bought some fast film."

"Granddad," asked Celeste, "are we really going back to the cemetery tonight?"

"Yes, sugar. I've made all the arrangements."

"What arrangements?" Mark inquired.

Justin turned down the volume on the TV and sat down in the armchair opposite the couch. "I went to the Basin Street graveyard and looked up the sexton — Mr. Lefebvre.... I told him you two were researchin' a book on local Voodoo practices, and that we needed to have access to Marie Laveau's tomb at midnight tonight."

"And he bought that story?" asked Celeste.

"No. He just laughed and said he's heard that one before."

"So, what'd you do then?" queried Mark.

"I used the direct approach," Justin said with a smile. "I offered him a bribe."

"Of course," replied Mark. "How much?"

"That's not important — a hundred dollars."

"A hundred bucks! Just to leave the gate unlocked?"

"Not exactly. Mr. Lefebvre said the police check the gate sometimes. That the best he could do is loan us a rope and look the other way."

"Look the other way!" exclaimed Mark. "Justin, you got took. For a hundred bucks, we could've bought a lot of rope."

"I realize that. But I was at his mercy once I'd revealed our intentions. At least the rope is already tied to the backside of the wall, waitin' for us. Lefebvre did walk me around the outside of the wall and show me where the rope will be hidden on top. And we'll be out of sight near the back wall of the cemetery. Passin' patrol cars won't see us."

"Granddad?" interjected Celeste. "What are we goin' to do, once we get inside the graveyard?"

"Look at the side of Marie's tomb at the stroke of midnight. What else?"

Celeste uttered a bitter little laugh. "You know that song about your dreams coming true? Somehow, I never thought I'd be wishing for a nightmare to come true."

Chapter Twenty-Nine

Julien, Emile, and Anton left New Orleans the morning after the duel with Manuel de Salcedo. Julien's hunch proved to be accurate. After the men reached Pointe Coupee, word reached them that Governor Carondelet had issued warrants for the arrest of both Emile and Anton. Monsieur Maree also reported that Spanish troops came to Julien's house in New Orleans not two hours after they had departed for Pointe Coupee.

The governor did not pursue the men, however. Always the politician, Carondelet knew arresting Julien's nephew would be most unpopular with the citizens of Pointe Coupee. And since the slave rebellion that spring, the popularity of the Spanish government was already at low ebb among the wealthy planters there.

Some ten months later, the governor recalled the warrants as a gesture of goodwill to Julien. In the meantime, Emile returned to Alma and to managing Julien's bank, while Anton was hired by Julien to inspect and report on the operations of the trading posts he had established on the upper Mississippi. Julien was quite pleased with the labors of both men, especially Emile, who proved to be an excellent banker, and had increased the bank's profits significantly.

A few weeks after the arrest warrants were cancelled, Anton Cuvillier returned to New Orleans. Julien was sorry to see Anton leave, as he had become rather fond of him. Emile, however, was forced to live in exile at Pointe Coupee. Even though the dueling charges had been dropped, the governor had warned Julien that, because of the grudge carried by Manuel, it would be best if Emile and Anton did not return to New Orleans, especially as Carondelet was to be replaced as governor by Manuel's father within a year. Anton, however, decided to risk returning, as he missed his family, and his father was reported to be in failing health.

Emile did not forget Aurora during his exile from New Orleans. She became his golden apple, the forbidden fruit he wanted all the more because it was out of reach. He corresponded with her for a few months, but Aurora's letters were only polite and perfunctory. They contained none of the impassioned language of Emile's letters. Eventually, Aurora stopped replying, which made Emile desire her even more.

It was not until the spring of 1798 that Emile would make his second visit to New Orleans. The occasion was the arrivals of Emile's half-brother, Benjamin, and that of the future king of France, the Duke of Orleans, Louis Philippe, who would be arriving later in the week from his exile in Boston.

Standing on the New Orleans landing with Julien, watching his brother's ship dock, Emile thought back on his own arrival some three years earlier, and how his life had changed so dramatically since then.

Benjamin was easy to spot among the disembarking passengers, even though it had been nearly four years since Emile had seen his younger half-brother. With his short stature, broad shoulders, and loose jowls, Benjamin looked like a bulldog in a suit, and he appeared more mature than his twenty-two years. Emile thought it somewhat serendipitous that Benjamin was the same age as him when he came to New Orleans.

Rushing to the bottom of the gangplank, Emile threw his arms around his brother as he stepped onto the dock. "Brother, welcome to Nouvelle Orléans. How was your voyage?"

"Long, but uneventful." Pulling back to look over Emile in his tailored silk suit, Benjamin added, "It appears you have prospered here in Nouvelle France?"

"Oui. Thanks to our uncle Julien. It is amazing what he has accomplished here. Come, he is also here to greet you."

Even though Julien had never laid eyes on Benjamin, he greeted the young man as if he was an absent son returning home, kissing him on both cheeks. Julien peppered Benjamin with questions about their relatives in France as the servants loaded his luggage in Julien's ebony landau coach. During the short ride to Julien's home in the Vieux Carré, Emile regaled Benjamin with descriptions of Julien's plantations, trading posts, bank, and other properties and business interests. Upon their arrival, Monsieur Maree greeted them at the front door and informed Julien that lunch was ready any time they were agreeable. Julien nodded and led the brothers into the dining room as the meal was brought in on silver trays. After the men were seated and the wine was poured, Benjamin stood and raised his glass in a toast.

"To Louis Philippe d'Orléans, the next king of France!"

Julien and Emile returned Benjamin's toast and chanted in unison, "To Louis Philippe."

Lowering his glass, Julien asked, "I suppose making such a toast in France could lead to our arrest for treason?"

Benjamin settled his short, rugged frame back down into his chair and immediately began to devour the meal set before him. "Excuse my manners, Uncle. But the food on the ship was nothing like this fare. In answer to your question, you are correct. Making a toast in honor of the crown could lead to one's arrest. However, you may be surprised to learn who would bring the charges."

"What do you mean?" asked Emile.

"It is not the Directory or the Jacobins that constitute the greatest threat to the monarchy now," answered Benjamin. "I fear France is to become a military dictatorship."

"Bonaparte?" suggested Julien.

"Correct, Uncle. So, you have heard of the 'Le Petit Caporal,' now General Napoleon?"

"You mean the general who conquered Italy and Austria?" asked Emile.

"Yes, Emile." After pausing to take another sip of wine, Benjamin continued, "For now, Napoleon supports the Directory. But he is becoming so popular with the people, and so powerful, that I fear it is only a matter of time before his army seizes control of the government."

"The people of France will eventually tire of dictatorship and constant war," offered Julien. "Until then, we must support the duke and wait for opportunity to favor us. When is he planning to call on me?"

"I am not privy to the duke's exact schedule, Uncle. Last I heard, he plans to visit Bernard de Marigny's plantation first, and then stop at Pointe Coupee as he visits planters along the Mississippi. I will contact Monsieur de Marigny and obtain the precise dates."

Observing Benjamin's fashionable suit and well-kept appearance, Emile thought the revolution could not have caused his younger brother too much privation. "You said Father is well?" asked Emile during a lull in the conversation.

"Yes, well enough when I left, although he suffered from gout this winter. He sends his love and said to tell you how proud he is of your success in New France. I have letters from him for you and Uncle Julien."

Spying Benjamin's empty plate, Julien asked, "Would you care for some more veal? We have plenty."

"No, thank you, Uncle. It was superb, but I'm quite full. I think I'll unpack. Perhaps later, you and Emile might give me a tour of the city?"

"It would be my pleasure," answered Emile. "We can look up my good friend, Anton Cuvillier. He knows all the points of interest in New Orleans."

"I'm afraid I have some appointments this afternoon," replied Julien. "But you two enjoy yourselves." With a slow wink, he added, "I won't expect you home for dinner."

It being a pleasant spring afternoon, Emile led his brother on a leisurely stroll through New Orleans. After viewing the Place d'Armes and the St. Louis Cathedral, the men found themselves on Chartres Street. Emile suggested they pay an impromptu visit to the home of Anton Cuvillier.

"Monsieur Cuvillier was your second in the duel with the new governor's son?" asked Benjamin.

"Yes. He's the friend I wrote you about. And what a swordsman! I wish I had half his skill with a blade."

"Does his skill exceed mine?" asked Benjamin somewhat peevishly.

"No, I did not mean to imply that, dear brother," chuckled Emile "Although it has been some time since I have seen you in action, I would still wager you are the best swordsman I have ever seen. I only meant that Anton is probably the best duelist in New Orleans."

Benjamin smiled and nodded. "I'll keep that in mind. Now, tell me more about the quadroon woman you wrote of. Did you really fall in love with her after a single dance?"

Emile felt the heat of a blush cross his face. "I do not recall writing that in my letters?"

"No, you didn't. That was Uncle Julien's interpretation of your actions. Why else would you fight a duel over a woman you had barely met?"

"Actually, the duel came about because of my extreme dislike for Manuel de Salcedo."

"Oh, really?"

"Yes. It was just my misfortune that de Salcedo was courting the same woman I desired."

The men halted their walk to view the garden of the Ursuline Convent. Emile pointed out that the convent was one of the few structures to survive the great fires of 1788 and 1794. Moving on down Chartres Street, Benjamin asked, "What ever happened to the woman you met at the quadroon ball?"

"Her name was Béluche, Aurora Béluche. I don't know where she is now. She stopped corresponding with me." Sighing, Emile added, "I've done my best not to think of her."

With a suspect look, Benjamin replied, "From the tone of your voice, I suspect you are failing in that regard?"

"Yes," admitted Emile. "I still think of her — and dream about her. I know it must seem foolish to you — to become so obsessed with a woman with whom I had such a brief encounter. But she was the most beautiful woman I have ever laid eyes on, and there was just this overpowering attraction I can't explain. I now know how Uncle Julien must have felt, when he had to leave the love of his life behind in France."

"I can hardly wait for the next quadroon ball. I must meet these women, if they have such amorous powers."

Halting in front of a well-appointed, two-story brick house, Emile pointed, "This is it."

Anton answered the door himself. He looked surprised to see Emile. "Emile," he said. "I... I had not heard of your return." After an awkward pause, Anton continued, "Excuse my manners. Would you gentlemen like to come in?"

"Yes, thank you, Anton," Emile answered as the men stepped into the hall. "We arrived only this morning. Allow me to introduce my brother, Benjamin de Lallande Poydras."

Extending his right hand, Anton said, "A pleasure, Monsieur Poydras, welcome to my home. I have been looking — "

The men's introductions were interrupted by the entrance of a young woman from an adjacent parlor.

"Aurora!" blurted out Emile. Composing himself, Emile continued, "Mademoiselle Béluche, may I ask what you are doing here?"

Aurora was stunned and bewildered by Emile's presence and question, so Anton quickly intervened and escorted her back into the parlor and closed the door. Turning to Emile, Anton answered for her. "Aurora is my mistress, Emile."

"What!"

"Yes. Aurora and I have lived together for almost a year now. I made formal arrangements with her mother."

Emile clenched his fists. Becoming livid, he demanded, "Anton, what is the meaning of this?"

"I'm sorry, Emile. I tried to write you many times. Each time I started, I thought how you might be upset and misunderstand my intentions. So, I decided to wait until I could tell you face to face. We never meant to — "

Emile cut Anton off. "No further explanation is needed! You knew how I felt about her. And yet, of all the women in New Orleans, you seek *her* out as your mistress?"

Anton slowly shook his head. "It wasn't like that at all, Emile. We kept seeing each other at the balls, and it just happened. Aurora told me your relationship with her had ended. Had I any idea you would feel that I betrayed you, I would have come to Pointe Coupee and — "

"Enough!" exclaimed Emile. "I demand satisfaction!"

Uttering a heavy sigh, Anton looked at Emile with sadness. "I will not fight you, Emile. There is nothing to duel over. And I owe your uncle too much to take up arms against you."

"Coward! Poltroon!" pressed Emile.

For the first time, anger flashed in Anton's eyes. "I am no coward, Emile. You of all people know that. You also know that you are no match for me in any duel."

The painful truth of Anton's rejoinder aggravated Emile's rage. He became flabbergasted and unable to reply for a moment. Finally, catching his breath, he pointed his sword cane at Anton's chest and said, "You are no gentleman, Monsieur Cuvillier, and no friend of mine — or my family. Mark my words! Someday you will be forced to give me satisfaction."

Part IV
Prescriptions for Deliverance

From ghoulies and ghosties and long-leggety beasties,

And things that go bump in the night, Good Lord, deliver us!

– Anonymous Scottish Prayer

Part IV

Prescriptions for Deliverance

Chapter Thirty

By 11:40 p.m., Justin, Celeste, and Mark reached the wall of St. Louis Cemetery No. 1 on Conti Street. From behind them, through the tenement's open windows, came the sound of someone's stereo at full volume playing James Brown's "Living in America." There were also the sounds of slamming doors and shouting.

Mark couldn't make out many of the words people shouted. The New Orleans' dialect was still a "foreign tongue" to him. But all were able to deduce that the cause of the shouting was the loud soul music blaring throughout the apartment complex.

"For da last time! Turn dat sucker *down*!" they all heard. Other residents of the housing project were heard interjecting various obscenities.

Justin halted and pointed up at the red and gray brick wall. "The rope's up there. It's attached just over the ledge of the wall."

Mark jumped, but he couldn't quite reach the top of the wall. He motioned for Justin. "Give me a boost, and I'll grab the rope for us." Justin bent over beside the wall, locking his palms at arm's length. With Justin's boost, Mark easily pulled himself on top of the narrow wall.

While Mark was letting the rope down the outside of the wall, Celeste suddenly felt uneasy — like something was moving behind her on the other side of the street. She turned around to see if anyone was watching them, but she saw no one.

With Mark straddling the top of the wall to give assistance, Celeste and Justin quickly scaled it and descended inside using the other end of the rope. After Mark pulled in the rope, they assembled on the inside of the cemetery. Justin untied a pillowcase from his belt and pulled out the new oversized flashlight and turned it on. Then he handed Mark the Polaroid camera. Leading the way with the flashlight, Justin silently directed the group toward the tomb of Marie Laveau.

Celeste felt more at ease as they proceeded into the cemetery. To her, the dark graveyard had a familiar look. The shadows cast by the tombs gave her a strong feeling of déjà vu.

For Mark, the cemetery had a completely different look and feel at night. Gone was the oppressive heat and bright reflections of sunlight. The white tombs now seemed to absorb and radiate the moonlight and the streetlamps outside the walls. The green-white light of the mercury vapor streetlamps gave some of the tombs an eerie, iridescent glow. The weird light and dark shadows made Celeste's dream seem much more realistic to Mark. He even had to suppress a shudder when he passed a defaced statue of a woman holding the limp body of a crucified Christ.

In less than five minutes, Justin led the party to the tomb of Marie Laveau. Handing his pillowcase to Celeste, he took the flashlight and walked completely around the tomb, closely examining each wall with the light. When he had completed his inspection, Justin said, "Just like in the daylight. No sign of writin' on any wall. What time is it?"

Looking at his digital wristwatch, Mark replied, "11:56."

"Let's get ready," said Justin. "Celeste, which side of the tomb does the child write on?"

Pausing to think a moment, Celeste pointed and answered, "The right side. She always runs around to the right side."

Retrieving the pillowcase from Celeste, Justin withdrew a legal pad, clipboard, and felt tip pen. "Is the camera ready?" he asked.

Switching on the Polaroid's flash, Mark observed the red ready light come on. "Ready."

"Good," replied Justin. Pointing with the flashlight beam, he added, "You stand over there, Mark, where you can focus on the entire side of the tomb." Turning to Celeste, he directed, "You stand where you always do, sugar, in front — as you do in your dream."

Justin switched off the flashlight. As he walked over to stand beside Mark, all of them heard the cathedral clock begin to chime midnight. That struck Justin as odd. He wondered how they could hear the chimes above all the neighborhood noise. After the chimes stopped, they all stood silently staring at the tomb. When nothing happened right away, Justin whispered, "What time is it now?"

"Four minutes af — " Mark started to answer, but he was interrupted by a call from Celeste.

"She's here," she stage whispered. "She's coming your way."

Mark and Justin waited and watched but saw nothing. Mark was just about to ask Celeste what happened, when Justin grabbed his arm and pointed at the tomb wall. There, appearing on the whitewashed wall, a letter at a time, was the message. The letters were written in a broad, deliberate script — like a child's handwriting. The color and consistency of the lettering varied, as if some were being written in paint with a small brush or a person's finger. Nevertheless, they showed up well on the white tomb, even in the dim light. The first two words of the message that appeared were "Mélanger dans." Justin thought to himself, *Mix in... Celeste was right. This is the recipe for the curse.*

Mark raised the Polaroid in his trembling hands to snap a picture of the first few words, but Justin pulled the camera down. "Wait until she's finished," he whispered. "The flash might scare her off."

With his clipboard and pen, Justin recorded each new letter of the message as it appeared on the tomb. Mark kept straining his eyes, hoping to see the apparition that was writing on the tomb. But no form or figure became visible to the men. However, Mark did notice that small drops of blood were starting to appear on the pavement beside the tomb, seeming to fall out of thin air.

When six long lines of script had been scrawled across the tomb, the writing stopped. Justin double-checked his draft of the message against what was written on the wall. Then he waited another minute to be certain that the writing did not continue. When no new letters appeared, he motioned for Mark to photograph the tomb wall.

The bright light of the camera's flash blinded the men momentarily. When they were able to focus again on the wall, the message had vanished, along with the drops of blood on the pavement

Calling out from the front of the tomb, Celeste asked, "Did you see her?"

As the men came around to the face of the tomb, they found Celeste standing in the exact spot they'd left her. "Didn't you see her?" continued Celeste. "I know she ran your way." The tone in Celeste's voice was one of disappointment and urgency.

"We have the curse," reassured Justin, holding up his legal pad. "Every letter of it."

"Yeah," added Mark. "I saw it too, babe. But we didn't ever see the little girl."

"What!" Celeste exclaimed. "You had to have seen her. She was right here."

"It's alright," said Justin. "We got the curse, that's the important thing.... Evidently, only you have the power to actually see the spirit of the child."

"But she was here," persisted Celeste. "It was just like in my dream."

"Perhaps you were havin' your dream — your vision — just now?" suggested Justin.

"How could... Maybe you're right, Granddad." Rubbing her forehead, Celeste added, "Now that I think about it, I must've gone into a trance or something, 'cause I also saw the priest and the other children in their Halloween costumes."

"The camera flash probably woke you up?" suggested Mark. "Anyway, I owe you both an apology. I never really believed all this Voodoo business until tonight. But I saw the blood writing with my own eyes. And we even got a picture of it."

"Let me see?" she asked excitedly.

Mark pulled the exposed photograph from the Polaroid and held it up to Justin's flashlight. The tomb wall was clearly visible, but it was a blank slate in the snapshot.

"This can't be!" cried Mark. "I saw it. The whole wall was covered with writing in blood!"

"Well, I still have my notes," said Justin. "Now, shall we go home and see if we can figure out what they mean?"

"Fine by me," answered Mark. "This place is giving me the creeps."

Retracing their steps through the cemetery, they soon reached the spot where the rope was tied to the wall. Mark helped Celeste and Justin up and over the wall. Then he climbed on the top of the wall, threw the rope back inside the cemetery, and jumped down to join them on the sidewalk.

Before the group had taken one step towards home, a threatening voice called out from behind them, "Don't move!"

As they turned around, they found themselves confronted by two tough-looking black teenagers, one of whom was holding a homemade pistol, or zip gun.

The youth without the pistol said, "See, I told ya, man. I told ya I seen three honkies climb dis wall."

The teenage boy with the gun didn't respond to his companion. He kept the gun pointed at Mark and glared. "Gi'me your wallets and jewelry. *Now!*"

Mark, Celeste, and Justin were too shocked to immediately respond to the hoodlum's demand. Shaking the zip gun at Mark's face, the robber pressed his point. "I said *now*, sucker! Dis gun may have only one bullet, but it sure can kill you dead."

When Mark — still frozen by shock — didn't respond, the gunman lowered the weapon at Mark's stomach. Celeste saw a flash of anger enter the robber's eyes. She sensed that he was really going to shoot the petrified Mark.

Before he could pull the trigger, Celeste jumped in front of Mark, grabbed the gun's pipe barrel, and pulled it to her chest. The startled robber pulled the trigger, and Celeste heard the click of the hammer striking home. But the pistol didn't fire. With Celeste still holding onto the barrel, the young mugger quickly cocked and pulled the trigger a second time. When the pistol still didn't fire, he let go of his grip on the weapon and backed up.

"You is one crazy bitch. That gun ain't never — "

The gunman was interrupted by his accomplice. "Benny! Come on! Run! Cop car just turned da corner."

Before turning to run after his fleeing comrade, Benny reached out and jerked the zip gun from Celeste's hands and said, "You ought'a be dead! You ought'a be dead!"

Chapter Thirty-One

Emile and Benjamin proceeded to debauch themselves after the heated encounter with Anton. Emile introduced his brother to one of New Orleans's best bordellos — one that prided itself on offering the most beautiful of quadroon women.

Having indulged in women and wine all night long, the brothers stumbled back to Julien's house just before dawn. When Julien, being an early riser, decided to roust his nephew from bed later that morning, Emile's temples were pounding from his hangover. Julien's rap on the bedroom door sounded like a bass drum echoing in Emile's pained head.

Entering the bedroom, Julien acted slightly perturbed when he found Emile still in bed. "Still in bed? It's after nine o'clock. You and your brother have already missed breakfast."

Emile groaned and said, "That's quite all right, Uncle. I'm not hungry."

Julien smiled at his stricken nephew but still feigned agitation. "I trust you two got your fill of carousing yesterday, for we have work today."

Emile struggled up in bed and leaned back on his elbows. "What work might that be?"

"We must issue invitations and purchase supplies for the duke's visit. We all must be fitted for proper clothes in which to receive him. Then, we must get back and see that all is in order at Pointe Coupee."

Shaking his aching head, Emile replied, "I hope all that need not be accomplished today?"

"Of course it *all* cannot be accomplished in what is left of today. But we must get started. Our visit to New Orleans must be brief, if we are to be ready to entertain the duke at Pointe Coupee."

Sitting fully up, Emile said, "I understand, Uncle. I'll accomplish all I can today."

"Good. Now, I must get your brother up."

As Julien turned to leave the room, Emile delayed him. "Uncle, a moment, please. I need to speak to you before Benjamin joins us."

"Of course," responded Julien as he turned back and sat at the foot of Emile's bed.

"I know you don't wish to talk about Voodoo in front of Benjamin."

"That is correct," Julien agreed. "For the time being, I think it best that we keep my ring and its secrets confidential.... However, we should warn Benjamin to be on his guard. And you must watch over him. We don't want him to also fall prey to a Voodoo seductress."

"I'll tell him about my experience with your slave — Sally Francis. That should get his attention."

"Very well," said Julien. "We will warn Benjamin of the pitfalls of Voodooism, but we won't mention my ring — or how it was created.... Is there something else you wanted to bring up?"

Hesitantly, Emile replied, "Yes... I need to ask a favor."

"Certainly."

"I need for you to arrange for me to meet Sanité Dédé."

"What!" bristled Julien. "Whatever for?"

"I need her help.... I want to place a curse on someone."

Julien shot up. Incredulously, he asked, "On whom, for God's sake? And why?"

Emile shook his head. "I can't tell you, Uncle. Just believe me when I tell you this man has wronged me greatly. He will deserve what happens."

"Then seek your redress in court — as a last resort, challenge him. But you must find some other remedy. I will not have you involved with Sanité Dédé — or murder by Voodoo."

"Then recommend me to some other Voodoo practitioner," pleaded Emile. "Besides, I do not wish to really harm anyone — only give back a little of the unhappiness he has caused me."

Sighing, Julien said, "I'm beginning to regret the day I ever told you about the power of Voodoo. I warn you, Emile. Once you become involved with the cult, it may have you as its servant for the rest of your life. Its power is most seductive."

"I'll take my chances, Uncle. From what I've seen, Voodoo can give one a real advantage in this new world."

"Very well," begrudged Julien. "If I cannot dissuade you, I will give you the name of one of the local Voodoo doctors. But only if you give me your word that you will stay away from Sanité Dédé?"

"Agreed," said Emile.

"My boy, you have become a real asset to me, and I love you as if you are my own son. Just be cautious. It will break my heart if some calamity befalls you."

***

The next afternoon, Emile rode out to Lake Pontchartrain. Following Julien's written directions, Emile had no trouble in locating the lakeside shack that served as the home of Doctor Beauregard — a doctor of Voodoo.

Julien had explained that while the Voodoo doctors occupied secondary positions in Voodoo hierarchy, many were nearly as influential as the Voodoo queens, and Doctor Beauregard had one of the largest followings of any of these Voodoo sorcerers.

Doctor Beauregard's one-room shack had only a tattered piece of canvas for a door and was weathered gray from exposure to the elements. When Emile knocked on the doorframe to announce his arrival, the loose boards rattled a reply.

Hearing movement from within, Emile took a step back from the door. Out of the shack came a pungent odor and the wildest looking creature Emile had ever laid eyes on. Doctor Beauregard was a tall, skinny black man wearing an old, black frock coat and battered stovepipe hat. He had long matted dreadlocks that hung down past his waist. Emile noticed that portions of Doctor Beauregard's hair were tied so that they formed a network of little pockets. In these receptacles the doctor carried some of his Voodoo paraphernalia. Emile observed such items as leather bags, shells, dried frogs, bird skulls, and a hoot owl's head.

Taken aback by the Voodoo doctor's appearance, Emile stumbled with his introduction. "Are... are you Doctor Beauregard?"

"I be him, man. What dis it you want?"

"My name is Emile Poydras. My uncle — Julien Poydras — said you might be able to help me."

Doctor Beauregard smiled and nodded. "Oui, Monsieur Poydras. I sure I can help you — for de right price." Pointing to a rough bench on the shady side of the shack, Doctor Beauregard motioned for Emile to be seated. "Jist tell me what you desire?"

Emile reluctantly sat down at the far end of the bench, not wanting to be too close to the odoriferous doctor and the weird assortment in his hair. "Do you have a charm that will break up a love affair?"

"Of course," the doctor replied. "I have a sure-fire charm for dat, but it will cost you two doubloons."

"What! Two gold doubloons! That seems rather high, *doctor*."

"Oui, monsieur. But de elements of de charm are quite rare and expensive."

"Very well," Emile grudgingly assented as he dropped the coins into the sorcerer's outstretched palm. "But, if your charm doesn't work, I'll be back to see you."

"Not to worry, monsieur. Now dis is what you must do." As he spoke, Doctor Beauregard began removing small leather pouches from their nests in his hair. "First, take dees nine magic needles — break each needle in three pieces. Den, write each lover's name three times on paper — write one name forward and de other backwards.... Next, put de needles and de paper in a tin plate under a doorway. Hang a black candle upside down on string over de tin plate and light it — make sure de drippin's all go in de plate." Handing Emile another leather pouch, Doctor Beauregard continued, "Next, put de paper, needles, and de drippin's in dis bag and throw it all into de river.... In three days, one of de lovers will leave."

Feeling lumps in the last sack he was handed, Emile asked, "What's in here?"

"Dung from a black and white dog."

"What?"

"It be special dung though. De charm won't work less'en it comes from de dog while he be runnin' and barkin' in de street."

Emile rose. Shaking his head in disbelief, he placed the items in his saddlebag. The thought entered his mind that Julien had played him for a fool by sending him out to see the bizarre Doctor Beauregard. Taking the reins of his horse, Emile asked, "I trust, doctor, that my visit today will remain confidential?"

"As you wish, monsieur. It will be our little secret."

As Emile started to mount his horse, he had another thought. He stopped and turned back to face Doctor Beauregard. "Do you also have charms that will cause someone to fall in love with a certain person?"

"But of course, Monsieur Poydras. But dat be an entirely different matter. Come back and see me anytime. I'll have what you want."

Chapter Thirty-Two

Luckily, the police car that had scared the two muggers off did not see Celeste, Mark, or Justin as they stood with their backs against the cemetery wall. The car pulled to the curb on Basin Street at the end of the block, and the two officers got out and headed toward the housing project and the blaring stereo. Apparently, the police were responding to a noise complaint and had not spotted the fleeing muggers or their intended victims.

When he was certain the police had not spotted them, Justin motioned for the party to leave the area. They walked as fast as they could, without breaking into a run. No one spoke a word until they had crossed Basin and Rampart Streets and were back in the relative safety of the French Quarter.

Mark reached out and grabbed Celeste, who was walking ahead of the two men. Pulling her back, he spoke. "Are you crazy?" he demanded. "Whatever possessed you to grab that guy's gun?"

"I knew he couldn't hurt me, Mark."

"What! He had a gun — "

"And I have the ring!" interjected Celeste, holding up her left hand. "Don't you remember the story in the diary about Julien Poydras? When he tried to shoot himself with Emile's dueling pistol?"

Mark could only muster a dumbfounded look in reply.

Justin walked up between them and took them both by the arm. "Come on. We'll talk about it when we get back to my house. The Quarter has big ears."

Upon reaching Justin's home, Mark and Celeste followed Justin into the kitchen and sat down at the dinette table. In silence, Justin passed out beers for everyone then took a seat and began examining the notes he had taken at the tomb of Marie Laveau.

Mark was sullen and looked worried as he stared down at his beer. Finally, Celeste broke the silence. "What's it say, Granddad?"

Justin looked up from his notes. "There are two or three words here I'm not sure of. I need to get my old French dictionary to translate them."

Celeste stood up. "I'll get it."

When Celeste had left the kitchen, Justin reached across the table and squeezed Mark's hand. "Don't worry, Mark. We'll get her out of this. We're very close now to havin' the answers we need."

Mark nodded but didn't look up. Nevertheless, Justin still caught sight of a single tear rolling down his cheek. "I feel like I'm losing her, Justin. First these lovemaking dreams with a dead man, then tonight… Celeste is becoming someone I don't know — someone else entirely."

Justin opened his mouth to reassure Mark, but at that moment Celeste came back into the kitchen. All he could do was squeeze Mark's hand again to comfort him.

With aid of the dictionary, it took Justin only a few minutes to complete his translation of the curse. "I believe I have it," he announced.

"We're all ears, Granddad."

Reading from his notes, Justin said, "The first line says, 'Mix in a bottle, bad vinegar, beef gall, gumbo filé, red pepper and… the blood of the goat without horns.'"

"Meaning the blood of a sacrificed child?" asked Celeste.

"Yes, the blood of a white child."

Mark joined the discussion by asking Justin, "Do you think Celeste is right? That the blood of the little girl who wrote on the tomb was used to make the ring?"

"We can't be certain," answered Justin. "My guess is that the ghost of the child represents either that child or another child sacrificed by Marie Laveau."

"What's the next line say?" Celeste prompted.

Justin looked back at his notes and continued, "Write the victim's name three times across each other — superimposed — and place them in the bottle."

"Victim?" puzzled Celeste. Answering her own question, she declared, "Emile Poydras!"

Justin nodded and continued reading his translation. "The next part says, 'Shake the bottle nine times and tell it what to do.'"

"Tell it to do *what?*" queried Mark.

"It's not specified," replied Justin. "The final section says to bury the bottle breast or chest deep in the cemetery — upside down. The last words are, 'Then the victim will be forever yours, upon his death.'"

"That must be a reference to Emile's spirit being trapped in the ring," added Celeste. "But how is the curse going to help us unless we know what the third part means? We don't know what Marie Laveau told the bottle to do."

"No, we don't," agreed Justin. "But I'll wager Mama Vance does. We'll take what we have to her first thing in the morning."

***

Celeste slept soundly that night, not dreaming at all. When she awoke, she lay in bed reflecting on the events at the cemetery. She surmised her grandfather was correct when he suggested she had acted out her dream while they were at Marie Laveau's tomb.

Later that morning, while Celeste was brushing her teeth, it occurred to her that she had not experienced the first part of her dream, where she makes love to Emile Poydras. Although she admitted it to no one else, Celeste felt somewhat cheated or disappointed about missing her lovemaking with Emile.

After a quick breakfast of sweet rolls and coffee, the group climbed into Justin's BMW and headed for Bayou Fatma. The bayou and Mama Vance's dilapidated old house did not look nearly as foreboding in the bright morning sunlight. Celeste thought it hard to believe that it had only been three days since her first visit to Mama Vance's. It seemed like weeks had gone by, so much had happened in those three days. Celeste felt so different now. When she first came to Mama Vance, Celeste had been absolutely desperate to get rid of the ring and put an end to her nightmares. Now, she felt at ease with herself — and her dreams. The thought crossed her mind that she would miss having her dreams, at least the ones with Emile. She even wondered if it might be foolish to give up the power and protection the ring could provide her and Mark.

They found Mama Vance as they had left her, sitting in her rocking chair. Her bizarre companion, Cupid, was not to be seen, and for that Celeste was grateful.

The thought of Cupid leering at her again was the thing Celeste had dreaded most about returning to Mama Vance's house.

Because of the summer heat, Mama Vance had unbuttoned the front of her housedress. There, between her withered breasts, hung the massive gold necklace. Mama Vance's state of undress made Mark uncomfortable. Celeste noticed he diverted his eyes from Mama Vance's exposed chest. Justin, on the other hand, focused on the necklace, as if he were trying to commit its design to memory.

Celeste gazed at the necklace as well. It was a truly impressive piece of jewelry. Its heavy links and ropes of gold were attached to a massive gold counterpoise in the shape of a lotus. The counterpoise was inlaid with red and blue lapis lazuli. It was also inscribed with columns of Egyptian hieroglyphics.

Mama Vance acted as if she had been expecting their arrival. She pointed to the kitchen chairs that had been set out for their use, and she made no effort to button her dress. After the amenities had been disposed of, Justin pulled out his translation of the curse. When he began to read Mama Vance his English translation, she stopped him and asked for the original Creole. Justin complied in a halting cadence.

When the reading of the curse was completed, Mama Vance gave no response, except to begin rocking in her chair.

Finally, Justin asked, "This is the curse you asked for?"

"Oui, Monsieur Noyan. It be de curse of Marie Laveau."

"Do you know what it means, Mama Vance?" asked Celeste. "I mean — the part about telling the bottle what to do."

"But, of course, ma chérie…. Marie simply told de bottle ta capture Emile Poydras's soul for her as soon as it start ta leave his body."

"Capture it and put it in his ring," added Justin.

"Exactly, Monsieur Noyan. Dhat where de soul of Emile Poydras now reside."

"But how did Marie Laveau know how or when Emile would meet his death?" asked Celeste.

"Perhaps, she not know for certain, ma chérie? Maybe she know de ring no longer protect him after he steal it back? Anyways, despite her curse, it was your family dhat ended up with de ring, not Marie Laveau."

"But, Mama Vance?" queried Mark. "I'm confused. If Emile took the ring back and thought he had killed Marie in the process, how did she survive to curse the ring and Emile?"

There was a long pause before Mama Vance responded to Mark's question. Finally, she stopped her rocker and replied. "You always full of de questions, Monsieur Richards, eh? You need not know all de answers. Suffice it ta say Marie was still protected by de ring's power when Emile and his brother try ta kill her."

"Mama Vance?" asked Justin. "Now that we have the curse, is there any way to safely release my granddaughter from the ring?"

Mama Vance nodded. "Oui, Monsieur Noyan. But, ta do so, we must also free Emile Poydras's soul from de ring."

"We understand that," agreed Justin.

"Do you also understand what de 'goat without horns' be?" asked Mama Vance.

"We do," replied Justin.

"No stronger curse exists dhan one based on de blood of de goat without horns. Ta break such a curse, one must also use de sacrificed blood."

"What!" interrupted Mark. "Are you saying we must sacrifice a child to break the curse on the ring?"

Mama Vance stopped rocking again and raised her voice in reply, "You must use de blood of de lamb — no matter what we attempt, I can do nothin' about dhat!"

"Please, Mama Vance?" interposed Justin. "We mean no disrespect. Just bear with us for a moment.... Suppose we could get the blood, you said, 'no matter what we attempt.' Are you sayin' we have options on how to break the curse?"

Justin's plea seemed to settle the ire of Mama Vance. She settled back in her chair and began rocking again. "Oui, Monsieur Noyan. Only, both options require de blood."

"What are the options?" asked Celeste.

"De only way I can guarantee your survival, ma chérie, is ta create a new charm of protection ta replace de ring of Emile Poydras."

"You could make such a charm?" asked Justin.

"Oui."

Remembering what Mama Vance had told them on their first visit, that the secret of making life charms died with Sanité Diable, Justin considered asking Mama Vance if she had made such a charm before but thought better of it.

Feeling bewildered, Mark entreated, "Please, Mama Vance. Don't get me wrong. I truly appreciate you trying to help us. But… how will trading one charm for another help Celeste?"

"De new charm will be free of de spirit of Emile Poydras," answered Mama Vance. "It be his spirit dhat entered de dreams of your wife."

"So, what's the other option?" asked Justin.

"You follow de plan given ta Celeste in her dream…. You must return de ring ta Marie Laveau in a conjure ceremony on All Saint's Eve."

"You said the only way to 'guarantee' Celeste's survival is by creatin' another charm. Are you sayin' the conjure ceremony is more of a risk?" continued Justin. "Or are you uncertain it will release Celeste from the spirit of Emile Poydras?"

"No, Monsieur Noyan. Dhat is not my concern…. I be afraid dhat she may not be strong enough ta survive de ceremony."

Chapter Thirty-Three

Due to the preparations for the Duke of Orleans's visit to Pointe Coupee, Emile was not able to remain in New Orleans to determine firsthand the results of the charm he had purchased from Dr. Beauregard. However, true to the promise of the Voodoo doctor, three days after Emile dropped the charm bag into the Mississippi River, Aurora Béluche left Anton Cuvillier. Anton returned to their empty cottage in Treme' to find only a terse note from Aurora saying that their love affair was over, and that she had returned to her mother's home.

When Aurora refused to see him or reply to his letters, Anton became desperate. Being without Aurora made him realize how hopelessly in love he was with her. Anton racked his brain to figure out what could have happened to cause Aurora to leave. They had seemed so happy together. In fact, the day before Aurora left had been the most joyous day of their relationship. Anton and Aurora had talked of having children, and Anton had even promised to recognize them as his legitimate heirs. Hence, Anton could not imagine any offense he had committed — certainly none that would cause Aurora to suddenly leave him without explanation. He had offered her all that he had short of marriage — which was out of the question.

Finally, Anton's desperation drove him to seek out Sanité Dédé — queen of the Voodooiennes. Anton was determined to make Aurora love him again, no matter what the price.

***

The visit of the Duke of Orleans and his two brothers to Pointe Coupee was a great success and a real social triumph for Julien. Julien felt a common bond with the exiled duke and made a generous contribution to his royalist cause. Following the duke's departure for Havana and Spain, Julien and his nephews remained at Pointe Coupee. Julien, Emile, and Benjamin toured all six of Julien's plantations, and Emile was given the task of helping educate Benjamin in the operations and management of Julien's plantations and other businesses. During this busy period,

Emile and Benjamin's visits to New Orleans were infrequent. Out of respect for Julien and his wishes, Emile avoided all contact with Anton during his trips to the city. However, friends had written him that Aurora had left Anton, but the realization that Aurora had betrayed him for Anton killed all ardor Emile had felt for her.

Even so, it was with surprise and some chagrin when Emile next saw Anton. For holding on to Anton's right arm was Aurora, beautiful as ever. Emile felt fortunate that he was across the dance floor of the Théatre d'Orléans. He had no desire to confront the couple, as he had promised Julien he would not provoke a duel with Anton.

It had been six years since Emile had seen either Anton or Aurora. So much had happened in those six years. It seemed like a lifetime ago. Julien's dream of seeing the Duke of Orleans restore the monarchy was dashed by Napoleon's coup of 1799. The duke was now exiled in England. It was the fifth year of the new century, and New France was now the territory of the United States of America as a result of the Louisiana Purchase of 1803.

Emile even found himself longing for Spanish rule once more. The Spanish at least acted with civility — most of the time. But the American heathen that came down the Mississippi appalled Emile. He regretted the day the river was opened to the Americans — no matter how much his uncle Julien was making trading with the new United States.

Over the past six years, Emile and Anton had maintained an unspoken détente and scrupulously avoided all contact. When Emile visited New Orleans, their "seconds" would meet to make sure the men's social schedules did not overlap. Anton had instructed his second to always defer to Emile's schedule. He wanted to make sure Emile had no opportunities to issue another challenge. In public, Anton might be compelled to accept Emile's challenge — depending on how Emile chose to issue it.

Emile had understood that Anton was not to be in attendance at this particular quadroon soirée. And to make matters even worse, there were far too many boorish Americans at the ball.

Being too stubborn to retreat from the ball, Emile thought a good tactic would be to step out back of the ballroom for a cigar. As fate would have it, Anton had decided on the same tactic. Emile found himself at a loss for words as he and Anton practically bumped into each other behind the Théatre d'Orléans. The men stared at each other, and each blinked in surprise. Finally, taking the initiative, Emile spoke first. "Monsieur Cuvillier, I understood you would not be attending this ball."

"I had no such understanding, monsieur," countered Anton. "In fact, I was informed this ball was not listed on your calendar."

As Emile turned and started to march off, Anton had a change of heart. "Emile, please wait! Is there no way we can end this feud?"

Stopping, but not turning to face Anton, Emile replied, "There is no way to forgive such betrayal."

"I can forgive, Emile. Why can't you? We were good comrades, once."

Spinning around, Emile shot back. "That's exactly my point, Anton. We *were* friends. And what do you mean by saying you can forgive me? I did not betray your trust and friendship. I harmed no one!"

"What do you call placing a Voodoo curse on an innocent woman?" Seeing Emile's surprised expression as confirmation of his misdeed, Anton continued, "What? You didn't know I found out about Dr. Beauregard's curse?"

"I… I did not know," admitted Emile. Emile felt like a schoolboy again, caught in misbehavior by his schoolmaster. "After seeing the two of you together tonight, I assumed nothing came of it. How did you find out?"

"From Sanité Dédé. I purchased a love philter from her to win back Aurora's affections."

"But how did she know? No one saw me with Dr. Beauregard."

"Emile, there are no secrets among the Voodooiennes — at least not from their queen."

Emile took a drag off his cigar and nodded his head. "Of course, of course, I should have guessed. But no matter. It seems the fates are with you and Aurora."

Anton held out his hand and said, "It's been six years, Emile. Isn't it time to put all this strife behind us?… No doubt you have been in love with other women since Aurora."

Emile looked at Anton's outstretched palm with disdain. "You don't understand, do you, Anton? It was never Aurora herself. What killed our friendship was you taking up with her — knowing that I still longed for her."

"But I didn't know, Emile! Aurora said your relationship had ended — that you stopped corresponding with her."

Emile nodded his head and replied contritely, "I know that, Anton. Nevertheless, you should have confirmed that with me."

"Emile, you hardly knew her," Anton answered with a sigh. "What will it take for you to forgive me, Emile? What is your price?"

There was an uncomfortable pause before Emile replied. He looked at his feet and finally raised his head to answer, "Oh, Anton, truth be told, it is I who should be asking your forgiveness. Except, it isn't in me to do so. Pride is a vicious mistress, Anton. So, let us accept our circumstances and acknowledge we can never be friends again."

"All right, Emile, so be it. But we don't have to be enemies, do we?"

"Anton, nothing has changed between us. I advise you to refrain from speaking of me and to avoid all encounters with me in public. Otherwise, I may be obliged to reissue my challenge." With that final rejoinder, Emile threw down his cigar, crushed it out with the heel of his boot, and walked off.

Chapter Thirty-Four

After Mama Vance warned Celeste about the risk of a conjure ceremony, silence fell over the group. Finally, Celeste got up her courage and asked, "What do you mean, Mama Vance? Why shouldn't I be strong enough to survive the ceremony?"

"Give me your hand, ma chérie."

As Celeste complied with Mama Vance's request, she began to feel weak — like she was a battery being drained of its power. Celeste also sensed her feelings of anxiousness and apprehension dissipate. It was as if all her emotions were being pulled from her body. As on her first visit, Mama Vance let go of Celeste's hand at the exact moment Celeste felt she was going to pass out.

Mama Vance gave Celeste a moment to recover her wits, and then said, "I feel your love for Emile Poydras, ma chérie. I sense you may not want ta give him up."

Celeste caught her breath, but she knew she could not deny Mama Vance's revelations. She was at a loss for a response.

Finally, Mark intervened. "What are you talking about, Mama Vance? Celeste is terrified of her dreams. That's why we came to you — to free Celeste from these nightmares."

Mama Vance ignored Mark's pronouncement and looked directly at Celeste. The old woman's vacant eyes suddenly came to life when she spoke. "You know what I mean, ma chérie. Don't you? You must give him up ta free yourself — and ta free his spirit. If you not strong enough ta give up Emile, you could die and your spirit be lost too."

"How is that?" asked Justin.

"Once de spirits be called forth, dhey must be reckoned with, or your granddaughter will surely die."

"I still don't understand?" persisted Justin.

"I fear dhat when de ceremony begin — and she start ta feel Emile Poydras' spirit separate from her — her passion for Emile may cause her ta stop or leave de ceremony."

"And not completin' the ceremony will kill her?" asked Justin.

"Oui, it kill her for sure."

Turning to face Celeste, Justin asked, "Do you understand what Mama Vance is sayin', sugar?" Celeste nodded her head without looking up at her grandfather. "Can you go through with the ceremony? Is there any doubt in your mind?"

Celeste looked up at Justin. Tears were rising in her eyes. She felt simultaneously conflicted, guilty, and ashamed. But it wasn't just her connection to Emile's spirit that was causing her doubt. She also relished the feeling of power the ring gave her. Turning to look at Mark — and seeing the hurt expression on his face — made Celeste feel all the more chagrined.

"I can do it," she declared. "I *want* to do it! But it must be soon. I'm not sure how much longer I'll be able to control myself. I don't think I can hang on until Halloween."

"All Saint's Eve is over four months away," said Justin. "Must we wait until then, Mama Vance? I share Celeste's concerns about delayin' things that long."

Mama Vance rocked faster, thought a moment, and answered. "No, I think not. De spirits are most active on All Saint's Eve. But St. John's Eve dis month. De spirits very frisky den too. I can summon dhem dhat night, provided you can furnish de blood of de goat without horns."

Justin let out a sigh and asked, "How much blood do we need?"

"Not too much. A pint or so will be a plenty. Just make sure it be fresh and from an innocent white girl child at de time she die."

Standing up to take his leave, Justin declared, "We'll get the blood, Mama Vance. Then we'll be back."

When they were back in the car heading home, everyone was silent. Finally, Celeste got up the courage to ask, "Granddad? Where are we going to get the blood of an innocent white girl?"

"I don't know, for sure. But I'll get it. We've come too far to give up now…. Just let me worry about gettin' it."

Wishing to change the subject, Celeste asked, "What did you make of her necklace?"

"It made me think of the necklace of Sanité Diable. You know, the gold necklace Julien Poydras described to Emile?"

"You mean the charm necklace Sanité Diable dropped the day Julien saved her life?" asked Mark.

"Exactly," answered Justin. "The necklace that's the Voodoo queen's charm of protection."

"Wait a minute," continued Mark. "You're not saying Mama Vance is Sanité Diable?"

"No, could be, but I think not. Supposedly, the necklace contained the secret incantations of eternal life, but I find it hard to believe anyone could live that long — no matter what kind of charm they had.... One thing struck me as odd though. When I was re-readin' the diary, I noticed Sanité Diable changed her name to Sanité Dédé."

"Why did she do that?" inquired Celeste.

"The diary doesn't say. Emile merely states that years after Julien received the ring, he went lookin' for Sanité Diable — tryin' to obtain a charm for Emile. When Julien found her, she was goin' by the name Sanité Dédé."

"Why would a Voodoo queen give up her name?" continued Celeste. "Their names and reputations were big assets to the queens."

"I suppose there could be many reasons," offered Justin. "Trouble with the law, fear of other queens. Or maybe people were beginnin' to wonder about Sanité Diable."

"How do you mean?" asked Mark.

"My father told me that ring not only gives eternal life and protection, but it retards the agin' process as well. Sanité Diable's necklace no doubt had the same properties."

"So, people probably began to wonder why Sanité Diable didn't age?" suggested Celeste.

"Exactly, maybe too many outsiders were askin' too many questions about why she never looked much older."

"And she changed her identity to throw 'em off the track," added Mark.

"It's possible," concluded Justin.

"Well," Mark continued, "Mama Vance sure has aged. No one would say she doesn't look her..." Mark caught himself before he finished his sentence.

Justin uttered a cross between a snort and a laugh and finished Mark's sentence for him. "Look her *age*, Mark? I don't know. How is someone that may be over two hundred years old supposed to look?"

Chapter Thirty-Five

When Emile and Benjamin docked their barge in New Orleans on the afternoon of October 27, 1811, they were informed that their uncle Julien's ship from Washington DC had arrived the day before, three days early.

Julien had just completed a term as congressman for the Territory of Orleans. Now, at the request of the territorial governor, Charles Cole Claiborne, Julien had returned to New Orleans for the territorial statehood convention. Beginning November 5, 1811, the convention was to meet to vote on the issue of statehood. If the vote was in the affirmative, a name was to be chosen, and a constitution drawn up for the 18th state of the Union.

Unlike many Creoles, Julien had welcomed the American administration of the territory, and he was wholeheartedly in favor of statehood. Julien's many enterprises prospered greatly under the American free trade policies, and as a Protestant in a land of Catholics, he appreciated the freedom of worship that came with the American government.

At the age of sixty-five, Julien Poydras was still a vital and vigorous man. In fact, he didn't look a day over forty-five or fifty. He would have passed for an even younger age but for his graying hair. Julien was still a bachelor though, and his marital status wasn't the only thing Julien refused to change. Through his entire term in Congress and after, Julien persisted in dressing like a member of the Court of Louis the XV. Even though knee breeches and queues had been out of fashion for at least twenty years, that was how Julien was dressed when Emile and Benjamin entered his home in New Orleans. His nephews had long since given up trying to convince Julien to convert to trousers.

Emile and Benjamin found their uncle gathering up papers from his desk as they entered his study.

"Uncle Julien," greeted Benjamin, "we did not expect you for another two days."

"Yes," added Emile, "you must have made record time. We regret that we weren't here to meet you."

Julien dropped his handful of papers on the desk and came out from behind it to hug both of his nephews. Though Emile was nearly thirty-nine, and Benjamin had turned thirty-five, Julien persisted in doting on them. "No apologies are necessary, my dear boys. It is good to see you both looking so well. How are things at Pointe Coupee?"

"We are having record harvests," answered Emile. "And your bank continues to prosper. I think you will be pleased with our stewardship."

"I have no doubt about that. But tell me? Has the fever epidemic reached Pointe Coupee?"

"Fortunately not," replied Benjamin. "But it has taken a heavy toll in New Orleans. I am told there have been over 240 deaths this month alone. They are calling it the saffron scourge."

"Yes indeed," confirmed Julien. "It may even delay the start of the statehood convention. In fact, I am on my way now to meet with Governor Claiborne about the convention."

"We won't delay you, Uncle," said Emile. "But please tell us. Is it true what you said to Congressman Quincy? The newspapers reported you called Massachusetts the witchcraft state, and that you said more ignorance and cruelty was tolerated in Quincy's state than any other part of North America."

"I did say those things," demurred Julien. "And I rather regret it now. However, Josiah Quincy threatened to lead Massachusetts from the Union if we were admitted. Then, on the floor of Congress, he raved and ranted about our citizens being 'heathens of that swamp country,' and that we were no better than apes or alligators."

"Then the tongue lashing you gave the scoundrel was well deserved," said Emile.

"And apparently very effective," agreed Benjamin, "as Congress passed your Enabling Act by a wide margin."

"Let us hope the citizens of the territory are as easily persuaded to vote for statehood. There is still much resentment of the Americans here."

"It would have helped if they had sent us a governor who at least spoke some French," added Emile.

"I agree," said Julien. "But Governor Claiborne is a good and honest man. We could do much worse. At any rate, I must leave for my meeting with him. Can we continue our discussions at dinner tonight?"

***

Because of the yellow fever epidemic, the Territorial Convention did not convene until November 18, 1811. Julien was the overwhelming choice for chairman of the convention. Due in part to Julien's popular leadership, in short order the convention voted in favor of statehood and chose Louisiana as the name for their new state.

By Christmas of 1811, proposed constitutions were being debated by the convention. The state's constitution was one of the most popular topics of conversation at Governor Claiborne's Christmas party that year. The other topic on most guests' minds was the possibility of another war with Great Britain. Julien and his nephews were discussing that very possibility with Governor Claiborne as they left the dining room to join the guests who had commenced dancing in the velvet draped ballroom.

"The English would not dare to go to war with America," offered the governor. "Not with Napoleon in control of Europe and threatening to invade Russia."

Emile had a generally low opinion of Charles Cole Claiborne. He found the thirty-six-year-old governor egotistical and vain, despite his rather plain appearance. But Emile agreed with Claiborne on the subject of challenging Great Britain to war. "I agree, sir. The English have their hands full dealing with the armies of France. If America declares war on England, they will mend their ways."

"The great Emperor Bonaparte has been no match for the English Navy," admonished Julien. "The English Fleet has swept the French Navy from all the seas. The few war ships America has cannot even begin to protect our major ports, let alone protect our merchant ships on the high seas."

"What would... vous avez... you have us do, Uncle?" queried Benjamin, struggling to speak English for the governor's sake. "We cannot allow the British to board our merchant ships and continue to impress our sailors. Are you accepting of the British dictating what countries you may freely trade with?"

"No one dislikes the English more than I," rejoined Julien with a stern tone in his voice. "You forget, as a young man I was taken from my ship and imprisoned by them. I am simply suggesting that before we declare war, we should be prepared to fight it."

Emile started to make another point in favor of challenging the British to war when his attention was diverted by activity on the dance floor.

Near the edge of the dance floor was an obviously intoxicated man attempting to dance with a young girl. The man appeared to be in his mid-thirties, while his petite partner didn't look a day over thirteen or fourteen. The man was so inebriated that he kept stumbling over his inexperienced partner's feet. What diverted Emile's attention was an outburst from the man when he stumbled and nearly fell.

"Damn you! Watch your step!" the man bellowed.

"Who the devil is that?" asked Emile.

Governor Claiborne sighed and softly answered, "Henri Noyan and his wife, Nicole."

"Wife!" exclaimed Emile. "Surely you jest? She's just a child."

"She's fully fifteen years of age," replied the governor. "They were married last month."

"Was it an arranged marriage?" asked Julien.

"You are correct, Julien. I've heard that the wedding date was accelerated because Henri Noyan was in need of the bride's dowry."

"No doubt Monsieur Noyan has wasted no time in restocking his wine cellar," scoffed Emile.

"His wife is certainly beautiful," offered Benjamin. "Her chestnut hair and fair skin remind me of the girls back in Nantes."

"Yes," agreed Emile. "If that stumbling oaf doesn't fall and crush her, she will no doubt grow into a true beauty."

No sooner had Emile finished speaking than the drunken Henri Noyan did in fact fall on his rump. His face beet red from drink and anger, Henri jumped to his feet and slapped his young bride's face. The sharp crack of the blow halted the other dancers and directed the attention of the entire room to the scene. Observing all the aghast expressions, Henri Noyan yelled, "What are you all looking at!" With that, he stomped out of the hall, leaving the embarrassed Nicole stranded in the middle of the dance floor.

When the bewildered Nicole remained frozen on the dance floor, Emile started to go to her aid. However, he held up after taking only a step, for another gentleman had come forward to offer Nicole his arm. Emile silently cursed when he recognized the gentleman as none other than Anton Cuvillier.

Chapter Thirty-Six

That evening, after their last visit with Mama Vance, Justin found the following article on the local page of the Times-Picayune:

Hit and Run Victim Near Death

Ten-year-old Elizabeth Villere was run down in a crosswalk on her way home from school. The collision occurred at 3:30 p.m. Tuesday at the intersection of Bonnabel and Homer. Two of Elizabeth's classmates, the only witnesses to the mishap, reported Elizabeth was struck by an older model, red pickup truck. The driver left the scene without stopping.

Elizabeth, the daughter of Charles and Evon Villere of Metairie, was rushed by ambulance to the trauma center at Metairie General Hospital, where she underwent emergency surgery for six hours. Elizabeth remains in a coma, and her doctors fear that she has suffered irreversible brain damage.

Friends of the Villere family report that no decision on the termination of Elizabeth's life support systems will be made until her parents are convinced that their child cannot recover.

The hit and run driver is believed to be a white male with dark hair. The witnesses' opinions on the driver's age varied from twenty-five to forty years old. Anyone with information concerning the driver or vehicle that struck Elizabeth is urged to contact the Metairie Police Department.

Accompanying the newspaper article was a school photo of Elizabeth Villere. Even though the newspaper printed the photograph in black and white, Justin could tell Elizabeth had fair skin and light brown or dark blond hair. She was in fact a beautiful child. Justin circled the article and photograph with a blue ballpoint pen. Then he separated the page from the rest of the paper, folded it, and placed it in his jacket pocket.

After a cold-cuts dinner in the kitchen, Justin excused himself from Celeste and Mark's company, saying he was going to the hospital to visit a sick friend.

Mark had been moody ever since they'd left Mama Vance's house. He hardly conversed during dinner or the remainder of the evening. Celeste suspected she knew the reason for his withdrawn disposition, but she was reluctant to bring up the subject. Finally, after she got ready for bed, Celeste decided she could not ignore the situation any longer.

Finding Mark in bed, his face buried in a copy of *Sports Illustrated*, Celeste asked, "Mark, honey? What's wrong? You've hardly said a word all evening."

Without removing his face from the magazine, Mark replied, "Nothing's wrong. I'm just tired."

Dropping her inquiry for the time being, Celeste finished brushing her hair. When she climbed into bed, she gently pulled the magazine away from Mark's face. "That must be some article, babe. You haven't turned a page in over five minutes."

Mark gave her a hesitant smile. "Okay, you want to know what's on my mind? I'll tell you.... I find myself feeling jealous of a man who's been dead for over a hundred and fifty years. At first, I told myself, hey, that's stupid. But today — at Mama Vance's — I saw it in your face. You really are in love with him? At least with his fucking ghost. Yeah, that's it. I've been shot out of the saddle by a fucking ghost."

"Well, you know what they say, babe," Celeste said as she leaned over and switched off Mark's bed lamp. "If you get knocked off your horse, the best thing you can do is get right back in the saddle and ride her again." With that, Celeste's head disappeared under the sheet, and Mark forgot all about being jealous of the ghost of Emile Poydras. After making love twice, Celeste and Mark fell asleep, exhausted, in each other's arms.

Celeste did dream that night, but her dream took a new and puzzling turn. It began as always, in Emile's bed, though he was not making love to her. They were sitting up in bed. Emile was squeezing her hand, talking to her with an imploring tone in his voice.

It was as if Celeste had just come to in the middle of Emile's speech, for she couldn't comprehend what he was talking about. He was saying, "Don't let it happen to you! Don't let him take it. Promise me, you won't let him take it!"

Then, before she could ask Emile for an explanation, Celeste found herself in the cemetery again. But this time, she was stark naked, and there was a bright bonfire beside her. Suddenly, Mama Vance was there with a huge, hissing python in her hands. She was motioning for Celeste to take the snake as she approached.

Celeste wanted to run, but her legs wouldn't budge. She opened her mouth to scream, but nothing came out.

Out of nowhere came Mark's voice, yelling, "Run, Celeste! Run! Call the police!"

The crash of Mark's bed lamp as it shattered against the floor made Celeste realize she was no longer dreaming. That Mark was not shouting to her in her dream world, but in their dark bedroom.

Bolting up in bed, Celeste could make out the forms of two men struggling and thrashing at each other on the floor at Mark's side of the bed. Lunging for her bed table, Celeste snapped on the light. The light coming on diverted Mark's attention from his adversary to Celeste. Again, he yelled, "Run! Run! He's after your —"

Mark never finished his warning to Celeste, for the other man picked up the base of the broken lamp and smashed it into the side of Mark's head, knocking him unconscious.

Celeste wanted to scream when she saw who was standing over Mark's limp body. But she froze, like in her dream, when she recognized Cupid, Mama Vance's tongueless servant. All Celeste could do was pull the sheet up over her exposed breasts and mutter, "No! No! Please, don't hurt us."

Cupid looked down at the floor, took a step, and bent over, retrieving a long butcher knife he had lost in the struggle with Mark. Pulling back his lips in a hideous grin, exposing his sharp canine teeth, Cupid started for Celeste's side of the bed.

Celeste never saw what happened next. She fainted from fright before Cupid reached her.

Chapter Thirty-Seven

In June 1812, only a few weeks after Louisiana was admitted to the Union, the United States went to war with Great Britain for the second time. President Madison, and the southern and western War Hawks who controlled the Twelfth Congress, led America into a war that nearly brought about the dissolution of the fledging United States of America.

The war was fervently resented in New England and Louisiana, where the English naval blockade had a devastating effect on commerce and shipping. The Creoles were already resentful of the Americans, calling all the newcomers "Kanitucks" — the lowest of the low. But when the Kanitucks forced the citizens of New Orleans into a war, their resentment began to turn into hatred.

To make matters worse, the war was not going well on any front for the Americans. The attempted conquest of British Canada was an abject failure. By December 1814, the British had already captured and burned Washington DC and were massing for the conquest of New Orleans. A New England convention to discuss secession and a separate peace with Great Britain was scheduled to begin December 15, 1814, in Hartford, Connecticut. The unspoken consensus of the nation was that the Union could not survive another defeat at the hands of the English. If New Orleans fell, it would be a deathblow for the United States of America.

Unlike many Creoles, Emile and Benjamin enlisted in the local militia. They joined, not out of real patriotism or great loyalty to the United States, but out of necessity. If the British had burned the nation's capital, they were likely to do the same to New Orleans and the surrounding plantations. While they held the Americans in contempt, their French blood boiled at the thought of any Englishman putting to the torch what they and their uncle Julien had worked so long and hard to build.

Andrew Jackson, military commander for all US territory from the Ohio to the Gulf of Mexico, came to New Orleans to take charge of the city's defenses on December 1, 1814. General Jackson was seen as another Kanituck who spoke not a word of French. When he asked Governor Claiborne for a local interpreter to be assigned to his staff, the governor called on the newly commissioned Captain Emile Poydras.

Both Emile and Benjamin had learned to speak English at their uncle's insistence. Julien had told them they need not like the Americans to do business with them, but they must learn their language if they wanted to make a profit off them.

Emile was taken aback on his first meeting with Andrew Jackson. A product of the American frontier, Jackson was tall and lank to the point of emaciation. No one would ever call him handsome. At age forty-eight, he had light blue, what-d'ya-want eyes, light brown hair, a pump-handle chin, and a long thin mouth that looked like it had been cut out with a knife. Emile thought he looked more like an executioner than a general and former Justice of Tennessee's highest court.

On the afternoon of December 23, 1814, when Emile was ushered into the general's quarters at 106 Royal Street, he found Jackson preparing to leave for an inspection of the city's defenses. Instead of a uniform gleaming with medals and gold braid, the Commander of the Seventh Military District wore a short Spanish cloak and uniform of faded blue cloth, devoid of insignia and decoration. A worn leather cap was on his head, and his boots were mud spattered and too large for his scarecrow legs. Emile looked more like a general in his shimmering blue and silver uniform of the Feliciana Dragoons.

Jackson took one look at Emile standing at attention in his dapper uniform and grinned. Then he asked, "Who in blazes are you?"

"Captain Poydras, sir."

"Who?"

"The new interpreter you asked Gov — "

"Oh, yes. Stand at ease, Captain. The governor didn't tell me he was sending such a dashing cavalry officer…. Have you seen any combat, Captain?"

"I'm afraid not, sir — I only received my commission two months ago."

Nodding his head, Jackson replied, "No matter. Most of the men in my command have yet to taste battle. You just make sure your local militia units understand my orders."

"Yes, sir."

"Come along, Captain Poydras. I was just on my way to inspect the fortifications on the Chef Menteur Road. The British fleet has taken Lake Borgne, and that road leads straight into the city from — "

General Jackson didn't finish his sentence. He was interrupted by a loud commotion outside his quarters. Both he and Emile heard an excited man yelling in French just outside the door. Directly, one of the general's guards came in.

"Sorry to bust in, General. But there's a couple of ravin' Frenchies out here demandin' to see ya. And I cain't make head nor tails tah what they're sayin'."

"Well, show 'em in, Sergeant." Turning to Emile, Jackson added, "Here's where you start earning your pay, Captain."

Emile immediately recognized the two men who flew through the open door. One was Major Gabriel Villeré, son of General Villeré, commander of the New Orleans Militia. The other was a merchant, Dussau de la Croix.

Gabriel Villeré was not in uniform. In fact, he was barely dressed, considering the cold and rainy weather. All he had on were trousers and a torn shirt, both of which were wet and covered with mud. He looked as though he had been dragged or chased through the swamp. It was apparent the men had run all the way to General Jackson's quarters, for both were nearly breathless when they entered.

Recognizing Emile, Major Villeré ignored the general and launched into a rapid, animated narrative in French. Soon, all three men were talking excitedly — in French — all at the same time.

General Jackson quickly tired of being excluded from the conversation and bellowed, "Christ Almighty! Will someone tell me what the hell you all are jabbering about?"

The general's oath silenced all the other men, and Emile answered, "It's the English, sir. They've captured the Villeré plantation. Major Villeré here barely escaped through the swamp to warn us."

Jackson's face turned pale. "What? The Villeré plantation. Why that's only..."

Emile finished the sentence for him, "Only seven miles downriver, sir."

The room fell silent again. Every man in it realized that the advance guard of the largest foreign army to invade American soil was less than half a day's march from New Orleans, and there wasn't a single American soldier between the British and their objective. The general had never dreamed the British Army could make it through the cypress swamps between Lake Borgne and the Mississippi. Now the English could march right along the levee and bypass all the fortifications Jackson had built along the Chef Menteur Road.

For what seemed like an eternity to Emile, Andrew Jackson stood silently before them, ramrod stiff, a blank expression on his face. Abruptly, he grabbed his saber from his desk and slammed it into his scabbard.

"By God, gentlemen!" he cried. "We'll fight them tonight! Right now!"

Chapter Thirty-Eight

When Celeste came to, both Justin and Mark were standing over her bed. Mark was holding a bloody hand towel against the side of his head, while Justin — still wearing his wet raincoat — wiped her forehead with a cool, damp washcloth.

Seeing Celeste's eyes flicker, Justin spoke first, "Celeste, honey? It's okay now. He's gone."

"Yeah, babe," Mark added. "It's all over. He didn't hurt you, did he?"

As she came back to consciousness, Celeste was still too addled to recall what or who Mark and Justin were talking about. Then suddenly the image of Cupid — his grotesque grimace — flashed across her mind. Celeste's whole body went rigid, and she let out a loud gasp for air.

Mark knelt down and took hold of her hand and gently squeezed it. "It's alright, babe. There's no one here but us."

Celeste sat up and threw her arms around Mark's neck, inspecting his wound as she hugged him. "Oh, Mark. You're bleeding. He hit you with the lamp! Are you okay?"

Mark shrugged it off. "It's nothing. Just a little scalp wound. It looks a whole lot worse than it is."

Becoming aware of her nakedness, Celeste sat back in bed and covered her chest with a pillow. "What was Cupid doing here?" she asked. "Why would he want to hurt us?"

Instead of answering her, Mark looked at Justin. With hesitation, Justin replied, "It was the ring he was after, Celeste. He's stolen the Poydras ring from you."

Celeste jerked her left hand to her face. When she saw her bare ring finger, she began to sob. "Oh, Granddad, what am I gonna do now?… What am I ever gonna do?"

After a moment of silent deliberation, Justin replied, "Get dressed. We're goin' to Mama Vance's. Right now."

"What!" exclaimed Mark. "She's probably behind the theft."

Justin shook his head. "I don't think so. She has no motive to steal the ring. She has the necklace of Sanité Diable. Besides, she's the only one who can find Cupid for us. We have no choice but to go to her. Come on, let's bandage you up while Celeste gets dressed. We should find Cupid as soon as possible."

***

The sun was just coming up as Justin, Mark, and Celeste left the French Quarter. During the drive to Bayou Fatma, Celeste asked, "How long do you think I have, Granddad?"

"Come again?"

"How… how long do I have to get the ring back… before it's too late?"

"We've got plenty of time," reassured Justin. "The protection of the ring does not dissipate immediately. Remember, Julien Poydras lived several months after giving the ring to Emile."

"And your grandfather Randolph only lived two days after mailing the ring home from World War I."

Justin had no reply to Celeste's rebuttal. He surmised that Celeste was also recalling their ancestors who did not die immediately after losing the ring — Jean Noyan and Julien Poydras suffered long fatal illnesses after giving up the ring. That their deaths were just as certain, only more agonizing and protracted.

"You know," continued Celeste, "Emile tried to warn me in my dream last night…. He told me the ring would be stolen, but I didn't understand him."

Deliberately changing the subject, Mark asked Justin, "What kept you at the hospital so late, Justin? Did your friend take a turn for the worse?"

"You could say that."

"Beg your pardon?"

Justin didn't respond to Mark's question for a moment. As he turned off Highway 23 onto Lapalco Boulevard, Justin replied, "Did you read about the little girl who was run down by a hit-and-run driver two days ago?"

"Seems like I remember hearing something about that on the news last night, why?"

"That's who I went to see."

Realization flashed across Celeste's face. She turned to Justin and asked, "The little girl isn't expected to recover, is she?"

"No. Unfortunately, the child is brain dead. If there is no improvement, her parents plan on turnin' off her respirator the day after tomorrow."

Now Mark caught on. "You talked to the girl's parents about…?"

"Yes, about takin' some of her blood."

"They didn't think you were crazy?" Mark continued.

"I didn't tell them the real reason I wanted the blood. I told Mr. and Mrs. Villere that I was a doctor involved in research on brain trauma…. I also told them I would pay all their funeral expenses in return for the blood."

"And they agreed?" Celeste asked.

"Not at first. Initially, they didn't want to face the reality that their daughter was not goin' to recover. When I told them my research might someday help save some other child, they changed their minds."

"Oh, Granddad," said Celeste, shaking her head. "How could you take advantage of those poor people… I understand you did it for me. But it seems so ghoulish."

"I suppose it is ghoulish. But in my heart, I don't feel that I have taken advantage of them. They can't afford all the medical and funeral expenses for their daughter. And I really didn't lie when I said the blood might help save someone else."

Celeste sighed and shrugged her shoulders. "Well, no matter how you rationalize it, it really doesn't matter now. Without the ring, we won't be needing that poor little girl's blood."

Mark ignored Celeste's pessimistic remark and asked Justin, "How are you going to get the blood? You aren't planning to try and fool the hospital staff with your research story, are you?"

"No. I plan on goin' back to the hospital late tomorrow night and drawin' the blood myself — if the Villeres have made up their mind to terminate the life support."

"You know how to draw blood?" persisted Mark.

"Yes. I was a medic in the Army, durin' World War II."

Justin could sense Celeste becoming tense as they turned onto the bayou road and neared Mama Vance's house. As he parked the BMW, he asked her, "You want to wait here until Mark and I check things out?"

"No, I'll go with you. I'd rather not be alone out here."

Before exiting the car, Justin reached under his seat and pulled out an Army issue Colt .45 caliber pistol. He chambered a round and stuck the weapon in his belt after he stepped out of the car. Mark came out of the backseat carrying a tire iron.

As soon as the group stepped up onto Mama Vance's porch, they sensed something was wrong. The screen door was ajar, and the inner door was wide open. Stepping into the house, they were immediately hit by a strong odor of kerosene. A broken kerosene lamp lay beside the toppled table it had rested on. Mama Vance's overturned rocking chair lay beside the shattered lamp globe.

Pulling his pistol from beneath his shirttail, Justin cautiously entered the kitchen. It too was in shambles. Broken dishes and overturned chairs gave evidence of some violent struggle. But what caught everyone's attention was the kitchen table. It was covered with blood. Puddles of fresh blood were also on the yellow linoleum floor beneath the table. In fact, blood was still dripping onto the floor from the edge of the old oak table. Bloody bare footprints crisscrossed the kitchen floor and led out the back door. In the center of the table, its blade buried in the tabletop, was a blood-smeared hatchet.

Celeste slumped against the kitchen door jamb. "Well," she said, "it looks like Mama Vance won't be helping me or anyone else in this world."

Chapter Thirty-Nine

Jackson's night attack at the Villeré plantation on the evening of December 23, 1814, did catch the British off guard, but it was no rout. The fighting was fierce, and mostly hand-to-hand. Both sides became confused and bewildered in the dark, moonless night. The night mist from the river thickened to a choking consistency as it combined with the gun smoke hanging in the stagnant air. The only light on the battlefield came from the flashes of musket fire.

Eventually, the superior discipline of the British troops turned the tide of the battle, and the Americans were forced to withdraw from the bloodied flood plain. General Jackson pulled his troops back upriver a short distance to the Chalmette plantation. Behind an irrigation ditch known as the Rodriguez Canal, Jackson re-formed his men and prepared a line of defense. Breast works were constructed of mud and bales of cotton, there being no trees or other natural cover in the bare cane fields that comprised the new field of battle. The flat open ground's only covering was the harsh dead stubble of the cut cane.

The engagement of December 23 was at best a draw for the Americans. But it had stalled the advance of the British and misled them into believing that the Americans had a much larger force than in fact there was. In the days that followed, each side reinforced themselves and did their best to prepare fortifications on the soggy, open terrain.

Andrew Jackson set up his headquarters in the Macarté house, which was located a few hundred feet behind the Rodriguez Canal. After attending all day staff meetings there on Christmas Eve, 1814, Emile set out that night in search of Benjamin, who was serving as a company commander with a local volunteer unit known as Beale's Rifles. Walking from campfire to campfire, Emile asked for directions to his brother's unit. He finally located Beale's Rifles at the extreme right of the American lines, next to the levee. Benjamin was warming his backside before a campfire when Emile sighted him.

"Benjamin!" Emile called out.

Recognizing his brother's voice, Benjamin came away from the fire, and the brothers embraced each other.

"Are you all right?" inquired Emile.

"I'm fine, Brother. What about you?"

"Hah! There was little chance of me being wounded. General Jackson has me confined to headquarters — he hardly lets me leave his sight. But you? You were in the thick of the fighting last night."

"Yes," agreed Benjamin. "Our men gave the English a taste of their own medicine in the fight. We'd have driven them back into the swamp if we could have seen what we were shooting at."

As the brothers conversed, a fine rain began to fall. Emile pointed toward the Macarté house. "Come back to headquarters with me for a Christmas toast. At least I can get you out of this weather for a while."

Benjamin nodded his acceptance of the invitation, and they began weaving their way through the campsites behind the Rodriguez Canal. The brothers didn't talk as they walked. Both withdrew into their own thoughts. The dismal weather and pitiful Christmas holiday put them in melancholy moods. Though neither would admit it to the other, they both felt qualms about the future battle in the pit of their stomachs. Despite their bravado with each other, they knew their ragtag army was greatly outnumbered and facing the most proficient army in the world. The British regulars they would face in full combat had defeated Napoleon and put the nation's capital to the torch. Could they really hope to defeat them?

After a while, the brothers came upon a Negro militia outfit composed of free men of color originally from Santo Domingo. Emile was about to comment that General Jackson was taking a big risk in arming Negros, but as he opened his mouth, the Dominicans' campfire exploded in flames. Apparently, someone had thrown grease or some other flammable liquid into the fire. The result was a burst of nearly blinding flames that shot ten to twenty feet into the air.

When the bonfire blazed up, a group of Negros encircling the fire began to chant:

He-ron mandé

He-ron mandé

Ti-gui li papa

He-ron mandé

Ti-gui li papa

He-ron mandé

He-ron mandé

Do se dan do-go…

As the Dominicans chanted, they began to slowly dance around the fire. In the center of the dancers, dangerously close to the flames, stood a tall black woman leading the chant. The woman wore a red tignon on her head. Her buxom figure strained the seams of a tattered blue dress. Draped around her neck and chest hung a massive gold necklace, which reflected the fire light with an iridescent glow.

"Who the devil is that?" asked Benjamin, pointing at the woman.

Observing the gold necklace around her neck, Emile knew instinctively who was leading the chant. "Sanité Dédé, queen of the Voodooiennes."

"What!" replied Benjamin with ire in his voice. "You mean they are holding a Voodoo ceremony on the eve of our Savior's birth? This is outrageous! Come, we must put a stop to — "

Emile grabbed his brother's arm. "No, wait. It might cause dissension among the Negro troops. We cannot afford that now."

"But, Emile! Those people are devil worshipers."

"Yes, but General Jackson doesn't care about that. He'd enlist Satan himself, if he'd fight the English for him."

As the brothers stood in the shadows and watched the Voodoo ceremony, the chanting died down, and Sanité Dédé began to sing in English to a background of soft drumbeats:

They think to frighten us,

Those English must be crazy.

They don't see their misfortune,

Or else they must be drunk.

I — the Voodoo Queen,

With powers yet untold.

I'm not afraid of their tomcat shrieks,

I will drink the English blood!

They think they have pride

With their big army,

But when they see my gris-gris

They'll run as frightened prairie birds.

Her song finished, the worshipers lined up, double file, before Sanité Dédé. They chanted together in low, indistinct tones, making the words impossible to understand.

As each pair of soldiers marched up to the queen, each man received a small leather bag on a cord, which Sanité Dédé placed around their bowed heads. Upon receiving the amulet, each soldier shouted, "Aie! Aie! Voodoo Magnian!"

"What's she doing that for?" inquired Benjamin.

Emile quickly decided against giving his brother a complete answer. He simply answered, "She's blessing her troops — and cursing the English."

After a short and somber Christmas celebration at Jackson's headquarters, Benjamin returned to his unit. Making sure that General Jackson had retired for the night, Emile returned to the camp of the Negro troops.

It was after midnight when Emile reached the camp. The bonfire had died down to smoking embers. Two sentries, sharing a jug of rum, stood watch over the fire. They did not bother to challenge Emile as he approached, nor did they try to conceal their liquor.

Emile asked one of the guards, a handsome white man whom he assumed was an officer, if Sanité Dédé was still in the camp. Without hesitation or speech, the guard pointed to a tent to the left of the fire pit.

As Emile neared the tent, he could see the glow of a single candle showing through the canvas walls. Pausing at the closed tent flap, Emile reconsidered what he was about to do. His promise to Julien — to stay clear of Sanité Dédé — nagged at his conscience. While Emile silently debated his dilemma, a voice came from inside the tent. "Come in, Monsieur Poydras. I've been expecting you."

Chapter Forty

Finding nothing further inside Mama Vance's house, Justin and Mark decided to search the grounds for evidence of what had taken place in the blood-spattered kitchen. Celeste knew the evidence they were looking for was a body — probably Mama Vance's body. Dreading that discovery, she begged off and locked herself in the car to wait while Justin and Mark did their search.

The bayou vegetation was so dense outside Mama Vance's cottage that the men could have been standing two feet from a body and not been able to see it. Spanish moss draped the trees and muted the sunlight. Vines, weeds, grass, and palmettos all grew together, thick and waist high. Standing about six feet apart, Mark and Justin poked their way through the tangled marsh ground.

Sweating and having grown restless waiting in the closed BMW, Celeste got out and crossed the road, walking toward the edge of the bayou channel where she could catch some breeze. The tall grass at her feet rustled unexpectedly as a young alligator made a run for the water. Celeste halted to let the timid creature get clear of her.

As she stood watching, two Cajuns motored by in a small aluminum fishing boat. Celeste heard movement in the brush again from behind her position. Expecting to see Mark or Justin approaching, Celeste turned to confront a large, young, black man. His feet and chest were bare, and he was dressed only in a tattered pair of blue jeans.

Celeste drew in her breath to scream for help, but the young man stopped in his tracks and held up a hand in a stop signal. Perceiving it was not a good idea to scream, Celeste abandoned her cry and froze in her half-turned stance.

The black man, not saying a word, pointed toward a mud bank at the edge of the channel, near where the young alligator had gone in the water. Celeste took a step or two toward the water to get a less obstructed view. She could see three gators lounging on the mud bank, soaking up the morning sun. Then she noticed something else. At first, she thought it was a log — a large piece of driftwood covered with mud. But then as she watched, a big adult gator reached over and took a bite of the log, shaking it with his powerful jaws. As the gator shook his prey, Celeste saw it was no log the reptile was eating, but a man. Rather, what was left of the torso of a man. As the alligator flailed the body, Celeste could see gaping wounds in the flesh, and that in addition to its head, one of the corpse's arms and both its legs were missing. Celeste spun around, but the young black man had disappeared. This time, Celeste did not hesitate to scream for help.

When Mark and Justin came running to her aid, at first Celeste couldn't speak. She just pointed at the body. Justin, spotting the body, waded through the tall weeds toward the mud bank, but he stopped well short of the water's edge, not wanting to get too close to the alligators. Mark stood by Celeste with his tire iron raised and ready to strike.

"What is it?" Mark asked.

"I can't be certain," answered Justin. "The gators have chewed him up pretty bad."

"Him?"

"Yes. It's a man — a black man."

Staring at the alligators still lying on the mud bank, Mark asked, "Do you think we can scare 'em off for a closer look? The water doesn't look too deep."

"We probably could, if I fired a couple shots at 'em, but we can't risk makin' the noise. I think we'd better leave before the authorities show up."

"What?" asked Celeste, finally bringing herself to speak. "We aren't going to call the police?"

Justin made his way back to Celeste before answering. "And what will we tell the police when they ask us what we were doin' here?"

"Yeah," concurred Mark. "We can't tell 'em the truth — they'd lock us all up in rubber rooms. And if we lie to them, they'll suspect we had something to do with the bloody mess in the kitchen, and that body out there. We'd better get out of here before someone comes by and sees us here."

"It's too late for that," said Celeste. "Someone has already seen us."

"Who?" asked Mark and Justin simultaneously.

"There was a young black man here. He pointed out the body to me. Then he ran off."

"He was on foot?" Justin asked.

"Yes. As a matter of fact, he was barefooted."

Justin put his .45 back in his belt and turned toward the car. "Come on! Let's get out of here. We'll sort this all out back at my house."

Everyone kept their thoughts to themselves during the drive back to the French Quarter. When they were almost home, Justin sensed Celeste's despondent mood. Trying to comfort her, he said, "At least it wasn't Mama Vance's body we found. Somehow, I just know she's still alive.... And we'll find her."

"Yeah," added Mark. "But something has been bothering me about Mama Vance. She evidently has had the gold necklace for many years, but she's blind and looks as old as Methuselah. How come the necklace hasn't done a better job of protecting her and keeping her young looking?"

"Yes," agreed Justin. "I've had the same thoughts. Assumin' Mama Vance is not some ancient Voodoo queen, maybe there are limits to the charm's protection — maybe it gives eternal life, but not protection from all forms of injury or illness? Or maybe she lost the necklace for a while and that's when she lost her sight? There's a lot we don't know about Mama Vance and maybe never will. But it really doesn't matter. We have no choice. We must find her and get the ring back..." *And soon,* thought Justin.

***

When the group got back to Justin's house, Mark and Celeste dropped onto the couch and turned on the TV. Justin shut himself in his study. Celeste dozed for a while on the couch, and the couple had some leftover red beans and rice for their only meal of the day. Justin didn't join them. Their only connection with him for the rest of the day was hearing his muffled voice through the study door as he made phone calls. Celeste was so emotionally and physically exhausted from last night's confrontation with Cupid and the trip to Mama Vance's house, she excused herself and went to bed at 8:15. In a few minutes, Celeste fell into a restless sleep and into a dream. It was unlike any dream she had thus far experienced.

Chapter Forty-One

During the days that followed the engagement of December 23 — or the "little Christmas fandango" as General Jackson called it — discord struck the American forces. In fact, certain members of the Louisiana Legislature had such little trust and confidence in Andrew Jackson, they conspired to contact the British commander — Major General Sir Edward Packenham — and negotiate the surrender of the City of New Orleans.

These Creole conspirators had no regard for the Americans and the "damned Yankee cause." They feared that the Americans, who were outnumbered two to one, would lose the battle at Chalmette. If that happened, the traitors reasoned that Jackson would burn the city rather than let it fall into British hands, or the British would put it to the torch as they had in Washington DC.

It was with some astonishment that Emile observed both Anton Cuvillier and Henri Noyan being escorted, under guard, into Jackson's headquarters on the night of December 29, 1814. Emile had not seen either man since Governor Claiborne's Christmas party two years earlier, at which the drunken Noyan had slapped his child bride, Nicole. Emile did not speak to his former friend as Anton and Henri were led past him. However, he did follow the prisoners as their guards marched them into General Jackson's office.

Jackson was seated, feet on top of the table, studying a map when the men entered. The soldier in charge of the detail — one of Jackson's own Tennessee volunteers — walked over and handed the general a fistful of papers. "I caught these fellers tryin' to sneak through the lines with these, Andy," he said.

After quickly skimming the documents, Jackson dropped them on the table and rose to address the two prisoners. In calm, flat tones, he asked them for their names. After receiving their replies, he said, "I could have you two shot for this."

Neither captive responded to the general's declaration. With blank, solemn expressions, they simply stared at the wall behind Jackson.

Unable to control his curiosity any longer, Emile walked over to the table and picked up the papers the guard had brought in. The documents consisted of a legislative petition and letters addressed to General Packenham, offering to surrender New Orleans in return for British protection. Anton Cuvillier and Henri Noyan were among the petition's signatories. Emile felt a flash of anger come over him when he realized the two men were seeking to betray him and all the denizens who had come out to fight for their city.

Dead silence pervaded the room as General Jackson deliberated the fate of the turncoats. Finally, he gave an order to one of the Tennessee guards. "Private, go fetch horses for these men — and an escort to take 'em back to the city."

Turning to the intimidated traitors, Jackson continued his orders. "You two shall return to New Orleans, under guard — tonight! Upon arrival, you shall report to Governor Claiborne and inform him of your actions and that I am ordering the legislature dissolved. Also, you are to tell the governor to report to me tomorrow. You shall inform him of every member of your conspiracy, and he shall inform me which of you have seen the light and decided to fight for his country."

Walking up and facing each man with a cold, intense scowl, the general concluded by saying, "And if I hear so much as a rumor that you — or any of the other traitors who signed that petition — have attempted to contact the British again, by the Eternal, the whole lot of you will end up in front of a firing squad! Now, get out!"

Both Anton and Henri saluted and marched out without uttering a word. Neither man made eye contact with Emile. After the room was cleared, Jackson turned to Emile. The expectant look on Emile's face begged the question, *Why?*

"I had to," replied General Jackson. "Arresting 'em now would probably have caused a mutiny among the Creole troops.... We'll deal with 'em after we drive the English back into the swamps."

Emile struggled not to show his disapproval of Jackson's leniency, saying only, "I know both those men, General. They are not to be trusted."

"Hell, I don't trust 'em, Captain. But, if I can force these traitors to fight to save their skins, I don't need to trust 'em."

The quick actions of General Jackson and Governor Claiborne nipped the Creole conspiracy in the bud. Once exposed, the conspirators renounced their betrayal. Many of them (including Anton) did join the American troops along the Rodriguez Canal to prove their newfound loyalty. Also, among the new champions of the "Yankee cause" was Henri Noyan, who ended up attached to Benjamin's unit — Beale's Rifles.

After taking time to concentrate their forces and test the American lines, the British made a full-scale assault on the Rodriguez line on the morning of January 8, 1815. General Packenham no longer had any misconceptions about the size of the American Army. He knew he outnumbered the Americans nearly two to one. That is, close to nine thousand battle-tested British soldiers were massed to attack some forty-seven hundred motley American volunteers (including pirates and Choctaw Indians) — many of whom didn't even have weapons.

What Packenham and Jackson didn't know was that fifteen days earlier, on Christmas Eve Day, the Treaty of Ghent had been signed, which ended the war and required the withdrawal of all British troops from American territory.

When the mist rolled away that Sunday morning, the sunrise revealed the British Army drawn up in two large columns, the middle of the field vacant except for their artillery in the rear. The Americans were not surprised by the attack. Their guns were loaded, and they were packed in close along the half-mile Rodriguez line. The New Orleans Municipal Band was even assembled. The band struck up "Yankee Doodle" as the artillery duel began and as the British troops commenced their advance with fixed bayonets. Barrages of British rockets flashed through the still dark sky.

The first ranks of advancing redcoats quickly began to drop in the face of the American cannon fire. Some were slammed backward as though hit by an invisible club. Others simply crumbled or slipped to their knees before toppling over. Their stone-faced comrades stepped delicately past the bodies, filling in the ranks, seemingly oblivious to the grape shot being fired from the American guns.

General Jackson and his staff, including Emile, were on horseback surveying the American lines. They had reached the extreme right — near the flèche manned by Beale's Rifles — when the cannonade commenced. Jackson pulled up next to Emile's mount and yelled into his ear as he pointed toward the position manned by Beale's Rifles. "Tell those men to hold their fire until the redcoats are well within musket range! Aim just above where their white chest belts cross!"

Although Emile felt certain the troops knew to hold their fire, he did not contest the general's order. He merely nodded that he understood, dismounted his horse, and headed toward Benjamin to relay the instructions. Rather than return to the rear of the lines, Emile decided to stay and fight with his brother as the redcoats were closing swiftly on their position.

The stubborn British troops maintained their advance in the face of the American artillery barrage, carrying fascines and scaling ladders with which to assault the canal's defenses. When they came within small arms range, the close-packed Americans opened up, not firing in volleys as a "civilized" European Army would have, but firing at will and reloading as quickly as possible. The American rifle fire built to a continuous roar, becoming one great wall of flame.

Redcoats no longer dropped just here and there. Now they fell in swaths, as though cut down by some invisible scythe. However, the British had concentrated their assault at the flèche manned by Beale's Rifles, and their focused attack breached the American lines at the river's edge.

Emile was standing shoulder to shoulder with Benjamin. After discharging both of his pistols into the faces of redcoats scaling the flèche, Emile turned and bent over to pick up the musket of a fallen American soldier. As he turned his back, a redcoat came over the top of the rampart and lunged at Emile's back with his bayonet. Emile saw the attack coming out of the corner of his eye, but not in time to avoid the bayonet completely. It pierced the calf of his left leg, breaking the fibula, as Emile lurched to get out of the way.

Screaming in pain, blood spurting from his leg, Emile rolled over, helplessly facing his attacker, watching in frozen fear as the British soldier raised his bayonet to make a fatal plunge into his chest. Just as the redcoat was about to drive his bayonet home, a shot rang out, and a musket ball shattered the Englishman's forehead. Blood and brains flew through the air as the redcoat's head snapped back. The dead soldier fell backwards and dropped his musket across Emile's bleeding left leg.

Emile turned over, expecting to see his brother, Benjamin, as his savior. Instead, he was surprised to see Henri Noyan holding a smoking carbine. Henri threw down his weapon and rushed forward to Emile's aid. Helping him to his feet, he yelled, "Come on! We've got to fall back!" as he helped Emile limp to the rear.

With the assistance of the adjacent 7th Infantry, Beale's Rifles rallied. Their combined countercharge drove the British out of the American lines. When it was all over, the British Commander, Sir Edward Packenham, lay dead on the cane

fields of Chalmette, along with nearly three hundred of his troops. Another thirteen hundred lay wounded on the field. One couldn't even see the color of the
earth for all the British soldiers that lay upon it. A solid blanket of scarlet and
Sutherland green covered the battlefield. Five hundred British troops were taken
prisoner by the Americans. American losses were thirteen killed and thirty
wounded, including Emile Poydras.

The actual battle had been so short — barely more than half an hour — that
nearly two-thirds of the Americans behind the Rodriguez line never had a chance
to fire a shot. Expecting a second wave, Jackson kept his troops behind their defenses as the British retreated from the field. No second attack came; the British
had had enough.

Lying on his back on the damp ground, inside a tent that served as the American field hospital, Emile worried that the cut-happy surgeons would want to am-
putate his leg. Emile unbuttoned his uniform jacket and put his hand down the
neck of his shirt. Glancing over his shoulder to make sure no one was looking, he
pulled out a small leather bag attached to a cord around his neck. Contemptuously,
he jerked the cord, breaking it free of his neck. Emile then tossed the bag and
broken cord over his feet and gazed at the ceiling of the tent. Silently, he prayed
that the bleeding from his leg could be stopped.

Chapter Forty-Two

Celeste arose about 7:00 a.m. the next morning. Pulling on her robe, she headed downstairs, looking for Mark. She found him with Justin in the garden, drinking coffee and reading the morning paper.

"Good morning," she said as she came through the open French dining room doors.

Looking up from his paper, Justin seemed startled by Celeste's greeting. "Good mornin', sugar. I thought you were still asleep."

Mark got up from the wrought iron table and gave Celeste a kiss on the cheek. "Morning, babe. Can I get you some coffee?"

"Yes, please."

When Mark went in the house to get Celeste's coffee, Justin asked, "Did… you sleep well last night?"

"You mean, did I dream last night?"

"Yes," admitted Justin.

"Yeah, I had a dream. But it wasn't the same." Seeing Mark coming back with her coffee, Celeste didn't continue until he joined them. She sat down and took a sip of the steaming black coffee before continuing.

"My dream was completely different last night.… At first, it seemed to start the same — I was in Emile Poydras's bedroom. But I was alone in his bed, and I couldn't sense his presence at all. It's hard to explain.… I felt distant or detached from him. Finally, I called out for him. And I heard him answer with my name, but it was a faint reply from far off — it sounded as if it came from outside the house. When I got out of bed and opened the bedroom door, I was suddenly transported to a bayou. I was lost in this swamp — with no idea of which way was out.… Then, I heard Emile's voice again, calling my name. So, I pushed my way through the tall weeds in the direction of his voice."

Celeste sighed and took a gulp of coffee. "It seemed like I walked forever through the swamp, but the sound of Emile's voice was no closer. Then, just as I was about to give up, I saw him. I'd come to the edge of a river, and Emile was standing on the opposite bank. I waved and yelled to him, but Emile didn't respond. He just stood there like a statue. The river seemed calm, and it wasn't very wide, so I decided to swim to him. But just as I put one foot in the water, a huge alligator rose up directly in front of me. I jumped back onto the shore. And when I looked at Emile again, he was walking back into the swamp. Before he disappeared from sight, he turned and said, 'Not without the ring. Not without the ring.' At this point, I felt so despondent, I sank to my knees and began to cry. Then I remembered Mama Vance and her advice."

"What advice?" asked Mark.

"At our first visit to her house. When I felt that we had no hope of finding out the curse on the ring, Mama Vance told me to pray to Marie Laveau for help."

"So?" continued Mark.

"So, I prayed to Marie Laveau — in my dream. I said I'd do anything if she'd just get me out of that swamp and help me get the ring back."

When Celeste didn't continue her narrative, Justin prompted her, "Then what happened?"

Celeste smiled. "I woke up."

Glancing at the open *Times-Picayune* lying on the table, Celeste asked, "Is there anything in the paper about the body we saw?"

Justin shook his head. "No. No mention of it."

Pushing her coffee cup aside, Celeste asked, "So... wha'da we do now, Granddad?"

"We must locate Mama Vance. You and Mark need to stake out her house while I make inquiries elsewhere."

"How do we know she's still alive?" chimed in Mark.

"We don't," admitted Justin. "But my gut tells me the body we saw in the bayou came from Mama Vance's bloody kitchen. She's out there somewhere layin' low. We just have to — "

Justin was interrupted by the ding-dong of his doorbell. "Who the devil would come callin' at this hour?" he said.

Brushing back his uncombed hair with his hand, Justin rose and headed to answer the bell. In less than a minute, he returned with a small, yellowed envelope in his hand. He held it out to Celeste.

"What's this?" she asked.

"When I got to the gate, no one was there. Just this envelope stuck in the bars. It has your name on it."

The old yellow envelope appeared to have been white at one time. It looked like old stationery that had aged in some dry attic for an unknown number of years. It had "Celeste Noyan" printed on the front in a crude hand. The envelope was not sealed. Celeste withdrew an equally yellowed and brittle piece of stationery and gently unfolded it. In old and flawed typewritten print, it stated:

If you want ring back

be at moon walk 3am

you must bring gris gris

cupid leave with you

ONLY YOU TOUCH GRIS GRIS

Celeste handed the note to her grandfather when she had finished. Mark scooted his chair so he could read over Justin's shoulder. Asking the obvious question, Mark said, "The note's not signed?"

"It has to be from Mama Vance," replied Justin. "Who else?"

Celeste nodded her head. Then she asked Justin, "What's the 'moon walk,' Granddad?"

"It's what they call the public access pier — across the street from Jackson Square — the place all the tourists go to get a close look at the Mississippi."

"What's this mean about bring the gris-gris Cupid left?" Mark inquired. "If he left something in our bedroom, I never saw it."

"If Cupid left a gris-gris, it won't be in your bedroom," Justin answered.

Mark look puzzled. "Huh?"

"Gris-gris is an amulet or charm used to transmit a curse," continued Justin. "The term is pretty broad, but when a Voodooienne wants to curse all the members of a household, they'll plant the gris-gris on or under your doorstep or entryway. So all who enter the house are cursed."

"What's it look like?" asked Celeste.

"It could be a small cloth or leather bag — filled with various powders and such. It could be an odd assortment of food or bones — or even a dead animal. You'll know it when you see it, because it will definitely look out of place."

"I'll check the front gate and door," volunteered Mark as he rose from the table.

"Okay," replied Justin. "That leaves the back door for me. Celeste can look around here. Remember! If you find something, don't touch it. Come and get me first."

Pulling the sash to her robe snug as she stood up, Celeste began her inspection of the garden. There were two sets of French doors leading into the garden. The ones that were open — into the dining room — and a set that led into Justin's office. Walking to the office doors, Celeste could see no place even a small charm or bag could be hidden. Outside the glass doors was a solid concrete patio. There were no doormats or planters next to the doors to conceal anything under. Celeste tried the doorknob, but it was locked.

Moving back to the dining room doors, Celeste lifted up the green AstroTurf doormat but found nothing. There were pots of red geraniums on either side of the doors, but there was nothing under them either.

Between the concrete patio outside the dining room, and the shaded area where Justin had placed his breakfast table, lay a walk of round flagstones. Celeste had given up her cursory search and was walking over the flagstones to retrieve her coffee cup. When she stepped on the edge of one of the flagstones, it wobbled, and her foot slipped off the edge. Looking down, she noticed that the stone was slightly out of line with the one in front of it.

Kneeling, Celeste could clearly observe that the flagstone had been moved a couple of inches or so to the right. The dirt of the garden floor had a circular indentation in it from the paving stone, and someone had moved the stone out of the center of its circle. Using both her hands, Celeste found she could pry up the heavy stone. In her first effort, the stone slipped and scraped her fingertips as it fell back down with a thud. For her second effort, Celeste gave the stone a quick jerk — with all her might — and the stone tumbled over.

In the dirt circle, staring up at Celeste, was a dead frog — a rather smashed dead frog. But what made Celeste let out a gasp was that the frog was crucified upside down on a small wooden cross. Several large sewing needles were driven into the frog's chest and head. Smashed pea pods formed an arch around the frog's head and the bottom of the cross.

"Guys!" Celeste yelled. "You can stop lookin'! I found it!"

Chapter Forty-Three

After his victory at Chalmette, Andrew Jackson became the most stupendous American hero since George Washington. In fact, the newspapers referred to him simply as "The Hero." Even the snobbish Creoles cheered the "Yankee General" and threw lavish balls in his honor.

Emile did not attend any of the victory balls. His dancing days were over. The surgeons had been able to save his leg, but the fracture healed badly, leaving his left leg stiff and over an inch shorter than the right.

The first social invitation that Emile accepted after his recuperation was to the home of Henri Noyan. As one of the few Americans wounded at Chalmette, Emile became a bit of a celebrity himself, but he had shunned all social events and invitations for public recognition. Emile, however, felt compelled to attend Henri's dinner party on April 4, 1815. After all, Henri had saved his life.

As the carriage carrying Emile and Julien neared the Noyan plantation house, Emile thought to himself, *Of all the people to owe my life to — that drunken lout Henri Noyan... The only worse savior could have been Anton. Luckily, he was elsewhere at the battle.*

Emile's thoughts were interrupted by an out-of-the-blue question from his uncle Julien. "Emile? Why did you not tell me you saw Sanité Dédé at Chalmette?"

Caught off guard, Emile could only offer a feeble response. "What?"

"Benjamin happened to mention yesterday that you two observed her perform a Voodoo ceremony for the Negro troops."

Frowning before answering, Emile said, "Yes, that's true. I guess it's not what I tend to remember most about Chalmette."

Julien was not deterred by Emile's attempt to change the subject. "Did you see her any other time while she was there?"

Emile didn't want to answer his uncle's question, but fearing he might be caught in a lie, he answered reluctantly, "Yes... I did."

Raising his voice, Julien responded, "You gave me your word! That you would not contact her!"

"I know, Uncle. I'm sorry. I can't really explain why I went to her. After I inadvertently saw her ceremony for the Negro troops, I felt this overpowering desire to go to her. I just couldn't get her out of my head."

"Oh, Emile, you *know* how I feel about her. I warned you, everyone who gets involved with her regrets it.… What happened?"

"When I saw her blessing the Negro troops — she was giving them all gris-gris charms to protect them in battle. Well… please don't think me a poltroon, but I decided to ask her about creating a charm of protection for myself."

Shaking his head, Julien asked, "And what did she tell you?"

"Basically what you did — that genuine charms like yours could not be created without a human sacrifice. However, she did sell me one of the gris-gris bags she had given to the Negro troops. She said it would protect me just for the battle." Slapping his bad leg, Emile continued, "I was a fool to believe her."

"You should have known better. A Voodoo queen will promise you anything to sell her wares. Most of their charms are pure superstitious bunk." Squeezing Emile's knee, Julien said earnestly, "Please! In the future, stay away from Sanité Dédé! No good will ever come from involvement with her. Give me your solemn promise on this, and I will leave you my ring when I pass on — I'll even give it to you *now*, if that's what it takes to keep you away from the Voodooiennes."

Emile snapped his head up and replied, "No, Uncle. You can't give up the ring. Doing so would mean your death."

"I've had a full and prosperous life in my sixty-nine years. Even so, no one wants to live forever. The ring protects my body from death, but I can foresee the day when my spirit will eventually grow tired of life's toils."

"Please, Uncle. Don't talk like — "

"Don't worry, my boy. I'm not ready to leave this world just yet. I'm just trying to make a point that — "

Emile held up his palm. "Say no more. I will keep my word this time."

But as the carriage stopped in front of the Noyan house, Emile pondered Julien's words. *If given my uncle's wealth and the means for eternal life, would I ever grow tired of life? Would I ever be willing to give it up — for anyone?*

Henri Noyan's dinner party was even more unpleasant than Emile had anticipated. Henri got drunk, as usual, and he was crass beyond belief. As the "guest of honor," Henri led Emile around the room like a crippled show horse. He would interrupt the conversation of each group they visited and regale his audience with his heroic deeds at Chalmette. By the end of the evening, not only was he claiming credit for saving Emile's life, but also for singlehandedly leading the counterattack that drove the British from the American lines.

Emile yearned for the freedom to inform the guests that before the battle, Henri had been apprehended trying to sell out the American Army to the British. Silently, Emile vowed to somehow repay Henri for saving his life. He refused to be forever in the debt of such a boorish Bacchanalian.

Emile noticed that Nicole Noyan did her best to steer clear of her husband during the evening. Remembering how Henri had humiliated her at Governor Claiborne's Christmas party, he surmised their marriage had not improved in the past two and a half years.

Emile also observed that Nicole's beauty had matured greatly since he had last seen her. Though she was yet to reach her nineteenth birthday, Emile concluded she had become one of the most beautiful women in New Orleans. All the other women in attendance paled in comparison. Nicole's hourglass figure, opalescent skin, and lustrous dark hair put them all to shame.

Realizing he had been staring at Nicole for some time, Emile looked around to see if Henri or anyone else had noticed. He decided they hadn't. But he couldn't help feeling a twinge of guilt about it. He felt himself becoming attracted to Nicole, but it could never be. He owed her husband his life.

Near the end of the party, Emile's supposition about the Noyan marriage was confirmed. As he was observing the couple from across the room, he saw that Henri was being churlish with his wife. However, he couldn't hear what he was saying to her. Suddenly, Henri threw the contents of his wine glass across the front of Nicole's white satin gown. With a wry smile, Nicole curtsied to her husband and left the room by the nearest door, which led out to the rose garden. Henri headed for the refreshment table to refill his wine glass, ignoring the stunned expressions of the guests who had observed his action.

When he felt no one was looking, Emile followed Nicole into the garden. He saw her standing alone at the end of one of the graveled garden paths. The crunch of Emile's limping steps on the gravel caused Nicole to turn around. "Oh, it's you, Monsieur Poydras."

"Yes, Madame Noyan…. I couldn't help but notice what just happened. Is there anything I can do?"

Nicole didn't answer for a moment. Then she said, "Why, yes. You could kill my husband for me."

Chapter Forty-Four

By 2:00 a.m., the activity in the Quarter was winding down. As Mark and Celeste crossed Bourbon Street, only some hard-core partiers and a couple of hookers were to be seen. The throngs of tourists were gone, having already eaten and drunk themselves senseless. In the distance, a loud rock and roll band could be heard playing in one of the few bars still open.

Mark and Celeste headed down Orleans Street to where it ended at St. Anthony's Square, the small garden behind the St. Louis Cathedral. The spotlight illuminating the garden's statue of Christ with outstretched arms cast a long, intimidating shadow inside the small park. As they cut over to Pirate Alley, walking beside the cathedral garden, Celeste recalled the stories her grandfather used to tell her as a child — about all the duels that were fought in St. Anthony's Square.

Stepping out of the alley into Jackson's Square, Mark stopped and let out a little sigh of relief, saying, "Whew. That's one spooky street."

"Yeah," agreed Celeste. "The walls of the cathedral keep it pretty dark in there."

"Where to now?"

Celeste pointed to the well-lit street on the other side of the square. "All we have to do is cross Decatur and walk up that concrete ramp. The Moon Walk is right behind that cannon on the observation deck."

Noticing that the Café du Monde was still open, Mark suggested, "We've got a few minutes. How 'bout a cup of coffee?"

After being served their café au lait and an order of beignets, Mark looked around the room. Besides them, there were two other couples and a group of obviously gay men in the café. The group of men all had on black leather attire.

"Doesn't this place ever close?" he asked.

"Nope, stays open twenty-four hours a day."

After consuming half a beignet in a single bite, Mark smiled. "These powdered donuts are great when they're hot."

"Ben-*Yays*, Mark," corrected Celeste. "They're not donuts. They're Ben-*Yays*."

Shrugging his shoulders, Mark changed the subject. "Sure hope your granddad doesn't get caught at the hospital…. I kinda wish…"

Celeste finished Mark's sentence, "… wish he were here? Me too. But he felt certain they would take the Villere child off life support early this morning — after the doctor's rounds."

"Yeah, I guess it was his last chance. After the shift change, there'll be too many people in the hospital." Mark took a swig of his milky, chicory-flavored coffee. "Wonder what the penalty for blood theft is?"

"He's not stealing anything!" scolded Celeste. "He's paying all their funeral expenses!"

Mark patted his chest once and looked around to see if anyone had heard Celeste's exclamation. "I'm sorry, bad choice of words. I just meant he could be in trouble with the law if the parents have been talking about his offer."

"I know." Celeste glanced at her wristwatch. "We'd better take the coffee with us. It's ten till three."

After they descended the observation deck and levee, Mark and Celeste had to cross the dark riverfront railroad tracks before they could mount the Moon Walk. The boardwalk along the river's edge was fairly well lit with streetlamps, and Mark could see no one standing or sitting on any of the benches as they approached the pier area.

As they stepped under a light on the boardwalk, each of them heard the sound of an outboard motorboat engine kick over. Looking out toward the dark river, they saw the red and green running lights of a small boat flash on. As the boat drew close, Celeste thought she recognized the dark red runabout's operator and sole occupant.

"It's the man who pointed out the body," she whispered.

"Huh?"

"The *body* we found in front of Mama Vance's house."

The young black man skillfully maneuvered the outboard boat parallel to the Moon Walk's pier. Grabbing the edge of the wooden pier with one hand, he motioned with his free hand for the couple to get in.

Celeste hesitated. "Did… did Mama Vance send you?"

The boat driver didn't answer. He just pointed toward the opposite riverbank.

"What's he pointing at?" asked Mark.

"Algiers Point," answered Celeste. Then she asked the driver again, "Is Mama Vance on the other side of the river?"

The black man nodded once and motioned again for them to board the bobbing runabout. After a questioning glance from Mark, Celeste said, "Let's go. We've come this far."

As soon as the couple was seated in the boat, the driver pushed off and gave the outboard engine full throttle. The shallow boat bounced across the murky water toward the lights of Algiers Point. In five minutes, they were there.

Tying the runabout up next to the Algiers ferryboat pier, the driver pulled out a flashlight and blinked it three times at the black shore. In less than a minute, two figures came walking out of the darkness. It was stoop-shouldered Mama Vance, on the arm of another young, well-built black man. Stopping at the edge of the pier, clutching a shoebox under one arm, Mama Vance said, "You must git out of de boat, ma chérie."

Mark rose to help Celeste out of the motorboat and started to follow her out of the craft, when Mama Vance said, "You need not come ashore, Monsieur Richards."

"What? How did — I'm not leaving…"

"No one is leavin' you, Monsieur Richards. As soon as ma chérie takes my hand, we both be boardin' de boat."

True to her word, after Celeste had climbed up onto the pier and taken Mama Vance's hand, the old queen barked an order to her companion. "Help me into de boat, Hector."

When everyone was seated in the runabout, Mama Vance issued a command to the driver. "Ajax, head back across de river." Ajax didn't verbally acknowledge the order, but he immediately backed the boat away from the pier.

"Your helpers don't talk much," commented Mark.

"Dhey speak when dhey need ta," replied Mama Vance. Turning her head toward Celeste's seat, she asked, "Did you bring Cupid's gris-gris with you?"

"Yes," answered Celeste, pulling a small brown lunch sack from her purse. She held it out toward Mama Vance.

"I don't want it, ma chérie. When we reach the middle of de river, drop it in de water — but make certain you drop it in with your left hand. Dhen, you must throw a coin in — over your left shoulder."

Mark thought that if Mama Vance was blind, she seemed to be seeing well enough in their dark boat. *How did she know Celeste offered her the sack?* he wondered.

"Come again?" Celeste asked.

"It's why I had you git out of de boat and join me on shore. It's all part of de ritual ta break Cupid's gris-gris…. Don't worry, ma chérie. I'll tell you what ta do, when de time come. Just git a coin ready."

Mark pulled a quarter from his jeans pocket and handed it to Celeste.

After riding in silence for a few minutes, Mama Vance yelled over her shoulder to the driver. "Ajax? We be in mid-river yet?"

Ajax didn't answer, but in seconds, he pulled the throttle back into neutral and let the boat idle in mid-channel.

"Now," Mama Vance continued, "drop de sack with your left hand." After Celeste complied with the instruction, Mama Vance said, "Bien. Now throw de coin over your left shoulder — and clap your hands three times." When Celeste had completed the ritual, Mama Vance added, "Bien! Bien! Now you all be free of Cupid's gris-gris."

"Mama Vance?" inquired Celeste. "You know Cupid stole my ring?"

"But, of course, ma chérie." She patted the shoebox in her lap with one hand. "I have it right here."

"You have it?" exclaimed Celeste.

"Oui, I have brought it for you. But I cannot give it ta you here."

"Then where?"

Mama Vance answered Celeste's question with her next command to the boat driver, "On ta Chalmette, Ajax."

"Chalmette?" questioned Celeste. "We're going to the National Battlefield?"

"Oui, ma chérie. We must enlist de aid of de spirits dhere — if you are ta wear de ring once more."

Chapter Forty-Five

In the years following Jackson's victory at Chalmette, the popularity of the Americans waned in New Orleans. Even by the fall of 1820, the city was still much more French and Spanish than it was American. Creole and Spanish were the languages mainly heard on the streets, and for the most part, the cliquish Creole society still excluded Yankees from the North. Though statehood had caused the city to expand in all directions, the heart of New Orleans remained the Place d'Armes, with its stately cathedral and cabildo, which would later be renamed in honor of Andrew Jackson.

One permanent change the War of 1812 did bring was even greater trade and prosperity for Louisiana. Julien Poydras and his nephews became wealthy beyond their dreams. The latest Poydras enterprise was the St. Francisville Steamboat Company, one of the first steamboat lines on the Mississippi. It was owned by Julien, Benjamin, Emile, and several other Louisiana investors.

The first ship of the new line was the 408-ton *Feliciana*. It was the *Feliciana's* inaugural arrival in New Orleans that brought Emile and Julien to the wharf on a sultry afternoon in late September 1820. They were there to greet Benjamin, who had sailed from the Philadelphia naval yard on the ship's maiden voyage.

It appeared to Emile that nearly the whole city had turned out to welcome the new steamship. A reviewing stand had been constructed for the mayor, steamboat company officials, and other dignitaries and important citizens. Emile looked out over the crowded docks from his seat near the top of the stands. He felt proud to be a Poydras. He didn't care if some Creole snobs laughed behind his back about his eccentric uncle. No matter that Julien still dressed like a French nobleman from the last century. He was rich as a French monarch, and Emile was no pauper himself.

A few minutes before the *Feliciana* steamed into sight, a small Negro boy wormed his way through the reviewing stand crowd and up to Emile and Julien's seats. The child came up to Emile and pulled at his jacket sleeve. "Monsieur Emile?" he asked.

"Oui, I am Emile Poydras."

Upon hearing Emile's answer, the boy extended a crumpled note with his hand. As Emile took the note, the boy turned to leave.

"Hold on!" Emile said. "Who sent you?"

Without answering, the little messenger pointed at the crowd at the bottom of the reviewing stand. Emile couldn't be certain, but it appeared the child was pointing to a statuesque young Negro woman, with long, curly black hair, for when she saw the boy and Emile look in her direction, she smiled and turned her back. Before Emile could ask any other questions, the child had made his way to the bottom of the stands.

Unfolding the wrinkled note, Emile read the neat French script with Julien looking over his shoulder.

Monsieur Emile Poydras,

If you wish to repay your debt to Henri Noyan, today is the day. An attempt will be made on Monsieur Noyan's life as he leaves the ceremony. Stand ready and close to him, and your life can be yours once more.

Your Servant,

Marie Laveau

"Who in blazes is Marie Laveau?" asked Emile.

Julien shook his head. "I know a planter upriver by the name of Charles Laveau, but he has no daughter by the name of Marie."

Realizing Julien had not noticed the young Negro woman the messenger boy had pointed toward, Emile asked, "Might Monsieur Laveau have an illegitimate daughter of mixed blood?"

"I'm sure I wouldn't know," replied Julien with slight indignation.

Standing up to get a better view, Emile surveyed the seats occupied by the Noyan family on the opposite side of the dais. Henri sat next to his gray-haired father, Paul Noyan. Nicole was conspicuously absent from Henri's party. But other than that, nothing looked out of order. Henri's seat was surrounded by those of other family members, friends, and upstanding citizens of Louisiana. Sitting back down, he said, "Henri appears to be in no danger to me."

"I believe I know who sent you the note," replied a frowning Julien.

"Who?"

"I didn't make the connection with the name Laveau. But I've heard rumors about a new Voodooienne priestess, a free woman of color, who calls herself the 'Widow Paris' — Marie Paris. Laveau was her maiden name I believe. She's very much in demand as a hairdresser among the ladies of the city."

"But how would she know about my desire to repay Henri Noyan for saving my life?"

Julien gave his nephew a knowing smile. "Perhaps she is Madame Nicole's hairdresser as well. I've heard women will tell their hairdressers about their most intimate affairs — things they would never confess to their priests."

Although Emile and Nicole had begun a clandestine affair after the 1815 dinner party, when Henri had left New Orleans on an extended business trip, he was uncomfortable discussing it with his disapproving uncle. He diverted the conversation back to Marie Laveau. "But that still doesn't explain why she would send me this note?"

"She wants something from you, my boy. Be sure of that. If her information is correct — and you benefit from it — there will be a price to pay. So, be on your guard. I strongly recommend you ignore this message."

As Julien finished speaking, the sound of a distant steam whistle brought forth loud cheers from the crowd. In another minute, the *Feliciana* steamed into sight, bedecked with red, white, and blue bunting and at least a dozen large American flags.

During the welcoming ceremonies and longwinded speeches by the mayor, Julien, and other dignitaries, Emile kept his eyes on Henri Noyan — looking for any stranger who might be moving close to him.

When the official proceedings ended, Julien rose to go welcome Benjamin, who was still on the deck of the *Feliciana*. When Emile didn't stand up too, he asked, "Aren't you coming on board with me?"

"Not now, Uncle. I want to stay close to Henri Noyan — just in case the note is true. Tell Benjamin I'll greet him at your house in a little while."

"As you wish," replied Julien as he started down the reviewing stand. After taking a couple of steps, he turned as if to say something more, but only shook his head and proceeded down the steps.

When the Noyan entourage started to leave the reviewing stands, Emile was quick to follow, staying approximately a dozen steps behind Henri Noyan. As the group crossed the still crowded levee, Emile observed a well-dressed mulatto man fall in behind and begin following Henri. When the mulatto began closing the distance between himself and Henri's back, Emile knew it was time to act.

Shoving his way through the departing crowd, Emile reached the colored man just as he raised a dagger behind Henri's neck. The scream of a nearby woman caused Henri to spin around, but he had no time to defend himself. The dagger was in motion only inches from his throat. Just as the weapon started to strike home, Emile struck the assailants' hand full force with the blade of his colichemarde. The blow sent the dagger flying and caused the would-be assassin to grab his wounded hand and scream in pain.

Two of the men in the Noyan entourage quickly grabbed the injured assailant and removed him from the levee. As the mulatto was taken away, he screamed at Henri, "All I wanted was my wife! You swine! All I wanted was my wife!"

Sheathing his sword, Emile asked, "What was that all about, Henri?"

A shaken Henri stared at the departing assailant. "He's a former Dominican slave who bought his freedom. I outbid him for his wife at a slave auction last year, and he's obviously gone mad over it."

Looking at Henri with reproach, Emile asked, "Why didn't you sell the poor devil his wife?"

"She's a very good slave. And he couldn't afford the full market price."

"Henri, you disgust me! I've waited five years to be able to tell you that, and now I can. Today, I've paid my debt to you in *full* — your life for mine. Now…"

"Not so fast, Monsieur Poydras!" interrupted Henri. "Our accounts are far from balanced. There is the matter of my wife."

"What do you mean?" demanded Emile, feigning outrage.

"Come now. Do you think I am such an ignorant cuckold that I haven't learned of your affair with Nicole?"

"I would think, monsieur, that your wife's fidelity would not be a topic you would discuss in public."

"I don't give a damn about my wife's fidelity — or her reputation, Poydras." Then, with a smirk on his face, Henri added, "But know one thing. I will never divorce her! She will *never* be free to live with you!"

Emile calmly replied, "Your wedding vows said until death do you part, Henri. Divorce is not the only way to end a marriage."

Chapter Forty-Six

The trip downriver to Chalmette was a short one. Scattered patches of fog lay on the river, but Ajax deftly piloted the small boat past and between the anchorages of several large tanker and merchant vessels, and in less than thirty minutes, he was docking the runabout beside the concrete-topped levee at Chalmette National Battlefield.

When everyone was out of the boat and standing on the deserted tour-boat dock, Mark asked, "What about guards? Isn't there a night watchman?"

"Oui," answered Mama Vance. "Dhere be one watchman. But he no problem. He be one of my followers."

All that separated the battlefield from the levee was a low, white picket fence. Entering by the open gate, the party proceeded to the antebellum Malus-Beauregard Mansion that served as the park's headquarters. No lights were on in or outside the house, and no watchman was in sight, but Mama Vance didn't attempt to enter. She sat down on one of the numerous park benches outside the mansion, resting the shoebox on her knees. Ajax and Hector walked out onto the battlefield and disappeared into the foggy darkness.

Celeste and Mark sat down on a bench facing Mama Vance. Celeste then asked, "What now, Mama Vance?"

"We wait for de dawn, ma chérie."

"Then what?"

"When de mist begin ta lift from de cane field, I will call de spirits."

"Whose spirits?"

"De spirits of de men who die here."

"You mean, the soldiers who died during the battle?" inquired Mark.

"Oui. All de English soldiers."

Celeste shook her head. "I don't understand, Mama Vance. Why do we need to summon these spirits?"

"Cause dhey be strong enough ta capture and hold Cupid's spirit."

"I'm sorry, I still don't understand."

Smiling, Mama Vance handed the shoebox to Celeste. Taking the box and resting it on her lap, Celeste waited for some explanation. When she realized Mama Vance was not going to say anything else, Celeste removed the box's lid. Suddenly, Celeste gasped and bolted up. The shoebox fell from her lap. As the box hit the ground, an object rolled out onto the grass. Mark's eyes didn't want to focus in the pale moonlight. He bent over for a closer look. Then he too jumped back, uttering his own gasp. On the ground lay a severed human hand. A white bone protruded from the wrist. On its second finger was the Poydras ring.

Mama Vance cackled at the couple's reaction. "Hee! Hee! Don't be worried. Cupid can't hurt you now. Just don't take de ring off his finger till I tell you."

Celeste wanted to escape, but she didn't know where to run. The flesh on the withered hand was beginning to decay, and it emitted the foul odor of a dead animal. All she could do was back away from it.

"So, that was Cupid's body we found outside your house?" asked Mark.

"Oui!"

Mark took a step to the side to get upwind from the rotting hand. Then he asked, "But… why didn't the ring protect him?"

"Hah! Cupid be a fool! Stealin' de ring don't steal de power. De protection only come when de charm be freely given and accepted."

Composing herself, but keeping her distance from the severed hand, Celeste asked, "You mean, I still have the ring's protection?"

"No. Not yet, ma chérie. De protection be lost when de ring was taken. We must free it from Cupid's spirit first and den return it ta your hand. De spirits of Chalmette make sure Cupid's spirit never escape ta haunt you again."

Mark wiped the sweat from his forehead with his bare hand and asked, "But, if stealing the ring didn't transfer the power, why did Cupid do it?"

Waving a hand, Mama Vance answered, "Cupid not know dhat. Dhat is secret of de ring. Cupid — he was my king — he thought he could use de ring ta shield himself and overthrow me."

"Is it the same with your necklace?"

Mama Vance gave a displeased smile and paused before answering. "So, you recognize my necklace, Monsieur Richards?"

"It's the necklace of Sanité Dédé, isn't it?"

"Oui. Dhat be true. And it is de same as de ring. It be no good ta him who take it by force. So, we must first cleanse de ring of Cupid's spirit, since he not give it up. Dhen, we can git de ring back ta your wife, and she be protected again."

"How can you be so sure about the ring protecting Celeste again? It looks like your necklace hasn't done that great a job of protecting you."

Mama Vance turned her blind eyes toward Mark and glared at him as if she had sight. "Monsieur Richards, you need ta keep your mind on your wife's predicaments; mine are no concern of yours."

Just then, from across the dark cane field, came the flash of orange flames, muted by the fog. As the flames rose higher, the outline of a tall obelisk became visible.

"What's that?" asked Mark as he pointed toward the fire.

"Pardon, monsieur?"

"Oh, sorry," said Mark, having neglected that Mama Vance was blind. "There's a fire out in the battlefield. In front of some monument."

"Oui, not ta worry. Dhat be Hector and Ajax, preparing for de ceremony." Standing up, Mama Vance held out her hands. "Please lead me ta it." Then speaking to Celeste, she added, "You bring de hand, ma chérie."

When Celeste didn't respond or move to pick up Cupid's severed hand, Mama Vance added, "You may carry it for her, Monsieur Richards. Just be sure you not touch de ring."

Mark kicked the hand back into the overturned shoebox and picked it up. Upon reaching the hundred-feet-high, white marble monument, Celeste noticed that the bonfire was burning inside a large white circle that was chalked on the ground. A campstool had been set up inside the circle, and Hector and Ajax stood next to it, tending the fire. Also, inside the circle stood another man — an older white man in a blue watchman's uniform. He had a snare drum strapped across his chest.

"What time is it?" asked Mama Vance, of no one in particular.

Mark turned his watch crystal toward the bright fire. "About, 4:55," he answered.

"Bien! It be time ta begin." After Hector helped seat her on the campstool, Mama Vance turned toward the watchman and commanded, "Begin de summons!" In response to her order, the watchman began to beat the drum in a slow march cadence.

Mama Vance put her hand on Celeste's shoulder and commanded Mark to give Celeste the open shoebox and then to join everyone else inside the fire circle. When Celeste, holding the shoebox at arm's length, followed Mark inside the circle, Mama Vance held her back and said, "Not you, ma chérie. You must stay outside de circle, facing downriver."

When Celeste stopped, but didn't move away, Mama Vance pushed gently on her shoulder and added, "You must git away from us, ma chérie — out in de battlefield. You must face de other way. In de direction de English come from. And whatever you do, do *not* come inside de circle. No matter what happen, understand?"

As Celeste opened her mouth to confirm her understanding, she felt a probing force enter her body, the same force she had felt on her visits to Mama Vance's house. She instinctively knew Mama Vance was reading her mind. So, she didn't bother with a verbal answer to Mama Vance's question. Suddenly, feeling no fear or apprehension — just numbness — Celeste turned and marched off toward the cane field. When she had gone about twenty paces, Mama Vance yelled, "Halt! Dhat be far enough!" This left Celeste standing at the edge of an abandoned drainage ditch. It was the old Rodriguez Canal that the Americans had used as a line of defense during the battle.

Mark gave Mama Vance a dubious glance. *How did she know how far Celeste had walked?*

Next, with Hector and Ajax on either side of her, holding her hands, Mama Vance stood up and began to moan. Gradually, the moaning grew louder and faster. The drummer picked up cadence to a quick march. Finally, the moaning turned into a chant:

He-ron mandé

He-ron mandé,

Ti-gui li papa,

He-ron mandé,

Ti-gui li papa,

He-ron mandé

He-ron mandé,

Do se dan do-go,

As the chanting and drumming continued, Mark kept his eyes on Celeste and the fog lifting from the battlefield. He was amazed that Celeste had removed Cupid's hand from the shoebox. She had discarded the shoebox, holding the hand by its severed wrist.

Standing next to the bright fire caused Mark's night vision to decrease. Therefore, he didn't see the movement on the battlefield at first. When he could focus, Mark didn't believe his eyes. He was sure he was hallucinating. For marching toward Celeste, out of the rising fog, came rank after rank of British redcoat soldiers. Their bright red and white uniforms looked as good as new, and their deployed muskets bristled with glistening bayonets. The troops' faces drew Mark's attention. They were so white and gaunt. Then Mark caught his breath. The soldiers had no faces. They were white skulls. Hundreds of marching skeletons were moving toward Celeste and the shallow, grass covered ditch she stood behind. Mark feared that if Celeste didn't retreat, she would surely be impaled on the outstretched bayonets of the ghost soldiers. But when the dead redcoats were less than ten yards from the Rodriguez Canal, the drumming stopped, and Mama Vance ceased her chant and threw some white powder into the fire. "Now!" she screamed at Celeste. "Now! Remove de ring and throw de hand at de soldiers."

Celeste slowly twisted the ring off Cupid's curled finger. When it was free, she slipped it on and threw the hand over the canal with a high softball pitch. As Celeste made her throw, Mama Vance yelled out, "Aie! Aie! Voodoo Magnian!"

Mark never saw the hand hit the ranks of fallen soldiers. There was a sudden and blinding flash in the air, and the bonfire flames rose like rockets above his head. When he could finally see Celeste again, the skeleton soldiers had all disappeared, along with the fog. Mark began a sigh of relief. But his heart quickly sank, for he saw Celeste slowly crumble and fall forward into the canal ditch.

Chapter Forty-Seven

Henri Noyan took Emile's thinly veiled threat to heart. A week after Emile had saved his life, Henri took Nicole and left for France, supposedly to inspect his father's business interests. But every Creole in New Orleans knew the real reason for Henri's hasty departure was his fear that Emile would challenge him to a duel. Under Benjamin's tutelage, Emile had become well known and feared for his dueling skill with pistols. And, even with his bad leg, Emile was a better than average fencer. Except for his one moment of glory at Chalmette, Henri's renown was that of an abject coward and bacchanal.

Emile was heartbroken upon learning of Nicole's sudden departure. Henri had prevented her from sending any prior notice to Emile. He considered following Nicole and Henri to France, but Julien and Benjamin convinced him that would be foolhardy because of the Noyans' political connections there. Emile coped with his loss by retreating from New Orleans's society. He spent the next three years running the Poydras' bank and other enterprises at Pointe Coupee. He visited New Orleans infrequently, and then only for business purposes.

Emile never met or heard from Marie Laveau again. However, he did send her a hundred dollars in gold and a note of gratitude for notifying him of the attempt on Henri's life.

In November of 1823, Benjamin took ill with a terrible fever. As he and Julien were delegates to the convention to nominate the next candidate for governor of Louisiana, Julien coaxed Emile to substitute for the indisposed Benjamin. Emile hated politics and most politicians, but he couldn't turn his uncle down. He was forced to admit that political connections were necessary for their continued success in business. And he also realized that the Creoles in the state had to be united or some uncontrollable Yankee might gain control of the statehouse. Thus, on a chilly afternoon, the 14th of November 1823, Emile accompanied Julien to the opening session of the delegate convention. It was held in the stately courtroom of the Cabildo in New Orleans.

The first order of business was the roll call and introduction of delegates. Political conventions had no committee on resolutions, nor much of one on credentials, since it was a dueling offense to question the right of a delegate to sit when he presented himself. Still, as a formality, after each delegate was introduced, the chair called for challenges from the floor.

Emile nearly dozed off in the warm courtroom during the protracted introductions and seating of the delegates. However, when the chairman called out the name of Anton Cuvillier, Emile quickly sat up and took notice. As the chairman was finishing Anton's introduction, Emile's spine became rigid, and his face flushed. He was suddenly overcome with a burst of rage he could not control or even comprehend.

"Monsieur Cuvillier has served his state and country with distinction, both in the state legislature and during the war with the British invaders. It is my honor to submit his name to you. Are there any objections?"

Julien grabbed for Emile's arm as his nephew shot to his feet, but Emile was too quick for him. The chairman had scarcely finished speaking before Emile yelled, "Oui! I object, Monsieur Chairman. This man betrayed his country and us all at Chalmette. He is not fit to serve!"

The old chairman's jaw gaped open at Emile's vociferous challenge, and after some murmuring, a hush fell over the hall. Finally, Anton pushed the chairman aside and pointed at Emile from the podium. "I demand satisfaction for those remarks, Poydras! Immediate satisfaction! You lying chacalata!"

Raising his colichemarde above his head, Emile replied, "You shall have it, monsieur! As soon as you wish!"

No adjustment could be reached over Emile's challenge. No one really even tried. The exchange between Emile and Anton had been so acrimonious and public, almost everyone feared it would only end one way — in a duel à outrance, a duel to the death. Julien reluctantly offered to serve as Emile's second, as Benjamin was still too ill. When he presented himself to Anton's entourage at the New Orleans wharf, Julien was quite surprised to see who stepped forward as Anton's second. It was a smirking Henri Noyan.

"Monsieur Noyan," said Julien. "I thought you were still in France?"

"I have recently returned — for the convention, Monsieur Poydras. Now, down to business, if you please?"

Waving the lace handkerchief he constantly carried, Julien replied, "By all means."

"Of course, there can be no adjustment," declared Noyan. Julien nodded his agreement. "Therefore," continued Henri, "as it was your nephew who issued the challenge, Monsieur Cuvillier is entitled to choose the weapons and place of honor. However, because of your nephew's disability, Monsieur Cuvillier has instructed me to defer those decisions to Monsieur Poydras."

"Foils," replied Julien without hesitation and with a firm tone in his voice. "Across the river, on the bank at Point Algiers."

"Foils!" exclaimed Henri. "Your nephew chooses Anton's favorite weapon? No one exceeds Monsieur Cuvillier's skill with the foil."

"We shall soon see," said Julien flatly.

Henri looked almost jubilant. "Yes, we shall! There will be much interest in this exchange. Now, as the ferry takes some time to cross, I suggest we not delay too long in scheduling the time."

Julien pulled a gold hunting case watch from his blue satin vest, opened it, and said, "Four-thirty should give us sufficient time."

"Very good. Monsieur Cuvillier and our party shall cross on the first ferry — yours on the second?"

"That is acceptable," agreed Julien as he made a slight bow and withdrew.

Dueling, of course, was still illegal under state laws. However, the law was not enforced on the other side of the Mississippi. In fact, at meetings between highly touted duelists, you would likely find police and other officials in attendance. Such combats became social gatherings, taking on a festive atmosphere.

As their ferry barge slowly steamed toward Point Algiers, Julien motioned for Emile to step away from their crowd of supporters. Crossing the open deck, he joined Julien at the side rail. "Just answer me this," began Julien. "This isn't over that damn quadroon girl — is it?"

"Aurora?" answered Emile. "No, Uncle. Not anymore. Our animosity runs much deeper than that. You know Anton was one of the traitors who signed the surrender petition at Chalmette. He is unfit to serve…"

"That was nine years ago, Emile! And Anton went on to redeem himself by fighting the British at Chalmette. So, why have you decided to suddenly challenge him now?"

"This wound has been festering all these years, Uncle. It's time to clean it out." When Julien didn't respond to his inadequate explanation, Emile continued, "Oh, I can't explain it, Uncle, not really. A rush of outrage just came over me. Part of it is that I hadn't seen Anton for years, and when he was unexpectedly presented at the convention, as a great patriot, it suddenly brought back all my old animosities for him. No doubt, I have acted *rashly* — again. But here we are."

Julien studied his nephew for a moment. "So be it. But, why in God's name did you instruct me to ask for foils? You are much better with a pistol than Anton. And with your leg, you are at a disadvantage using a foil."

"Everything you say is true. I deliberately choose to fight on the terms most advantageous to Anton. That way, when I kill him, no one can refute the justice of my victory."

"Kill? No, remember the Code, Emile. I will not be a party to murder. This contest ends at first blood."

"Unless the combatants choose to go on," corrected Emile. "Somehow, I don't believe either of us will choose to terminate the contest at the first wound."

"Do you know that Henri Noyan is acting as Anton's second?"

Emile shrugged his shoulders and made a slight sneer. "So I hear."

"You do not find that surprising? I never knew those two to be friends."

"I was told that Henri volunteered immediately after the challenge was made." When Julien did not respond, Emile continued. "Henri does not have the courage to challenge me himself. So, I dare say, he thinks serving as Anton's second is the next best thing."

As Emile turned to speak with one of his well-wishers, Julien shook his head and spoke softly to the air. "May God have mercy on both you fools."

At that moment, the ferry pulled alongside the Algiers wharf. Julien looked out over the crowd assembled on the mud-cracked riverbank. With the sun beginning to set, the temperature had taken an uncomfortable drop. Anton and his entourage were standing in front of a fire of driftwood, warming themselves. Julien searched for Henri but didn't spot him at first. When Julien did spy Henri, a cold chill ran through his heart. For Henri was off to himself conversing with none other than Marie Laveau, the current contender for Voodoo queen of New Orleans. When Henri spotted Julien, he gave Julien a malicious smirk and tilted his head once in the direction of Marie Laveau. Julien at once realized why Henri was so eager to be Anton's second. *But how on earth did Henri know a duel would occur today?* he mused. *It cannot be coincidence that Henri has a Voodoo queen in attendance? Was some Voodoo conjuration placed on Emile to cause his abrupt challenge today?*

Pulling Emile aside, Julien asked his nephew to remain on the barge until everyone else had gone ashore. When they were alone, Julien held out a closed hand to Emile, saying, "Here, take this."

With a puzzled look on his face, Emile extended his open palm. With that, Julien dropped his gold alliance ring into his nephew's hand. "Uncle! Your ring! Put it back on at once."

"It's too late for that," said Julien with a shake of his head. "I have freely given the ring to you."

"But! I cannot possibly accept it. Why are you doing this? I am fully capable of acquitting myself in this duel."

Shaking his head, Julien answered, "No, you are not — not this time. Henri is here with the new Voodoo Queen, Marie Laveau. I can tell they have conspired against you and cursed you. You were at a disadvantage dueling Anton to start with. Now, I'm convinced you have no chance of surviving this duel."

"But, Uncle," pleaded Emile. "You will die without your ring."

"I told you once before, no man wants to live forever, and who's to say how long it takes for the protection to dissipate. Besides, as I said, I cannot take it back. For in my heart, I have given it to you. Now, you must decide whether to accept it…. It will surely save your life today. But, once you put it on, you cannot remove it until you are ready to confront your own mortality."

Emile froze, for he didn't know what to do. He surveyed the crowd for Henri and Anton and, spotting them together, stared at them awhile. Finally, Julien took the ring from his palm and slowly slipped it onto Emile's left ring finger. "There, it is done. Now, go forward to your victory — to your destiny."

The crowd was stunned. Emile, stiff leg and all, made short work of Anton. With a sharp parry and vicious lunge, Emile's foil punctured Anton's right lung.

It was not a mortal wound, but the surgeon attending Anton declared the combat at an end. Anton had finally met his match with a sword. Emile's victory gave him little satisfaction. Although many in attendance congratulated him and praised his skill, Emile felt isolated and empty — like a dark pit had opened and pulled his soul into it.

As Emile and Julien walked back to re-board their ferry, they observed Henri Noyan in an animated conversation with Marie Laveau at the far end of the pier. A few feet from the pair, the surgeon was frantically attending to Anton's wound. They weren't close enough to make out the conversation, but Julien could tell it was not a pleasant one. It concluded with Henri shaking his fist at the Voodoo queen and abruptly following the stricken Anton onto their ferry.

As Emile and Julien continued walking toward the pier, the young Voodoo queen blocked their path and struck a defiant pose, hands on her hips. Quickly glancing at the hands of the Poydras men, she declared, "Ah-hah! It is as I suspected. Monsieur Emile now wears the ring."

"That's right!" replied Julien. "Your curses are no match for it."

Eyes flashing, Marie retorted, "We shall see, Monsieur Julien! We shall see! Only you won't live long enough to know the final outcome. Will you?"

Chapter Forty-Eight

As Mark, Celeste, and Mama Vance were encountering the spirits at Chalmette Battlefield, Justin was entering Metairie General Hospital. At 5:00 a.m., the only open entrance was through the Emergency Room. Justin waited until the desk nurse left to refill her coffee cup, and then he slipped in wearing a white lab coat and carrying a new black doctor's bag.

Taking the stairs to the third floor, Justin was able to reach Elizabeth Villere's room unnoticed. He had timed the nurses' rounds on his prior visit to the hospital. They checked the child's vital signs and IV every thirty minutes on the hour and half-hour. Glancing at his watch as he entered the private room, Justin estimated he had about fifteen minutes before the next nurse's check.

The hospital room was nearly dark, illuminated solely by a dim night light above the child's bed. The only sound was the rhythmic hum and click of Elizabeth's respirator machine. From out of the dark corner beside the bed, Evon Villere leaned forward to see who had entered the room.

Justin spoke first. "Good mornin', Mrs. Villere. How's Elizabeth?"

The child's young mother didn't answer at first. She rubbed her eyes with one hand for a moment and shook her head. Then she finally replied with a mournful tone in her voice. "I know you're not a doctor. What do you really want with my child's blood?"

Justin froze for a second, not knowing what to do. Then he sat his black bag on the foot of the bed and pulled up a chair facing Evon Villere. Looking directly into the woman's grief-stricken eyes, Justin said, "You're right, Mrs. Villere, I'm not a doctor, but — "

"Who are you? Our doctor said we were to call the hospital security at once, if you showed up again."

After being interrupted, Justin pulled a small piece of paper from his shirt pocket, unfolded it, and handed it to the woman. Evon held it close to her tired face so she could read it in the dim light. "This is a cashier's check for six thousand dollars!"

"Yes," answered Justin. "And it's yours — whether you turn me in or not. All I ask is that you give me a chance to explain."

Evon nodded her consent, still holding the check in both hands.

"As I said, I'm not a doctor. But I wasn't lyin' when I told you your daughter's blood would help me save a life — my granddaughter's life. I can't tell you any more than that. I swear, I mean your daughter no harm. And what I need to do will cause her no pain.... It's your decision. If you say no, I'll leave now, and not trouble you again."

Looking at the check again, Evon Villere let her hands drop into her lap. Then she looked over at her motionless daughter and the respirator hoses taped to her face. "I don't know why," she said in a forlorn voice. "But I believe you. If Elizabeth's blood will help save your granddaughter, take it. Take as much as you need. They're turning off the life-support this morning anyway."

Justin reached over and squeezed Evon's limp hand. "Thank you, Mrs. Villere. Thank you." Looking at his watch, Justin noted he had less than five minutes until the next scheduled nurses' rounds. "Mrs. Villere, it will take me a good twenty to twenty-five minutes to draw the blood, and the nurse will be in here to check on Elizabeth any minute now. Is it okay with you if I conceal myself in the bathroom until the nurse is gone?"

Without looking up, Mrs. Villere choked out softly, "Yes."

As soon as Justin heard the nurse leave, he moved quickly. First, he raised the foot of the hospital bed as high as it would go. Then he tied off the child's free arm with a rubber tourniquet and inserted a large gauge needle into the vein bulging at her arm. The needle was attached to a long plastic tube, which was connected to a pint glass bottle Justin placed on the floor. The blood spurted and flowed slowly into the clear plastic tube. When Justin released the tourniquet, the stream of scarlet liquid stabilized, but the flow was slow — too slow. Glancing at his watch, Justin realized that there would not be enough time to collect a second bottle.

When the bottle was filled, he pinched the tube off with his fingers and withdrew the needle. Blood trickled out of the needle puncture in the child's arm. Justin wiped it off with a cotton ball and put a band-aide over the wound. Then he put a black rubber cork into the bottle's neck and loaded the blood and the dripping tube and needle into his open doctor's bag. As he did this, he looked over to Evon Villere. She had slumped back in her chair, staring at the blank wall on the opposite side of the hospital room.

As he opened his mouth to say a parting word of thanks, Justin was cut short by a woman's voice behind him. "What's going on here?"

Justin spun around and saw that the question came from a stern looking nurse standing in the doorway.

"Just drawin' some blood for the lab," he replied.

"The hell you are! I've never seen you before, and there's no orders for lab work. Where's your ID badge?"

Realizing his bluff had failed, Justin slammed his bag shut and tucked it under his arm like a halfback carrying a football. He lunged for the door, shoving the nurse aside with a stiff arm to her left shoulder. As Justin forced his way out of the room, the nurse screamed, "Security! Someone call security!"

Never looking back, Justin raced for the stairs, running down them two at a time. In a matter of seconds, he reached the fire escape door leading out to the rear of the hospital. Without slowing down, he hit the red door release with his shoulder and exited into the dark service lot. From behind him came the harsh clanging of the fire door alarm.

Halting beside a row of green trash dumpsters, Justin caught his breath and whipped off his lab coat, throwing it into one of the open dumpsters. His heart was pounding so hard he could hear and feel its rapid pulsations in his ears. Justin took a couple of gulps of damp air and looked in all directions. No one was to be seen.

Sprinting across the nearly vacant parking lot, Justin avoided running directly under any of the lot's light poles. When he reached the street and sidewalk behind the hospital, he slowed to a fast walk, still keeping his doctor's bag tucked under his arm. After zigzagging three or four blocks, Justin was home free. He made it to where he'd parked his BMW on a secluded residential street.

As Justin pulled in front of his house, he noted the lights were on in the living room, and the front gate was standing open. *Good*, he thought. *Celeste and Mark have made it back.*

Bypassing the front door, Justin walked quickly through the garden. Coming in the French doors unannounced, Justin was immediately grabbed around the neck by a huge black man. Letting out a gasp, Justin dropped his doctor's bag and pulled at the muscular arm choking off his breath. He heard Mark call out, "It's Justin!"

"It's alright, Hector," came Mama Vance's voice from the living room. "Dhat be Monsieur Noyan."

After being released from Hector's chokehold, Justin walked into the living room. Mama Vance was seated in an easy chair. Ajax sat cross-legged on the floor at her feet. Mark was also sitting on the floor, beside the sofa, with a washcloth in his hand. On the couch lay the limp body of Celeste, who was motionless and unconscious.

Part V
Death and Redemption

And forthwith Jesus gave them leave. And the unclean spirits went out,
and entered into the swine: and the herd ran violently down a steep place
into the sea,... and were choked in the sea.

– Mark the Evangelist, Mark 5:13

Chapter Forty-Nine

After Emile's duel with Anton, Julien returned to Pointe Coupee. *To await my fate*, he told himself. Before he left New Orleans, he made Emile promise not to tell anyone about the secret of the ring — not even Benjamin. He reasoned that if the power of the ring became known to others, Emile would be subjected to numerous schemes to take the ring from him. Besides, they already had Marie Laveau to contend with. How she'd found out about the ring, he didn't know.

Emile remained in New Orleans after his uncle's departure. The reason he gave Julien was to check on their steamboat business and other interests. Without challenging him, Julien was astute enough to know that Emile must have another reason to remain behind. Julien was reasonably certain that Emile was going to rendezvous with Nicole Noyan. But it didn't dawn on Julien that Emile had more than one reason to remain in New Orleans — to see Sanité Dédé.

Once he saw Nicole again, Emile could not bear to be without her. Their passion for each other had not diminished during their separation. Henri made no attempts to obstruct their affair. He had not the backbone to challenge Emile. After seeing what short work Emile had made of Anton, who was supposedly the best swordsman in New Orleans, Henri knew better than to confront Emile, especially since Marie Laveau's gris-gris had failed to protect Anton.

Occasionally, Emile would feel pangs of guilt for not visiting Julien. He did write his uncle and Benjamin and inquire repeatedly about Julien's health. Yet, he knew intuitively that conditions might not be as well as reported. He felt their letters were evasive at times. But whenever he was with Nicole, Emile could not focus on his responsibilities. Nicole was a very demanding woman. Even though she had lessened her badgering about freeing her from her marriage to Henri, Emile felt her unspoken entreaties. He was also uneasy about leaving Nicole in New Orleans, not knowing what Henri might do to her if he wasn't around. Though Emile realized Nicole was using him to liberate her from her dreadful marriage, he didn't care. He loved her even so. He devoted all his time to Nicole, and before he knew it, the weeks of his stay in New Orleans stretched into months.

Emile's life went blissfully along until one day, in June 1824, when he received a cursory letter from Benjamin:

Dear Emile,

You must return to Pointe Coupee at once. Uncle Julien is gravely ill. I fear he will not last the month.

Please hurry, Emile. Uncle Julien has been asking for you.

Your Devoted Brother,

Benjamin

Notwithstanding the open secret of their affair, Emile and Nicole still had to keep up appearances somewhat. And despite the fact that Henri kept himself absent from New Orleans a good deal of the time, their liaisons could not take place in public or at Julien's New Orleans residence. So, Emile rented a modest cottage for them on St. Ann Street a block east of Rampart Street. The day after receiving Benjamin's letter, Emile met Nicole at their cottage to tell her he had to go to Point Coupee.

Nicole sensed Emile was troubled the second she entered the house, for Emile did not rise from his desk to greet her. "Emile, my love, is something the matter?"

Nodding his head and holding up Benjamin's letter, Emile answered, "It's Uncle Julien. He's dying. I must leave for Point Coupee at once."

"Oh, Emile, I'm so sorry. What has happened?"

Lying, Emile said, "I don't know. Benjamin just said to hurry — that the end is near."

"Dear one, do you want me to go with you? You must be devastated. I know how you adore your uncle Julien."

"No, thank you. I think I best go alone for this. It's just that — "

"It's all right, Emile. I know your uncle does not approve of our relationship. I have often worried that I have caused an estrangement between the two of you.... I'm sorry."

Rising from the desk and embracing Nicole, Emile consoled her. "No, no, dear. What has happened between me and Uncle Julien is far more complicated than our affair. I can't explain it all right now. But it's not your fault, I promise you."

Looking up into Emile's eyes, Nicole nodded. "If you say so. Nevertheless, please convey my sympathy to your uncle and brother. And please return to me as soon as you can. I don't know how to live without you."

***

Upon his arrival at Pointe Coupee, Emile was greeted by his solemn-faced brother. As he stepped off the river barge at the Alma Plantation, Emile asked sheepishly, "I'm not too late? Am I?"

With a look of disdain, Benjamin replied, "If you mean, is Uncle Julien still alive? The answer is, yes."

By the tone of his voice, Emile could tell his brother was quite piqued with him. This intensified Emile's feelings of guilt and delinquency. "What ails him?" he asked as they walked toward Julien's house on the banks of the False River.

"The doctors don't know. They say it's his age. He simply grows weaker by the day.... But you'll soon see, he certainly has not lost the desire to live."

"I had no idea," Emile began. "Why didn't you write me sooner of his decline? There was no mention of Uncle Julien's failing health in any of his or your other letters."

"He forbade any mention of his condition, and he refused to really explain why. He would only say he didn't wish to worry you." Benjamin stopped in his tracks and confronted his brother, "Why haven't you come once to check on Uncle Julien in all these months?" Insight flashed across Benjamin's face. "Uncle Julien has not been the same since he returned from New Orleans last fall. Did anything happen between the two of you there?"

Emile feigned ignorance. "No, I can't think of a thing. Unless it had something to do with my duel with Anton Cuvillier?"

Benjamin shook his head and walked on. "No. That doesn't make sense. We both have been involved in duels before. Something else must have happened there."

Emile shoved his left hand into his coat pocket, hoping his brother would not notice that he now wore Julien's alliance ring. The brothers walked in silence the rest of the way to the modest white plantation house.

They found Julien in his bedchamber, fully dressed, propped up on pillows in his four-poster bed. Emile was shocked at his uncle's appearance. Although Julien had recently reached his 78th birthday in April, he had become a gaunt shell of the vigorous man that left New Orleans seven months earlier. His eyes were sunken and his skin pallid, and there was a labored wheeze to his breathing. When he realized that Emile had entered the room, he dismissed his houseboy with a wave of his hand.

Taking his uncle's trembling hand into his, Emile sat down on the bed. "Oh, Uncle! Can you ever forgive me for taking so long to come to you?"

"Nonsense," Julien said with a weak smile. "There is nothing to forgive. You have your own life to lead."

Tears welled up in Emile's eyes. "I would have nothing, but for you, Uncle."

Looking up at Benjamin, standing at the foot of the bed, Julien requested, "Benjamin, please fetch my will. I want to go over it while you both are here." With a nod of his head, Benjamin left the room, closing the door behind him.

After Benjamin's footsteps faded down the hall, Emile spoke. "After you left New Orleans, I tried to find Sanité Dédé, but she was not to be found. Some said Marie Laveau banished her in her campaign to become queen of all the Voodooiennes. Others said she just decamped to Baton Rouge or elsewhere. I'm sorry — "

Julien sighed and cut him off. "There's nothing she could have done, even had you found her."

"She might have had a way to safely return the ring to you, or she could have made you another ring."

"No!" said Julien with all the strength he could muster. "There must never be another ring — not even if it costs all our lives. It would be a mortal sin to ask for another such charm, knowing that an innocent child must die to create it."

Dropping his head, Emile replied, "I know, Uncle. But I would gladly give my soul to save you now. I feel so ashamed that I let you give me your ring. I was so selfish. But now I shall return the ring to — "

"No! I will not accept it! It's too late for me now. The ring was mine to give, and I really gave you no choice in the matter. Now that the die is cast, I only ask that you use the ring not only for self-gain, but for the benefit of others as well. And when the day comes that you are ready to give it up, make certain that the one you entrust it to has moral intentions. Better to throw the ring into the river than let it fall into the hands of evil. Will you make this your final and lasting promise to me?"

Before Emile could answer, the men heard the approach of Benjamin. As the door began to open, Emile whispered, "I promise, Uncle. I promise."

When Benjamin entered the bedroom, Julien instructed him to hand his will to Emile for him to read and ask any questions he might have, as he and Benjamin were designated co-executors of Julien's estate. Emile was astounded by his uncle's philanthropy. Aside from the generous bequests to him, Benjamin, and other relatives and servants, Julien provided for the New Orleans Female Orphan Asylum, which he had helped establish seven years earlier. He left the orphanage houses and land worth more than $100,000. He also bequeathed $30,000 each to the Parishes of Pointe Coupee and West Baton Rouge to set up trust funds to provide dowries for the girls of the parishes, with those in "pitiable circumstances" to be given preference. Also, Pointe Coupee was bequeathed $20,000 to establish an academy or college for local children. The New Orleans Charity Hospital received many valuable properties as well. The list of beneficiaries seemed to be never ending.

But when Emile read the article dealing with the disposition of Julien's one thousand slaves, he was utterly amazed. "Uncle?" he questioned. "I can understand your wish that the slave families not be split or separated from your plantations. But do you really want us to free *all* the slaves twenty-five years after your death? And give each of them twenty-five dollars?"

"Yes, I'd free them all today if I thought the other plantation owners would stand for it. You know how they have chastised me over the years for being too lenient in my treatment of our slaves. I can only hope that in twenty-five years our society will have matured enough to understand the insidious evil that is fostered by slavery. There must — there will be a better way someday."

"It will — " Emile started to say but was interrupted by Julien.

"Quick, boys! Put my shoes on and stand me up. I feel another spell coming on."

Emile looked puzzled and turned to Benjamin, who quickly slipped Julien's silver buckled shoes on him. Benjamin answered Emile's unspoken question. "Uncle Julien believes a man cannot die on his feet. That is why we keep him fully dressed and servants constantly at his side. Whenever he feels an attack coming on, he has us stand him up so he can touch the floor. You'll have to pull him up under his arms. He's too weak to do it himself."

As Emile and Benjamin held their uncle up, his arms limply around their necks, he grimaced and tried to speak. But the only sound that passed through his lips was the rush of his last breath leaving his lungs.

Chapter Fifty

As Mark quickly explained the fantastic events that took place at Chalmette, and how Celeste became unconscious, Justin knelt beside Celeste and took her wrist in his fingers. Her pulse was slow and somewhat irregular. Pulling open her eyelids with his thumb, Justin observed that Celeste's pupils were dilated and slow to react to the lamplight above her head. He then noted that the Poydras ring was back on Celeste's left ring finger.

Turning to Mama Vance, Justin asked, "What happened to her, Mama Vance? She's in a coma."

"I not be sure, Monsieur Noyan. It tricky business takin' de ring by force. It may be de ceremony not free de ring of Cupid's spirit — or he jump into Mademoiselle Celeste's body instead of de dead soldiers."

"I don't under… Look, we must get her to a hospital. I'm afraid her heart may stop."

Mama Vance shook her head slowly. "Your doctors cannot help her. Only ting dhat save your granddaughter be ta hold conjure ceremony right away, dhat free her body of *all* de spirits dhat possess her."

"How can she survive the ceremony like she is?"

"You have no choice, Monsieur Noyan. Unless we free her of Cupid's spirit soon, she will die, I fears."

Rising to his feet, Justin asked, "Wait, what about the ring? Now that she has it back, won't it protect her from Cupid?"

Shrugging her stooped shoulders, Mama Vance answered, "Maybe. But I fears not. Cupid's spirit must'a git in her before she git de ring back on. And now he takin' his vengeance on your grandchild."

"What vengeance?"

"As Monsieur Richards say, I had ta kill Cupid ta git de ring back. I curse his spirit too."

Justin closed his eyes and rubbed his forehead as he tried to process the dreadful turn of events he had encountered. Finally, he turned to Mark, who was still wiping Celeste's forehead with the damp washcloth, as if he could wash her coma away. "What do you say, Mark? She's your wife."

Not looking away from Celeste's face, Mark answered, "Whatever Mama Vance says. After what I saw this morning, I'll believe anything she suggests."

"Alright, then," agreed Justin. "We proceed with the conjure ceremony. How soon can it be done?"

Mama Vance pondered Justin's question before answering, "Be best ta wait for St. John's Eve.... Not sure I can call up de spirits now. But I not sure she last three more day. So, we do it tomorrow tonight. At midnight," replied Mama Vance. "If you have de blood of de goat without horns?"

"I have it," answered Justin as he walked to the entry where he had dropped his black medical bag during his struggle with Hector.

As he bent over to pick up the bag, Justin noticed a large puddle of dark liquid had seeped out of the satchel onto the entryway's gray tile floor. Jerking the bag open, Justin's fears were immediately confirmed. The neck of the bottle containing Elizabeth Villere's blood had broken off when Justin dropped the bag on the tile floor, and since the satchel had landed upside down, all the blood had drained out.

"No!" he screamed. "No, it can't be!"

Mark left Celeste's side and ran to Justin. Seeing the spilled blood, he too cried, "Oh God! No! This can't be happening."

Rising to her feet with the help of Ajax, Mama Vance asked, "What be wrong?"

"The bottle broke!" wailed Justin. "All the blood has spilled out on the floor. Quick, Mark! Fetch the sponge and dishpan from under the sink. Maybe we can salvage most of it."

"Don't bother," interjected Mama Vance. "If de blood not be pure, it be no good. Must have fresh pure blood for de conjure to work."

Justin slowly sank to his knees. Kneeling in the pool of blood, he put his face into his hands and began to sob.

Chapter Fifty-One

After Julien's death, it took Emile and Benjamin over a month to even begin to put his estate in order. Thus, Emile did not see Nicole again until the first of August 1824. Emile found that his guilt over Julien's death had somewhat cooled his ardor for Nicole. Nonetheless, they resumed their affair without hesitation.

After Emile had been in New Orleans about six weeks, a coach, heavily loaded with baggage, pulled up to his late uncle's house. The coach's sole passenger was a woman in a bright blue dress with matching satin hat. Her face was obscured by a thick white veil.

Having observed the arrival of the woman from the parlor window, Emile rushed into the foyer. Shoving the houseboy aside, he opened the front door as she came onto the porch. "Nicole! What is the meaning of this? You can't just move in here."

Without answering, Nicole raised the opaque veil covering her face and neck. Emile flinched upon seeing her face. Her left cheek and lower lip were purple and swollen to twice their normal sizes. Both her eyes were blackened, and there were coin size bruises up and down her neck.

"My God, Nicole! Did Henri do this to you?"

Nicole nodded and replied, "Yes. Now, are you going to keep me standing out here for the whole city to see? Or may I come in?"

Emile meekly stepped aside. Turning to the gawking houseboy, he said, "Didier, have the coachmen take Madame Noyan's trunks up to the back bedroom, overlooking the garden." Then, gently taking Nicole's arm, he led her into the parlor and closed the door.

Nicole collapsed into a green velvet chair and removed her hat and veil. Sitting down in the matching chair beside her, Emile asked, "What happened?"

"I'm pregnant, Emile."

"What?"

"It's your child." Nicole lightly rubbed at her swollen lip with her fingertips. "When Henri found out, he nearly beat me to death. He's hit me before, but never like — "

"You told him *first*!" interrupted Emile. Narrowing the focus of his eyes on Nicole's face, he asked, "Why did you do that, my dear?"

Nicole dropped her eyes and looked at her folded hands. "I had to. I'm pregnant with your child."

"Yes, yes. But why tell Henri that in person — and alone? You must have known he would react violently?" When Nicole gave no answer, Emile continued with his accusatory tone. "You wanted him to beat you — didn't you? So I would be compelled to take you in?"

Nicole still didn't answer Emile, but tears began to roll down her bruised cheeks. A discerning look came across Emile's face. "Or were you trying to provoke Henri into finally issuing a challenge to me? Or me to him?"

Nicole slid to her knees, wrapping her arms tightly around Emile's legs. "Yes! Yes! I did it, for all those reasons. I had to do something! I can't bear to be married to him another day."

"Oh, Nicole, is that all I've ever been to you? A way to escape your marriage to Henri?"

Looking up Nicole answered, "No, no, my love.… But if you are asking have I *used* you? Then, yes, I suppose I have. People can use someone and still love that person. What about you? I know you loved your uncle Julien dearly. But didn't you use his wealth and business connections to make your success? Deep and lasting relationships are built on more than one motive."

Emile cradled Nicole's tear-streaked face in his hands and softened his tone. "You're right; I'm being hypocritical. Besides, you made it clear on the night we met what you wanted from me. I think I'm really angry at myself for not calling Henri out sooner. You should not have been forced to subject yourself to this."

"He still swears he will not give me a divorce. And when I scorned him as a coward and a cuckold, he still refused to challenge you. He said he would never be fool enough to do that."

"He will challenge me," declared Emile as he pulled Nicole to her feet. "I promise you. I have to catch Henri and his father together in some public place. And that will be the end of it. Paul will force Henri to challenge me."

"Why not simply issue your own challenge — send him a note today?"

"No," said Emile, shaking his head. "Henri could always refuse my challenge, saying I was beneath his station — or no gentleman. Besides, I want the choice of weapons for this duel — pistols. I will not make the same mistake twice. This time it *will* be a duel to the death."

Nicole forced her swollen lips to smile. "Yes, a duel à outrance it must be. Come, shall we drink to my soon-to-be late husband?"

Emile closed his eyes and sighed, silently criticizing himself. *Oh, Uncle Julien. I should have listened to you. I'm glad you are not here to suffer the shame I have brought to our family.*

Chapter Fifty-Two

Mark bent over and pulled Justin out of the puddle of blood. As Justin stood up, Mark saw that the knees of his white hospital trousers were soaked scarlet from the blood on the tile. Even after standing, Justin was not in control of himself. He just stood there above the bloody floor and stared at it, wiping at his dwindling tears with his fingers.

Mark was about to lead Justin back into the living room when the telephone rang. The clanging of the kitchen wall phone startled Mark. Realizing that Justin was in no shape to talk, Mark ran to get the phone. He grabbed it before the third ring was complete.

"Hello?"

"Mark? Is that you?"

Not recognizing the voice, Mark answered cautiously, "Yes. Who's this, please?"

"It's Amy, Mark. I'm sorry to call so early. But I've been tryin' to reach you all for days, and I never get an answer."

Doing his best to control the panic that was seizing him, Mark replied, "That's okay, Amy. Sorry, I didn't recognize your voice. It sounds different over the phone."

"No apology is needed, hon. I probably woke you up. Anyway, you've got plenty of time to learn your mother-in-law's voice."

Mark forced a polite laugh. "Hah. Sure thing, Amy. Is everything alright?"

"That's what I called to find out. Justin called me the day after you all got to N'aw Arlens. But I haven't heard a peep out'a you or Celeste. Are you both okay?"

"Oh sure, Amy. We're both fine. I'm sorry we haven't called. With all the sightseeing and job interviews, I'm afraid we just lost track of time."

"That's alright, hon. Just as long as everybody's okay. Is Celeste handy? I'd like to talk to her a sec."

Even though Mark had anticipated Amy's request from the start of their conversation, he felt he hadn't come up with a very good answer. "She's still asleep. I'll wake her if you want, but…"

"But what?"

"Well… to be honest, we both had too many hurricanes at Pat O'Brien's last night. Celeste was up half the night puking. I kinda hate to wake her just now?"

"Oh sure, hon, I understand. Just have her call me when she's up and feelin' better."

Glancing through the kitchen door at the comatose Celeste, Mark answered, "I sure will, Amy."

"Well, I bet you'd like to git back to bed too. So, I'll let you go. Give my love to Justin."

"Sure Amy, bye now."

Mark hung up the phone with a sigh of relief. When he walked into the living room, he saw that Justin had made it into the velvet side chair next to Mama Vance. As he entered the room, he heard her say, "… dhere's no substitute for de blood of de lamb — 'cept maybe dhat of a saint. You know any saints, Monsieur Noyan?"

Justin looked at his wristwatch. "It's only 7:05. Maybe I can get back to the hospital before they cut off the life support?" As soon as Justin uttered the proposal, he knew it was impossible. He realized by now every nurse and doctor in the hospital had his description, and hospital security would be at the door to Elizabeth Villere's room.

"I know," continued Justin. "I'll follow the body to the funeral home and draw some blood there."

Mama Vance shook her head. "Dhat no good neither. De blood must be taken while de heart be still warm. It no good less'n be fresh."

Justin threw up his hands. "What do you suggest, then?"

"You have only two choices, Monsieur Noyan. Let your granddaughter die, or sacrifice de new lamb to save her."

Justin slumped back in his chair and stared into Mama Vance's blank eyes. "You're suggestin' we murder some innocent child?"

"De choice be yours, Monsieur Noyan, not mine." Turning her head in Mark's direction, Mama Vance added, "Yours and Monsieur Richards. Jest don't take too much time decidin'."

Chapter Fifty-Three

True to his promise to Nicole, Emile did compel Henri Noyan to challenge him. The week after Nicole moved in with Emile, he found Henri and his father, Paul Noyan, together at the New Orleans slave market on Esplanade Avenue at Moreau.

Emile marched up to the men, in the middle of an auction, and called Henri a coward, announcing, "Only a villain and a coward would beat his wife in place of challenging the man he believes wronged him!"

Henri responded with contempt for Emile and his illegitimate background — saying it was beneath his family's dignity to favor such a mongrel with a challenge. When Emile then offered to purchase a colored wench for Henri to vent his anger on, now that Emile had his wife, Paul Noyan could take no more of the public humiliation. He took his son aside and ordered Henri to challenge Emile or he would do it for him, adding that if he had to do so, Henri was not a Noyan and would be disinherited.

The next morning, Paul Noyan greatly regretted having forced Henri into the duel. Having chosen pistols for their duel, Emile avoided Henri's first two fires and dispatched Henri with a precise shot to the heart on their third exchange. After he knelt beside his son's lifeless body, Paul approached Emile and all but begged Emile to proclaim that the child Nicole carried was Henri's, so the Noyan family would have an heir if a son was born. Out of pity and guilt, and the promise that the child would inherit the Noyan family wealth, Emile agreed to Paul's request. It proved to be a fatal decision for both him and Nicole.

Nicole and Emile settled in New Orleans and were married five days after the duel with Henri. Nicole gave birth to a son the following spring, on March 12, 1825. Despite her initial protests, the boy was christened Jean Baptiste Noyan II, after the martyred hero of the 1768 revolution against Spain. Even though Nicole was furious with Emile for having agreed to give their child the Noyan name without consulting her, Emile was able to convince her it was better for them and their son socially if no one could claim Jean was the product of an illicit affair. Also, there was the added benefit of the Noyan family inheritance promised by Paul Noyan.

Emile always assumed he and Nicole would have other children to carry on the Poydras name, but after five years of marriage, little Jean was their only child. Paul Noyan doted upon the boy, visiting the child nearly every week and lavishing him with expensive gifts. Emile felt Paul's love and concern for Jean were genuine, and he came to believe that they had even transcended the bitter memory of Henri's death.

Then on the evening before Jean's fifth birthday, Paul made an unannounced visit to Emile's home in New Orleans. He found Emile alone in the parlor after Nicole had taken the boy up to bed. Emile was lounging on the sofa with a brandy when Paul came in. "Ah, Paul, come sit down. We did not expect you until Jean's birthday party tomorrow. Will you join me in a cognac? After chasing after a spirited five-year-old all evening, I feel the need of a drink."

Remaining standing, Paul replied coolly, "No thank you, Emile."

Sensing something amiss, Emile sat straight up and asked, "What is it, Paul? You seem upset."

"Not at all; it's about Jean. I want to take him home with me."

"But of course. We are always happy for Jean to visit you. He — "

"No! You don't understand," interrupted Paul. "It's not for a visit. I want to adopt the boy."

"What!" declared Emile as he rose quickly from the couch. "You're not serious, are you?"

"I am quite serious. The boy is a Noyan — my grandson — my heir. He belongs with me."

"Have you gone mad? You know the boy is *my* son. I have never objected to sharing Jean with you. But I will *never* give him up. Not to you. Not to anyone!" Emile pointed his finger at Paul's face for emphasis as he spoke.

Unfazed by Emile's declaration, Paul stood his ground and replied with a sinister tone in his voice. "I strongly suggest you and Nicole think about it. It would be in your best interests to let the child go with me."

Raising his voice, Emile responded, "How dare you threaten us! Now, leave my house at once. And do not return until you renounce this preposterous demand."

Paul turned on his heel and walked briskly to the door. As he exited, he turned back to face Emile. "Think about it, Poydras. If you don't value your own life, think about your wife's. I will not fail if you force me to act."

Chapter Fifty-Four

Mark fanned himself with his white bucket hat. He and Justin were in a rental car, parked in the hot Louisiana sun outside an elementary school in Gentilly, Louisiana, a northern suburb of New Orleans.

"Damn, it's hot," declared Mark. "How much longer? I think the brown dye in my hair is starting to run, I'm sweating so much."

Justin, wearing a New Orleans Saints baseball cap and oversize sunglasses, glanced through the steering wheel at the inoperable clock on the dashboard of the rented Chevy Impala. Then he looked at his wristwatch. "It shouldn't be more than five minutes. The superintendent's office said all summer school classes let out at three."

Looking down at the closed grocery sack and doctor's bag laying on the passenger floorboard, Mark added, "I'm not sure I can go through with this, Justin. Not even for Celeste."

"Look, Mark. We've been through this from every angle. And we agreed on what we had to do. Don't go soft on me now!"

Mark dropped his chin to his chest and exhaled. "I'm sorry. I thought I could do it. But now…"

As Mark was speaking, the front doors of the red brick school flew open, and children came running out and past their car. Mark put his hat on and put his head down, but Justin intensely scanned the groups of kids leaving the school building. His eyes locked onto a girl with her blond hair cut in a pageboy. She was dressed in blue shorts and a pink T-shirt, and she appeared to be ten or eleven years old.

Starting their blue Chevy, Justin said, "I've got one. Get ready."

Justin and Mark slowly followed the blonde-headed girl and her companions for three or four blocks. At the next intersection, the group of children split up. The blonde-headed girl was left alone, except for one other dark-headed girl in a denim shirt and skirt.

Giving Mark a stern look, Justin pulled up beside the two girls, keeping the car engine running. Mark leaned his head out the open passenger window and spoke. "Excuse me? Would you girls know where Pratt Park is? I'm supposed to meet my niece there."

The two girls looked at each other, and then the dark-headed girl answered, "Sorry, mister. I've been there before. But I don't know how to give ya directions."

Looking to the blonde girl, Mark asked, "What about you, honey? Can you tell me how to get there? I've got a city map here."

The blonde-headed girl shook her head. "I'm real sorry, mister. But my folks don't allow me to talk to strangers."

"That's real good advice," added Mark. "And I wouldn't want you to disobey your folks — maybe I could ask them? Do they live nearby?"

"Yes'um," she answered, "'bout five blocks from here."

"Oh, that far. Well, you see," said Mark, holding up the grocery bag, "my family's having a cookout at the park, and I'm late getting the hot dogs there. If you girls could just show us where we are on this map, I'd sure appreciate it. We'd even give you each five dollars?"

"Five bucks!" exclaimed the dark-headed girl. "Sure. Let me see your map."

Mark opened the back door to the Chevy from the inside and began unfolding the map. The dark-headed girl slid into the backseat, but the blonde girl remained standing on the sidewalk. So, Mark encouraged her. "Don't you want to get in too? We've got the air conditioner on."

"Yeah… I guess," she answered hesitantly. "As long as it don't take too long."

As soon as the blonde-headed girl got in the car, Mark quickly exited the front seat and got in the back seat with the girls. As he handed them the map, he slammed the car door and locked it. With that, Justin quickly accelerated from the curb.

The two girls gave each other startled looks and began to scream.

Chapter Fifty-Five

A month had passed since Paul Noyan had demanded custody of little Jean. Paul had returned to his plantation upriver and remained there. Emile surmised that Paul would soon miss seeing Jean, drop his demand, and make amends. He told Nicole about Paul's demand to adopt their son, but not about the veiled threats he had made against them.

Emile had almost put the matter out of his mind when he received a hand-delivered letter on June 13, 1830. Taking the envelope into his study and closing the door, Emile broke open the red wax seal and read the message in private.

Monsieur Poydras,

This is your last opportunity. If Jean is not delivered to me by week's end, it will be too late to save you and Nicole.

May God have mercy on your souls if you disregard this warning.

The note was unsigned, but the envelope bore the personal seal of Paul Noyan. The message so infuriated Emile, he considered issuing a challenge to Paul. But he immediately realized that the elderly Noyan could not accept a challenge, and he would only lose face by issuing one.

Emile unlocked the desk drawer he kept his diary in and slipped the letter inside the cover of his leather-bound journal. He started to close the drawer but stopped and took out his diary and made an entry about Paul's threating note and his planned response. He concluded with: *Nicole was right all along. Paul was not to be trusted. It must have been his plan from the beginning to take Jean from us when it suited him.*

He decided it would be best to keep Paul's threat to himself for now and do his utmost to guard his family. With that in mind, Emile went upstairs and instructed Nicole and the servants to begin packing immediately. He told Nicole the entire family was steaming the next day to St. Louis on business, with a stop at Pointe Coupee to inspect his plantation and visit Benjamin.

On Sunday, the second day after they reached Pointe Coupee, Nicole took ill with a fever. By Wednesday night, Nicole was dead. The doctors said it was yellow fever, and that it was very odd how she had succumbed so quickly. There had been no reported cases of fever in the area that year.

Since Nicole's family lived in New Orleans, Emile and Benjamin took her body downriver for burial. As one of their company's sternwheelers, the *Iberville,* steamed through the morning mist, Benjamin found his brother on the bow of the riverboat, staring at the reddish-brown water. Though it was only half-past eight in the morning, Emile was drinking whiskey from a large water tumbler.

Emile ignored his brother's approach and kept gazing at the ripples in the water being cut by the bow of the *Iberville.* After a moment, Benjamin broke the silence. "I feel so useless, Brother. I wish there was some way I could help you bear your grief."

Emile drained the rest of the bourbon from his glass and intentionally dropped the glass in the river. After a long pause, he finally responded to his brother. "There is something you can do for me."

"Name it."

"Promise me — if anything happens to me — you won't let Paul Noyan obtain custody of Jean. That you won't let Noyan *near* Jean."

"As you wish," answered Benjamin slowly. "But what happened? You, Paul, and the boy were so close? What has caused this estrangement?"

Emile looked Benjamin in the eyes for the first time. "I... I can't explain it all now. But Paul is responsible for Nicole's death. And he would kill me as well, if he could."

"What! Emile, Nicole died of the fever. How could — "

Emile interrupted Benjamin by grabbing his shoulders with both hands. "You must believe me, Brother! After the funeral, take Jean back to Pointe Coupee with you. If I fail to come for him, the answers to your questions are in my diary. It's locked in my study desk."

"But — "

"Please!" implored Emile, dropping his hands from Benjamin's shoulders and turning back to face the river. "You must trust me for now. When this is over, I promise to tell you everything."

"Very well, Emile. I will see to it."

Benjamin started to withdraw, but Emile did a quick about-face and stopped him. "One more thing, Benjamin."

"Yes?"

Holding up his left hand, Emile added, "If I don't... If something should happen to me, make certain Jean gets Uncle Julien's ring. Promise me you will retrieve it immediately, and that no one will put the ring on before Jean."

This request struck Benjamin as odd, but he did not question it out of consideration for Emile's grief. He simply repeated, "As you wish, Brother."

After Benjamin left him, Emile stared at the ring, rubbing it between his right thumb and index finger. He wondered if it really would protect him from Paul's deadly plot, or if its powers were limited. Or worse yet, were they just a figment of his and Julien's superstitious imaginations.

Chapter Fifty-Six

Before returning the rental car, Justin parked it in a remote area of the New Orleans Airport short-term parking garage. While Mark replaced the stolen license plate with the one that came with the car, Justin put on leather driving gloves and began to wipe their fingerprints off the car's interior. Turning his attention to the backseat, Justin noticed some small blood spots on the seat edge and on the carpeted transmission hump. "Damn!" he said.

"What is it?" asked Mark, poking his head through the open rear door.

"Some of the blood missed the drop cloth. There's a bottle of alcohol in my medical bag. Get it, please."

Justin dabbed at the bloodstains with gauze and rubbing alcohol. It lightened the stains, but it did not remove them from the gray upholstery and carpet. Giving up on the bloodstains, Justin went to the open trunk of the Chevy. There, he unzipped a large, soft-sided suitcase. Inside were a blood-spattered drop cloth, four used syringes, an empty vile of phenobarbital, and the New Orleans city map. He added the stolen license plate, his medical bag, and the brown grocery sack. Justin dropped Mark and the suitcase off at his BMW, on the bottom parking level, before returning the rental car.

It was nearly 6:30 when the men returned to Justin's house in the Quarter. Ajax met them at the gate, unlocking it from the inside. Upon entering the foyer, Justin carefully set the suitcase down flat on the tile floor. Having second thoughts, he picked it back up and laid it on the carpeted floor of the coat closet. Then he zipped it open, removed the two plastic pint bottles of blood (one only half full) from his black doctor's bag, and headed for the kitchen. After placing the bottles of blood in the crisper drawer of the refrigerator, Justin joined Mark in the living room. Seeing that Mark was alone, he asked, "Where is everybody?"

"Beats me," answered Mark with a shrug. "Maybe they took Celeste upstairs and put her in bed?"

As the men walked to the bottom of the stairway, they heard footsteps on the landing above them. First to come into sight was Hector, carrying Mama Vance down the stairs in his arms. When they saw who was following Hector down the stairway, the men blinked in disbelief. It was Celeste, eyes open, walking unassisted, with a blank expression on her face.

Mark held out his arms and cried out a greeting as she came to the bottom of the stairs. "Celeste! Are you okay?"

Celeste paused on the last step to glance at Mark, but didn't respond or change her fixed, expressionless gaze. Then she walked right past Mark and Justin, following Hector into the living room. Stunned for a moment, Mark ran after Celeste, grabbed her shoulders from behind, and spun her around to face him. He stared into her vacant eyes and implored her to recognize him. "Celeste! It's me, babe, Mark. Don't you know me?"

Receiving no response, Mark released Celeste and ran toward Mama Vance, whom Hector had seated in one of the velvet armchairs. "What have you done to her?" he demanded. "What have you done, you witch!"

Unperturbed, Mama Vance answered, "I've saved her life, Monsieur Richards. At least for de time being."

"Saved her?" thundered Justin. "You've turned her into one of your damn zombies!"

"Oui, dhat be true. But it was dhat, or leave her dead. She stop breathin' thirty minutes after you leave us."

"Oh no," cried Justin. "This can't be happenin'. Not after what we just did. We've got the blood, but now it's too late."

"It not too late," corrected Mama Vance. "Madame Celeste's body and soul may be separated, but I can put dhem together again, with de blood of de lamb."

Chapter Fifty-Seven

On June 23, 1830, the morning after Nicole's funeral, Emile returned to the St. Louis Cemetery, located just outside the city's ramparts. Stopping at the cemetery gate, he read the posted list of death notices. Nicole's family had listed her burial under the name Noyan, rather than Poydras, as one final statement of their disapproval of her affair and remarriage.

Emile cradled a dozen red roses in his arms as he marched past the rows of neatly whitewashed oven vaults in the Catholic section of the graveyard. As the hour was still early, he encountered no other visitors in the cemetery. Emile still wore his black funeral suit from the day before, now wrinkled from his fitful night of sleep in it.

Turning the corner before Nicole's family crypt, Emile froze in his tracks. Dropping the roses, he ran the last few steps to the tomb. The ornate brass cross, which had topped the crypt's pinnacle, lay in pieces at the base of the tomb, among the melted stubs of black candles. The marble slab that had covered Nicole's vault was leaning against the crypt's wall. Nicole's oven was vacant, casket and all.

Searching behind the tall crypt, Emile found Nicole's empty mahogany casket. Fresh drops of blood were visible on the white satin pillow and lining of the coffin. A decapitated rooster lay beside the casket lid.

Clenching his hands into fists, Emile kicked the dead rooster against the wall of an adjacent tomb. Blood splattered against the crypt's whitewashed bricks. Turning to leave the empty casket, Emile took only two quick steps before his path was blocked. A figure had suddenly appeared on the narrow path between the stacked oven vaults. It was a tall, slender colored woman in a ragged purple dress.

Momentarily startled, Emile did not recognize the woman at first. Then, as a sly smile came across the young woman's face, Emile recognized her. It was Marie Laveau. "You did this! What have you done with Nicole?" he demanded.

Standing her ground, Marie answered, "She has risen, Monsieur Poydras."

"Damn you, woman! Where is my wife's body?"

"She is a corpse no more. Your wife now serves me."

"I don't believe you," answered Emile.

"It is easy enough to prove, Monsieur Poydras. Come to my camp on Lake Pontchartrain tonight. See for yourself."

Finally accepting the idea that Nicole could be Marie Laveau's zombie slave, Emile asked, "Why? Why have you done this? I have never wronged you."

"For a price," replied Marie with a wave of her hand. "It is merely business."

"Paul Noyan? He paid you to do this?"

"He paid me to dispose of you and your wife, oui. But not to make Nicole my slave."

"Then, why have — "

"Because you have something I want. You know what it is?"

Insight flashed across Emile's face. "Uncle Julien's ring? Never! It's the only thing that prevents you from killing me as well."

"I have no desire to harm you or take sides in your quarrel with Monsieur Noyan. I only want the ring."

Emile defiantly closed the distance between him and Marie. Holding his left fist and ring in the Voodoo queen's face, he declared, "You shall *never* have the ring, witch. I'll see you in Hell first!"

Marie laughed at his threat. "Hah! Oui, Monsieur Poydras. Perhaps we shall see each other in Hell someday. But, for now, it is I who has your wife in Hell. And the ring is the only thing that can buy her tortured soul peace." Lightly stroking Emile's cheek with the back of her long fingers, she added, "I'll see you tonight, Monsieur Poydras. Tonight is St. John's Eve. After tonight, we shall see what you have to say."

Chapter Fifty-Eight

Celeste found herself in bed with Emile once more. He was on top of her, making love to her. Their intercourse had never seemed this intense — this real — before. As she reached her climax, Celeste placed her arms around Emile and pulled hard on the small of his back. As they both came, Celeste let out a loud, sustained moan.

Other things in the dream seemed different this time as well. Instead of leaving the bed after their lovemaking, Emile rolled over on his side and brushed at the hair on Celeste's sweaty forehead. Celeste lay quietly for a few moments, afraid to speak lest Emile become an apparition once more.

Finally, Emile spoke to her. "That was wonderful, my love. It is so good to have you with me like this."

"How is it you're still here?" asked Celeste. "In all my other dreams, you have always disappeared from the bed after our lovemaking."

A look of concern came across Emile's face as he answered. "This... this is no dream, my love. We are together now."

Celeste's eyes widened as she sat up in bed. "What do you mean, this is no dream? My dreams always begin with our lovemaking."

Emile reached out and took her hand into his. His hand was warm to the touch. "Your spirit is free now, Celeste. Our souls are no longer separate and restricted to those brief encounters in your dreams. We are in the same world now. I shall be with you always."

Celeste's voice cracked with panic. "We can't! We can't be in the same world. You're dead."

"Yes," Emile confirmed. "And you are with me now, my darling."

Chapter Fifty-Nine

At 10:30 on St. John's Eve, Emile and Benjamin finally reached Marie Laveau's temple on the swampy shore of Lake Pontchartrain. Their arrival had been delayed because the narrow dirt road was choked with the carriages of all the Orleanians who came out to observe the grand festival of Voodooism held each year on the night of June 23.

It wasn't that the Creoles and other upper class Orleanians in attendance were followers of the cult. It had merely become fashionable entertainment to visit Voodoo ceremonies and to hire the services of Voodoo practitioners for solving personal problems and matters of the heart. St. John's Eve always drew the biggest crowd of sightseers, as the ceremonies were the most elaborate, and the Voodoo queen herself would preside.

Marie Laveau's Voodoo temple was little more than an open-walled hut, roofed with mud and straw. By the time Emile and Benjamin reached the chapel, the ceremony had already begun, and the crowd of onlookers was so large no one else could get inside the hut. Emile noted that the throng of observers greatly exceeded the number of ceremony participants.

Because of the large crowd, Emile and Benjamin remained in their open carriage to get a better view of the ritual proceedings. A ring of torches on poles lit the dirt floor of the temple. Seated on the floor, with their legs crossed beneath them, were about fifty Negro men and women. Emile could see no white person among the seated devotees. None of the men wore shirts, and the women were scantily clad as well. But each female wore a bright purple or blue tignon on her head.

Shaking his head in distaste, Benjamin surveyed the gathering. "You really expect to find Nicole here? If Marie Laveau really stole her corpse, she would not be fool enough to display it in front of all these people."

"I don't know what to expect, Brother. But I believe the witch has Nicole. Why invite me here if she doesn't have some sort of proof to display?"

"I will never understand why you and Uncle Julien got involved with this Voodoo cult. I find it all repulsive."

Sighing, Emile replied, "Please bear with me, Benjamin. Look, the ceremony is resuming. Let's just see what happens"

In the center of the temple floor, at the foot of a raised altar, the acolytes spread a long, white linen tablecloth. At the corners of the tablecloth were placed burning red and black candles. For a centerpiece, there was a tall, round Indian basket sitting before what appeared to be a painting of St. John the Baptist. Diminutive piles of white beans and corn were placed around the basket, and just outside these were laid a number of bleached, white bones. Emile couldn't decide if the bones were human or animal. Bunches of feathers in curious shapes were placed next in line, near the edge of the cloth, and outside of all were several saucers with small cakes in them.

On a crude platform that served as an altar, a striking café au lait woman with fierce dark eyes sat down in a wooden chair as if she were taking a throne. As a scepter, she held a crude black cross. Two handsome black male attendants were at her feet.

Benjamin leaned toward his brother and asked, "Is that Marie Laveau?"

Emile answered his question with a nod of his head, never taking his eyes off the crowd as he scanned it for a glimpse of Nicole.

At the foot of the altar stood an old Negro man, whose wool was white with years, scraping on a two-stringed sort of fiddle with brightly mottled snakeskin. Two young mulatresses beside him were beating little drums made of gourds and covered with sheepskin. These tam-tams produced short hollow notes of primitive sound. Suddenly, a voice from behind the altar yelled out, "À présent commencez!"

Rising from the crowd of worshipers and stepping upon the altar appeared a tall and burly Negro man. He had the physique of a Greek god — *a black Hercules,* thought Benjamin, but his head was shaved, and his face was covered in a pattern of scars that made him look grotesque. Hesitantly, and with lack of emotion, he commenced to sing in a low, loud voice:

Mallé couri dan déser,

Mallé marché dan savane,

Mallé marché su piquan doré

Mallé oir ca ya di moin!

Sangé moin dan l'abitation ci la la?

Mo gagnain soutchien la Louisiane,

Mallé oir ca ya di mion!

"What is he singing about?" questioned Benjamin. "What does it mean to wander in the desert and walk upon the golden thorn?"

Shrugging his shoulders, Emile answered, "I don't know. I've never heard this song before."

As "Hercules" continued to sing, he became more animated in his performance. He became combative, flailing his arms out in wild abandon as he turned in circles, and his eyes took on a wild, frantic look. The tam-tams and fiddle kept time to the repetitive song, giving it an eerie and mind-numbing accompaniment. Suddenly, Hercules stopped dancing and pointed with both his arms at the disciples at the foot of the dais. Then all the worshipers, except the queen, rose to their feet and began to dance around the altar, joining Hercules in his song as they danced wildly.

Benjamin thought the jerking, twisting motions of the dancers were comical at first. But as the tempo of the song quickened with the tam-tams, the movements of the dancers turned into disturbingly frenzied contortions. Emile and Benjamin observed two of the women and one emaciated man fall to the floor, seemingly unconscious. Some of the Negresses began to pull open their dresses as they made lascivious motions with their hips.

When the dance was at the peak of delirium, there was the sudden entrance of a lithe, chestnut-haired white woman, who whirled around the room in the arms of a muscular, coal black Negro man.

Benjamin grabbed his brother's arm and declared, "My God! Emile, it's Nicole!"

Emile sprang to his feet and then froze. He stood in the carriage and watched as Nicole, the wife he had buried the day before, danced in the depths of depravity. Her pallid, wanton face radiated carnal desire and at the same time menace. Emile thought, *La Dame aux Camélias*, in her wildest hours, could not have displayed more complete moral abandonment.

As the maddening whirl escalated, Nicole threw her arms and legs around the neck and buttocks of her partner as he spun her, his face buried in her exposed breasts. Gasps and loud murmurings rose from the crowd of sightseers.

Then Queen Marie Laveau rose from her chair. The music and dancing abruptly halted. She raised her hand, and a shout of "Voodoo Magnian!" clamored from the worshipers who had been gyrating at her feet. With that, all the lustful dancers ran out of the temple to consummate their avarice in the dark.

Emile watched with horror as the half-naked Nicole ran out into the night, hand in hand with her soon-to-be black lover. Turning his attention back to the altar, he saw Marie Laveau staring right at him, hands on her hips, roaring with laughter.

Chapter Sixty

On June 22, the morning after obtaining fresh blood for Celeste's conjure ceremony, Justin awoke to a foul and pungent odor that permeated the entire house, even past his closed bedroom door. Pulling on his blue terry robe, Justin opened his door and stepped out into the hall. The odor was much stronger there. It had the stink of rotting fish and burnt toast and was really quite nauseating. Justin surmised the smell was coming from the kitchen and headed down the stairs to investigate.

He found Mark had already come down to determine the cause of the stench. In the kitchen, Mama Vance was stirring a large copper pot on the electric range. Hector was standing by her side to assist. The bubbling soup pot was definitely the cause of the foul smell. The contents were a ghastly yellow-green color, and bits of fish, herbs, and unidentifiable objects churned in the chowder.

"Good Lord, woman!" implored Justin. "What are you cookin'?"

Mark answered his question. "Zombie food."

"What?"

"Yeah, zombie food. She expects Celeste to eat that shit."

"Say what you wish, Monsieur Richards," defended Mama Vance. "It be what she need now ta sustain her. Her body be different now dhan yours."

"What do you mean different?" asked Justin.

"When you separate a soul from de body, it needs become different — ta stay live."

"Where... What...," stumbled Justin. "You've *actually* removed Celeste's soul from her body? I assumed that was hyperbole — an exaggeration?"

"No, I had ta separate dhem, ta keep her body alive. Otherwise, I not be able ta control her body's organs. It be my spirit dhat tells your granddaughter's heart ta beat now. Hers had give up."

Justin eased himself into one of the dinette chairs before continuing. "Where then is Celeste's soul?"

"In de ring. It be safe dhere 'til we can rejoin dhem. De ring keep her spirit safe 'til we ready — when her body free of Cupid."

"The ring?" questioned Mark. "But that's where Emile Poydras's spirit is."

With a sly smile, Mama Vance answered, "Ah, de jealous husband, no? Oui, Monsieur Richards. Your wife be with Emile Poydras's spirit. You not want her be lonely, do you?"

Closing his eyes and shaking his head, Mark added, "I can't handle this — excuse me, or I'm gonna puke."

With that, Mark hurriedly left the kitchen and ran through the dining room doors to the fresh air of the garden. Before Justin could think what to do next, he heard Mark call from the garden patio. "Justin! You'd better get out here. A car just pulled up, and it looks like a cop car."

Chapter Sixty-One

On the afternoon of St. John's Day, Emile called on Marie Laveau at her cottage on St. Ann Street. It was a low, faded, white clapboard house set behind a high board fence, which concealed most of the premises from the banquette. All one could clearly see from the street was the sloping red tile roof. As Emile entered the front gate, he encountered a yard filled with banana trees and tall bamboo plants. Getting a good look at the house, Emile deduced it was several years old and built during the years of Spanish rule.

Stepping onto the portico, Emile rapped beside the open door. The front room of the house was dark. Heavy black drapes covered all the windows. In the room's far corner, he observed a small Catholic shrine with a single white candle burning before it.

Emile's knock was not answered by Marie, but by a handsome, middle-aged white man. Emile thought he looked vaguely familiar. The man spoke in English with a Creole accent. "Good afternoon, Captain Poydras. You are expected."

"No one has addressed me as 'Captain Poydras' in years. Do I know you, monsieur?"

"No. I doubt it. But I remember you from Chalmette. I was on guard the night you came to visit Sanité Dédé. My name is Glapion, Louis Christophe Duminy de Glapion. I am Madame Marie's... husband."

Emile was at a loss for words upon realizing that Marie's spouse was from a noble family. As Louis finished his introduction, three colored children came laughing and running from the side yard onto the porch. There were two girls and one boy, and their ages appeared to range from five to two years. Louis headed them off before they could enter the house. "Go play in the back yard, children. Your mother has a guest now."

Without missing a step, the parading children veered off the porch and ran around the other corner of the house. "Handsome children," commented Emile. "Are they yours?"

"Oui, mine and Madame Marie's. Now, please come in, and I will tell Marie you are here."

Emile stepped in as Louis disappeared through a door leading to the back of the cottage. As the windows were all closed and draped, it was uncomfortably warm in the house. Emile remained standing near the open door and unbuttoned and fanned his tailored gray waistcoat, exposing a pistol in his cummerbund

Marie Laveau came into the parlor wearing a modest blue smock and stained, white apron. Louis Glapion did not return with her to greet Emile. "Ah, Monsieur Poydras," said Marie, wiping her hands on her apron. "Please excuse me. I have been preparing supper." Pointing to a worn, leather armchair, she added, "Won't you sit down?"

"No, thank you, madame. What I have to say will not take long."

"As you wish, monsieur."

"I've come to meet your terms. I have but one condition."

"And what is that?"

"Before I give you the ring, you must release my wife and return her to her grave."

Marie snorted a laugh. "So, monsieur would rather see his wife in her grave than in the arms of a colored man?"

"Damn you, woman! Don't taunt me, or I'll kill you where you stand!"

Without really relenting, Marie replied, "It will be as you wish, monsieur. I will return your wife to her tomb this very night. But is there nothing else I can do for you?"

Emile started to answer with an immediate no but caught himself. "Oui, madame. There is something else you can do. You can curse Paul Noyan with the same fever that killed my Nicole. That is only just."

"I don't know about white man's justice, monsieur. But what you wish can be arranged, for a price."

"Price? I'm giving you my uncle's ring!"

"True. But that is the price of your wife's eternal peace. The death of a man such as Paul Noyan will cost an additional five hundred dollars — in advance."

With a grudging nod of the head and a sarcastic laugh, Emile agreed. "You amaze me. You are undoubtedly the most mercenary creature I have ever encountered. Very well, I will bring you the ring — and the money — at noon tomorrow. Once I have verified that Nicole is at rest in her tomb."

"I shall trust you, Monsieur Poydras, and you must trust me. For, unless you keep your bargain, I shall have to summon your wife from the grave once more and send her to greet your son."

Chapter Sixty-Two

Justin sprang from the kitchen table and ran to the French doors leading out to the garden. He motioned for Mark to come in the house.

"Have they seen you yet?" he asked.

"No. I don't think so. They're still in their car," answered Mark.

"Good. Stay inside — out of sight. And keep the doors closed. I don't want them seein' Mama Vance or smellin' her chowder."

Justin remained out of view on the patio until he heard the front doorbell ring. He pulled his robe tight and counted to ten before answering the bell.

Standing at the gate were two men in their late thirties. One man, with unkempt sandy hair, had his blue-plaid sport coat hooked in his thumb and draped over the shoulder of his short-sleeved, white shirt. The other man was short and stocky and had his black hair cut in a flat top. He wore a wrinkled khaki suit with white socks and black shoes.

Justin put a pleasant smile on his face and said, "Good mornin'. Can I help you, gentlemen?"

The sandy haired man answered, "Good mornin', sir. Are you Mr. Justin Noyan?"

"I am."

"I'm Detective Sergeant Phillip Cuvillier, and this is Detective Stan Barski." Pulling a combination badge and ID card from his coat pocket, Detective Cuvillier added, "We're with the N'aw Arlens Police Department. Could we speak with you a moment?"

"Certainly," answered Justin as he opened the gate. "How can I assist you?"

"Excuse us for callin' so early, sir," began Detective Cuvillier, "but did you rent a blue Chevy sedan at the airport yesterday?"

"Yes, a blue, four-door Impala. What about it? Excuse my manners," added Justin, pointing at the garden table. "Please, sit down. Can I offer you some coffee?"

"No, thank you," answered Detective Cuvillier as the men took seats at the white, wrought iron table. "We've had plenty this mornin'."

"Now, what's this about the car I rented?"

Speaking for the first time, Detective Barski answered tersely, "A car fitting the description of your rental was involved in a kidnapping yesterday."

Hoping he was showing the right amount of surprise and concern on his face, Justin replied, "A kidnappin'. My God! Who was kidnapped?"

"Two young schoolgirls," said Barski, laying school photos of the girls on the table. "They were abducted as they walked home from school yesterday in Gentilly. Have you seen them?"

Picking up the photos with steady hands, Justin studied them a moment and said, "No. No, I haven't. I wasn't near Gentilly yesterday. I'm afraid I don't follow you. Someone says they saw my rental car in Gentilly yesterday?"

"Well, not necessarily your car, Mr. Noyan," answered Cuvillier. "But one like it."

"Did they get a license number?"

"Unfortunately, no. The witness was another school child," replied Barski, picking up the photographs and returning them to his suit pocket.

"However," said Detective Cuvillier, "we believe the car was a rental, because the witness did see a yellow sticker on the rear bumper. And all of A-1 Rental cars have yellow bumper stickers on them with their name and logo."

"I see," said Justin flatly.

"Would you mind telling us where you went in the rental car, sir?" asked Detective Barski.

"No, not at all. I made one trip from and one return trip to the N'aw Arlens Airport — from my home here in the Quarter."

Taking out a small note pad, Phillip Cuvillier asked, "And what route did you take, sir?"

"US 61 — both ways."

"I see. And why did you rent the car?"

Justin felt the urge to become defensive as Detective Cuvillier continued his questioning. But he thought better of it. *Innocent people have nothing to hide*, he thought.

With a sincere and unguarded tone in his voice, Justin answered, "Well, I had gone to return some plane tickets for my granddaughter and her husband. When I came out, my car wouldn't start. Somehow, I'd hit the headlight switch when I got out, and my battery was dead. Since I had a luncheon engagement, I couldn't wait for the auto club to come jump-start my car. So, I rented one."

"I see," said Cuvillier, writing in his notebook. "Did anyone travel with you in the rental car?"

"My granddaughter's husband — Mark Richards — made the return trip with me that evenin'. To help me get my car started. We had jumper cables and planned to use the rental car to start mine."

"You returned your rental car at approximately 5:40 p.m.?"

"That sounds about right."

"And when did you jump start your car?"

With a wave of his hand, Justin answered, "I didn't have to. The car started without assistance. I guess lettin' it sit awhile let the battery recover enough of a charge to start."

"Is Mr. Richards here, sir?"

"Yes, but I believe he and my granddaughter are still in bed. Do I need to wake him?"

"No, that won't be necessary, for now. Could you give me his age and general description?"

"I believe Mark is twenty-two years old. He's about six foot-two, blond hair — probably weighs a hundred and eighty pounds."

"Thanks. Now, did you or Mr. Richards notice any stains in the back seat of the rental car?" Cuvillier looked up from his notebook as he asked this question, looking Justin directly in the eyes.

"No. I don't recall either of us bein' in the backseat," answered Justin coolly. "What kind of stains?"

"Well, the lab work's not done yet, but there appears to be some blood stains on the back seat and carpet."

"Sorry, I never noticed."

"That's okay. Now, one more thing," continued Cuvillier, "and we'll let you go. Did you and Mr. Richards wear gloves when you drove the rental car?"

Justin fought hard to suppress a sudden rush of panic. His stomach felt suddenly light. "Why no, who would wear gloves in this weather? Why do you ask?"

"It's just that we couldn't find a single fingerprint inside the car, except for a couple smudges."

"Really? Perhaps the rental company cleaned it after I returned it."

"Their garage man said no."

There was a lull in the conversation as the detectives waited for a response from Justin. "Sorry, gentlemen, I can't help you. After I returned the car, I don't know what happened to it."

"May we ask who your lunch appointment was with, sir?" inquired Stan.

Justin looked uncomfortable for the first time. "Is that really relevant, gentlemen?"

"Just trying to tie up all the loose ends," continued Stan.

"Well, if you must know, my appointment was with a lady friend. Ethel Stern, she — "

"Madam Dauphine?"

"Yes, so I hope that disclosure is not made public? It's a private matter."

"Sure," replied Stan with a smile and a dubious tone in his voice. "But one of us will probably contact Ethel to confirm your appointment."

"Gentlemen, what's going on here? Am I a suspect in your kidnappin' investigation?"

Philip intervened, "No, sir, we have no suspects yet. We're just workin' our leads." Phillip Cuvillier stood up and closed his notebook. Stan Barski followed suit. "Well, thanks for your time, Mr. Noyan. We'll let ya get back to your breakfast now."

Detective Barski forced a smile and added, "Yeah. Thanks for your trouble."

"No trouble a t'all," answered Justin as he showed them out the gate. "I hope you catch who you're lookin' for."

"Oh, we will," answered Phillip Cuvillier. "I just hope it's in time to save those two little girls."

When the two detectives were back in their unmarked black car, Stan asked, "Well, what da ya make of him?"

"I'm not quite sure," answered Phillip. "He seemed on the level, but the description of this Mark Richards seems like it could fit."

"Except for the blond hair," corrected Stan.

"Hair can be dyed. Too bad our witness didn't get a look at the driver."

"Yeah, and since the rental car company failed to record the mileage before Noyan took the car, we can't verify his travel. I guess we check out his alibi with Ethel and see if that holds water." Picking up a clipboard from the car seat, Stan added, "Okay, next on our list is — "

Staring through the windshield, Philip interrupted, "There's somethin' strange goin' on in that house. I just can't put my finger on it."

"What da ya mean?" asked Stan as he laid down the clipboard and started their shopworn Dodge sedan.

"Every once in awhile, while we were talkin', I got a whiff of a real bad odor comin' from the house."

"Yeah, I smelled it too. Kinda like fish chowder gone bad."

Phillip nodded. "Yeah, but not quite. I've smelled that odor before."

"Where?" asked Stan as they drove off.

"When I was a kid and visited my grandma. She had this old mammy cook who lived out back. Mammy cooked crap that smelled that bad."

"So?"

"Grandma claimed it was witches' brew and told me to stay clear of her shack. She said Mammy was a Voodooienne."

Chapter Sixty-Three

Marie Laveau kept her bargain, and so did Emile. After verifying that Nicole's body had been returned to her tomb in the St. Louis Cemetery, Emile went back to Marie Laveau's house and gave her Julien's ring — and five hundred dollars. Before accepting the ring and placing it on her finger, Marie made Emile declare that he was giving it freely and unconditionally to her.

That night, after seeing Marie, Emile and Benjamin removed Nicole's casket from her tomb and shipped it upriver to Pointe Coupee. The brothers had Nicole reburied under a false name in the St. Francis Church Cemetery on Bayou Sara.

Two weeks later, on July 10, 1830, Emile was back in New Orleans. Among the stack of mail waiting for Emile at his French Quarter residence was a letter with a black wax seal and no return address. Emile sighed with apprehension as he opened the letter and read:

Monsieur Poydras,

I trust all went well with the new burial arrangements for your wife.

While I appreciate your previous remunerations, I find myself in need of additional compensation for our transactions. I believe the sum of five thousand dollars, in gold, will suffice for now. Please have this sum delivered to my residence at your earliest convenience. Otherwise, I cannot promise that word of our dealings will continue to be kept private and not fall into the hands of your enemies.

Your Servant,

M. L.

Emile crumpled the letter immediately upon reading it and threw it into the vacant fireplace in his study. *Uncle Julien was oh so right about not trusting Voodooiennes. He always said extortion was a Voodoo queen's stock in trade. I'll see Marie Laveau in Hell before she gets another cent from me!* Emile declared to himself.

Ten days after reading Marie Laveau's blackmail letter, Emile and Jean were back in the New Orleans cemetery, this time to attend the funeral of Paul Noyan. It seemed the elder Noyan had succumbed to a fever he contracted shortly after

Emile and Benjamin had left for Pointe Coupee. People said it was strange, as there hadn't been any reported cases of the fever in the city yet that summer. With little Jean sobbing at his side, Emile felt a twinge of guilt. The young boy had lost his mother and grandfather in a month's time. It was more than any five-year old should have to bear.

As soon as the graveside services ended, they started to walk away from the Noyan family crypt, hand in hand. Jean stopped and looked up at his father. With tears in his eyes, he asked, "Papa? You're not going to die too, are you?"

"No, son," answered Emile as he squeezed the boy's hand for emphasis. "I'm not going to die. I promise you." Emile wondered if he could keep his promise after giving his ring to Marie Laveau. *My plan must succeed*, he thought.

"Are you certain, Papa? If you should die, there would be no one to take care of me."

"Of course there would, Jean. Your uncle Benjamin loves you very much. You could live with him on his big plantation at Pointe Coupee."

Unsatisfied, Jean shook his head. "But I only want to live with you, Papa."

Emile didn't get the chance to give further assurances to Jean. Their conversation was cut short by the abrupt appearance of Anton Cuvillier. Anton had aged somewhat in the six and half years since the men's duel. His hair was nearly gray now, and his face was lined and starting to sag a little.

Emile's old adversary struck a defiant pose, blocking the path and pointing at Emile with his cane. "How dare you come here!" began Anton. "You have the audacity to come to the funeral of the man you had murdered!"

Startled, Jean looked up to his father for an explanation. After a moment, Emile answered coolly, "You don't know what you're talking about, Monsieur Cuvillier. At any rate, if you have a dispute with me, I ask you to have the decency to not bring up such matters in front of my son."

"Hah! Decency? I, for one, believe your son should know his father is a murderer and a Voodooienne."

Losing his temper, Emile threw the riding gloves he held in Anton's face. "That is enough. Have your second contact my brother and set the terms. We shall settle this on the field of honor — once and for all."

Bending over to pick up one of Emile's gloves, Anton arose with a sly smile on his face. "I gladly accept your challenge, monsieur. For this time, the outcome will be much different. This time you don't have the Poydras ring."

That evening, Emile recorded the day's disturbing turn of events in his diary, including:

Jean is inconsolable about Anton's accusations. He is reeling from the sudden loss of his mother and grandfather. And now he must try and understand his father being accused of murdering his grandfather. I fear my lie that Anton only did it to taunt me into a challenge is not fully believed. I rue the day I ever became involved with Voodoo.

No doubt Marie Laveau told Anton about the ring and my loss of its protection. I am somewhat surprised she shared this knowledge with Anton. However, I suppose Marie may not have told Anton all the secrets of the ring. No doubt she does not fear the potential threats from lesser mortals. At any rate, she is proceeding to make good on her threat to take my life for refusing her extortion by having Anton provoke a duel. She will regret that! Benjamin and I will thwart her scheme and punish her for it. Voodoo queens are not the only ones who can deal in treachery.

If I am truly being honest with myself now, which I am finding it most difficult to do, I also deeply regret Anton and I becoming enemies. It was foolish of me to allow my infatuation with Aurora to cost me his friendship. Now Anton is bent on vengeance because of my past aspersions, and because he now knows our first duel was dishonorable; its outcome predetermined by Voodoo trickery. Thus, I must kill my former friend to protect my sullied reputation and to repair my son's opinion of me.

Chapter Sixty-Four

That evening, after the visit by the police detectives, Mark returned to Justin's house at about 6:00. He carried in two brown paper sacks and set them on the kitchen table. Jerking a paper towel off the counter dispenser, Mark wiped the sweat off his forehead and the back of his neck. Grabbing a bottle of Dixie beer from the refrigerator, he walked into the living room.

Justin was sitting on the couch watching the local television news. Mama Vance was in one of the armchairs with Hector at her feet. Celeste sat rigid and motionless next to Justin, her glassy eyes seeming to stare off into space.

Justin looked up as Mark entered the room. "Did you have any trouble finding Chicken Man's Voodoo shop?" he asked.

"Nope, I got everything on the list." Noticing the news broadcast, Mark asked, "Anything new about the missing girls?"

"Just that they haven't been found yet."

"It's only a matter of time," added Mark as he sat down on the arm of the sofa beside Justin. "Did you get ahold of Madame Dauphine?"

"Yeah, she said she'd confirm my alibi. She didn't even ask why."

"You buy all de candles I tell you?" Mama Vance asked Mark.

"Yeah, yeah, all four colors. What's the difference, anyway?"

"Big difference, Monsieur Richards. De blue is ta protect us from harm. De red ones is for victory over our enemies. And de yellow candles drive de enemies clean away, if dhey try come back."

"And the black candles?"

"Dhey bring Li Grand Zombi forth. Dhey be for his work."

"So, the blue robe I got is supposed to protect Celeste during the conjure ceremony?" asked Mark.

"Oui."

"But what's with the silver sewing needles?"

Mama Vance smiled. "All in good time, Monsieur Richards. It be clear ta you at de ceremony tomorrow."

After taking a long pull off his beer, Mark asked, "Why can't we do the ceremony tonight? Those cops may be on to us by tomorrow night."

"Must wait for St. John's Eve. Dhat be when I can call de spirits for sure. Dhey not come out tonight."

"Shit!" said Mark in uncertainty. "Should we have waited until today to get the blood?"

"I don't know," replied Justin. "But school's not in session on the weekends. It's not goin' to do any good worryin' about that now."

Turning to Mama Vance, Justin asked, "Will the blood still be good? Is there anythin' else ya need for the ceremony?"

"De blood be fine. You have de wood for de fire?"

"Yes, I arranged that with the sexton, and for a key to the cemetery gate."

"Bon, but de key not needed. I can git us in with no key."

Justin was just about to ask Mama Vance to explain how she could unlock the gate without a key, and whether Sexton Lefebvre was a member of her cult, when the doorbell rang.

Mark and Justin looked at each other and froze for a moment, not wanting to answer the door. Both feared it was the police returning with warrants for their arrest.

When the bell rang a second time, Justin got up and walked to the front window and peeked out the edge of the drapes. "Oh, no!" he exclaimed. "This is *all* we need now."

"What?" asked Mark excitedly.

"It's Amy — Celeste's mother."

Chapter Sixty-Five

Two days after Paul Noyan's funeral, Emile returned to Marie Laveau's cottage on St. Ann Street. It was dusk when Emile approached the high fence around the house. He looked over both shoulders before opening the gate, making certain no one saw him enter.

Stopping behind one of the banana trees in the yard, Emile reached inside his black frockcoat and checked to see that the percussion caps were still in place on the two matched pistols in his belt. Gripping his colichemarde in his left hand like a club, he crept up onto the vacant portico of the house.

Because of the summer heat, Emile again found the door of the cottage wide open. Besides the candle burning before the shrine, an oil lamp was lit on the table in the center of the room. No one was to be seen in the front room, but Emile could hear the chatter of children's voices coming from the kitchen. He also heard Marie's voice reprimanding her children. "Quiet, now! Supper be ready soon."

He waited and listened outside the door nearly a minute but never heard or saw any sign that anyone was in the house except Marie and her children. Emile knew Louis Glapion was not home as he had observed him walking off toward a local tavern a few minutes earlier.

As Emile waited in the shadows on the porch, Marie's two little girls came running into the parlor. The older, taller girl was holding a rag doll over her head, which her younger sister tried to recover with repeated jumps and lunges.

"Mére! Mére!" the young child screamed. "Make her give it back!"

As Marie came out of the kitchen to scold her squabbling children, Emile stepped quickly into the front doorway. His sudden appearance startled the children into silence.

Without addressing Marie by name, Emile announced, "You betrayed me!"

"What do you mean, Monsieur Poydras?" replied Marie defiantly. "How dare you come — "

"You told Anton Cuvillier about the gris-gris I paid you to kill Paul Noyan with, and you told him about the Poydras ring."

"I never promised not to," rejoined Marie with a smirk. "And you failed to respond to my letter regarding the additional payment you owe me."

"Owe you?" shouted Emile. "I owe you nothing! You have betrayed me." With one quick jerk, Emile drew out the blade of his colichemarde. "The ring!" he demanded. "Give it back, *now!*"

Turning her face up to the ceiling, Marie laughed scornfully. "Hah! You fool! You cannot harm me now. I have the ring."

Stepping quickly forward two steps, Emile grabbed the arm of the youngest child. The little girl pulled and cried to be let go, but Emile kept a firm grip. The older girl ran and grabbed her mother's skirt for protection.

"The ring does not protect your children, witch! Hand it over, or I'll cut her throat before your very eyes."

The look of defiance vanished from Marie's face. She studied Emile's face hard for a few seconds before answering in cold, flat tones. "No, I think not, Monsieur Poydras. I know you much better than you think. You would not kill an innocent child — even to save your own life. If I am wrong, so be it. I can have other children. There is only one ring."

"You don't know everything about me," replied Emile as he released his grip on Marie's young daughter.

Marie was about to boast about Emile's failed bluff when she sensed sudden movement from behind her. She started to turn toward the kitchen door, but before she could see who it was, Benjamin struck her from behind with an iron poker. Benjamin's first blow tore a gash in Marie's cheek as she turned to face her attacker. As Marie raised her hand to cover her wound, Benjamin struck again, hard, on the back of her head, near the base of the skull. The tip of the poker punctured Marie's neck, and Emile heard her spine crack. Blood spurted into Benjamin's face and down the front of his white, lace shirt. The blow sent Marie reeling forward and spread eagle on the floor, motionless.

Seeing their mother fall face down in a spreading pool of blood, the two girls went screaming past Emile and out the front door.

Looking to his brother, Benjamin shook his head. "I pray to God you are right about this, Emile. I have just committed murder for you. I would not have believed any of these Voodoo superstitions were real had I not seen Nicole at that Voodoo ceremony after her death."

"Oh, it's real, Brother. Uncle Julien's ring is real."

"But, not *real* enough to protect this witch, it would seem. I suggest you practice your marksmanship before your duel with Anton tomorrow."

That evening, after putting Jean to bed, Emile recorded the grisly events of the day in his diary. Little did he know it would be the last entry he would ever write.

Chapter Sixty-Six

Amy Noyan stood at the locked gate, suitcase by her side. She gave Justin a perturbed look as he came to open the gate.

"Amy! What a surprise. How was the drive here?"

"Never mind that, Justin, I want to know what's goin' on here."

Justin unlocked the deadbolt on the gate and picked up Amy's suitcase. When she got no response from him, Amy asked, "What's wrong with Celeste?"

Leading the way into the house, Justin answered, "What makes you think somethin's wrong with Celeste?"

Amy slammed the door shut behind her. "She hasn't called since she and Mark came here. And yesterday... Yesterday, I discovered that... that *damn* diary was missing from Jim's trunk. Now, what the hell is goin' on?"

With a sigh, Justin pointed toward the now empty living room. "Come and sit down, Amy. We've got a lot to talk about."

Justin's explanation of Celeste's supernatural predicament was somewhat disjointed and cryptic. He began with Celeste's accidental discovery of the Poydras ring and its powers and afflictions. But when he described the ceremony needed to reverse the curse, he deliberately left out any mention of the blood of the "goat without horns," and how he and Mark had obtained it.

He explained the situation slowly and as calmly as he could, so as not to exacerbate Amy's agitated state. But when he finally told Amy that her daughter had "temporarily become a zombie," she refused to listen any longer. Throwing up her arms and rising from the sofa, Amy demanded, "Take me to her, Justin! Take me to her *now!*"

Silently, Justin led Amy upstairs to the guest bedroom. Without knocking, he pushed open the door and stepped aside. Amy rushed past him into the room. Celeste was lying on the bed, motionless, her eyes closed. Mark, seated at the foot of the bed, looked up with a helpless expression as Amy came in the room.

Amy froze upon seeing her cataleptic child. Then, noticing Mama Vance sitting with Hector in the corner of the room, she lashed out at her. "You witch! You did this to my baby." Amy ran and dropped to her knees beside Celeste. Taking Celeste's limp hand into hers, she pleaded, "Celeste, honey? It's Mom." Tears began to stream down Amy's cheeks. "Please, baby. Please... Please open your eyes and look at me."

Without uttering a sound, making only a slight pulling motion with one hand, Mama Vance commanded Celeste to open her eyes and sit up in bed.

Amy started to smile at her daughter, but when she saw the vacant look in Celeste's eyes and realized that Celeste didn't recognize her, she dropped her head and began to sob heavily. Without looking up, Amy ordered, "Get *out*! All of you! Get out and leave us alone."

"Dhat not be good idea, Madame Noyan," replied Mama Vance. "Your child need me nearby ta stay alive."

Amy looked up meekly at Justin. He confirmed Mama Vance's statement with a nod of his head. "Oh, Amy," Justin added regretfully, "I wish you had delayed your trip another thirty hours. This nightmare would have been over, and we could have spared you all this grief."

Amy was not consoled. "Damn you, Justin!" she said, her eyes red from crying. "Your obsession with the... the family curse cost me Jim's life. And now it's turned my child into a goddamn zombie."

Justin looked stunned for a moment, then comprehension flashed across his face. "You knew about the ring?"

"Of course! I never told Jim — or anyone. But, after he left for Vietnam, I read the translation of Emile Poydras's diary." Seeing the look of surprise on Justin's face, Amy added, "Jim hid a copy in our closet. I found it one day while cleanin'. I thought... I had no idea the ring was in the trunk. I assumed you had the ring."

Shaking his head, Justin said, "All these years, you knew I talked Jim out of wearin' the ring?"

"No, just the opposite. I thought the ring was pure bunk, and that you convinced Jim to take the ring with him. I... In the back of my mind, I always thought that's what got Jim killed. That maybe he took chances because he believed the ring would protect him." Amy stood and looked back down at Celeste. "Now, I see it was the reverse. Jim died because he didn't wear the ring. Now… now my baby's a walkin' dead person because she *did* wear the ring. No matter how you look at it — or use it — that damn ring is cursed. It's cursed us all."

Chapter Sixty-Seven

Anton chose the plantation of Louis Allard as the site of the duel. It was to be under "The Oaks," the same live oaks Emile had killed Henri Noyan under in their duel six years earlier.

The contest between Anton and Emile was not scheduled until one o'clock on the afternoon of Tuesday, July 27, 1830. Arriving at the Allard plantation at five of noon, Emile was somewhat surprised to see a large crowd already gathered under the giant oak trees. Groups of men and families had brought lunch baskets and spread their picnics out on blankets in the shade afforded by the oaks and Spanish moss hanging from the trees.

Looking out the open window of their approaching coach, Emile commented, "I had no idea my tilt with Anton would draw such a crowd."

Seated across from Benjamin and Emile was a plain man about their age, Bernard Marigny, a member of the State Legislature and a renowned duelist in his own right, despite his short, five-foot stature. Viewing the crowd out his own window, Bernard explained, "There were two other duels fought here this morning. The good citizens of New Orleans have come out to make a day of it."

"Hah!" snorted Benjamin. "Look at them. Eating and drinking — waiting for the next event of bloodshed. No doubt, in ancient times, they would have purchased tickets for the Colosseum."

Leaning back into his seat, Emile seemed totally at ease. Smiling at Bernard, he spoke. "Did Benjamin tell you? Cuvillier has chosen pistols for this duel. My weapon of choice."

"Oui," replied Bernard. "Anton intends there be no repeat of your last encounter. One of you will surely be killed this time. It is almost certain with a firing distance of only ten paces."

Slightly annoyed with Bernard's statement, Emile leaned forward and raised his voice slightly. "*One* of us, Bernard? Surely you don't believe Cuvillier is my equal with a pistol?"

"Normally, I would agree with you, Emile," said the unperturbed Bernard. "But you haven't heard about his new pistols, have you?" The blank looks on Emile and Benjamin's faces bade Bernard to continue. "Anton has a pair of those rifle-barreled Belgian pistols. In addition to being deadly accurate, they're damn delicate. The slightest jar and they misfire. He's been practicing with them for the past two days I'm told."

"The devil with his Belgian pistols!" rejoined Emile, squeezing his left hand into a fist and feeling the reassurance of the Poydras ring between his fingers. Emile settled back into his seat once more as their coach slowed to a halt. No sooner had the men exited their coach than they were confronted by a stout man approaching on horseback. Despite the midday heat, the rider wore a dark, three-piece suit and tall, black felt hat.

Emile pulled at the collar of his open white blouse and spoke first. "Good afternoon, Sheriff Lindoe. What brings you so far out into the parish?"

Pulling up his chestnut gelding, but without dismounting, Charles Lindoe replied, "I'm here to place you under arrest, Monsieur Poydras."

"On what charge?" exclaimed Emile.

"Dueling — if you attempt to go forward with your meeting with Monsieur Cuvillier."

"Now, Sheriff," interposed Bernard. "You know dueling is like getting married. The more barriers erected against it, the surer the parties are to come together."

"Joke if you will, Marigny, but the law will be enforced this day. I'd advise you all to leave the premises at once." With his admonition completed, Sheriff Lindoe jerked his mount into a turn and rode back towards the crowd.

"What do you make of that?" asked Bernard. "The man has no doubt just observed two other duels but threatens to arrest you."

"Off hand," replied Emile, "I'd say someone was trying to prevent this duel. Perhaps Anton has lost his nerve?"

To himself, Emile speculated that Anton had somehow found out that Emile had recovered his uncle Julien's ring. *Of course,* he thought, *Marie Laveau's death has been reported.*

"Leave the good sheriff to me," said Bernard. "I shall remind him who appropriates his salary for the coming year." With that declaration, Bernard marched off after the sheriff.

When he was certain Bernard was out of earshot, Benjamin looked his brother in the eyes with an analytical gaze. "Emile, you're acting too cocky about this duel. Ring or no ring, I won't be party to another of your risky sideshows. You must promise me you will fire at Anton on the first volley."

Emile waved his hand. "Never fear, dear brother. No harm will come to me this day."

"You place entirely too much trust in that cursed ring Uncle Julien gave you. It didn't save Marie Laveau last night when I bashed her head in."

Ignoring Benjamin's admonitions, Emile turned to his left and pointed at an approaching carriage. "Look. Here comes Anton. Who's that riding with him?"

Benjamin stared at the open carriage as it came toward them. When it reached a bend in the road, he got a clear side view of all the occupants. There was Anton, his second, Harnett Cane, the young publisher of the *New Orleans Times*, an elderly Italian surgeon by the name of Furioso, and a tall, statuesque woman of color with curly black hair.

Benjamin stared in astonishment for a moment, his jaw dropping open slightly. "My God! It can't be! I killed her with my own hands."

Emile didn't appear to be surprised at the apparent resurrection of Marie Laveau. Without taking his eyes off her, he replied, "We have nothing to fear. This merely confirms the ring's power of protection."

Anton's carriage pulled up alongside Emile and Benjamin. Focusing on Marie's face and the back of her neck, Benjamin was stupefied. There was no sign of the mortal wounds he had inflicted less than twenty-four hours earlier.

Acting nonchalantly, Emile spoke first. "Welcome, Anton. I see you brought your Voodoo witch for protection. You will need her. Sheriff Lindoe will not be stopping this duel."

"That is most unfortunate for you," shot back Marie. "For you will die in this duel. The ring will not protect you now."

"Let's get on with it," demanded Anton, looking less than self-assured as he jumped down from the carriage. Without uttering another word or looking directly at Emile, Anton, his second, and Dr. Furioso brushed past the Poydras brothers towards the dueling field and waiting crowd.

Marie Laveau lingered to speak to Emile. "This is your last chance, Monsieur Poydras. Return the ring to me, now. And I shall forget that you broke your bargain with me — and that your brother tried to murder me."

"Hah! Never, witch. You shall never lay hands on this ring again." Emile shook his left fist and ring finger in Marie's face as he spoke.

"Then you shall die," replied Marie coolly. "And when you die, I shall take your soul. You shall *never* have peace until the ring is returned to me." Her threat delivered, Marie glared at Benjamin and sulked off after Anton and his companions.

Benjamin and Anton's second, Harnett Crane, wasted no time in preparing for the duel. They quickly staked off the firing distance and proceeded to load Anton's Belgian dueling pistols. Benjamin insisted that the duelists choose their weapons prior to loading so he could personally load Emile's weapon. There would be no tampering with the pistol loads as in the duel with Henri Noyan.

As the seconds loaded the guns, Emile limped out to his firing position and calmly surveyed the crowd. Bernard Marigny stood next to Sheriff Lindoe. The sheriff did not look happy. When Bernard caught Emile's eye, he gave a thumbs up sign. The good sheriff had been persuaded not to interfere with the duel.

Marie Laveau stood off by herself, her back leaning against one of the massive live oaks. She fiddled with a necklace in her hands, an odd sort of chain made of chicken bones. The Voodoo queen scowled at Emile, never taking her eyes off him as she muttered to herself.

Among the crowd of sightseers, Emile noticed money changing hands. Bets were being taken on who would survive the duel. The sightseers laid aside their picnics and focused on the dueling field as the time drew near.

Benjamin delivered the loaded pistol to Emile at the stake marking his firing position. "Hold it gently, Brother. It has a hair trigger."

Nodding, Emile took the weapon with his right hand and pointed it at the ground. Whispering, Benjamin added, "I'm calling the fire. It will be a quick count, so be ready."

As Benjamin marched away, Emile turned his right side toward his adversary, making as narrow a target as possible for Anton.

"Gentlemen, aim your weapons!" ordered Benjamin.

Emile sighted down the barrel of his pistol at the anxious face of his former friend. For some reason, a vision of their joint duels with the Spaniard, Manuel de Salcedo, flashed through his mind, and how Anton had saved his life thirty-five years earlier.

"Ready! Fire! One, two...," counted Benjamin.

As soon as he heard the word fire, Emile started to squeeze the trigger of his pistol. But something — some force — stayed his hand. Before he could comprehend what was happening, the air was filled with the thunderous discharge of Anton's weapon.

The .65 caliber pistol ball struck Emile right below his armpit, shattering a rib, ripping through his right lung, and lodging itself deep in his chest. The impact threw Emile backwards, flat onto his back. His pistol discharged harmlessly into the air as he fell.

Benjamin and Dr. Furioso were the first to reach Emile. Emile didn't need a doctor to know he was mortally wounded, but the expressions on the faces of the doctor and Benjamin confirmed his self-diagnosis.

"Sen... d him away," sputtered Emile, blood streaming from his nose and mouth. "Keep them all away."

The solemn-faced doctor silently obeyed Emile's request and directed the rest of the crowd to step back.

With labored effort, Emile pulled the alliance ring off his left ring finger. With his bloody hand, he pressed the ring into Benjamin's palm. "Ta... ke this for Jean. Tell him I love him, and that I'm sorry I could not keep my promise. When he is old enough to understand, give him my diary and the ring. Promise me! Promise me you will do that?"

Crying unashamedly, Benjamin held his brother's hand and the ring in a steady grip. "If that is your last wish, dear brother, it will be done."

"Paul's family…" Emile grimaced as he struggled to speak. "They may try to take Jean."

"Don't worry, Emile. I will take Jean to Pointe Coupee immediately. No one will get custody of Jean. Besides, the sheriff there is in debt to our family."

"And beware tha… t witch, Marie Laveau. You must never bring Jean back to New Orleans. You… can never be safe from her here."

"I understand. But why didn't you fire, Emile?"

Emile heard his brother's question, but he couldn't answer. At that very moment, his soul was leaving his lifeless body. He felt as if his spirit was being pulled in some unnatural direction, being compressed into some dark void. Then he was confronted by a blinding double ring of light and the sound of a woman's laughter — the hideous cackle of Marie Laveau. Emile screamed, but no one could hear him. No one but Marie Laveau.

Chapter Sixty-Eight

Phillip Cuvillier rang Justin's doorbell for the third time and looked up at the lighted second story window.

His partner, Detective Stan Barski, peered through the locked iron gate at the dark garden. "It's ten-thirty. You'd think someone would be home by now."

"Yeah," agreed Detective Cuvillier, "someone's in there. I just saw a shadow move past that upstairs window."

"So, whada we do?"

"We go back to the car and wait. We can't bust in without a warrant. Anyway, I've got a feelin' they may be comin' out pretty soon."

As they walked back to their car, Stan asked, "Don't you think we're jumping the gun, Phil? We've got no real physical evidence; the O positive blood stains in the rental car could belong to anybody, and we don't have witness identification of Noyan or Richards."

"Yeah, I know, but all our other leads were dead ends. And ever since we interviewed Noyan and that smell hit me, I've had this hunch — call it a sixth sense — that there's somethin' sick and unnatural goin' on in that house."

"You mean Voodoo?" scoffed Stan as the men got back in their car.

"Yeah, Voodoo. Laugh at me if you want, but tonight is St. John's Eve. So, if these people are up to anythin' weird, it could happen tonight."

"Okay, I'll play along, Phil. But you have to be the one to tell the captain you think this kidnapping has something to do with a Voodoo ceremony."

"Yeah, okay. We'll postpone that conversation until we see what happens tonight."

Nearly an hour later, a gray paneled van pulled out of the alley beside Justin's residence and headed north. At the wheel was Amy Noyan. Next to Amy, riding shotgun, was Justin, holding his .45 pistol in his lap. "Head toward the interstate," he directed Amy. "I want to see if we're bein' followed." Turning around in his seat, he looked at Mark, who was sitting on the floor of the dark van. "You did remove all of that bumper sticker, didn't you?"

"Yeah and switched the plate. No one should be able to identify this van as a rental."

"Lot of good your precautions will do," chimed in Amy, "if the police were watchin' us leave. Someone rang your doorbell."

"I know," answered Justin. "But we couldn't wait any longer." Looking at his watch, he added, "We've only got thirty-five minutes to get into the cemetery and prepare for the ceremony. Besides, we can't be certain it was the police at the gate."

From the rear of the dark van came Mama Vance's high-pitched voice. "Need be dhere soon, Monsieur Noyan. Must begin exactly at midnight, St. John's Eve, or conjure might not work."

Taking her eyes off the road to look at Justin, Amy asked, "Why did you bring the gun, Justin? You still haven't really explained why the police are investigatin' you."

Not looking at Amy, Justin answered, "I told you. We were held-up last time we went to the cemetery. The police suspect Mark and I broke into the cemetery. That's why they're askin' questions."

Amy really didn't buy Justin's explanation but decided not to press the issue right then.

Sitting on the van floor on either side of Mama Vance, like matched bookends, were Mama Vance's two young helpers, Hector and Ajax. Celeste lay stretched out, her head in Mark's lap, dressed only in the blue chenille robe Mark had purchased for her.

After driving east on I-10 a few miles, Justin said, "Take the next exit and double back. I don't think anyone is followin' us, but we'll know for sure when we turn off."

Justin kept his eyes trained on the van's side mirror as Amy exited at the Gentilly Boulevard interchange and looped back onto I-10 heading west. "All clear," he said. "No headlights followed us."

Squeezing the steering wheel of the van and shaking her head, Amy replied, "I don't know whether to thank you or curse you for all you're doin' for Celeste. I thought Jim's death was my worst nightmare. But this…"

"I know, Amy. Not a day goes by that I don't regret convincin' Jim not to wear the ring. You're right, if he had taken it to Viet Nam, Jim'd still be alive, and Celeste would never have had to go through any of this livin' nightmare. If I could trade places with her, you know I would. And don't worry about the police. If there are any legal repercussions over what we're doin', I'll protect Celeste and Mark."

Amy pulled the van up in front of the Basin Street entrance to St. Louis Cemetery No. 1 at precisely 11:45. Hector and Ajax quickly threw open the rear doors of the van and began unloading Justin's black doctor's bag, two grocery bags, Mama Vance, and Celeste.

Quickly throwing the gearshift into park, Amy grabbed Justin's arm as he began to open the passenger door. "Please, let me come with you? She's all I've got left, Justin."

Squeezing her hand on his arm, Justin tried to comfort her. "It's goin' to work, Amy. I promise you. You'll have your little girl back when you pick us up."

"But I want to go with her."

Justin shook his head. "You can't, darlin'. Only members of the cult can attend the ceremony. It would jeopardize your life *and* Celeste's." Justin slid out of the van door. Shutting it, he spoke through the open window. "Remember. Don't wait here. It's not safe, and it would draw attention to the cemetery. In an hour, park across the street. I'll signal you with my flashlight."

Amy nodded solemnly, put the van in gear, and drove off.

When Justin turned around, the gate to the cemetery was already standing open. Except for Ajax, waiting just inside, no one else was in sight. Justin pulled the black iron gate shut behind him and locked it with the sexton's key.

Ajax and Justin caught up with the rest of the party at the tomb of Marie Laveau. As they walked up to the three-tiered oven vault, Hector was lighting two black candles he had placed in the green flower holders affixed to either side of the white crypt. Celeste was standing in the center of the walk before the tomb, and Mark was bent over, drawing a circle on the sidewalk around Celeste with a piece of yellow chalk.

Mama Vance stood to the left of the tomb, next to a pile of twigs and scrap lumber. Ajax walked over and drew a large double circle around Mama Vance and the firewood, using red and yellow chalk. Meanwhile, Hector arranged the red, blue, and yellow candles in a diamond pattern around both circles.

Once the candles were all placed and lighted, Mama Vance motioned to Justin. "Bring me de blood of de goat without horns."

Justin walked over to his black medical bag, pulled it open, and removed the full plastic bottle of blood. When he handed it to Mama Vance, she twisted off the cap, spat into the bottle, shook it up, and took a deep drink. Wiping the blood from her mouth with the back of her hand, she handed the bottle back to Justin. "Now, you drink," she said.

"Wh... Whaaat?" stammered Justin.

"Drink. All must drink de blood. It protect our souls from de evil ones."

"You mean from Marie Laveau?"

"Oui, she be one."

Closing his eyes, Justin put the bottle to his lips and let a small sip of the cold blood flow into his mouth. He held it for a second or two before forcing himself to swallow.

Hector and Ajax took the bottle, and each downed a large gulp of blood without hesitation. Mark was another matter. With two shaking hands, he gripped the bottle. When he attempted to drink, he choked and sputtered out the blood. On his second attempt, he compelled himself to ingest a thimbleful of the dark blood.

Taking the bottle from Mark, Mama Vance hobbled inside the yellow circle, feeling for Celeste with her free hand. While chanting under her breath, and with Hector's help, she held the bottle to Celeste's lips, making certain Celeste took a long drink from the bottle. Pulling open Celeste's robe to expose her breasts, Mama Vance poured the rest of the blood over Celeste's head and chest. Dropping the empty bottle, she made a small cabalistic sign over her blood-drenched hair.

Mama Vance's next procedure made Mark cringe. She removed the packet of silver needles from the pocket of her yellow housecoat. By touch, she proceeded to push a needle sideways through each of Celeste's exposed nipples. Celeste stood perfectly still during this torture, never flinching or changing her blank expression.

Needles inserted, Mama Vance and Hector moved Celeste's left hand to her breast. Then they took her ring finger and slipped the needle in her right breast between the Poydras ring and her finger. Celeste stood like a bloody statue ready to say the Pledge of Allegiance, only her hand was over her right breast instead of the left.

Making a different cabalistic motion with her hands, Mama Vance backed out of Celeste's circle. "Now," she announced, "no one may enter ma chérie's circle. No matter what happen, no touch her." Turning toward Justin and his doctor's bag, she continued, "Hand me de rest of de blood — everyone remove dher shirts and do like Hector and Ajax."

Pulling off their shirts and throwing them on the firewood, Hector and Ajax each walked up to the face of Marie's tomb, rapped on it three times, and drew the sign of the cross with red chalk. They proceeded to kneel before Mama Vance, who anointed their heads with blood from the second bottle. Holding her hand out towards Mark and Justin, she said, "Now, you come be purified."

Mark and Justin gave each other a befuddled look and went through the steps of the purification as demonstrated by Hector and Ajax, kneeling before Mama Vance.

"What be de time?" asked Mama Vance.

Turning his wristwatch toward the candlelight, Justin answered, "Nearly midnight, only a couple minutes to go."

"Dhen, everyone git inside de double circle and light de fire. Remember! Once de fire burn and de ceremony begin, not ta leave de circle. Do so on pain of death."

Chapter Sixty-Nine

The crowd of mourners trying to enter the narrow gate of the Saint Louis Cemetery poured out into Basin Street. Across the street, standing on the corner of Conti and Rampart Streets, a mature besuited man and his black male companion observed the throng entering the cemetery. The man's sculpted face was accented by a pencil mustache and dark circles under his eyes. His black associate was dressed in the formal black attire of a manservant and stood with his arms locked in front of his chest.

"The crowd is very large, Monsieur Jean," remarked the black man. "Are you sure you want to go in?"

"Yes, Marcus. I must. But let's wait here until the crowd clears the gate."

Jean Noyan opened the newspaper he had carried under his arm and re-read the short death notice he had circled.

Marie Philomen Glapion, age 62, passed away June 11, 1897. A funeral mass will be held Monday, June 14 at two o'clock in the Chapel of St. Anthony of Benedict (the Mortuary Chapel) on N. Rampart Street. Interment to follow in St. Louis Cemetery No. 1.

Jean closed the newspaper and sighed. Marcus shook his head and broke the silence.

"I recall standing here in June, sixteen years ago, for another funeral, Monsieur Jean. Why are you so sure it is her this time? People are saying this is Marie Laveau's daughter's funeral."

"I know because my dreams have changed this time — I saw her die this time! Besides, when the Widow Paris died, I still saw Marie, alive, in my dreams. Marie tried to fool us into believing she had died then. But the old woman buried in that tomb in 1881 was not Marie, the dark queen of the Voodooiennes. Perhaps she assumed her daughter's identity or took possession of her body? I don't know. But, I'm — "

Marcus scoffed and interrupted, "Oh, Monsieur Jean, when will you be done with this absurd crusade!"

"Enough, Marcus! During the war, I would have had you whipped for such insolence."

"Yes, but during the war, I was your slave. Now you have to put up with my mouth if you want to keep me around. Also, my wool is white now, and my bones are getting tired. While you have hardly any gray in your hair and keep me up all hours of the night with your nightmares."

Sighing again, Jean replied, "I'm sorry, Marcus. I know this has been wearing for you as well. But I am seventy-two years old now, and I must get this done before my time runs out. You know she cursed and murdered my father. I must make certain her reign is finally at an end. Remember, she came back from the dead before she cursed my father."

"Very well, Monsieur Jean, we will see this through. Look, the crowd has cleared the gate. We'd better hurry if you want to see them put her coffin in the tomb."

Jean raised his left hand and kissed the gold alliance ring on his ring finger. "Yes, let's go."

***

The following afternoon, Jean and Marcus returned to the cemetery. Outside the sexton's office, they encountered a burly and shirtless young man breaking up jagged blocks of concrete with a sledgehammer. As they came up behind the young man, Jean spoke first.

"Excuse me, monsieur. Is Sexton Lefebvre in?"

The workman let his sledgehammer drop and turned to face Jean, wiping the sweat from his brow as he replied. "No, the sexton is out of town until next Monday. I'm his assistant, Victor — Victor Ardoin. Is there something I can help you with?"

Jean hesitated before answering. "No, thank you. I think not. My business with Monsieur Lefebvre is of a personal nature."

"Of course, Monsieur Noyan. But didn't I see you gentlemen at the burial yesterday of Marie Laveau?"

Jean gave Victor a suspicious look. "How do you know my name, and what do you know of Marie Laveau? Has Monsieur Lefebvre discussed my personal affairs with you?"

"Oh no, Monsieur Noyan, he only told me to make his apology if you called. He was compelled to leave town for a family emergency."

"That still doesn't explain how you know my identity and why you have mentioned Marie Laveau?"

"Well, sir, Sexton Lefebvre described you well. I assumed your identity. You rather stood out in the crowd of mourners yesterday. And here you are again. I can only conclude you have an interest in the tomb of Marie Laveau."

"You are being rather presumptuous, monsieur. Good day."

As Jean turned to leave, Victor made an apology. "I meant no disrespect, sir. You see, I am quite familiar with the followers of Marie Laveau. I only wish to be of service to you, if you wish?"

Jean held up and turned to face Victor. "You said your surname is Ardoin. I knew an Adrien Ardoin from Basile during the war. He was an officer with the Second Louisiana Cavalry. Are you related?"

"I'm his son, sir."

"You are Adrien's *son*?"

"Yes. No doubt you are wondering what the son of such a prominent family is doing breaking concrete in a graveyard in New Orleans?" When Jean did not respond, Victor continued, "You see, my father and I have had a falling-out, a disagreement over my religious affiliation."

"You are a Voodooienne?"

"Yes, sir, after a fashion. So, if you have a question about Marie Laveau's burial, you are welcome to ask me. I promise you my complete discretion in the matter. I assume you would not want your interest to become known to any of the newspaper reporters who were at the burial."

"Humph! You don't say. Very well, Monsieur Ardoin, did you observe the corpse before it was interred?"

"No, I did not personally view the body. However, I feel certain there is a corpse in the coffin, and I overheard some of her followers discussing the condition of corpse."

"And what did you overhear, pray tell?"

"Of interest to you… that the expression frozen on Marie's face was one of abject terror, and that Marie's gold necklace was missing when her body was discovered."

"Necklace! What do you know of the necklace?"

"Well, sir, as I suspect you are aware, Marie was nearly a hundred years old when she died — many say she was much older than that."

"And?"

"The gold necklace was a charm of protection and immortality, passed down among the Voodoo queens. A new queen rules now, and she is the one who somehow took the necklace and killed Marie."

"And who is this new queen?"

"She is called Mama Vance. I can tell you where to find her, if you wish?"

"No, that won't be necessary. I have already met Mama Vance."

Nodding once, Victor replied, "Ahh, I see."

Marcus interjected himself into the conversation for the first time, gently placing his hand on Jean's arm. "Monsieur Jean, is this wise — "

Jean cut him off. "It's all right, Marcus. I think we can trust this young man." Turning back to Victor, Jean continued, "I have no interest in the necklace or Mama Vance. My only concern is making sure Marie Laveau does not leave her tomb."

"I'm afraid I don't follow you, sir? Marie Laveau is quite dead."

"Then your knowledge of Voodoo history is obviously lacking. Sixty-seven years ago, Marie Laveau was killed by my uncle. Yet, she came back from the dead, cursed my father, and caused his death. Now, I intend to make certain her spirit never leaves her tomb — or stays in Hell. She must never rise to harm any of my family ever again."

"Very well, but I don't know what I can do? I am but a novice of the faith."

"I have a powerful gris-gris I need placed in Marie's coffin." Jean pulled out his purse and poured four twenty-dollar gold pieces into his hand and held them out to Victor. "Will you take care of that for me?"

Taking the coins, Victor agreed, "Of course, sir. But I cannot open the vault until after the cemetery closes for the day. Have you brought the gris-gris with you?"

Jean looked at Marcus and nodded his head. Marcus pulled a small burlap bag, tied with a black ribbon, from his coat pocket.

"Show it to him, Marcus." Marcus took a step forward and placed the charm bag in Victor's open hand, on top of the gold coins. Victor's nostrils were immediately hit with the pungent odors of vinegar and rotting flesh.

Victor grimaced. "Where did you get this?"

Jean studied Victor a few seconds before replying, "From Mama Vance herself. It is a binding charm. It will keep Marie Laveau's spirit in her tomb forever."

"If you say so. But everything eventually turns to dust in these oven vaults, even bones. What makes you believe that this charm will last forever?"

"Because, among other items, it contains a lock of Marie Laveau's hair and a piece of her flesh." Jean nodded at Marcus again, and he retrieved the charm bag from Victor's hand.

Victor turned his face to the side and took a deep breath of fresh air. "There is something else you should know, Monsieur Noyan. The rent on Marie's vault has only been paid for a year and a day. If no one continues the rent payments, her remains, and your gris-gris, will be removed or broken up and dumped into the bottom receiving vault."

"Then I shall buy the vault and pay for its perpetual care. Can you take care of that?"

"But of course. It will take a little while for me to draw up the documents."

"Fine, I will have Marcus return at closing time to pay you and supervise the placement of the gris-gris in the coffin. And, Monsieur Ardoin, as you surmised, I wish to remain anonymous in all these transactions. Will that be a problem?"

"Not at all, sir. I just need a name to place on the vault deed. Whose name shall I use?"

Jean smiled wryly. "Emile de Lallande Poydras. Put everything in the name of Emile Poydras."

Chapter Seventy

Detectives Cuvillier and Barski sat in their parked car on Conti Street, beside the wall of St. Louis Cemetery No. 1. "Now what?' asked Stan. "We lost the van in the highway traffic. We don't know for certain they're in there."

"Yeah, but the patrol car reported seein' a light-colored van pull away from the front of the cemetery just fifteen minutes ago."

"But the gate is locked, and we haven't heard a thing. Besides, they found the girls hours ago, and they couldn't ID either Noyan or Richards in the photo lineup of their DMV photos."

"Sure, the kidnappers wore disguises and kept the girls drugged and blind-folded, but…"

"But what, Phil? This is nuts! What are we doing here?"

***

Everyone acknowledged their understanding of Mama Vance's warning about leaving the circle by carefully stepping inside the red and yellow chalk lines. Immediately, Ajax poured a pint of rum over the pile of shirts and firewood. When he put a match to it, the liquor ignited with a whoosh, and intense flames blazed up.

The heat from the fire became uncomfortable in no time at all. Justin and Mark turned their backs to the blaze and stood with their toes on the line of chalk marking the inner circle's boundary, putting as much distance between themselves and the fire as possible.

At precisely midnight, they heard the cathedral clock striking the hour. That's when Mama Vance began to chant:

L'Appé vini, le Grand Zombi,

L'Appé vini, pou fe gris-gris!

As Mama Vance began the third repetition of her chant, Justin was startled by the sound of wings flapping behind him. He turned just as a black rooster fluttered down off the top of a neighboring oven vault and dropped at Mama Vance's feet.

"Where'd that come from?" whispered Mark.

Justin shook his head. "I… I don't know. We didn't bring it with us."

Hector picked up the docile rooster and handed it to Mama Vance, who continued to chant. The old Voodoo queen held the rooster upside down by its feet. She pulled a straight razor from her pocket, slashed off the bird's head, and threw its twitching body into the flames. Although there was not a breath of a breeze in the graveyard, as soon as the fire began to consume the rooster, the flame of every candle went out simultaneously. Every candle, save the black ones on the tomb of Marie Laveau. Smoke with the pungent odor of burning feathers stung Mark and Justin's eyes. Nevertheless, they turned to face the fire and Marie's crypt.

As Mama Vance maintained her monotonous chant, one of the black candles grew brighter than the other. The intensity of the light increased until it looked like a hundred-watt light bulb. Justin detected movement within the bright light. It looked like a small head with two eyes.

"My God!" uttered Mark. "It's a snake. There's a snake coming out of that candle holder."

"Le Grand Zombi," replied Justin.

The thick, black snake slowly emerged from the green flower holder and slithered down the face of the tomb, its forked tongue darting out periodically. Fully egressed, the serpent appeared to be over ten feet long. It proceeded down the crypt wall onto the sidewalk and curled into a semicircle around Celeste's chalk circle.

Mama Vance changed her chant:

Eh, yé, yé Mamzelle Marie,

Ya, yé, yé, li konin tou, gris-gris;

Li té kouri lekal, aver vieux kokodril;

Oh, ouai, yé Mamzelle Marie…

This new chant caused the second black candle to light up like the first. This time, instead of a snake rising up from the light, the head of a cat appeared — the head of a giant, black cat with glowing green eyes. Once the cat had pulled itself free from its side vase, it leaped up to the crest of the tomb, humped up its back, and emitted a threatening hiss and yowl.

The cat's yowl seemed to cue Mama Vance to cease chanting. Justin took the opportunity to ask a question. "Is that the spirit of Marie Laveau?"

"Oui, dhat be her."

"Celeste must give the... the cat her ring?"

"Oui, her spirit. But not yet."

"And will that reincarnate Marie Laveau?"

"No. It take de body of a living soul — and de ring — to do dhat. We not let dhat happen. De blood of de lamb will stop her from entering any of our bodies."

No sooner had Mama Vance finished her last sentence than the cat focused its green eyes on Celeste. Suddenly, the amplified sound of heartbeats filled everyone's ears, and two beams of bright emerald light pulsed in unison out of the cat's eyes. The green light enveloped Celeste in a translucent, glowing cocoon. A look of concern came over Mama Vance, and she demanded Justin describe for her what was transpiring.

"No! No!" screamed Mama Vance. "Dhis can't be!"

They all stood frozen, mesmerized by the glowing Celeste. In a few seconds, the green glow surrounding Celeste changed to red, and smoke and heat began to radiate from her exposed skin.

"What's wrong?" demanded Justin. "What's happenin'? It's like she's startin' to burn!"

Before Mama Vance could answer, the beam of a bright flashlight hit Justin in the face. The voice of Phillip Cuvillier rang out, "This is the N'aw Arlens Police! Y'all are under arrest!"

Throwing back his head, Justin screamed, "Not now! God, not now! Why now?"

"They found the two little girls locked up in that abandoned warehouse," answered Stan. "You abducted them, didn't you?"

Grabbing his arm and thrusting her face into Justin's, Mama Vance shrieked, "You fool! You not kill de child? De blood come from a livin' child? You ruin everythin'!"

Tears streaming from his face, Justin blubbered, "I… I'm sorry. I just couldn't do it. Not even for Celeste. I… I thought if you never knew the — "

Mama Vance cut him off, "Idiot! Look at your grandchild. You have damned her for *eternity*! And Marie will kill you all!"

As Justin looked back to Celeste, her face now showed the agony she was suffering. Her eyes were active now, and she seemed to be aware of her surroundings. Spotting Justin, she cried out, "Granddad! Help me! I'm burnin' up!"

As she cried for help, Celeste's smoldering hair and robe exploded into flames, and she let out blood-curdling screams from the pain.

Instinctively, Justin bolted from his circle and ran to Celeste. He beat at the flames with his bare hands and tried to smother them with his exposed chest, taking care to keep Celeste inside her circle. Abruptly, the fire completely transferred from Celeste to Justin. Celeste's body appeared to be unscathed, but the fire turned Justin into a human blowtorch. He crumpled and fell backwards in a ball of flames. It reminded Mark of all those news spots he had seen of Vietnamese monks who immolated themselves with gasoline. Only now, he could smell the burning flesh and hair.

Celeste wailed out, "Granddad!" and started to go to the aid of Justin.

Mark yelled, "No! Stop! You can't leave the circle. It's too late for him. Don't move!"

The two police detectives were absolutely flabbergasted and immobilized by the bizarre, violent scene they had come upon.

Stan Barski muttered, "Sweet Jesus."

Phillip Cuvillier lowered his flashlight and stared at Justin's flaming corpse in disbelief.

Before either detective could recover, the black cat shot out two more blasts of green light. The first pulse struck Stan in the center of his chest, blowing his heart and pieces of a lung out the back of his body. Phillip didn't fare any better. Even though he sensed the attack coming and dove for cover behind a low crypt, the bolt of light hit the side of his head as he went down, shattering his skull and blowing out the right side of his brain.

Mark felt a rush of panic and wanted to run but thought better of it, remembering Mama Vance's admonition about leaving the circle. As he looked up at the black cat, he saw it leap off the top of the tomb onto the bare back of Hector.

The big man screamed and tried to shake and pull the clawing animal off, but to no avail. Fright finally got the best of him, and he made a run for it. No sooner had Hector stepped out of his circle, the cat plunged its entire body into a bloody cavity it had clawed and chewed out of Hector's back. Instantly, Hector froze in mid-step and whirled around to face the people remaining in the circle. Mark saw that Hector's eyes now blazed with green light like the cat.

Pushing past Mark, Hector slammed into Ajax, throwing the second man up against the front of Marie's tomb. As Ajax struggled to break the chokehold Hector had on his throat, the top capstone on the tomb began to glow with pulsating green light. It was Celeste's nightmare come true. The glowing capstone burst open, and the hands and arms of a skeleton appeared. The long bony fingers came up behind Ajax's head and grabbed it. There was a violent jerk, and Mark heard the snap as Ajax's neck was broken.

Mark glanced at Mama Vance. She appeared to be in a trance, oblivious to all the violence around her. But Mark could see that Mama Vance had focused her now blazing eyes on Celeste, as if she were concentrating her thoughts in the direction of his terrified wife.

When the green-eyed Hector turned from Ajax's body and took a step toward him, Mark could stand still no longer. He made his move, leaping to join Celeste in one quick jump. Once inside the circle with her, Celeste threw her arms around Mark's neck. Instantly, Mark felt weak, and his knees buckled. Celeste gasped and jerked her hands back, but it was too late. She had felt Emile's spirit pass from her and the ring into Mark's body. At the same time, she felt free of Cupid's presence. When she looked Mark in the eyes, she could tell he was different. Celeste knew instinctively that it was Emile looking back at her.

While this transference was taking place, the zombie of Hector turned to the opening in Marie Laveau's crypt. The zombie stood at attention while the mortal remains and bones of the great Queen Marie continued to emerge from her tomb. There were patches of leather-like flesh left on her face, and a few strands of her long, curly hair remained. Except for a remnant of her burial shroud, she was nothing more than a stark, white skeleton.

The skeleton of Marie grabbed the head of Hector with both of her bony hands and gave it a violent twist. There was another blinding flash of green light when Hector's head separated from his body.

When Celeste's eyes recovered from the bright flash of light, she found herself looking not at a skeleton or Hector. There stood Queen Marie Laveau in all her prime and glory. Her long, curly black hair fell across the shoulders of her favorite purple dress. And she was smiling — smiling wickedly at Celeste. Marie extended her hands and moved toward Celeste. "Now," she said in a menacing, clear voice. "Now the ring is mine. Give it to me!"

Mark stepped in front of Celeste as Marie came within their circle. The great queen hissed at him and slapped both her hands around his throat. Grinning, Marie slowly, but surely, began to strangle him. Mark pulled frantically at Marie's hands, but he was powerless to break her supernatural death grip. Mark's eyes began to bulge, and his face was turning blue from lack of oxygen. Without a second thought, Celeste pulled the Poydras ring off her finger, grabbed Mark's flailing left hand, and shoved the ring onto his finger. Instantly, Mark was filled with the power of the ring, and he was able to pull Marie's hands free of his throat and separate from her.

"Now, witch," he declared, holding his ring in her face. "The only person who will leave this circle alive is the one wearing the ring. Back to Hell with you — where you belong!"

Marie and Mark grabbed each other and struggled and twisted within the circle, but Mark adroitly placed his leg between hers and shoved hard, knocking Marie backwards out of the circle. She hit the pavement on her rump, her green eyes flashing. Clenching her raised fists, she cried, "No! No! Not again! Not this — "

Before Marie could complete her sentence, her body was picked up and pulled backwards through the air, as if caught in some strong, invisible vacuum. This unseen force sucked her kicking body back through the hole in her tomb. Once Marie was back inside the vault, the fragments of the shattered capstone rose up and replaced themselves over the opening. In less than a minute, it was as if the tomb had never been opened.

Mark turned to Celeste, who was still standing within her circle. "My darling," he said, "what have you done? You have saved my life, but you are doomed the minute you step out of the circle. I must give you back the ring, and you must accept it."

"No, wait!" called out Mama Vance. "Dhere be a way for you both ta live."

With halting steps, Mama Vance felt her way and walked up behind Celeste. Reaching beneath her loose housedress, Mama Vance brought forth her massive gold necklace and fastened it around Celeste's neck.

Celeste looked down at the dazzling pendant lying on her breasts and turned to face Mama Vance. "No, Mama Vance, you'll die without your necklace. I can't — "

"Hush, ma chérie. De gift be complete. Truth be told, I never wanna see Marie come back. If she got de ring, she could 'ave. I send her ta de tomb ta start with, and now I know she not escape. Besides, I tired of dis world. Now, you and your lover *both* be immortal. Live forever in pleasure. But beware. Never take de necklace off. A false lover trick me inta takin' it off once, and I end up a blind old hag."

Turning to Mark, Celeste studied her husband's eyes and asked, "Mark? Mark, is it you or Emile with me now?"

"It's either, or both of us, my love. Whichever you want."

Smiling, Celeste replied, "I'll take you both."

THE END

Acknowledgments

I began this novel in the 1980s, pre-Google and the internet. So, I did my research the old-fashioned way by going to the New Orleans' libraries and museums, and by rummaging through French Quarter book shops. By my side the whole time was my wife, Debi, who was my research partner and first editor. Without her help and encouragement, The Poydras Ring would never have been written. That's why this novel is dedicated to her.

I finished the draft of this book around 1988 and put it up on the closet shelf, where it lay for over thirty years. Then, after I retired from my law practice, I dusted it off and decided to see if this story was worth trying to publish. Needless to say, as a novice writer, my manuscript had numerous issues that needed to be addressed. But I had the great good fortune of finding a local editor, Linda Ingerly, who took me by the hand and gave me the directions I needed to turn The Poydras Ring into a complete and compelling story. Linda has also been with me during the long journey to publication. She even found the publisher who accepted this book. So, thank you, Linda! You made my dream of being a "published author" come true. And don't go anywhere. My next novel, Laffite's Ghost, needs your help too.

I am also grateful to Histria Books for accepting a book from an agent-less, first time novelist. There aren't many publishers these days willing to take the time to develop new authors. So, thank you to their whole team, especially Assistant Director, Diana Livesay.

Of course, there have been others who encouraged me to get my book published, like our children, Katelyn and Alex. I take delight in knowing that Debi and I have infected them with the "New Orleans Bug." They make their own pilgrimages to the Big Easy now.

I thought about trying to list all the source materials that educated and inspired me in developing the plotlines about Julian Poydras, Voodoo, dueling practices and the rich history of New Orleans and Louisiana I've tried to portray in this novel. But I'll give you my favorite: Gumbo Ya-Ya, the WPA Louisiana folk tale collection by Lyle Saxon, Robert Tallant and Edward Dreyer. This book is my go-to source of inspiration and plot ideas for stories about New Orleans and Louisiana. Check it out sometime. It's a classic, and it's in the public domain and available on-line.

So, until next time, look for us in the piano bar at Pat O'Brien's, and laissez les bons rouler!

HISTRIA FICTION

Other fine books available
from Histria Fiction:

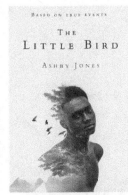
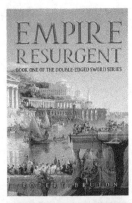

For these and many other great books
visit

HistriaBooks.com